QUAKER SUMMER

LISA SAMSON

Published by
THOMAS NELSON
Since 1798

www.thomasnelson.com

Published in Nashville, Tennessee, by Thomas Nelson, Inc.

Thomas Nelson, Inc. titles may be purchased in bulk for educational, business, fund-raising, or sales promotional use. For information, please e-mail SpecialMarkets@ThomasNelson.com.

Scripture quotations are from the HOLY BIBLE, NEW INTERNATIONAL VERSION®. NIV®. Copyright © 1973, 1978, 1984 by International Bible Society. Used by permission of Zondervan. All rights reserved.

Publisher's Note: This novel is a work of fiction. Names, characters, places, and incidents are either products of the author's imagination or used fictitiously. All characters are fictional, and any similarity to people living or dead is purely coincidental.

Library of Congress Cataloging in Publication Data

Samson, Lisa, 1964–
    Quaker summer / Lisa Samson.
        p. cm.
    ISBN-13: 978-1-59554-207-6 (soft cover)
    ISBN-10: 1-59554-207-8 (soft cover)
    I. Title.
PS3569.A46673Q35 2007
813'.6—dc22   2006033474

Printed in the United States of America
07 08 09 10 11 RRD 5 4 3 2 1

For Erin Healy,
my partner in crime.

He has showed you, O man, what is good.
And what does the LORD require of you?
To act justly and to love mercy and to walk humbly with your God.

—MICAH 6:8

Part One

The Fool on the Hill

ONE

Five months ago I raised Gary and Mary Andrews from the dead. I took a wrong turn trying to find a Pampered Chef party to benefit Will's eighth grade trip to New York City, and there it stood as close to the road as ever, their old house. Superimposed over the improvements of the recent owners, a small bungalow with cracked siding, smeared windowpanes, and a rusted oil tank figured into my vision. The mat of green grass dissolved into an unkempt lot of dirt and weeds supporting a display of junk: an old couch, a defunct Chevy, and rusted entities the purpose of which I never could say.

What happened inside that house remains there. All I know for sure is that Gary and Mary Andrews climbed onto our school bus every morning and never waved good-bye to anybody. We'd pull forward in a throaty puff of diesel, away from that little frame house, its once-white paint as gray as the dirt that always outlined Gary's hands and shaded behind his ears. As a sixth grader, I didn't realize children weren't responsible for their own cleanliness, that Mary's hair never glinted in the sunshine or smelled like baby shampoo because nobody helped her wash it; nobody thrust their fingers into her curls and scrubbed away the dust of a tumble in the yard with the dog; nobody applied a nice dollop of cream rinse to untangle knots from windy hours outside. I never stopped to think nobody in that house cared about them.

God help me.

So I sit now in the anonymity of my car, praying somebody steps out. Perhaps they'll look around, notice me sitting here, walk forward and ask if there's a problem.

No. No problem. I just knew the people who used to live here. Might you know where they live now?

No movement, no fluttering of the drapes, no shadows behind the blinds. Always quiet here. It always was.

I pull off the side of the road, the heavy tires eating the gravel. I turn for home. I'll find myself back here again soon. It's become the way of it.

I'm sorry. I'm so sorry.

I fell asleep last night to the eerie strains of "Blackbird," my last conscious thoughts of broken wings and sunken eyes. Waiting for moments to arrive when broken wings fly and sunken eyes see, waiting for that moment of freedom, flying into the light.

If I had to listen to one musical artist or band or composer for the rest of my life, I'd choose the Beatles. Their music encompasses all the emotions, all the moods, and all the tempos I'll ever need, taking me back to my childhood when my father would slip an album on the stereo, set the speed to thirty-three, and push the lever up to automatic. The fact that my father was younger and definitely cooler than the other dads around only helped the Fab Four become *the thing* to an elementary school girl who should have been listening to Bobby Sherman or the Osmond Brothers. I never really did go for the teen sensations.

Lying on my stomach, I would watch from eye level, chin resting on the back of my hands, and stare, gaze stuttering in and out of focus as the record fell to the turntable on the floor by the couch, the arm lifted, swung backward then forward, diamond-tipped needle poised with promise over the smooth outer rim of the vinyl disc. As it dropped with slow precision, I held my breath wondering if it would really make contact with the disc this time. Those old hi-fi systems didn't miss the mark often, but they did enough to glue your eyes to the entire process and make your heart skip a few beats until the needle found its groove.

And then, after the static and scratch, Paul sang about his mother, Mary, comforting him, telling him to "Let It Be."

I was a daddy's girl, my mother having left him when I was two and then died not long after in a motorcycle accident with one of her precursor-hippie boyfriends. Nevertheless, I closed my eyes for the duration of the song, wishing she still existed and could lift her hand and rest it on my shoulder. She must have done that long ago.

Or maybe not.

During the strains of "Blackbird," I dreamt of my father for the first time in many months, his dark, winged hair breezing back from his wide forehead. Snuggled in the comforter freshly snapped down off the line yesterday afternoon, I wallowed in the numbness of slumber as he returned anew. Nobody told me how precious dreams of the dead become, how our own subconscious somehow gifts us with the time and space to once again be with those who have left us behind.

And so I lay basking in my father's presence, wishing so much for more time. But isn't that always the way? There he was, living in that little house in Towson, and I only saw him once a week. How differently I'd do things if I'd known he was slated for an autumn death. An accident at work. He was a plumber, a fact that used to embarrass me, an expert at redoing historical houses during his last decade. Nobody knew that wall was ready to fall down. They were just doing the initial walk-through. He was only fifty-five.

The cool morning air spirals the window curtains, and I inhale the breeze off Loch Raven to the bottom of my lungs. At the crest of the hill beside our home, earth—turned over and ready for planting by the farmer who lives next door—casts its loamy smell over the yard. As yet, the sun rests below a horizon unadorned but for the crabbed Dutch elm standing long past its expiration date. I hate that bleached thing. Why my neighbor, a sweet widower nicknamed Jolly, doesn't pull it down is as much a mystery as his very name. As far as I know, nobody knows Jolly's real name, and Jace and I wonder if Jolly even remembers. Maybe it actually is Jolly. Jolly Lester. I always figured it was John or Jacob or maybe James.

Jolly tries to live up to the name. Lord knows the man tries. But some days, especially when the rain falls in a light slick from a platinum sky, his sepia eyes tell me he misses his Helen with the longing of someone who loved one person all of his life and was content, even honored, to do so. And Helen loved him back.

The distant buildings of Towson peek over the trees, and farther yet, Baltimore lies hidden to me here. But life is beginning again in those places that formed me into this woman I've become, for good or for bad.

I should pray. My father taught me to pray.

Jace stirs. "You awake, Hezz?"

I sit up and grab for my robe. "I need to get that turkey in the oven so it's ready for sandwiches for the party this afternoon."

"What party?"

"We're having the end-of-the-year party for Will's class here, remember? I've got a ton of stuff to do. At least I decorated the cake already."

"Forgot. Would you like the shower first?"

"Nope. You go on."

"What kind of cake?"

"Triple chocolate with white chocolate buttercream icing."

"Mind if I take a piece to the office?" His mouth stretches into a smiley ribbon. He closes his eyes and I stare at my husband. Most women imagine that plainer women who've stolen a handsome man as their own must feel smug and superior having scored an undeserved hottie. Obviously, we've got brains or money or an extraordinary sense of humor to have nabbed such a prize.

Let me say, it isn't as easy as it looks. I know what people think when we walk into a restaurant. Tall, lean, good-looking Jace with his wavy brown hair and smoky eyes, his easy assurance, his ruddy skin warming up the room. They must wonder how on this green earth a little old roly-poly like me ended up with a movie star like him.

For the first ten minutes I'm conscious of myself in ways Jace has never made me feel. But he's just Jace, even in posh restaurants, placing his hand on the rounded waist that expanded with the growth of his child, smiling into eyes wrinkled from many afternoons squinting in the sun at swim meets, and laughing at my jokes that are only funny because of context, not content.

And they don't know that cucumbers give him terrible gas, that he can be a real jerk when he's sick, that he shuts down when he's mad, and that he still draws stick figures. They don't know that he doesn't call his parents nearly enough . . . that he gets upset about my spending habits, which I must admit are sometimes a little over the top. But it's too beautiful a morning to think about that.

I give his head a quick scratch. "I'll get you a cup of coffee, sweets."

Eyes still closed, he smiles. "I don't deserve you."

"Well, looks notwithstanding, that's probably true. Because I'm a good Christian woman, I seek an almost-perfection from the rising of the sun to the going down of the same. I volunteer at school; I once hosted a foreign exchange student; I color my hair, exercise at least three times a week to keep my temple from collapsing; I wear lipstick. Sometimes I wear two colors at once to manipulate the perfect coordinating shade with whatever Eddie Bauer or Talbots dreamed up for the season."

He squints. Why not continue?

"I tote a Vera Bradley purse with matching change purse, cell phone case, and makeup bag—which, honestly, I've never liked, Jace, but the Vera rage burned a couple of years ago at church, and I convinced myself a quilted handbag with a Noah's ark theme was not only a fine idea, but a potential witnessing tool, like a Jesus fish or a cross necklace."

"It's just a purse, hon." Jace leans up on one elbow. "You sure you don't want to shower first?"

"You know, I figured if I wore it steadily for three years, it would come to about ten cents a pop, and surely that's not bad, is it?"

Jace shakes his head, throws back the covers. "No, Hezz, it isn't." Under his breath he mumbles, "That purse is the least of it."

I wonder how long it'll take before he sees the new deck furniture. I'm glad I remembered to hide those bags from T.J.Maxx.

The coffeemaker is burbling like the creek on the west side of our property, the one that soaked Will clear down to his skivvies after he played in it at least four afternoons a week once the warmth of spring overlaid the fields and the woods.

Every so often that stream floods, and I am frightened for my son. Good reasons for this abound. Will was a wandering, curious tot with a certain "Don't you know I must be about my Father's business?" air about him.

Six thirty in the morning, and the forty-five minutes before I must awaken my son stretch in front of me like a sun-warmed path to the beach. I'm never alone, it seems, even with just one living child (and I wanted ten, but those thoughts are definitely for another day, or maybe next year). I feel so confined, as if my skin has thickened, hardened like the dried-up skin of a past-due tangerine, and inside this shell I'm fighting to be free, to be young and full of hope that I'm made for something more.

More than motherhood?

Justifiably so, the women at my old church would never understand these thoughts. Any woman who wanted more than motherhood wanted too much. But something inside me claws with puckered lips and shiny-bright eyes, believing it will drag not just me but all those I love right along with it onto a new roller coaster with longer drops to go speeding down but greater vistas from which to view the world.

I don't know how I know this, other than I've known it for years, known I was created to do something out of the norm; known that only one pregnancy out of five actually took because I wasn't cut out to be the mother of many nations; I wasn't destined to think that Elisabeth Elliott and her daughter have it all sewn up.

Gary and Mary Andrews fit into this somehow. See, right now

I'm living in a puzzle, the box lid having just been taken off, and I stare down onto the pieces, some clear, some hidden, and they work together somehow, but I'm just looking at them, smelling the woody pulp, and wondering, all the while knowing it's designed to do so, how in the world I'll make it all fit together and look like something real. Even the box lid sports no picture to guide me.

But first, the turkey.

Sliding the small bird out of the refrigerator, I lay the chilled pan on my soapstone counter. Just had to install those soapstone tops after a particularly enlightening episode of *Martha Stewart Living* on HGTV. Oven, 375 degrees. Rack in the lower third. Good. Poor bird, forced to give up its life for us. We'll eat every bit. After all, through no choice of its own, the creature sacrificed its life for our protein consumption, so how can I casually pitch it into the garbage without giving it some kind of meaning?

Thus the plethora of soups and casseroles that line the extra freezer in the basement; I long to give them away, but without a church home, who would I give them to?

Thus my weight problem.

But, honey, I can do more with a can of cream of mushroom soup than Paul McCartney ever could have hoped to do with two guitars, a bass, and drums. Although he did have Ringo to train. I have to allow for that.

I'd better vacuum a bit before we leave for school.

How do I live like this? The kitchen and family room alone spread out before me, larger than our first place down in Anneslie, a pea-sized second-floor apartment in an arts and crafts bungalow with a galley kitchen and a living room/dining room combo. But ah, the woodwork.

I insert the hose into the wall vacuum.

Less to vacuum there in Anneslie too.

Every year I think there must be more to life. And every year—despite a new car or a trip to a new land, new milestones and triumphs in my son's life, or a redone deck, a pool, a spa, or an entertainment system—I take stock and think once again, *I was made for more than this.*

But I love my stuff.

The hose jumps to life and I scrape the head back and forth over the cream-colored carpet.

Of course there's always church and God. And Jesus.

Something smells funny. Is the unit going up already?

Now Jesus, I get Him. I just wish I didn't forget Him when I open my eyes each morning and the day descends.

But church? Well, we left ours a year ago and still haven't found a place to settle. The praise songs had become so repetitive, the messages more of the same old "practical living advice" with a couple of Bible verses thrown in for good measure; and I was tired. Really, Jace and I were both just tired out. And there never seemed to be hope that a break was coming, that we wouldn't spend the rest of our lives doing this "stuff."

When Jesus said, "I will give you rest," I tend to think He meant the whole gamut, not just spiritual.

I finish the family room and the area rugs in the entry hall.

Jace enters the kitchen and refills his coffee.

"Jace, do you ever wonder what it was like for Jesus when He woke up each morning? Did He dread opening His eyes? Did He think, *Oh, Lord, all these people! People, people, people everywhere. How did it come to this? And why am I always the one who does the nice things? When was the last time anyone, especially one of these disciples, thought to do something nice for Me?* I have a feeling He didn't. He had no sin. He didn't carry around this darklight in His chest."

He pauses, coffeepot held midair. "Heather, are you okay?"

"Yeah. I just wonder about stuff like that sometimes."

"I'm a little worried about you. You seem really stressed."

"I'll feel better once the school year's done and this party is over."

"That fund-raising gala really took it out of you." He sets his mug down, walks over, and puts his arms around me. "I really love you, hon. You know that, right?"

I just burrow my face into his shoulder. I can't look at him when he starts making loving proclamations. If his professions are an accurate indication of his emotions, Jace adores me. So if he backs them up with candles and flowers and that sweet smile, why can't I believe him? With these sponge cake hips? This raggedy C-section scar? Come on, man! Where are your standards?

My hair is so greasy, and here I am snuggling into him. How can he stand it? "You know, Jace, with your looks, money, position, and exposure to the female kind in your practice, you could locate some remix of Martha Stewart with a little Gwyneth Paltrow thrown in for good measure. Some days I wonder why you don't."

"I don't know what more I can do to prove to you how much I love you, Heather."

He kissed me awake yesterday morning and whispered how much he loved me. When he got into the shower after I pretended to enjoy his lovemaking, I cried.

"What's wrong with me, Jace? Why can't I believe you? Why have I never believed you?"

"I don't know, Hezzie."

"It's not you."

"I know. I've always known that."

"It's got to be getting a little old."

"I'd be lying if I said it wasn't." He pours me a cup of coffee, and we stand on the side porch as the sun rises on this final day of school, peering through a misty sky, lighting the world as though nobody has given it permission and it doesn't want to overstep its bounds.

I turn around and refold myself into his tallness, and his arms surround me. I do love him.

"We need to get away together, Hezz."

"Yeah. Far away."

See, we fritter away our lives making enough to provide ourselves with four-star accommodations when we crawl home each night, and when all that isn't enough, when our bones are pitted and our muscles wasted, when our hearts are emptied out and imploded, we just want to get away from the reminders of our own foolishness.

My foolishness. Deep in my heart, I know this life on the hill over the lake is mine.

Jace never wanted any of this.

TWO

When Will went off to kindergarten, one mom did the Snoopy dance right at the end of the driveway as her last child climbed aboard the bus. There stood us first-time mothers crying our eyes to an angry, pulsating red, and Mary Jane, a veteran mom sending off her fifth and final, shuffled like Mr. Bojangles.

I understand now. In September my son will begin high school. And though I don't want to wish his youth away, I'll be dancing like Mary Jane did that day. School would be great if there weren't other children around being so mean and snobby and all. Just like their parents.

Will shuffles in, sleepy eyes weighed down by what looks like a dirty-blond Pomeranian atop his head. He lays his backpack against the desk. "Morning, Mom."

It's his birthday. We don't mention his birthday. After all, he says, he really had nothing to do with it, and if nobody is going to give me gifts as his mother, the woman who carried him for nine months, labored seventeen and a half hours, and went through major surgery to release him to the arms of the world, why should he get any? He simply showed up—invited, yes—but unable to accept or refuse. Fifteen years after the day he was born, I still can't wrap my mind around this eccentric soul. Now my heart is another matter entirely, of course.

I run my fingers through his hair. "Good sleep? Need a haircut?"

"Yes and no. I'll fix the eggs if you pour me a cup of coffee." He smiles with Jace's mouth and speaks with my father's voice, only a tad higher. Dad loved his grandson who inherited his artistic side. Dad painted murals on my bedroom walls, changing them with my interests. Now a man who can paint fairies one year and butterfly brides the next automatically qualifies as someone abnormally special.

Will opens the refrigerator door and leans down. Because we decided he should repeat second grade, he's three or four inches taller than most of the boys in his class, but probably weighs twenty pounds less. "Want cheese in your eggs?" He speaks with his new-found man-voice. And he smiles again, sending the love of my father right into the center of my heart.

"I wish you'd have known your grandfather better," I say.

"Me too. I loved going over there to spend the night. It must be a bummer to have no parents living."

"Yeah." A big bummer.

And now I feel like going shopping again. I'm not stupid. I know my incessant buying is trying to fill holes that purchases were never meant to fill. But I just feel so much better afterwards. Jace can't possibly understand. He's got the luxury of having living parents to take for granted and a satisfying career that actually helps people.

Laney, another room helper, helps me get sodas together for the party.

"Heather, do you ever feel like running away?" She leans against the counter, pulling the cans out of the plastic rings. She's pretty much the only room mother I really relate to. Unfortunately, I haven't taken the time to get to know her this year. That fund-raising gala took more than my money, that's for sure.

Laney's gorgeous. Figure that out. "I want to run away five days out of seven. It's those kids." Her oldest, Nicola, from her husband, Cade's, first marriage, is in Will's class and looks like her real mother, who isn't bad but is no Laney. The other four, who look like Laney, are under five and include a set of twins. And she's pregnant again. "Is that horrible?"

"No, it's understandable. We all feel that way sometimes." I heft a bag of ice out of the freezer.

"What about you? Do you ever feel like that?"

"Sometimes I look at my Suburban and wish it would turn into a sporty import, top down, so I can drive her away with no planned destination, no seat filled by a warm body, no music on the radio, no familiar bends, or houses, or ponds, or service stations." I lean my forearm on the cold bag. "Just drive and drive and drive. Why don't you start on the vegetables?"

"Sure." Laney reaches over to a head of cauliflower and begins to slice up florets for the fresh veggie tray that Carmen, the head room mother who terrorizes the rest of us, insisted we have even though we all know there isn't an eighth grader alive who will voluntarily touch the stuff. "Where do you end up in your dream?"

"I don't know. I never get that far, I guess."

I lied. Somewhere at the other end of the journey awaits a spare white bedroom with a single bed, a student desk and chair, and a reading lamp with a pale yellow shade. On the other side of the bedroom door a Purpose sits waiting on a straight-back chair, gray felt fedora beside him on the mission-style occasional table, hands folded over the brown leather grip of a banker's satchel. Occasionally he glances at his watch and wonders when I will wake up and emerge from inside.

This from St. Matthews Day School's Volunteer of the Year!

But I want to drive away to that white shell of a room and sit on the side of the institutional twin bed with its beige bedspread, gazing out of the small window overlooking a vacant lot dusted with some gum wrappers, a soda bottle or two, and an old dish towel twisted and squashed like a braided donut left for a week in the box. I'd sit that way until I garnered the courage to open the door and talk to my Purpose sitting in his chair.

He'd squeeze aloft his hat, stand up, hold the hat in both hands, and clear his throat. "Good then, Mrs. Curridge. There's still plenty of time left. Shall we?"

So I follow him out the door of the boardinghouse and onto a city bus. We ride for a long time, and I fall asleep to the cadence of the tar lines crossing the road. When I awaken, I find he's carried me into a small, tidy abode with a galley kitchen and white walls. The cupboards only hold eight plates, bowls, glasses, and mugs. All white and simple with that Palmolive shine. Or wait, does Palmolive soften your hands while you do the dishes? I can never remember.

He shows me each of the two bedrooms, small bedrooms probably 10 x 12. Seven sets of clothing hang in each person's closet, easy clothing, mix and match.

"This way, Mrs. Curridge."

We walk through the living room to the sliding glass doors, and on the balcony sit Jace and Will in molded white plastic lawn chairs. Jace stands. "Welcome home. We decided to get rid of all the extras while you were gone."

I say "Amen" to that.

I pour bagged ice over the sodas in the cooler.

"Laney, do you ever feel like you're going crazy?"

"Only all the time."

"But you've got more of an excuse."

"Yeah, those kids."

"But you look so gorgeous."

She begins to place the florets on a segmented tray, haphazardly without a care for effect. I like it. "It's genetics, Heather. I'm not going to age well, I can tell you that. Thin faces are fine midthirties. But with these cheekbones, I'm going to end up looking like that Madame puppet."

I bark out a laugh. "For me it's one minute you're a smooth-skinned twelve-year-old; the next you look like somebody rolled you around in beer batter and deep-fried you to a puffy golden brown." Thanks to the tanning bed in the exercise room in the basement. I had to have it after giving my sunlamp away to a man from church suffering from depression. "Brown fat is prettier than white fat, I always say. I've avoided the bathing suit department for years. I lie and say I don't swim, that I'm photosensitive."

"I think you're perfect. And sexy too." She grabs the carton of grape tomatoes. "Hey, I think we're pretty good for each other. We need to hang out more."

"You said it."

Me. Sexy. The girl must have standards as low as Jace's!

She scratches her cheek and tilts her head to the side. "Do you have these kinds of conversations with everyone?"

"I try to limit myself to two a day." I shake my head. "No, not usually. They just seem to be happening more and more. I don't know what's wrong with me."

"Just wondering." She reaches for a head of broccoli and pushes back a heavy, wavy chunk of burnished hair. "So how much of this stuff do you think will be eaten?"

"At least half, because Carmen will eat it herself just to prove she was right."

Laney raises a single brow. "But she'll be sneaky about it."

"Exactly."

We keep on chopping Carmen's veggies.

I reach into the fridge for the red peppers. "I watched an episode of *Oprah* a few years ago about a woman who found herself allergic to practically everything. She ended up living in a tent in the middle of the forsaken desert, away from cleaning products, paper products, new clothes, varnished furniture, anything with chemicals in it."

"I saw that too." Laney picks up a cucumber.

"And I envied her! I kept thinking, *Now wouldn't I like to trade places with her for a couple of weeks.* I haven't read a good novel in fifteen years! Not since Will was born."

"I read poetry."

"Me too, Laney. All the bang in less than five minutes. Unless it's epic, in which case, who cares? I just flip over to the short stuff."

"My favorite poem is 'The Highwayman,'" Laney says.

"'And the highwayman came riding, riding, riding . . .'"

"Yep, pretty much."

"Do you ever feel like you settled, Laney?"

"Yeah, a lot. I love my family, Heather, I really do, but I've got my PhD in biblical studies, and here I am with all these kids."

"Wow."

"I know it's a choice I made. But talk about guilt. When I feel good about being a mother, I feel guilty about not using my degree. When I'm studying to keep up on things, I feel guilty about not being a good mother."

"It's a never-ending cycle."

"And at church they could care less about my theological training."

"Really? Why?"

"Because I've got girl parts, I guess. I mean, what other reason could there be?" She lowers her voice to mimic some unseen pastor or elder. "'With your training, Laney, you should really be teaching. How about taking the Primary class?'"

"No."

"I kid you not, Heather."

"We left church a year ago and haven't found a home yet. I don't know what it is I'm looking for, Laney. I feel lost. I'd honestly rather stay home, read the Sunday *Sunpaper*, and eat homemade sticky buns."

"You're not the only one. I'm seeing it more and more."

"Am I ungrateful?"

"No. You're tired. We're all just tired of doing all this stuff and feeling as fractious and unhappy as ever before."

Lancy heads out to buy more ice. So the vacuuming's finished, I've dusted the furniture and the blinds, and now I just have to make sure the pool and the yard are in good shape.

Jace calls. "How's it going?"

"Almost ready. Just some last-minute things to take care of. To be honest, I'm kind of glad to be having something here. With church I could justify all this with the youth group and the ladies' groups meeting here, but it's been hard to live in a place like this just for us."

Church helped me justify this mammoth house. I mean, the

big-screen TV, the pool table, and the game systems were perfect for youth nights here on the bluff.

More. More. More.

How about a pool? Two years ago, there it finally lay, in blue sparkling California coolness, umbrellaed tables at the ready for the fellowship of God's people. Pool toys galore for the children—got those cheap at Tuesday Morning, though.

Built-in outdoor barbecue palace with a refrigerator and an ice-maker. Definitely a necessity.

"Still planning the tennis court, hon?" he asks. The tone is so slightly sour you'd only hear it if you'd been married to the guy for seventeen years. I pretend I don't.

"They break ground in July."

"Uh-huh. Hey, gotta go. I've got an afternoon surgery. I'll be home around eight."

I place the phone back in the cradle and head out to the upper deck leading off from the family room. Who could have told me that more, more, more is never enough, enough, enough? We have those dreams when we're tucked in those small apartments, thinking that lives lived in stone houses on hills overlooking lakes are surely free and easy. But those old days were exciting. I could put a gorgeous room together for under two hundred dollars, set a meal on the table for five bucks, buy a pair of jeans at the Salvation Army, and make the greatest skirts you've ever seen. Creativity proliferates in such circumstances, as I found in Jace's medical school years when we lived just fine all year on what we now pay for Will's tuition alone.

Great years, though, even with the limited income. How could I have known what a life we'd have when Jace first sat down in my chair at the hair salon for a buzz cut? Of course, I refused to clipper off those curls.

So, the deck furniture padding.

I open the doors to the pool house and start pulling out the golf-green cushions. This new furniture, more substantial, will last for years, I'm sure. A family from school told me about relatives who lost all of their furniture in a fire, so I gave them our patio furniture.

They picked it up yesterday. It was only a year old, so I didn't feel bad about handing it over as if I were giving away some second-rate castoffs.

Folks at school know me as someone willing to help out in such circumstances. It's really the only true ministry I've got these days.

Laney slips through the French doors. "I'm back. Here, let me help."

"Pads are in the pool house. Thanks for everything, Laney."

"Sure. I need the time away from home. I'll have to pick them all up soon enough. Are you sure you don't mind driving Nicola home after the party?"

"Positive."

At least my Suburban's good for something. I drive schoolkids everywhere. I'm the first pick for field trips because I always have drinks and snacks on board. However, I don't let the mean kids into my car. Will isn't the coolest kid on the block, and he suffers for it. I learned a long time ago that my being nice to the bullies does not make them behave any more nicely toward Will. So forget them.

The cushions distributed, I suggest a cold drink is in order. Cokes in hand, we settle on loungers by the deep end.

"So you had a life before all this, I'm guessing." Laney sweeps her hand over my vista.

"I had bigger dreams for myself, I suppose. I was a stylist, but I planned to major in business and have my own salon. I would have just called it *Heather*."

Heather.

A classy sign with simple raised gold lettering on a white oval, and tasteful heather floral arrangements to welcome my clients once they ventured inside. Good coffee available, fresh fruit and chocolate, wine in the evenings. Haircuts, spa treatments, community, a nurturing place in a busy world. "I miss talking to my clients, the other stylists, hearing the ins and outs of ordinary lives. It's all so big and important when it's somebody else's life, isn't it?"

"What happened?"

"I married a med school student."

"Well, at least he didn't dump you after he finished."

I raise my soda. "Here's to that, that's for sure. How long have you and Cade been married?"

"Six years."

"You happy?"

"Sometimes. I just want to get the child rearing over with. I miss the classroom so much, and here I sit with this belly out to here again."

"When are you due?"

"They say late July, early August. I lost track of when my last period was. And I refuse to get an ultrasound. My midwife doesn't like it, but she's a natural-type woman, so she understands."

"I'd say you have other stuff to think about."

I pull back up to the house around two thirty with a car full of kids intensely aware of the opposite sex, and ten minutes later their shouts ricochet off the waters of the pool and the slate patio. Two of the moms with lifeguard training stand on deck, chatting and getting browner by the minute. They look good in their suits. Not great. But darn good. Normally their volunteerism extends only to the sports program.

The girls have congregated around the edge of the pool, their skinny legs swallowed just below the knee by the water, chatting and gossiping while the majority of the boys, arms and legs loosely hinged, splash and dunk each other, hollering in their mid-change voices, thrashing about like clownish wildlife.

Will wants to join in, but he can't. He volunteered to man the grill, and Carmen is standing there looking over his shoulder. It's one thing to *be* the nerd; it's another to know you *are* the nerd. My heart breaks that he is the gangly, artistic oddball of the group whose voice changed sooner than the others. Yes, yes, I know he will do wonderful things someday, but that he's not welcome in this part of his world, a part I'm paying $20K a year for, mind you, makes me just plain angry.

And there's Ronald P. Legermin, the ringleader, whom I could absolutely strangle.

"I hate that child."

Laney whips her head around. "What?"

"Ronnie."

"So does Nicola. She can't stand him."

Whoa. I can't believe she didn't call me down for that one.

Carmen, dressed in the tropical theme of the party, pats Will on the back, then breezes in from the deck. Her skin glows like golden oak. "Burgers and dogs are almost done. Let's get the food out, ladies!" She clicks on her lime green slides over to my fridge, her derriere shaking like a Latin dancer's, and she yanks open the door. As she slides out Laney's veggie tray, a frown ages her brow. "Okay, then. Well. Heather, did you slice the turkey yet?"

"Yep. It's on a tray with the deli meats."

"And did you arrange it nicely? Please say yes." Laney reddens. Mercy, Laney, you're a PhD, for gosh sakes!

"Whether or not it's up to your standards, Carmen, I can't say." I point to the kitchen table where it's displayed. "Is that all right?"

She gazes over. "Oh yes. Relief. The cake is gorgeous too. You're almost professional at it, Heather."

Almost.

She clicks on over to the ice chests and peers in, nods—in satisfaction, I hope—then clicks over to the bathroom. She peeks her head back around the doorjamb. "Do you have any cleaning wipes?"

Laney and I exchange looks.

"I cleaned the bathroom this morning, Carmen."

"Really?"

"Are you that rude?" My hand flies to my mouth. Mercy!

Laney coughs into her hand.

Carmen reels backward. "Well, no, but I . . . well, I just thought I'd help out."

I cross my arms. Might as well keep going with it. I am losing it a bit after all, right? "Because I'm getting a little sick of your snide way of making the rest of us feel so unworthy."

Laney lays a hand on my arm. "Don't listen to her, Carmen. She's tired. She's married to a heart surgeon, you know, and they're never home." She squeezes.

"Right." I turn toward the refrigerator. Salad dressing. We need some for Carmen's veggies. Carmen clicks back toward the French doors.

I set the dressing on the table. "Do you think I'm losing it, Laney?"

"Maybe. Would that we could all lose it like that."

After Laney arranges the rest of the food, the kids file in, and Ronnie Legermin pushes his way through the crowd. I wish he wasn't so good-looking. His dark hair is richer than any color I ever applied in the salon, and his wide shoulders loom above slender hips. "I'm first. Get out of my way, folks!"

He shoves Will, who almost loses the platter of grilled meat.

"Hey!" I say.

Will looks at me with eyes that say, *Please, Mom. Don't.*

"Ladies first, Ronnie. Get back in the back of the line."

He stalks back, and soon the group of boys are laughing and pointing at me.

After setting the platter on the table, Will slinks up to his room.

Carmen claps her hands, her bracelets jingling, and gives out a list of at least ten instructions, ending with, "I just cleaned the bathroom, so you're all good to go."

That sneak!

A kid shouts, "Literally!"

Somebody, please, anybody, get me out of here.

Nicola loads two plates and disappears up the steps.

Jace arrives home after the crowd has filed away, all except Nicola, who's playing Super Smash Brothers with Will in the study. She's kicking his butt, and he's letting her with nary a clue. Jace throws his keys in a delft bowl placed on a half-moon table near the garage entry.

"How'd it go?"

"Good. They're almost all gone." I reach into the fridge for a V-8. "I'm going to run Nicola home in a while. She and Will are having a good time."

"Does he *like her* like her?"

"I think so." I hand him the drink.

"And do we approve?"

"Definitely."

THREE

An hour later, we drop Nicola off at that bustling city row house Laney makes a home by utilizing an enthusiastic palette on the walls and decent finds at Goodwill. Nicola, brilliant in math, receives a healthy scholarship to St. Matthews. Laney, baby on hip and another tugging on her T-shirt, invites us in for something to drink but is visibly relieved when we decline.

Her husband, Cade, slogs in from the kitchen, one of the twins, a boy named Reid, wrapped around his foot like a sniffling moon boot. "Thanks for bringing her home, guys." Cade peers with aquamarine eyes from a face pitted and scarred long ago by a youthful battle with acne. He's the same height as his wife, with a paunch thicker than the lenses of his glasses, and Laney loves him. Talk about an unstereotypical couple: a house painter/carpet layer and a woman with a doctorate together caring for a passel of children. He loves her more, though. There's always the one side of a couple who loves more. It's Cade in this case.

After the good-byes, we find ourselves lost in a crumbling downtown neighborhood. Jace fell asleep two seconds after I turned out of Laney's neighborhood in hopes that signs to the Jones Falls Expressway would appear. I still haven't figured out who loves who more in our case. I don't want to.

Jace's snore practically shreds the upholstery. He's so good-looking, and then this snore rips out. It's like Mickey Mouse cussing or something.

I should have brought Will. He wanted to come, but Jace and I spend so little time alone we suggested he watch a movie instead. So now he's asleep, and wow, what quality time this has turned out to be.

I pull over and nudge Jace. "Hey! Wake up!"

"What's the matter, hon?"

"Look. I got us lost."

He sits up. "Huh? How?"

"I've only been to the Petersons' once before."

"Do you have any idea where we are?"

"Last thing I remember is North Avenue."

"North Avenue? Why would you turn on North Avenue?"

I've got to admit, it's getting a little scary around here. "I was looking for Charles Street. I just sort of recall those wacky street-lights that line the road. But I think I turned the wrong way. So I went down a side street to turn around and bottomed out into this one-way street, and now I have no idea where we are."

"Okay. Pull into that gas station there and I'll get directions."

"It's got bars on the window. Let me drive to something else."

"Hezz . . ."

"Okay, okay."

Jace and I have switched male/female genes when it comes to get-ting directions. I am off the charts masculine, because really, if you drive on long enough, you're going to recognize something eventu-ally, aren't you? And I am the expert at taking long drives and find-ing my way back home again.

He hops out of the car, the anemic light from the awning over the gas pumps encouraging his light brown hair to turn a sickly sort of green, and yeah, look at how much more white glitters along his temples. Mercy, Jace! Getting to be an old man there!

A man saunters up to him in drawers with the crotch practically scraping the cracked pavement. He gestures in such a way that it seems he's offering something. Jace shakes his head and says, I think, that he just needs directions. He points over at our Suburban.

Okay, Jace, big mistake there.

"Hi, Mr. Drug Dealer, we're rich whiteys from the country just ripe for the picking!"

My scalp freezes as I watch the man, all of twenty-two, reach out and put his finger in Jace's face. Jace instinctively backs up. The man laughs, clapping his hands.

The radio is playing "Wake Me Up Before You Go Go."

I have two choices here.

Stay in the car. Jace would approve, wanting me to be safe; getting out would be a ten-regiment assault on his masculinity.

But he's a surgeon, not some tough guy.

He's brave every time he operates, but this is different, right?

Maybe if I just beep the horn. Or should I get out?

But before I can, he steals a glance my way, parallels his hand to the blacktop, and quickly slides it back and forth.

Okay. So stay put.

But I promised to stand beside him through thick and thin. I put my hand on the latch in readiness. My mouth dries out.

At least I can lower the music and roll down the window to hear what's going on, because like George Michael, I'm not planning on going solo either.

"I'm just looking for directions," Jace says.

"And I just want to see what you got to offer me for those same said directions."

"Are you threatening me?"

Man, his voice is really calm. Guess when you've stopped someone's heart with the full belief you'll start it back up again, this is mac 'n' cheese.

An inky Mercedes pulls up, blacked out and flat except for the chain motif around the license plate. Florida plates. Heaven help us, this is probably the big dude. Now the hair stands up at the back of my neck.

Cell phone! Cell phone! I'm an idiot! Cell phone!

I root through my purse as a very short, impeccably dressed man, his warm brown suit a shade lighter than his skin, slides out and walks over in a smooth, unhurried stride.

"Are you giving my man trouble here, man?"

Oh no.

I knew I should have cleaned out my purse. I thrash my hand around inside among the Noah's ark animals, feeling at least ten lipstick tubes, a can opener (a can opener?), loose change, hoping I'll hit the keypad and the phone will light up.

There.

And as I drop the phone into my palm, ready to dial, a new voice, female, pulls my eyes away from the phone and back to the scene.

"Ezekiel Campbell, you'd better leave that man alone!"

A woman taller than Jace strides into view, her nun's veil flying behind her.

The first guy holds up his hands. "Sister J, I was just talking to the man."

She turns to the Mercedes man. "You, you rascal, you get out of here."

"This is my corner, nun lady."

She doesn't flinch. "No. You'd *like* it to be your corner. I'm telling you, get in that dang sleazemobile and scram!"

"And if I don't?"

Her pale, wrinkled skin reddens, and she jerks her head toward Ezekiel. "Tell him what will happen, Zeke."

"She took in Knoxie Dulaney when his grandmother died. Practically raised him."

"Shoot."

"Yeah, man. You'd better get outta here."

The man holds a finger up to his lips.

Sister J points to him. "My corner. You got that?"

He steps into the car, shuts the door, and leans out the window. "How could a nun raise a devil like Knox Dulaney?" He drives off slowly, not in the scraping peel I expected.

"Go home, Zeke," the nun says. "You're better than this bull." And she kisses his cheek. She whispers something in his ear, and he shakes his head, smiles, then shuffles away.

I finally clamber out and Jace waves me over.

I run toward them. "Mercy! Are you okay?"

Jace whooshes out some relief.

I turn to the heroic nun. "Thank you so much!"

"No big deal." She waves a chapped, man-sized hand.

"Was that guy really dangerous?"

"Who, Zeke? No. He's just stuck. He's not such a rascal once he knows you. Now that other guy, I don't know who the heck he is. D'you see those Florida plates? His corner! His corner, my rear end!"

"Thank you, sister," Jace says. "I'd like to say I could have handled it, but that was way out of my league."

"Frish, but this place is out of most people's. Never mind that."

Frish?

"I'm Sister Jerusha."

"Jace Curridge."

"Heather."

Her speech hails from a more northerly location than Baltimore. Sounds like it grew up in the Bronx or someplace once upon a time, but I'm no expert on these things. And it kind of explains a nun using the word *bull*. Call me old-fashioned, but I didn't expect that.

Jace shoves his hands in his pockets. "Where did you come from? It seemed like you appeared from nowhere."

Sister Jerusha tilts her head to the left and points to a decrepit old hotel across the street. "There. I was almost home from visiting with one of my ex-clients when I saw what was going on. I was just about to go inside when I heard 'Wake Me Up Before You Go Go' coming out of your car. Frish, but I always loved that song."

Frish?

"Then I saw Zeke talkin' smack, so I waited a minute until that Florida boy pulled up. I may be sixty-five years old, but these boots are still made for walkin', if you know what I mean."

"You live there?" I ask.

"Run the place, doll."

A sign above the aluminum-framed glass doors reads "The . . . Hotel." The original name is covered over in electric blue paint.

"What do you do there?"

"What don't we do there is the better question. Meals—three a day. A nurse comes in once a week. Showers. Food pantry. Clothing center. Fourth floor we use for recovering addicts. Displaced women whether prostitutes or battered women—third floor. Families transitioning from homelessness—second floor. And then there's the big room where guys hang out during the day and have a meal or come in off the street on cold nights. We open that up when it hits below thirty-two degrees. Otherwise it's up to them to find shelter. City rules."

So she's given this spiel, what, at least a thousand times?

"Come on over and I'll fix you a cup of tea. I'm sure you could use something to calm your nerves after those thugs tried to put the make on you."

I look at Jace. It's late.

But he's all over it. "Good idea. If you don't mind."

"'Course not. Hold on, just let me tell Jaleel inside you're leaving your truck here for a little while."

She walks into the store.

Jace turns to me and blows out a whistle. "I pictured a bullet in my head more than once."

"I didn't know what to do. I was just about to dial 911 when the nun came running over."

"She's unbelievable, isn't she?"

"How tall do you think she is?"

"At least six-two."

"No wonder they listen to her."

The bell on the convenience store's door clangs against the glass. Sister Jerusha flies through like a bat. "It's all okay. Just leave that thing right there and follow me." Her glance slides along the Suburban. "Good Lord, that truck's a monster."

We cross the street, and she shoves a key into the lock of the double doors. "We lock up at nine in good weather. Plus, that's the curfew for our residents unless they have a work pass." She ushers us into a large room with pink-and-salmon-colored checkerboard floor tiling, strips of fluorescent overhead lighting, square tables, and chrome chairs. A long table stretches across the back of the room, presumably where the food is brought during meals, but I can't be sure. A desk sits perpendicular to the door, and an African-American man who must weigh four hundred pounds, with a head bigger than a Halloween pumpkin, a long thin nose, and one gold chain with a crucifix hanging around his forty-inch neck, says, "Good evening, Sistah J."

"Mo, this is . . . frish, but I already forgot your names, now, didn't I?"

Jace shakes his hand. "Jace Curridge. This is my wife, Heather."

Mo's hand swallows Jace's, and all I can think is, "Don't crush that hand! It makes lots of money!"

Pathetic but true.

Sister Jerusha tucks in a wisp of gray hair that escaped her veil. "What do you know about that rascal with the Florida plates? Big black muscle Mercedes?"

Mo leans back in the office chair, and I pray the springs hold. "Knoxie brought him on. Some distant cousin on his mother's side."

The hardened face of the nun softens for a second. "I don't like him."

"If he's working for Knoxie, he's not supposed to be likable."

"Have you seen Knox lately?"

Mo shakes his head. "Good riddance to bad rubbish."

"Don't talk about my godchild like that, doll."

"Godchild or not, Sister J, he deserves more than a name like that."

Sister Jerusha turns to us. "Knox went south. I tried, but what can you do? When his grandmother passed away, he was already fifteen. I was too little, too late."

Mo rolls his eyes. "You was a lot too late. He was already bad seed, and I should know." He taps the desk. "So you giving these folks the fifty-cent tour?"

"Heck yeah. It's payment for me saving their lives!" She laughs. Her smile blesses us with a loveliness previously unseen. Sister Jerusha was actually a beautiful woman in her day, I'll bet, very big but very beautiful. "Follow me. We'll start right here." She sweeps a hand around the room, empty except for two men in sweat suits filling out paperwork or something. Hard to tell.

"This room is a hodgepodge of scrap. The floor in these lovely designer shades came from the Dumpster at Color Tile, and the paint from the Dumpster at Lowe's."

Hmm. "Not a bad shade of blue."

"I know. Lucky for us."

"Is that right? You get a lot of stuff from Dumpsters?" Jace.

"You bet. We haven't been Dumpstering enough lately. But what can you do? I only have so much time in the twenty-four hours the good Lord gives me each day. You wouldn't believe the things you can find out by the malls, though. We're thinking of selling them on eBay to raise money for operational expenses."

She laughs. So do we.

"I'm serious, doll."

"What about government funding?" Jace asks.

She pushes through a swinging door, and we find ourselves in the kitchen. "Not a dime. We're privately funded." She is proud of that. "We're pretty much the last stop on the line for a lot of our clients."

Clients.

"Yep. We're here when all the principalities and powers have failed them and only Jesus'll do. God's Spirit keeps us humming."

The kitchen needs a good scrubbing. The stainless steel work-table is covered with crates of broccoli and some canned goods. The industrial stove . . . well, let's hope the Health Department doesn't inspect the place anytime soon.

"Kitchen. As I said, three meals a day, seven days a week. In the past ten years we've served over two million meals."

"Is that right?" Jace gazes at the Peg-Board holding colanders, spatulas, and other utensils. He's a gadget guy—can actually deep-fry a turkey if you please. "All that from right here?"

"The Christmas and Thanksgiving meals have become their own entity. Lots of volunteers during those times. And believe me, we'll take whatever we can get whenever we can get it. A lot of people doing what we do get all high and mighty about the holiday do-gooders. Not us! No sirree. If you show up, we'll put you to work, no questions asked."

"Where do you get that kind of money for food?" Jace.

"Almost all our food is donated. We don't buy anything except food for the holiday meals. Got to have turkey and dressing for the holiday meals—five thousand people we feed that day in four shifts. I make the stuffing myself. And I make a good stuffing. My mother's recipe, God rest her."

I readjust my purse on my shoulder. "Restaurants and stores donate?"

"You bet. It can get a little lean some days, and we have to do a lot of soup, crazy soup, and then some days there's caviar. It's a crazy way to run a place. Anyway"—she points to a doorway—"that's my office and my quarters back there. Nothing to sneeze over. Not even worth the steps it takes to get over there. Unless, of course, you're a collector of crucifixes like me or you have a thing for duct-taped recliners."

How could we resist a combination like that?

We head back out to the main room.

Depression hangs like an ocher fog. The plaster is so old the walls buckle and bubble and crack, and somehow sadness has oozed like black mold into those crevices to stay. I guess there's only so much hope, so much sweat that can keep it from taking over completely.

Sister J ambles over to a corner where a Bunn coffeemaker rests on a card table. "I'd marry this thing if I wasn't already married to Jesus." She laughs at her own joke. "It was donated by Jack Billing, who owns Baltimore Coffee. Boiling hot water anytime you want it. How about that tea?"

We nod and she plucks some chipped mugs from a nearby shelf, mine celebrating *200 Years! Bicentennial USA!* thirty years too late, and Jace's apparently a year-round tribute to Kwanzaa.

As she fixes our cups, she rambles on about all of the refurbishment that has taken place over the years, how the Hotel looks like Buckingham Palace compared to what it was when they held hands out front, praying to the Spirit for strength and declaring that redemption had come to this neighborhood. I had no idea nuns could be so spiritual. Who ever heard such talk?

Finally we sit down at one of the tables in the now-empty room. "We're a Catholic Worker community."

"Dorothy Day," Jace.

She nods, brows raised. "You bet. You've heard of her?"

"Big time." He turns to me. "The Catholic Worker movement started in the Depression, hon."

"Some people call us leftist crazies because we hate war." Sister Jerusha barks out a laugh, then reaches into her pocket and draws out a white hankie she begins to fumble. "We call ourselves a ministry of presence. The first step is to be here, to be present. So anytime anybody wants to come in and just hang out with the clients in the main room, we relish that. You don't have to work your fingers to the bone in the kitchen, although we can always use an extra pair of hands. Our first step is to just be around."

"Interesting." Jace looks up at the ceiling. "Need some new tiles there."

"Heck, yeah. We need a new administrator if you ask me. I can only get so excited about facilities and fund-raising." She points to a set of steps to the right of where we came in. The newel post is long gone, but with some rubbed-down wooden carving and a bit of gingerbread, it's easy to tell it was once a hotel staircase. "I love being with the people. That's my thing, getting into their heads, seeing what's in their hearts, stealing them back from the devil. Ha! Anyway, upstairs it's like I told you. Getting late, so I won't take you up there."

"And you've been here ten years?" Jace asks.

"Eleven in October. We've also got the food pantry and clothing ministry like I said, around the corner in a warehouse. Plus, people can do laundry there. Got a phone there by Mo's desk for clients to use. We do a lot for the working poor too."

The working poor?

"Lot of 'em can't afford to install a phone line, so they can use this one. We try to provide those little things most people have learned to take for granted. Frish, but it's hard to get a good job if your clothes aren't clean, isn't it?"

"What about classes and job training?" Jace asks.

"Lots of that with the families in transition and our former street people upstairs. But as far as the homeless gang that comes in for meals most days, well, remember, we're the last stop on the line. We can only give them food and respect in exchange for a little bit of nothing. A lot of them don't want to be helped other than that, and God forbid we shove them aside because of it. A ministry of presence is what we do. I can't explain it any better than that."

I brighten. "And who knows what God might do in their lives in the future?"

Sister Jerusha shakes her head. "Oh, doll, I wish I had that kind of optimism left. Most of the downstairs folk die of overdoses or exposure or AIDS or whatnot. As I keep saying . . . last stop on the line. But somebody's got to be around for the least of the least."

"Thank you for the tour." Jace drains his cup, then stands up. "It's late, and we don't want to keep you."

"Thanks for coming over. I love showing people the place. And we can always use any help anybody's willing to give. Time is always of the most value. Money only goes so far."

She walks us to the door. A loud knock vibrates the aluminum frame. Sister Jerusha peers through the glass, shakes her head as she twists the bolt and opens the door.

A loud, shrill voice gushes over us like ice water.

"Sister J, I'm so sorry, I didn't mean to be late. I waited for the bus for over an hour."

"Don't lie to me, Krista. I can smell your breath. You know the rules."

She's seven months pregnant if she's a day.

"But I swear I'm telling the truth."

"Out. Back out there. Come back at eight for breakfast, and we'll talk then."

"Please don't send me out there."

"This is the fourth time, Krista." She turns to Mo. "Right, Mo? Four times."

"She's right. Now you know I can't let you by this desk, so come back in the morning."

Krista begins twisting a thread of expletives so foul even Jace raises a brow. Sister J and Mo remain like stone.

Mo stands to his feet. "Do I have to escort you out?"

Krista flips him the bird and backs out. "I ain't never coming back here. You love your rules more than you love people!" More cankered words and a jabbing finger at Mo. "You are no brother to me, sir!"

The door shuts her out.

We turn to face the pair of them. "Wow," I say.

"Will she be back?" Jace.

Mo sits back down. "Shoot, yeah. If not tomorrow, then the next day. They almost always come back. She's not herself right now. Krista's not all that bad when she's not strung out. In fact, she's downright sweet. You all be careful driving home."

As we swing through the door, I hear Sister Jerusha say to Mo, "Bread delivery will be a little late in the morning. Is the nurse coming?"

And we are already forgotten.

We practically run to the car, jump in, and press the lock button right away.

What a couple of milksops!

"Mercy, Jace!"

"Wow, some evening. Can you believe that place?"

"Can you believe you might have been shot?"

He turns the key in the ignition, the car engine humming a timely tune of departure. "I don't know. It all seems a little weird, like some contrived way Sister Jerusha gets volunteers. Wait for people to get lost, sic Ezekiel on them, and come to save the day so she can do a tour."

"Pretty much."

"Seriously, she's a whirlwind, isn't she?"

"I'm still reeling from all that energy." I turn in my seat to face him, adjusting the shoulder strap. "It's hard to believe one person can do so much."

"Right. I know exactly what you're saying." He pulls out of the gas station. Good-bye, Jaleel, who watches us from inside.

"And turning that girl back out on the street. I didn't understand that, Jace."

"Imagine trying to run a place like that and not have your rules mean something, though."

"Yeah, that's probably true. You know, we really should send them a donation, don't you think? Fix that ceiling, redo the plaster on the walls, put some decent shelving in the kitchen?"

"Big time."

We are quiet the rest of the way home, leaving the city behind and returning to the soft darkness of the hill over the lake where the only lights are those of the fireflies who've never seen Jaleel, Jerusha, Krista, or Mo, and probably never will.

Three days later we find ourselves at a large church inside the beltway, its campus spreading like jam over a twenty-acre plot. The band plays with perfection, its singers in coordinating outfits looking like they just came home from lunch at the club or a day at work downtown. Tasteful ficus trees dot the auditorium, spilling a few brown leaves on the understated beige carpet.

Everything is so perfect. Just so perfect.

Turning into the parking lot of Gibby's Restaurant, I say to my family, "Do you picture Jesus as perfectly coiffed or kinda messy?"

"Messy," Jace.

"Most definitely messy," Will.

"I'm kinda messy, at least on the inside. Is there a church out there where people can be messy?"

Jace pulls into a space near the back of the lot. "Everybody's messy, hon."

"Okay, then, Mr. Smarty-Pants. Is there a church out there where we can admit we're messy?"

"I'd like to think so."

Jace hates the church-shopping we're doing. But right now, at this point in my life, the thought of settling down with another bunch of Christians makes me want to scream. He wasn't tripping the light fantastic down the aisles either, if I remember correctly. It was such a big church, you see, the faithfuls working their fingers to nubbins so the other 75 percent could sit in the pews without feeling at all uncomfortable.

As far as I remember, the gospel isn't all marshmallows and cream. But who am I? Just another woman in Christendom who's trying to figure out why she feels so defeated all the time and is coming up with a long list of problems but a short list of answers.

Is it the church? Is it me? Is it Jesus?

We all go down for a nap, our bellies full of crab cakes, crispy fries, and a snappy coleslaw. But I do not sleep. I wait for Jace's ripping snore and tiptoe into Will's room. Yep, his nose-whistle assures me he's slumbering, dreams of Nicola probably sashaying across his pubescent brain.

Time for a drive. I resist the urge to drive by Gary and Mary's house. There's time for that tomorrow or the next day or the next. I just want to drive and find my little house with white rooms, white plates, and an 8 x 8 plot of lawn with white rocks in the flower beds and some angled Japanese shrubbery that points a jointy finger, saying, "Less is more, my friend. Beauty in simplicity is still lavish and full of grace."

Okay, maybe not.

An hour is all I safely own, so I turn right out of the driveway and head out on Jarrettsville Pike. So many whispering trees and staunch white fences, hay fields and horse pastures, still ponds and winding creeks. Hess Road beckons me onto its twists and turns, and before I even realize it or know quite how I got there, I am in the veterinarian's office parking lot and the Andrews's house rests in a puddle of shade from the oak trees surrounding its sides and back. And no one is home again.

FOUR

Well, at least summer throws most of Will's school and extracurricular activities into hibernation. We zip around like bees all year long, and now summer's arrived, no school play, no band practice, no Japanese. No. No. No. No art class. No fund-raisers and cleanup days at the school. No "cooking with kids" at the community college.

I love this.

Okay, except for swim team. That party's just getting started.

Lark calls. "Hey, Heather."

Lark is the closest thing I have to a best friend.

"Hey, Lark."

"Summer's begun. You ready?"

"Yeah. Pretty much."

"Bring Will down for lunch tomorrow. Leslie needs some fresh faces around here."

"How's your mother doing?"

"The cancer is progressing, unfortunately. Six months, they're telling us."

"Poor Leslie."

I can picture her waving a hand.

"Oh, you know her. She's not admitting anything is wrong. She hired a new housekeeper and is giving the poor person fits."

Yeah, they're loaded.

"Nobody can replace Prisma."

"Obviously. This is number five since Prisma moved. So you coming tomorrow or what?"

"Why not? We could use a drive down into the city."

"Good. See you around lunchtime. This new housekeeper's a great cook. Not that Mother appreciates it." Her voice changes, dripping with aged Southern honey. "'I'm sick of field greens, Larkspur. If everything's as bad as you all say, then please get me off this heart-smart stuff so I can enjoy myself to the bitter end.'"

"She's got a point, Lark."

"You may be right about that. See you around noon."

"We'll be there. Hey, who gets the Christmas stocking this year?"

"Don't know yet."

She's always embroidering a stocking. One a year. Intricate needle-work that leaves everybody guessing all year long who will be the lucky recipient.

Ha. Right. I wonder if it's for me.

Lark Summerville and I crossed paths a few years ago at a fund-raiser for her late father's charitable foundation, the Summerville Foundation. One of Jace's surgeon friends dragged us along. I experience a guilty pleasure at these sorts of engagements, I have to admit. I grew up staunchly in the lower realms of the middle class. Dad supported us in our little brick row house on Joppa Road in Towson where our neighbor transformed his small front yard into the formal garden of Versailles. I always knew what the male anatomy looked like, thanks to Mr. lo Fabro. But my dad's idea of a high time was a Colts game with buddies from work and dinner afterwards at Johnny Unitas's Golden Arm Restaurant.

She was trying to brush her crazy mane of kinky hair in the bath-room when I first saw her. I thought she was a child at first—she's that tiny. And as women sometimes do, we just hit it off, were laughing within thirty seconds and revealing our souls. I've always felt sorry for men because I don't believe that happens to them very often.

We ditched the fund-raiser and opted for tea at Starbucks, her treat. I caught our reflection in the plate glass window of the storefront as we searched for a table outside in the summer air. With my height and weight next to hers, well, we'd have been the perfect choice for the casting director of *Of Mice and Men: A Female Review*.

Mercy! I was Lenny.

The tea was bitter yet weak, and I didn't care.

She pulled out her embroidery, that year's Christmas stocking, and we talked until Jace, after a frantic cell phone call, picked me up to go on home. Lark said, "Oh, lucky you. You get to go home with him. I get to go home to Mother."

I belt out a laugh as we travel down 695 toward Charles Street and the home Lark shares with Leslie, Leslie Strawbridge Summerville, a socialite's socialite in her day. That woman's royal bearing settles in a subtle cloud of expensive perfume around all who draw near, but according to Lark, she has mellowed a bit in her old age, or as Leslie herself calls it, her "dotage."

"What's funny?" Will asks. I tell him the story. Will likes to read. He gets literary references but fails to see how I could be Lenny under any circumstances. He likes the Beatles too.

"Does Miss Lark still play the organ, Mom?"

"No. She gave that up a few months ago. Had to because of her crazy schedule with her dad's charity."

Lark was the organist at St. Dominic's for years. She plays a mean organ. A raging river of an organ that will pull you downstream if you're not careful. How that little person can birth such resplendent sound from those childlike hands and feet is about as mystifying as a five-thousand-square-foot house on a quarter-acre lot. She rebelled against her parents' wealth and situation by impregnating herself via a wild boy from her posh set, running away from home to play keyboard with his rock band and then, after the divorce, running into the arms of the church.

I believe she looked at her music as God's open arms.

"Maybe she'll play something for you at the house." We fly under the overpass for York Road. I always fly places. I have to ease up on the gas pedal one of these days. Jace ribs me for the way I drive. And he's totally right. Not only do I drive too fast; I'm not really very good at it. I had two accidents in beauty school, one *not* my fault. Only the grace of God and an enervated guardian angel keep Will and me alive, and the other people on the road as well. When I see someone walking with a stroller alongside a busy road with no sidewalks, I want to yell, "Don't you know there are people like me on the road?"

I turn to Will; he points my gaze back to the road. "You glad school's out, bud?"

"Most definitely. I don't think my crotch could stand another month."

"What!" Oh, dear God. "What do you mean?"

"Wedgies, Mom."

"They give you wedgies?"

He just nods.

After what I sowed with Gary and Mary Andrews in school, I hoped to counteract any rotten crops that could be reaped by my own children. I volunteer every chance I get, show my face all the time like that bee that won't go away no matter how hard you bat the air.

"I'm sorry."

"I don't know what more I can do to get those kids to leave me alone."

"There's nothing you can do with kids like that, believe me."

"Were you bullied?"

"In the early grades."

"What happened after that?"

"Julia B. moved in. She liked me and she created a new regime."

"Oh. Were you one of the mean ones after that?"

"No," I lie.

"Phew. Good. I'd hate to think of my own mother like that. I think I'd lose all respect for you if you were once one of them."

Does Will suffer because of my sin? Does God say, "See how it feels to see someone you love ridiculed and ostracized?" He wouldn't do that to a good boy like my son, would He?

Maybe it's easier to ride past that house instead, begging for-
giveness. From Gary and Mary and Will. And God. Again and again
and again.

"Do you want to go to public school next year?"

He taps his fingers on his thigh. "No. They're jerks, Mom. One
day they'll look back on what they've done, maybe when they've had
their own kids, and they'll pay. I'm a big believer in justice if we only
have a little patience."

"I'm sorry."

"And Nicola's cool. We're already planning to hang out all the
time next year. She doesn't take anything from anybody. Especially
Ronnie Legermin. He won't come near her!"

"That's good."

"Most definitely. Those guys have problems to begin with, Mom,
if they keep having to reach down into another guy's drawers to make
themselves feel better."

"Yeah, but it's your drawers." I really am going to talk to the prin-
cipal about this.

Did I say I hated Ronnie Legermin?

We pull onto Greenway, a street in Guilford, one of Baltimore's old-
money enclaves. Not that Lark's dad hailed from old money, but
Leslie sure grew in a womb of privilege! Generations of money. Horse
money, tobacco money, land money, trace-your-lineage-back-to-John-
Smith money. Virginia money so old it hasn't had its own teeth for
well over a century. Lark's dad, James Summerville, founded
Baltimore Machinery Parts with a thousand dollars and his brain.
Since he could never be old money on his own, he married it. And
Leslie never let him forget it! Oh, that woman is a real stinker. But one
of those lovable old stinkers who would drop everything to help you
at first beck and call. Lark tells me she wasn't always this way.

In the three years Lark and I have been friends, Will and I have
visited the house many times. Lark prefers rambling within the city

limits, and the chauffeur—yes, chauffeur—would rather be garden-
ing, so instead of inconveniencing him, she ends up catching the bus
or a cab to most of her appointments. That's Lark in a nutshell.

We turn through the gate in the stone wall surrounding their city
acre and pull up to the parking pad at the side of the house. Fashioned
of local granite with an olive cast, the house on Greenway is one step
away from a haunted manor house in which Mary Shelley would feel
quite at home. Perhaps Percy as well. Talk about going against the
flow, those two!

The door, slightly medieval and masculine with wrought iron
hinges and a ringed latch, fools the first-time visitor about the
innards of the house, and Lark once told me what I'd suspected to
be true. Her father built the house before he met Leslie Strawbridge.
She has never liked it and doesn't mind saying so. She calls it "my
medieval monstrosity."

Inside, well, it holds everything you'd imagine a gracious Southern
woman would deem worthy of her home. Impeccable. Expensive but
not flamboyant like something you'd find in a casino or on the
Trinity Broadcasting Network or, heaven help us all, in a *Yankee's*
home. Tasteful reds, greens, and yellows, every stick of furniture an
antique or handmade. No Pier 1 or Pottery Barn fare on Greenway.
I doubt if Leslie has even heard of those lifestyle purveyors.

I yank on a cord leading to a bell mechanism housed somewhere in
the stalwart facade. A Quasimodo bong shivers our eardrums. Leslie
must hate that thing. As we wait, the sound of Charles Street traffic
borne on the breeze of a waning morning caresses our eardrums. I've
always loved the city for some reason.

Finally the door is jerked open, and there stands quite the most
rough-and-tumble-looking man I've seen in a long time. Grizzled,
he smiles, his missing left front tooth reminding me of the cook in a
stereotypical western, only twice the size and with that Fu Manchu,
a little more motorcycle around the edges. "Welcome!" And he
bends at the waist in one of the most awkward bows I've ever wit-
nessed firsthand. Come to think of it, I believe this is the only bow
I've ever witnessed firsthand.

". . . Thanks . . . ?"

A voice calls from the stairway, and Leslie's slender feet in bone-colored Grasshoppers descend the runnered steps. "Lloyd! For goodness' sake, we don't bow around here. Who do you think we have visiting, the Archbishop of Canterbury? Just let them through the door, if you please."

Lloyd steps aside in his hiking boots. So this is the new housekeeper. I had pictured my grandmother or Hazel, the nutty housekeeper on the old sitcom I used to love as a tot. Mr. B.! Mr. B.!

Maybe I need a housekeeper.

"Hi, Mrs. Summerville." I hurry over and circle my arms around her bony shoulders. She smells like lemon balm today.

She kisses my cheek and pulls back. "I do enjoy a hug from you, Heather, and truth to tell, I'd rather visit with you than the Archbishop, but it's your boy I've been most looking forward to seeing."

All this in that buttered rum accent.

Will adores Leslie and throws himself into her arms. He accepts her warm embrace like a sort of tonic to the past year in school.

"Let me introduce Lloyd to you. Heather, this is Lloyd Harmon; Lloyd, meet Heather Curridge and her son, Will Curridge."

We shake hands.

"Lloyd started a couple of months ago. He thinks it's some kind of palace or something. You're not the first people he's bowed to like a darned footman."

Lloyd shrugs. "Sorry, Mrs. Summerville. I'm just a highway flagman at heart, I guess."

"But can he cook." She places a bumpy, simply manicured hand on his shoulder. "And we always watch *Wheel of Fortune* together, don't we? He's a whiz, I don't mind telling you!"

"So what's for lunch, Mr. Harmon?" Will asks Lloyd.

"Fresh salmon and asparagus with hollandaise. Wanna come help? I'll be grilling outside. And I'm just Lloyd."

"Okay. What are you marinating it in?" Will follows Lloyd back past the stairs, and I hear Lloyd respond, "No marinade per se, a spicy herb rub . . . ," and into the kitchen they fade, where they will become one in the nirvana of food preparation. Will has been out-cooking me since last Christmas.

Leslie tucks her arm through mine. "Why don't you come back out to the patio while we wait for Lark? She said she'll be down in a minute. Honestly, Flannery brought home a straightening iron and she's trying it out. I told her it would take more than a couple of minutes to handle that head of hair, but"—she flutters her hand up in the air—"what does a silly old woman like me know about these modern beauty conveniences?"

Flannery is Lark's fabulously artistic twenty-seven-year-old daughter.

She leads me through the formal living room, where a fancifully carved organ—Lark's organ—looms in the shadows of abstinence, into the walnut-paneled family room complete with requisite plaid furniture a million years old. Although I could be wrong.

The brick patio supports a few new iron chaises, their celery green padding freshly placed. Oh, the colors, the life, the living going on before my eyes as birds bathe in the birdbath and a squirrel steals seeds from a birdfeeder across the lawn. I breathe in to the bottom of my lungs, believing with all my heart that the city fumes stop where their yard begins.

"Please have a seat."

I obey. For some reason, everybody obeys Leslie without question. As always, her clothing rests without pucker upon her slender frame: ivory pants and blouse, a light sweater in a heathery plum. Pearl jewelry and close-cut silver hair complete the flawless, classic senior-citizen ensemble. I'd hope to look as good at her age, but I don't look as good now!

"Now tell me how you've been."

"Heather!" Lark's voice streams through an open window upstairs. "I'm in the bathroom. How are you?" A hand waves from between the sashes.

"Fine!"

"I'll be down in a few!"

Leslie lays a hand on my knee. "So really, honey, how are you?"

Leslie owns the title to personal questioning with more certainty than her Bentley, which she refuses to drive nowadays, much preferring her granddaughter Flannery's old Toyota.

"Great. Good. Fine. Okay, I guess. Sometimes not so good. But fine. Really."

"Well, you've sold me on it." Leslie smirks, then crosses her legs on the chaise. "Oh, come now, Heather. Let's be honest enough to admit the truth, all right? I won't tell a soul. We're all playacting 80 percent of the time, aren't we?"

"What are we doing the other 20 percent?"

"We're either with someone very safe, or we're alone."

"But what if we're the unsafe ones?"

"Then you've got a far larger problem, honey."

Lloyd appears with a tray of iced tea, lemon and orange slices floating in the pitcher.

Leslie frowns. "Oranges! Lloyd, whoever told you to adulterate iced tea with oranges!"

"My mother did that until the day she died."

"Well, God rest her soul, then." Leslie picks up two glasses, hands one to me. "Bottoms up!"

Plain to see, Lloyd has already cracked the code to Leslie. He winks at me, and I thank him. I take a sip as he walks away. "This is pretty good if you ask me."

Leslie watches until the screen door shuts entirely. "It's ghastly, truth be told. But I'm not about to speak ill of the dead. Not at my age, anyway."

"Seems to me you've settled down, haven't you?"

Leslie wrinkles her nose. "I was a handful, certainly. Daddy relied on me quite a bit, Mother being the glorious drunk she was."

Mercy!

The dame waves it aside. "But I'm too old to worry about a woman like my mama. She's been dead too many years to lay the blame about much at her feet anymore."

The patio door slides open. Lark steps out. "Look!"

Leslie actually hops to her feet. "Goodness gracious, Larkspur. I don't . . . quite know what to say!"

"Isn't it pretty?"

In actuality, Lark looks like Cleopatra via shrink-ray. Did she really think straightening all that hair would make it lie flat and shiny?

Lark turns like a little girl in a swingy dress. "What do you think, Heather? Isn't it cute?"

"Well, it's certainly—"

"Holy mackerel, Miss Lark! What did you do to your hair?" Will emerges with a platter of raw salmon in one hand and tongs in the other.

Lark folds into laughter, then does the ninety-degree-angle Egyptian dance.

"Isn't it horrible?" Lark cries. "What was Flannery thinking?"

Leslie sits back down. "Thank heavens I didn't make a mess of that one."

A tension always seems to run like a fine thread between these two. It's my one beef with my friend. Doesn't she realize how wonderful it is to have a parent at all?

Lloyd grilled enough salmon to feed both of our families for two days. He divided up the spoils into Styrofoam take-home boxes.

"Wherever did you find those?" Leslie asks when he brings them to the table as we wrap up the feast with some hot drinks: tea for Lark and myself, coffee for Leslie and Will. I've never before seen Leslie Summerville embarrassed, but for some reason, the sight of those Styrofoam take-out boxes on her magnificent burled walnut dining table deepens the pink in her face.

"Costco, Mrs. Summerville."

"Oh, that Costco. I hate that place. It's the ghastliest store I've ever been in. In my day, shopping was a personal experience."

Lark rolls her eyes. "Mother, in your day, everybody came to you."

"And it was so much nicer that way."

Thirty minutes later, the two Summerville women wave us on. Leslie grabs Lark's hand and sags into her a bit as they turn and walk inside the house.

I start the car. "Four years ago they couldn't stand each other, Will. Now at least they don't crash on the rocks with every interaction."

"Maybe they both realize how little time they have left together."

"Let's hope so."

"Can we stop at Towson Art on the way home?" he asks.

"Sure." I take a right onto Charles Street. "I can't imagine having wealth like that."

"You'd never know Miss Lark was rich." Will pulls a small sketch-pad out of the glove compartment.

"No, not at all."

"Mrs. Summerville's a little bit what you'd expect." Next comes a pencil bag filled with drawing implements, his car bag. "But I like her!" Will rolls down his window a bit and spits his gum out. Dear Lord, please don't let it fly into someone else's car. "She's got great gams for an older gal."

I turn and look back at him despite my seventy-five-miles-per-hour travel speed. "Great gams?"

"Yep. I just call it like I see it."

Mercy! He would be fifteen now, wouldn't he? And she does have some great gams.

Still. "That Lloyd can really cook, though, can't he?" I jerk the wheel to the left, crossing two lanes to skid into the turn lane for Towson Boulevard at the last second.

Yes, I am *that* person.

Will draws a bold line with the side of his pencil point and he's nailed Leslie's jawline. "Most definitely."

I love him. As much as I love Jace and even God, I never realized that love like this existed until I had Will, and each year turns it into something so much deeper, I cannot begin to climb down into the well.

Knowing I wanted a dozen, God only blessed me with one. In a kingdom of children He might have given me, He was merciful enough to give me the prince.

I tell Will to clean his room before he watches TV.

"But you watched TV all the time growing up, Mom! You've even said so."

"I was a child of the '60s and '70s. We didn't know how bad it was for you."

"Please. I'll bet you watched at least four hours a day."

"Definitely. In the morning, after a soft-boiled egg on toast or cold cereal, I watched *The Little Rascals* with my father; after school I watched reruns of the old *Mickey Mouse Club*, *The Boys of the Western Sea*, *Speed Racer* via *The Captain Chesapeake Show*, and then *Gilligan's Island* came on before dinner."

"See? It's hardly fair, Mom."

"Wait, it gets better. By the time I made it to late elementary, *The Brady Bunch* came into the afternoon lineup. Then in the evenings, military comedies like *Gomer Pyle USMC* and *Hogan's Heroes* were on. I'd watch them with dessert, usually junket or 1-2-3 Jell-O. My dad always made dessert, believe it or not. He actually was a good cook."

"What about *McHale's Navy*?"

"*McHale's Navy* came on Saturdays. I hated *McHale's Navy*."

I still hate *McHale's Navy*. Everyone must hate it, surely.

"It is a little stupid." Will.

Come to think of it, I really didn't enjoy *Gomer Pyle* all that much either. I liked Jim Nabors, true, but that Sarge needed an enema or, at the very least, a big old Valium.

Will places his foot on the first of the steps leading upstairs from the kitchen. Yes, we have two staircases. Because I enjoy vacuuming steps so gosh darn much. The thought of that housekeeper returns.

"So what did Mrs. Summerville's husband do? What's that foundation you guys are always talking about?"

"He was a great humanitarian."

"In other words, he put his money where his mouth was?"

"Pretty much."

"Cool."

"Are you going to go back sometime to that hotel you and Dad found?"

"I don't know. Why?"

"I'd like to go if you do."

And he's gone. Will doesn't hang around for the pleasantries.

I decide to look up the Summerville Foundation online instead of just taking Lark's and NPR's word for it that it exists. An easy Google.

"Dedicated to bettering the human condition."

Yeah, I'm all for that. Who isn't?

But there's enough of that distrusting evangelical church lady in me that suspects any organization that uses such words. Are they . . . liberal?

I click away down the menu sidebar, suddenly privy to all sorts of poverty issues, wrongful imprisonment, torture, human trafficking, medical experimentation on street children.

Female genital mutilation and honor killing or mutilation by throwing acid.

And there's more.

Rape camps in California. Dear Lord, please. Some of these girls are only seven!

I shut my laptop.

And it had been such a nice day.

How does Lark do it? Day after day after day?

Well, her daughter's grown, for one thing. She's from money and has no financial concerns, for another. Lark doesn't live in the real world.

I wake Jace up in the middle of the night.

"You okay, Hezz?"

"I'm having a personal crisis. I think so, anyway."

"What is it, hon?"

"I saw Lark today and looked at the Summerville Foundation website. Lark does a lot to fight injustice, and I'm sitting here wondering how she does it."

"How do you think she does?" He's going to drift back at any second. I can tell.

"Her faith is very simple, I can tell you that."

His voice emerges thick. "Maybe because she's God's answer and she realizes that He has a plan for all these horrors, a plan of redemption and that He uses people to carry it out."

Maybe.

I focus on the lace edging of my pillowcase, such as I can see it in the darkness of the room.

"I've battled with God for years over the fact that if He is good, why do some children grow up without love, abused every day? Why do they pass it on when they know how bad it feels? Why are seven-year-old girls servicing dozens of men every day? And why do some of them, having lived such horrors, never even grow up at all, but are snuffed out before love has come?"

The snore begins. But I am not finished.

"I say I've battled," talking to the pillowcase. "I haven't really. I've only skirted around the issues because I'm scared that God will ask more of me than I feel like giving. Not so much time—I'm used to not having time. But my life, my comfort."

I look at my husband sleeping peacefully, a man strong in his faith who isn't cracked with fissures of doubt like I am, and I realize these are questions I must answer on my own. And I remember my father, a man who took a little girl without a mother and gave her the best childhood he could. He was my answer to the hand I was dealt.

FIVE

This morning I found I just couldn't stand my towels. So mismatched. Pretty, yes, but all those patterns and trims, everything from ribbons to ball fringe, unnerve me every time I open up the linen closets. I threw out everything that wasn't white. Well, actually, I packed it up for Goodwill.

All white towels. Peaceful, easy, uniform. Simple.

The good feeling lasted exactly nine minutes until I thought about the Summerville Foundation all over again. And I'll need to stop by the Linen Loft during swim team and fill in the gaps my purging left behind.

And I still haven't written that check to the Hotel.

So to cheer myself up, I bake a cake. Will took some misdelivered mail next door earlier in the day, and Jolly invited him for Salisbury steak and mashed potatoes—English peas from the garden too. Jace is working late, so I'm going straight for the dessert.

Pride may not be becoming, but I make the best cakes most people have ever eaten. No hunch on my part, this, because they tell me all the time. Why mine turn out so well using the same recipes as anybody else, however, is a topic for *Unsolved Mysteries*. Jace says I have "the gift of cake." Maybe he's right about that. It does seem a smidge supernatural, and they do look professional despite what Carmen thinks.

Sitting up in bed against the mound of pillows I bought from some ridiculous catalog, the same pillows that enable me to make the bed in five minutes as opposed to one, I dig into a slice of triple mocha cream cheese torte. Mercy, but this one turned out smoother than Lauren Bacall's voice. Cream cheese comforts your tongue like nothing else can. A cup of decaf coffee rests on my nightstand, the last rays of sunlight lying across the walnut surface. Can't do tea with chocolate.

When faced with the fact that seven-year-old Mexican girls are ending up in rape camps in Southern California, this all feels just a bit silly, not to mention full of denial, not to mention, and dare I say it to myself, downright sinful.

I set the cake aside and try to picture that little Mexican girl in the video clip online, try to remember Will at that age and the girls in his class. And as the tears begin to collect like salty mist, the phone rings.

The Mighty and All-Powerful Phone!

Its shrill alarm shatters the sun and the sweat and the tears. I may just be having a real moment with the Holy Spirit here, and what do I do?

"Hello?"

"Hi, Heather. It's Carmen."

"Hey, Carmen."

"Are you all right?"

I take a sip of decaf. "Oh yeah. Just allergies."

"Seems to be the worst season yet for allergies. And you know what they say about Maryland."

Everybody dubs her state as the worst allergy state in the U.S.

"Listen, Heather. I know you're really busy these days, so I went ahead and ordered professional bakery cakes for the welcome dinner for the new ninth graders and their families. Remember that new family that enrolled their child last year that owns that new bakery on Stevenson Lane? I thought we'd throw a nod their way, get them involved."

I pick at the Battenburg edging of my sheet. "Ah, they're doing it for free?"

"No. But they did offer a 10 percent discount." She clears her throat.

Okay, some things really are just funny.

"I hope you don't mind," she says.

"Of course not!" Of course so! My cake tastes better, I love doing it, and it's free. What is she thinking?

"They're delighted to help, of course," she says.

Help? No. It's a sale.

"I'm sure they are."

"Oh, good. I'm glad you're not offended."

"No. You know me, Carmen. Just glad to help out."

It's like the powder room to-do never happened! Or is this retribution?

My mask is pretty much superglued to my face right now. Mercy! I feel like I'm at church!

"I figured you'd be fine."

Just a thought, Carmen. Maybe a quick run-by first would have better served the overall grand scheme of your purposes. "Listen, Jace is due any minute. He had an emergency surgery this evening. I'd better go."

"Oh, sure. Thanks, Heather."

So I lounge here in my six-hundred-count Egyptian cotton sheets, look at my cake, and think about flour and eggs, cream cheese and chocolate, and it pretty much comes up short when compared to the doings of people like James Summerville, who not only wrote checks but rolled up his sleeves and dug ditches and spirited endangered human beings away in the night with no thought for his own safety. The stories Lark tells.

I call Lark.

"Hi, Heather!"

"Thanks for yesterday. It was really great."

"Mother loves it when you guys come. She feels a little useless in her dotage."

I bark out a laugh. "That woman in her dotage? What a crack-up. Hey, where are you going to church on Sunday?"

"I've been going to this small Catholic church. St. Peter Claver. I take a cab." Defiance weighs down her words.

"So are you jutting your chin out over the cab drive or the Catholicism?"

"Please. I was the organist at a Catholic church for years."

"The cab ride? Oh, Lark! Come on."

"Easy for you to say. You just get in your car and drive like a bat out of . . . you know where, Heather. And I have to fight to even get one foot out the door. Of course I'm defensive."

Lark lives inside her anxiety like other people would live inside their underwear if it were made of fiberglass insulation but somehow can't imagine wearing anything else.

"How about if I drive down and we go in the cab together?"

"Shoot, if you're going to drive all the way down here, you might as well just drive. I'm defensive, not stupid."

"What time should I be there?"

"Eight forty-five. Mass starts at nine thirty."

"Okay. I'll pick you up then."

"Why don't you want to go to your church?"

"We left a year ago, Lark. Too big, too busy, a lot of activity but not a lot of Jesus."

"How come you didn't tell me?"

"I'm still processing."

"Oh gosh, Heather, that sounds so jargony. Okay. I'll see you when you get here." And she clicks off.

When Lark's done talking, she's done.

I need to take a lesson from her.

SIX

My tea is pretty much fabulous. I normally go for spare, but today I started thinking about Gary and Mary and drizzled in I don't know how much honey.

"So what do you think?" I ask Lark. "Do you think I should take Will out of that school?"

"Beats me." Lark, looking out the car window, sips on the tea I brought her. To say her hair is downright massive this morning would be like saying Billy Graham did a little preaching. "I'd just start praying that something bad happens to Ronnie Legermin."

"Oh, Lark!"

"Seriously, though, Heather. Will is so gifted in art. What does that school have to offer him?"

"Not a whole lot."

"You might want to check out Baltimore's School of the Arts. I would have killed to go somewhere like that."

"It might give him an in when he applies to Maryland Institute."

"What about you? You know, I have no idea what your college major was, Heather."

"I didn't go to college."

Her brows raise, and I'd love to pluck those hamsters. "Really?"

"Why's that so surprising?"

"Well, you seem so, I don't know, prep school like."

"Nope, Joppa Road gal born to and raised by a plumber. I'm a trained stylist. I was pretty good. I was going to major in business and open my own place someday, but with Jace and medical school,

I found myself on a different path. I upped my hours in the salon instead of going to college." I pause for effect. "I sold Mary Kay, too."

"No way!"

"Yeah. I did well enough, and it was fun, sort of like being a cheerleader in high school long after the fact. It was cool while you were there, but a few years down the road it feels oddly embarrassing."

"Did you get the pink car?"

"No!"

"Sorry for not taking you up on the offer to do my hair. Why didn't you tell me you were trained?"

"It's a little embarrassing in my current circles."

"Oh please. All of our families started out humbly. Why that's such a crime I don't know. We all have to go to the bathroom and shave our underarms, you know?"

We are silent for a moment, sipping our drinks as we whiz by the brick row houses with their white granite stoops. Every once in a while the aroma of frying bacon from a restaurant wends its way into the car. Mercy, but I love bacon.

Lark taps her knee. "Well, maybe Mother doesn't have to shave her underarms." She turns toward me in a quick movement. "So if you could do anything you wanted to do, what would it be?"

"I don't know the answer to that question anymore."

"Look out!" she yells, and I swerve the truck back into my lane, waving with the zippy hand of apology to the pedestrian I almost plastered against my jumbo bumper.

Lark and I enter the small church, the smell of lemon wax high on the air. I've never been to a Catholic church before. The chapel seats perhaps seventy-five people, and there's no automatic projection screen that I can see. Some statuary, candles, a podium, and a broad table carved with Gothic arches embellish the sanctuary. The honey-hued wood, almost living despite the fact it was removed from its roots years ago, warms the sacred chamber where a trail of people dressed in white shirts with black skirts or pants now file into the choir loft. I watch with little expectation because, heaven help me, church hasn't done it for me for years. Yeah, there are a couple of praise songs that make me cry. But I used to look up at my pastor, who was ten years younger than me and light-years cooler, and most Sundays I heard, *Wok, wok, wokka wokka wok.* I was usually worrying about the turkey in the oven back home or wondering if everything was going okay in the Junior High Breakout Jam (yes, they actually called it that) where the kids learned all about the issues they were facing these days, not about being like Jesus, being wise, being loving, or, *gasp*, being meek.

That's right, folks, let's make it all about *you* and then go have pizza.

Still, I sent Will every week because I was too lazy and maybe a little too overwhelmed to take his spiritual education into my own hands.

Lark leads me to a back pew on the far left near a window with St. Francis of Assisi glowing in stained glass.

I sit in a rainbow glow pulsating through the window at my left, and I'm wondering who Peter Claver was and why he was canonized, and I'm hearing this congregation, mostly African-American, sing—

> *Lamb of God, you taketh away the sins of the world;*
> *Have mercy on us.*
> *Lamb of God, you taketh away the sins of the world;*
> *Have mercy on us.*
> *Risen Lord, you taketh away the sins of the world;*
> *Grant us peace.*

They draw out the word *grant*, rising upward on the scale, and the rest follows in a glorious crescendo until the word *peace* is sustained and resolved in a note of stunning power when sung from the lips of those around me and the choir in front of me, who all look upon Jesus as the suffering servant and take comfort from His birth in obscurity, His death on the cruel cross, and all of the poor wanderings, with no place to rest His head, that happened in between.

I watch and listen with expectation, caught up in the reverent hush that fills the sanctuary.

The sanctuary.

Oh, so that's why they call it that.

I was taught mostly to hope in the power of Christ's resurrection and glorification. Those are wonderful doctrines, but they hold little meaning if He didn't dirty His hands and feet, didn't get sick, didn't cry, didn't long to scream in pain and frustration but couldn't, not with the eyes of His children looking to Him to show them the way. He has grace on us because He gave Himself little.

Father Norman talks about what it means to be a peacemaker, and the concept is so new. A peacemaker? What about "Onward, Christian Soldiers"? Aren't we at war with those who oppose God? Put on the armor and all that?

"Jesus never once lifted his hand against the body of a living soul," the young black priest says, his skin smooth, his hands moving in punctuation. "My brothers and my sisters, we may be pressed, persecuted, and cast down, but only one Man, one Man, showed us the holy response. And the Lord Jesus Christ is all we have to go on.

"Pressed . . . but not crushed.

"Persecuted . . . not abandoned.

"Cast down . . . but not destroyed."

Amens bless his words.

Lark leans toward me. "It's a Baptist Catholic church."

"I love it."

And then we recite the creed and agree that someday Jesus will come again. But we are united in more than these beliefs. I'm not exactly sure what it might be. But that knowledge is newly secure.

I remember Sister Jerusha.

Jace and I lounge by the pool on the new furniture he still can't get over I bought. Will and Nicola swim in the pool, doing handstands, seeing how long the other can hold their breath. Her black hair contrasts with his hemp hair, her olive skin with his cream, and he's falling for her, dear Lord, I can see that a mile away.

"Jace, what do you think Jesus really meant when He said, 'Deny yourself, take up your cross and follow me?'"

"Jesus never minced words, did He?"

"That kinda bugs me about Him."

"I'm sure His contemporaries felt the same way."

"What does it mean to follow Jesus? Surely it means to act like He acted, walk where He walked, and love like He loved. But that seems like an extremely tall order, doesn't it?"

"Yeah, it does. It really does. I can't help but think of Sister Jerusha."

"Me either. I'm going to send a donation tomorrow."

"You do that." He looks down at his book and repeats in a whisper, "Yes, you do that." A minute later, he sets his book aside, and soon after I hear his car wind down the drive. Maybe I'm not the only one with a twisty life right now.

Man, I wish God wasn't starting to shake us up like this. Wouldn't it just be easier to care about stuff like dinnerware, golf, school uniforms, and getting to that new restaurant that just opened?

I fall into bed with no piece of cake at the ready. Nobody wants my cake anyway. "Oh no, mine's not good enough anymore, thank you, Carmen."

Mercy, these sheets feel good, all smooth and clean. And I just shaved my legs today too.

Jace sets down his Tozer book. He's a huge Tozer fan. Tozer all the time. He worships Tozer almost as much as those intelligentsia folks worship C. S. Lewis, like he's another incarnation or something. "What's that, hon?"

"Nothing. Just thinking about the cake for the freshman welcome dinner at school."

"As if you don't have better things to do with your time." He picks the book up again and settles his reading glasses on his nose. "Like buy more stuff."

"I'm sorry about the patio furniture. But those people really needed it."

"I'm not questioning your motives, Hezzie. I don't mind helping people, you know that. But where does it all end? I'm working as hard as I can as it is."

"Is this about the tennis court?"

"Partly. I have dreams, hon."

"We're not enough?" Okay, so that wasn't fair. And it was really lame. I hope he just ignores that, because he should.

"I don't want to talk about it right now. I've got two surgeries tomorrow, and when we argue I can't sleep."

"But this is important."

"Yes. And so is the money those surgeries will bring in. Much too important, if you want my opinion."

I want to tell him I'll cancel the order for the tennis court. But I can't yet.

I lean over and pluck *An American Anthology of Poetry* off my nightstand. We read in silence for a while.

He lays down his book. "You know, it's okay if you want to do something for yourself now, Hezz."

"What do you mean?"

"Maybe you need a bigger purpose?"

"What if I like things the way they are?"

"Then that's good."

"Right?"

"Right, Heather. Right."

"Just get back to Reverend Tozer, Jace."

"I don't know. You probably wouldn't like what he has to say."

Nope. I probably wouldn't.

Five more minutes go by and I'm reading some Poe; he lays his book down again. "Do you ever think your spending habits come from a lack of direction? I mean, your heart breaks over those websites and TV shows, and all you can think to do is write a check. Don't you want more?"

"You know, you're starting to bug me."

"Just food for thought, hon."

Five more minutes; a little Longfellow.

I lay my book down. "I'm sorry, Jace, about your dreams going unfulfilled."

"And yours haven't?"

"That's true, but I guess I'm used to taking care of things here, worrying about Will and you. I don't even know what those dreams are anymore. I used to think it was the salon. But now, well, I really could start one up, we can afford it, and I'm smart enough to get it running on a profit in the first year. I actually was thinking maybe when Will graduates from high school, I could do it. But now Sister Jerusha and James Summerville and Lark are throwing a big fat monkey wrench into my plans."

"You never told me you were thinking about opening up a salon."

"I know. Can you imagine? One of the area's leading cardiac surgeons married to a salon owner?"

He sits up. "You don't think I'd think that, do you?"

"No. But everybody else would."

"Oh, Heather. My gosh. I never realized."

"So yes, I'm trying to keep up appearances, I admit it. But please at least admit there's every reason why I should."

I cannot believe I'm throwing this back on him, like it's so uncomplicated, like he isn't partially right that I'm a bored suburbanite with no greater purpose than to make my life look like an episode of *Martha Stewart*.

He peels off his reading glasses. "Who convinced you you had nothing to offer in and of yourself? That you needed all this to make yourself worthy? Please tell me it wasn't me, hon."

"No, Jace. Never, never you."

"A tennis court isn't going to make you the picture-perfect country club lady."

"I know."

"In fact, if we have a tennis court and a pool, why do we need to be members in the first place?"

"Beats me."

"Right. We've got to figure something else out, Heather. I can't keep working these hours; you can't keep up this Jonesin' stuff, because at the end of the day, we're both still miserable even though we, quote, have it all."

"I know," I whisper.

He lies back down.

"What are your dreams, Jace?"

"Not tonight, hon. I've really got to get some sleep."

If that isn't the male version of "Not tonight—I have a headache," I don't know what is.

At 3:00 a.m. his pager beeps. He quietly pads downstairs to call the hospital. I follow him.

An emergency surgery. The lady he did a bypass on three days ago went into cardiac arrest. "I'm going to have to crack her back open, I think."

"Poor thing."

And three minutes later he's zipping down the driveway.

SEVEN

I dropped Will off at swim team practice and didn't feel like going back home, so I'm wandering down the aisles of T.J.Maxx, where a fabulous white sale has drawn in the bees of the cul-de-sacs in search of new looks for their bedrooms, baths, and kitchens. The prices are rock-bottom, folks. I fill up the cart with white bath towels, face towels, and washcloths, then head down the sheeting aisle.

Oh, why not? I'm tired of those brightly colored comforters in the spare rooms, and I know Sister J would appreciate them more than I do. One room holds two sets of twin beds, the other a queen. Today I'm laying aside the boldness of greens, reds, and golds and going for white down comforters and sheets so pure and crisp you'd think God sent them down like manna while you were asleep.

I load up another cart, then the car. Jacé never goes into those rooms.

I feel like I'm going to throw up. I could take these things back right now.

But I don't.

Before I pick up Will, I drive by the old house on Joppa Road. The Versailles garden still anchors the block, and my old neighbor bends down onto his knees to plant . . . looks like impatiens . . . in a shady spot near the front steps. Next door, our house hides behind overgrown shrubbery and drawn blinds guarded from the outside by the same shutters, but now they shirk beneath peeling layers of black paint.

Some things change. Some things don't.

We pull up into the driveway. He's home!

I tiptoe in, arms loaded, and hurry up the stairs, dumping my booty into the closets, already thinking I've got to get the steaks marinating. I pause by his study door, cracked open an inch or two. His bass voice carries.

"Yes, Bonnie, I'm definitely interested, but I have more than a few details to work out here. It's something I miss, I can tell you that. I've never forgotten the ship."

Bonnie Reynolds, his old friend from the hospital ship, is apparently on the other end of the line. She has kept up with medical missions, something Jace did before he started at Johns Hopkins.

He didn't go to med school until he was twenty-six. After he graduated from college and earned his RN, he traveled around, worked on a Mercy Ship, and saw the world. He realized he wanted to be a physician, so he came back and I met him the summer just before he began.

"It's going fine. I enjoy surgery, but the lifestyle is eating me alive. I never saw this as my life. I feel like I'm living somebody else's life."

His dream.

"Heather's fine. She's really involved at Will's school and keeping up appearances here at the house."

That wasn't nice.

"But I can't blame her. She sacrificed for so many years for me. I told her she needs to start doing things for her own sake, but I don't know if she can, or if she even knows what that is."

Bonnie's an old friend and a dear woman. I guess he has always confided in her. She's also happily married, so no worry there. Still, I feel an itch of betrayal at the base of my brain.

"You're right about that. How can I pull her away from all this?

She and her dad just scraped by. Her things give her great comfort. That's definitely part of it."

It's true.

"I'll get back to you about Chicago. I just don't know how to tell Heather about all this. I almost did last night, but I just couldn't."

He stands up. I back away from sight but continue listening.

"I know, I know, Bonnie. Just pray for me, okay?"

Jace didn't want this life we have—all the stuff, the cars, the big house. It was all me, Heather Reeves, trying to get out of that little Towson row house for good, trying to run away from the life she really deserved.

All is still. My eyes opened rather suddenly and I felt the slick of mucus and a raw throat. Darn these allergies. I tiptoe to the bathroom, fumble in the dark for the Benadryl, and try my best to turn on the water quietly.

It sounds like Niagara Falls.

I swallow the pills and pad into Will's room, a testament to the fact that he has always been no frills. Dark blue walls surround a platform bed, a dresser, and a desk with matching hutch. On the walls hang his artwork through the years in craft store plastic frames. Simplicity and neatness, however, do not go hand in hand. I move aside some books and a pair of sweats to sit down next to his sleeping form on the bed.

You're something, bud.

I lay my hand upon the blanket resting atop his thigh, and he feels so warm and substantial underneath. So much to learn, so much to learn. He breathes, a gentle puff escaping his lips on the exhale.

I hope he won't get waylaid like we did. We owe it to him to show him there's more to life, but what is it?

What are we doing? Have we really drifted so far off course? We have it all, don't we? We get along, live comfortably. But what's it all really for in the long run?

And still, from here in my strawberry fields, I dream about that little shop every so often. I can smell the heather. Jace dreams too, of parched plains and dying people.

"Hezz?" Jace stands at the doorway. "Are you all right?"

"Yeah. Just thinking about things."

"Want a cup of tea?"

"What time is it?"

"Five thirty."

I stand up and cross the room. "Mercy, I thought it was a lot earlier. Yeah, tea would be nice."

"Why don't you go ahead and jump in the shower first this morning, and I'll fix breakfast."

A nice turnabout. I love that he never takes our arguments with him into the next day.

Ten minutes later, my hair still wrapped up in a towel, I sit down at the breakfast table. Jace's scrambled eggs enjoy their own renown. He overdoes it on the cheese, which is why they're so delicious. I sip my tea, steeped and black.

"You know, Jace, I think this is one of my two favorite moments of the day."

"The first sip of tea, huh? What's the other?"

"Sliding in between the sheets at night."

"And all the in-between?"

Mercy, that prickles.

I lean back to the kitchen desk and grab the handout from yesterday's service at St. Peter Claver. "Look at this, Jace. Look at all this church does to help people."

He sits down and takes the bulletin out of my hand. He holds it way out and his eyes scan the activities: crisis pregnancy clinic, food bank, mentoring, after-school tutoring, to name a few.

He grabs my hand, his eyes burning.

"I miss the hospital ship, Hezz. There was something so stimulating about that kind of environment. I felt closer to God there than I ever have anywhere else."

"I know."

"We were of single purpose, really committed to the suffering and to the gospel. I don't know if God has that kind of life charted out for everyone, but man, I miss that kind of hard-core commitment."

"We tend to fit the gospel into our lives and not our lives into the gospel, Jace."

"Right. We sure do." He lets go of my hand and picks up his toast. "That's what we've done, isn't it?"

I nod.

We eat for a bit and I feel so married. Those moments hit me every so often when I realize that I'd do anything for this man.

"Jace?"

"Yes, hon."

"Would things be better if we just settled down at a new church? Maybe that's the reason life feels so confusing."

"If the answer was that easy, the church would be saving the world."

"What's going wrong?"

"We've sold our souls by selling our time to the highest bidder."

I look around me, copper pots, soapstone counters, high-end furniture, and I know he's exactly right.

"This place is a far cry from the Hotel, isn't it?"

Jace nods. "This place isn't real, Heather. You know that, don't you?"

"I think I'm starting to figure it out."

I decide to give him a chance to talk about Bonnie. "I got a support letter from Bonnie awhile back. How's she doing?"

"Well, she and Rob are doing really well." He looks at the clock above the doorway. "Hey, I'd better get a move on. I've got to make early rounds."

EIGHT

Jolly's wife, Helen, collected dolls. Dolls in flapper dresses, tuxedos, Southern belle gowns, gowns with bustles, gowns with shawls, gowns with matching coats, hats, gloves, and parasols. Dolls looking through painted-on eyes or realistic glass orbs. And some of them are the most mutated-looking bits of porcelain and wax and plastic I've ever seen. Horror movie prop people, if they realized what a gold mine sat here on the bonnie banks of Loch Raven, would be knocking down Jolly's door.

Oh, but Helen. With her gleaming coffee-bean skin and her tight battleship gray curls, her smiling garnet mouth—well, you never wanted to leave her kitchen table. Especially when she made scalloped potatoes, fried fish, and biscuits. And her lasagna made you almost want to give up on life because it just had to be all downhill from there.

The walk to Jolly's house feels like an enchanted step back in time. Years ago, the daughter of the MacFees, the family who built our original house, and Jolly's grandmother convinced their fathers to lay down a stone path that meanders close to the drop-off down to the waters of Loch Raven so they could easily get to each other's house, even on rainy days. For some reason, though several families have come and gone since the days of the MacFees at the turn of the century, we've all kept up the path, kept the slate pavers clear. We even planted moss in between the stones several years ago. Several telltale signs of romance festoon the walk. I pass maple trees with initials carved into their trunks. A squat concrete bench that's now crumbling but which no one can find the heart to remove and a line of honeysuckle bushes that perfume the humid air surely supported a marriage proposal or two. A muscled wisteria vine that spills its morning-sky purple over the banks undoubtedly witnessed its share of stolen kisses.

I wanted to live right here all of my life. The waters of Loch Raven hold a great deal of mystique for me, a girl who grew up with a chain-link fence separating the concrete patio from the concrete alleyway behind the house. And I'd be lying if I didn't say the multi-gabled stone house hardly looks like it belongs to someone like me—someone who walked to school with the other kids wearing clothes from Two Guys, someone who vacationed for a week every summer on the Magothy River in a small sea-green bungalow with a rotting pier and a rowboat even my father couldn't propel in a straight line.

The euphoria lasted about two years from the time we moved in.

Jace is from a "better" family, to use the adjective in the most presumptuous of vernacular. But for some reason, he never seemed to notice that. And certainly they give the chintziest Christmas gifts I've ever seen. Give me Dad the Plumber any day, who saved up all year for a rousing buyout of Toys "R" Us. The fact that I laugh with Jace and reach for his hand is, he said, "something I never knew I needed so badly, and something I'd never want to live without again."

Jace's family belongs here on the shores of Loch Raven, but they're still tucked down in Hampton, a cushy late-'50s neighborhood that was *the* place for rich city folks moving out to the county. They still do martinis at five.

I push through Helen's rose garden and skirt the grape arbor.

Jolly is the last farming holdout in the area. His house sits back from the cliff. A real beauty—its Palladian windows line the front, and several grand chimneys poke through the slate roof for the many fireplaces inside. But as Jolly says, "It's just a big old farmhouse, you know."

I need people like Jolly speaking into my life with their actions, particularly actions like having the same sofa for the past thirty years or so.

He planted anyway this year, although he threatened not to when Helen died. We stood by Helen's grave and he said, "I do believe the life has gone right out of me." But Jolly not planting is like me not making cakes. It's simply what we do.

I open the porch screen door on the side of the house, cross the indoor-outdoor carpet, then rap on the kitchen door Helen painted a parrot green a couple of years ago.

The door swings open, and there he stands with eyes redder than the potted geranium he placed by the porch. He clears his throat and smoothes a hand over his hair, thinned out and looking as soft as a closely sheared sheep. "Come on in, Heather."

"You been crying?"

"Appears so."

I step into the kitchen that's so Helen. Pink walls and gray countertops complement pictures of rose bowers and gardens. A large square table with a white lace cloth covered by a sheet of clear plastic dominates the center of the room.

Jolly scratches a bristly, caramel-colored cheek. "Coffee?"

I pull out a chair. "You got some made?"

"Nope. But I was planning on making some sometime today."

He wasn't. "That's fine." He needs the coffee or at the very least something do to while I take up space in his echoing kitchen.

He turns on the faucet and half fills an aluminum pot with water. I feel the hollowness in his heart as the water smacks the cavern of the old coffee pot. I can't imagine losing Jace, something I don't take for granted, believe me. Doctors die younger, you know, the irony of which never escapes me.

Everything appears the same as the day Helen left it all to go to the hospital for routine surgery and ended up having a massive stroke on the operating table. Scary the way that happens. But Helen herself breathed life into her crazy possessions and even the very air in this old home. When Helen was alive, it just felt loved and taken for granted, haphazard and clean, a reflection of the lady who was a special education teacher for years and years.

They never had children, and I never asked why. With Helen gone, I doubt I'll ever know.

"Jolly, did your family build this house?"

"No. The original family fell on hard times after the war, and so my great-granddaddy bought it real cheap—after he'd been freed a good while. Grandpop Mercer had the Midas touch."

I reach for the *Field and Stream* sitting on the table next to the place he's already set for his next meal, coffee cup looking down in its saucer. "You getting your fishing license soon?"

"Yep. Even Helen's death can't stop me from doing that."

"She's probably jealous she can't go with you!"

He nods. "Yep, you're right there. She was a mighty fine fly fisherman."

"Jace said she was sheer poetry."

"Think Jace'll want to go out on the Gunpowder soon?"

"Definitely. So what are you going to do today?"

Jolly spoons some instant crystals into a couple of coffee cups. Ah, well.

"Jolly, you got a tea bag?"

"Yep, sure do. Want that instead?"

"If you don't mind."

"'Course not. Anyways, I'm going to work my garden and do a lot of mowing."

"Will can come over and help if you'd like. It's summer now, and he needs something more to do than play video games and swim."

"Like that boy. Sure. Send him on over."

He pours the hot water over the tea bag and the coffee crystals. Then he looks up at me. "I'm trying to keep on going, Heather."

"I know."

I take a picture of his face, storing in my mind that look of pain mixed with a somewhat hopeless determination. I love the lines of his face, the vertical folds of his whiskery skin, the droopy hazel eyes so different these days. I wish he wasn't sad. But with the life of love he lived, how could he be anything else? And I surely wouldn't want *that* taken away from him.

He blinks, then taps the tabletop. "But some days . . . well, you of all people know that Helen and I were a real pair."

"I do." Rarely did just one of them show up on our doorstep. If

Helen canned some beans, Jolly helped deliver. If Jolly thought some corn shocks might be nice to decorate for autumn, Helen carried over a pumpkin as well.

"Sure. Send the boy on over. Life has gotten a tad dull."

He sits down catty-corner from me. "On a good note, though, I've been selected to go to art school."

"Really?"

He pulls out a folded-up newspaper. "Look here. If I can draw this, I can go to this art school, they said." He winks. "I sent it in and they accepted me, surprise, surprise."

I take the paper. "Hmm. Looks like it could be fun."

"Why not? What else have I got to do?"

"Let me know how it goes. Will can help you, you know. He loves to draw."

Jolly winks again and points to the wall surrounding the now-defunct kitchen fireplace. Pictures Will taped up in a slapdash manner surround the chimney. "I gathered that a good bit ago."

We slurp our beverages in mostly silence—a little talk here, a little talk there, and despite the freakish dolls in the other room, the peace that Helen always brought to any situation still remains here in the old house.

"I sure did like the way she canned peaches, Jolly."

"She did a good job of it, didn't she? Helen never did much halfway, though."

"No, she sure didn't." My gaze slips over to the dolls in the other room.

"You know she bought the dolls she felt sorry for."

"I never knew that, Jolly."

"No, most folks didn't."

I want to hug him to me, but I can't make Jolly a project. Like I need one more thing to do. But I do enjoy sitting with him. How could a person not? Jolly is like your favorite chair. His 1930s existence makes my soul yearn: tending his garden, talking to the boys down at the old store on Jarrettsville Pike, the last vestige of Loch Raven in the old days before people like us began buying up the place.

It seems like people in my parents' generation knew how to keep from overloading themselves. Or maybe they just didn't complain about it like we do. Haven't figured out which.

Jace calls me on my cell during my walk back home. "I was just on our bank account on the Internet. Five hundred dollars at T.J.Maxx, Hezz? Are you kidding me?"

"I'm sorry."

"Right. And here I thought our talk was a breakthrough. Man, Heather!"

"I said I was sorry, Jace."

"Maybe you should have thought *Sorry* before you walked into that store. Shoot, I'm being paged. I won't be home until late."

I slide some ground beef out of the freezer and lay it to thaw on a paper towel on the counter. My hands shake. Jace never gets mad like that. I hope it will all be blown over by the time he gets home.

Laney had her baby a few weeks early, and Will and I are going to deliver a meal. If her kids grow up to be just as nice as their mother, well, the world will be that much closer to what it should be. And isn't that important, God? To be around and raise decent children in a safe and loving environment?

Okay, so I'm crying and crying. I shouldn't turn on the TV this late at night, but I just couldn't sleep, and now an infomercial about what I can do to fight starvation in Africa is about to claw my heart right out of my chest.

I pull out my laptop, hop on the organization's website, and fill out a monthly pledge to help one child get enough food, clothing, and even schooling to hopefully grow up.

I'm feeling rather burdened, to use the church vernacular.

I bought the cutest outfit for a black-tie fund-raiser we attended tonight for the Make-A-Wish Foundation. All black with a touch of sparkle, it shaved off at least ten of my extra pounds. I'd just had my hair colored and styled it to look tasteful yet fancy. I try not to be overly concerned about my outward appearance to the point of obsessing, but you know when you've raised your personal bar. And believe me, church women can be so utterly obsessed by outward appearance it makes me want to just get old and be done with it. Maybe I should let all the gray hang out. My earlier years still haunt me, reminding me of how I never really fit in no matter how much I did, and following me to the clothing store all the time.

As a stylist, I could have worn all black, all the time.

My favorite rationale for excess Sunday fussiness is, "Well, I get dressed up and try to look my best on Sundays to give my best to God."

Jace, who was back to his old self when he came home last night, tied the bow tie for his tuxedo. "You look distressed."

"Ah, my. God was so impressed I had matching pumps and purse to worship Him, I'm sure. And when I sang "Shout to the Lord," He listened to my praise more than the poor schmoe up in the balcony with secondhand shoes, mismatched socks, and heaven help us all, faded blue jeans."

"You look beautiful, hon. A new outfit?"

"Yeah. It's new." I couldn't lie, now, could I?

"Pretty."

It's the guilt talking. I know he feels bad for yelling at me.

So I traipsed down the steps in my pristine high heels, smelling so fresh after a midafternoon shower, a very rare happening unless we're going out on the town.

"Whoa, Mom!" said Will. "Lookin' pretty good in that new dress!"

"Thanks, bud."

"Where'd you get it?"

"Nordstrom. And not the Rack either."

"Whoa."

Jace came down looking his typical dashing, easy self, the creep. He kissed my cheek. "I'm sorry." I tucked my arm through his and pulled him into the formal living room. "I dropped six hundred bucks between the dress, the shoes, the purse, the special bra, and the trip to the hair salon."

"Oh, Hezzie."

"At the time I rationalized it in a most stunning fashion. Ready for this? *Well, we don't have car payments. This is about the same amount as a car payment.* I'm sorry, Jace. I feel so out of control."

Jace, as usual, put his arm around me and didn't say a word. I knew what he was thinking, how he felt, how he feels. Can he not trust me with the truth?

"Aren't you mad?"

"Let's not talk about it. Let's just go and have a good time."

Which being interpreted means: I can't believe you did that, Heather. When will enough ever be enough? Do you even possess an enough?

And now here I sit in front of the TV in the family room at 3:00 a.m., eating New York Super Fudge Chunk ice cream, and if I figure it up right, everything I spent so I could look good and go give money to support a charity could, by my calculations, feed, clothe, and educate a child in Africa for almost two years.

Argh! Who wants to think stuff like this? I'm too busy. And we do enough, don't we? If I added up all the hours I worked for the church all those years, and that means working for God, I'm more than covered.

Absolutely more than covered.

I pick up the remote and click off the TV. Yes, enough is enough. I'm only one woman. I'll send off a check tomorrow. It's more than a lot of people would do.

"It's not your money we need. We need you. A ministry of presence is what we do here."

Oh, shut up, Sister Jerusha.

NINE

So I thought we'd try some smells and bells, as they say. We went to the early service at a little Episcopal chapel, stone with red doors and wrought iron hinges, and I swear, there must have been a memorandum sent out by the Archbishop of Canterbury around the turn of the century that made this a "must do." Prayers and Communion, no music, a tidy message of five minutes . . . and old people: men in jackets and ties, women in dresses and pantyhose. No smells. No bells. I guess they reserve those for the later service.

Or maybe they don't do that sort of thing anymore? I don't know much about Episcopalians.

Will and Jace sat in a peaceful quiet and went home to study more of Romans while I drove to Klein's to pick up something for lunch. Of course, it took me an hour and a half because I took the extremely long way home. I managed to steer clear of Gary and Mary Andrews's house. I did.

For some reason, Will let me sleep in. He left a note on the counter and headed next door to help Jolly with his art school assignment.

So I threw on some sweats from the old days and am now sitting in a special spot I always hope and pray no one else knows about. Many decades ago in the woods to the east of our house, an old lime kiln was carved into a hill. I keep meaning to find out the purpose of lime kilns, but so far I keep forgetting to look it up. But

I love sitting in the bowl of land that cradles it, and I know that at one time people came here for one reason or another to do that lime kiln sort of thing.

I spread out a blanket and lie down on my back, trying to summon up a picture of what life was like around here a century ago. Slower, kinder, more intimate with nature and people. Harder? Perhaps.

A June morning shouldn't be this chilly. But it rained last night after I turned out the light. Rained and rained and rained, washing away the heat, the humidity, the dust. It is stark. It is blue. It is clear. Simple.

I miss my father, his whiskey-voiced words, his gentle spirit, his gratitude for life's inherent blessings.

My dad used to bring me to Loch Raven Dam, and we'd watch the waters of the Gunpowder River flow over the graceful cement curve and out of the reservoir. Some evenings when the weather was nice, just he and I would drive out that way in his old Barracuda. I loved that car. We'd park across the road and I'd hold his hand as we crossed the street to the dam. My father had rough hands. Always warm. He loved to doodle when he was talking on the phone.

Carp the size of French poodles used to swim around behind that dam, and from the observation platform I'd throw bread in so those ugly fish might live to see another ugly day. I loved feeding those fish that seemed excited about a crust or two of stale bread.

I often think about the conversations my father and I had—Dad, the local history buff.

"There are towns buried beneath these waters, Heather," he said one day, forearms resting on the wrought iron railing, gray eyes looking out over deep waters.

I think I was about seven when he first told me.

"They built the dam, poured the cement, and unfortunately, at least from what I've heard, there's a worker buried in there."

"Oh no!"

"It always seems to happen when they're pouring the cement for dams, Heather. Somebody invariably loses their balance and falls in. Quite a few are buried in the Hoover Dam, if I recall correctly." And he put his hand over mine and squeezed a bit of comfort into my bones.

Looking back now, I realize there's metaphorical significance to this. How somebody always has to suffer so humankind can move forward. It feels so fallen.

Dad kept on with his story. "Once the dam was completed and they rerouted the river back to its original course, the water began to collect and rise. It took awhile to fill up the valley, but eventually it covered these towns up completely, and there they lie."

"Are there bodies still down there?" I asked him. I remember feeling the heat beneath my hat. It was cold that day, and he remembered earlier to tell me not to forget my mittens. I curled them around the railing.

He laughed a little. "Oh no, Heather. The people got plenty of warning. They were paid by the county for their property and they relocated. But"—he leaned forward, and his eyes sparkled like they did when he was up to something—"some people say that if the water flows just perfectly and you're standing in just the right place, you can hear a church bell ringing."

"A church bell. In the water!"

"Yes. Maybe someday you'll hear it."

And I've been listening for it ever since. Maybe someday, here on my hill above the waters, I'll hear the church bell calling to me.

Nobody knows this, but my father's ashes are in a container in an old hat box in my closet. He somehow would have understood my confusion these days. Dad understood the world was sometimes wonderful, sometimes frightening, but always broad in scope and wide open with possibility.

"Mom?"

I open my eyes, shielding them against the sunlight. Drat. "Will?"

He appears through the brush. "What are you doing here?"

"Just thinking." I sit up.

"Don't you love this spot?" He plops right down on my private blanket like he owns it or something. "It's my favorite place on the property." He lays his head in my lap.

Well, maybe it's okay if it's just him and me. "Mine too."

"Really?" He looks up into my face. "I thought I was the only one who knew about this place."

"Me too."

And it's good.

"Do you know what a limestone kiln did?" I ask him.

"I looked that up awhile ago. They'd burn limestone at a really high heat and ended up using the stuff that resulted to make plaster and mortar and stuff."

"Oh. That's cool."

"Yeah. Kinda strange that stone can be burned like that. I mean, who'd want plaster when you can have stone?"

"Plaster's easier to mold, and bricks without mortar are pretty useless."

He closes his gray eyes against the sun and folds his hands over his stomach. "Yeah. Don't ever go inside there, Mom. It could all come down on you."

"Thanks for the good advice." I keep quiet about the fact that I've been in there many times.

It's a pretty sad day when your fifteen-year-old is smarter than you are. I touch his hands, running a finger over the protruding knuckles. They were baby hands yesterday, little balloon digits, dimpled and supple. Dimpled and supple and sweet.

TEN

Lark always answers on the first ring, and I'm not sure how she does it with such dependability. She completes most of her foundation work from home and seems to be able to remember to take the cordless phone with her from room to room, unless, of course, there are phones in every room in that house on Greenway.

She's glad to hear from me. I can tell this because she doesn't ask me to get to my point even though, this time, I do have one. I've given up, you see, and figure I it owe to myself and Jace to at least see what's going on down there at the Hotel and not just throw a check at the problem.

The impish portion of me wants to prove to him I'm more than what he thinks I am, thank you, Mr. Hospital Ship.

I watch Will from my bedroom window as he and Jolly mulch the flower beds near the pool. "I'm calling for a specific reason, Lark. Do you know about Sister Jerusha and her hotel down somewhere off of North Avenue?"

"I've heard of her. Never been there, though. She's one of the Sisters of Charity, I believe."

"Jace and I were over there the other night. We got lost—okay, *I* got lost—and ended up getting a tour of her place."

"So what's this got to do with me?"

"There's something special going on there. I was wondering if you'd like me to come pick you up tomorrow; we can go out to lunch and then see the Hotel."

"It's a sad place, isn't it? I hear it in your voice."

I grip the phone and swallow. Jolly hands Will a rake. "I haven't been able to stop thinking about it since we were there."

"Okay. What time?"

Lark would outlaw crowds if she could. "How about eleven? We can eat early and then go over."

"Sounds like a plan."

Outside, Will says something, and Jolly begins to laugh, shakes his head, and lays a bony brown hand on my son's shoulder. I open the cupboard after hanging up the phone. Look at all those plates in various colors. Three sets, actually. Not one all-white plate in the bunch. Well, that's going to change too.

I gather up the old sheets, towels, and comforters and throw them in the back of the truck to take to the Hotel tomorrow. Maybe soon I can find nice white plates and take my old stuff down there too. Just white plates, a fresh surface every time, the food itself a lovely sight.

I don't know why excitement dances around inside me like Fred Astaire and Ginger Rogers, but for some reason, I can't wait to get back down to the Hotel. When Jace sees me doing this, he'll open up and tell me about the doings of Bonnie Reynolds and Co.

So I set out to bake a cake. A full-figured cake for the "clients" at the Hotel. And I'm going to decorate it too; diverse colors, bright as a populated beachfront, on chocolate icing maybe.

I open my favorite cookbook, *Let Them Eat Cake*, pour myself another mug of coffee, and start to flip through as I sip.

Devil's food. A family favorite.

Hot milk cake. Fabulous.

Lemon chiffon. I think I hear the Hallelujah Chorus.

So why pick? I'll make one of each.

Will slides into the kitchen on the wood floors, socks grayer than old wash water. Why he doesn't go barefoot like the rest of us is beyond my understanding, but Will is just Will and it rarely occurs to him to be anybody else. "What're you doing, Mom?"

"Gagging at the sight of those socks."

"No, really."

"Making up a grocery list for cake baking." I give him the scoop.

"Okay, you definitely need to do a chocolate mousse cake while you're at it. Hey!" He opens the fridge. "Can I get Jolly to come over and help? I think he'd like that. He was crying again yesterday when he didn't know I was looking."

"Sure. Go on over."

Will grabs a small plastic container of orange, well, liquid stuff, really, and pops it open. "What time?" He chugs the drink.

"I just need to run up to Klein's to get the ingredients. I'll be back in about thirty minutes."

"I'll get him. Hey, he's a pretty good sketcher too. You should see his bunnies. And I taught him how to do a killer robot."

I've got to admit it, Will draws great robots.

An hour later, both ovens heating up, Will and Jolly hack up baking chocolate squares and separate eggs.

"You're doing a good job there on those eggs, Jolly. I'm impressed." I begin measuring cake flour into four separate mixing bowls, and my hand will ache tonight after all this sifting.

"You know how Helen was on her baking days."

"I liked her." Will inflicts upon us the weird tongue motion he commits whenever he's concentrating on something like cutting or drawing or sculpting, and quite frankly, the face frightens me and I always hope and pray he doesn't do it in school but don't see how he could possibly avoid it.

"Everybody liked Helen," I say.

Jolly looks up. "That's the truth, Heather. I don't know of one person who didn't like Helen, and that's a fact."

Wish I could say the same about myself.

The little gray house with the diamond door comes to mind, and Mary Andrews's hair blows around all knotty inside my skull. I wonder what she thinks of me. Does she hate me like she should, like I hate Ronnie Legermin? And if I hate him, does that prove I'm better than I was way back when, when demanding the social upper hand was more important than anything else?

I can't believe what I said to her, what I did. I can't believe I was so cruel.

"Almost done with that chocolate, Will?"

"Yep."

Jolly pushes two bowls before me, one containing egg yolks and the other egg whites. "Mind if I make us a little coffee?"

"Not one bit. We can sip and talk while the cakes are baking."

Jolly stands with hands on hips before the coffeemaker. "Now how in the world do you use the likes of this?"

Will jumps right in.

Fifteen minutes later after he takes a sip, Jolly declares, "I think I'm going to get me one of those things. Will, want to head over to . . ." He looks up at me. "Now where would I get a coffeemaker like this?"

Will pats his shoulder. "Don't worry, I know where to go. You ever been to Target?"

"Well, now. I haven't had the pleasure."

"Oh, you're gonna love this place, Mr. Jolly. They have video games and even gardening tools."

"That so?"

I'm watching something special right now: a fifteen-year-old boy saving the life of a seventy-some-year-old man. Tell me God doesn't care.

The cakes are perfect. Almost. The 13 x 9 lemon chiffon now measures 9 x 9 because I lopped off an end to send home with Jolly. Will and I expressed ourselves in whatever way we saw fit, employing every last decorating tip and dye I own.

I tell Will about the Hotel. He wants to go to lunch too. Big surprise there.

"Oh yeah. Carmen called, Mom. She asked if you'd do the decorations for the freshman welcome dinner at school. She said to call back if it was no; if she didn't hear from you, she'd figure it was a yes. Then she went into a big spiel about you calling her back to get the color scheme, the theme, and something else. But I can't remember what it was. Cost maybe?"

"So much for not calling back."

"Yeah. She's a little high-strung, isn't she?"

"You think?"

I call her and get the details. Mercy—Carmen and her themes. We're going with a tiki party, and they'll give away the centerpieces to the new parents. Like these people need more junk.

Next call, the administrator of the school.

I look to the left and to the right. I'm not sure where Will is, but just in case, I tuck myself into the coat closet and shut the door. I crouch down at the end of the coats, leaning up against the wall, cupping the mouthpiece with my hand. "I have something I need to discuss, Mr. Maddock."

"Yes, Mrs. Curridge?"

"Have there been many complaints about Ronnie Legermin?"

"A few. Why?"

"Apparently he was giving Will, well . . . wedgies . . . almost every day last year. I just found out about it."

"Oh my!"

"I know. Is there anything we can do?"

"Certainly. I can't go into detail, but as I said, you're not the first to complain."

"And it won't come back onto Will at all, will it?"

"I'll do my best to protect him. But if it comes down to his father demanding the evidence, Will may have to come in and see me."

I grip the phone and crush it to my ear. "You don't think they'd retaliate with anything violent, do you?"

"No, Mrs. Curridge. Are you aware of Ronnie's situation?"

"Not really."

"His father's raising him on his own. His mother died years ago."

Oh great. Just great.

"Yes, ma'am. It's one of the reasons we were trying to give him a break." He sighs. "But if he's being physical . . . Well, you know as well as any other parent at St. Matthews that violence is something we simply do not tolerate."

"Yes, I do. Thank you."

Great. A boy without a mother. Life is never straightforward, is it?

I slip out of the closet and find Will in his room working on a watercolor. "Do you know about Ronnie Legermin's home situation?"

"Duh, Mom."

"Okay. I get it." I sit on his bed. "How do you stand it, though, even if you do feel sorry for him?"

"First of all, the guy's, like, four times the size of me. I really don't have a choice. It's the other things that keep me from hating him. Not that I like the guy or anything. He's still a jerk."

So okay.

I won't call Mr. Maddock back, though. Let the chips fall where they may.

Is that wrong?

I call Laney to arrange for Nicola to come spend the day later on in the week. So that's all set. After coordinating the necessary arrangements, I ask her about social upper hands. I've been thinking about that a lot the past few hours.

"What do you think, Laney? It just changes appearance when we're older?"

"I have no idea what you're talking about, Heather."

"Well, I was part of the cool crowd during a large part of my schooling. We worked hard to keep that upper hand, doing what it took to feel good about ourselves, be the best. Whatever that was."

"Okay, I'm tracking now."

"So as an adult, how does that look? Is it the nice car, the big house, the great clothes, the good schools? Is that the same thing, really? Only we let our stuff, our ability to travel and spend a fortune on our kids' education, speak for us?"

She's quiet.

"Are you still there?"

"Yeah. Uh, Heather, do you realize if I say yes what it is I'm saying to you?"

"Oh, right. Sorry."

"What do you think?"

"I don't know. I tend to think yes."

"Well, that could be," she says. "But honestly, I think people accumulate for different reasons. I don't know what yours is. And it could be a lot of reasons thrown together. Only you can say for sure."

"You're right."

We ring off and I wonder. I guess the only way to find out would be to start getting rid of stuff. Then I'd know for sure.

Okay, that's definitely something to think about tomorrow. Or the day after that.

Will and I stand on the pathway between our house and Jolly's. He places a hand on my shoulder and leans into me; the golden afternoon sun, warm and glowing like a welcome-home window in the dark clouds surrounding it, casts a vast circle upon the gray waters.

I tell him the story of the church bell and ask him if he's ever heard it.

"No." He whispers in a voice heavy with awe. "They drowned some towns?"

"That's what my dad told me." I never wanted to share this with anyone before. It was like giving away a piece of my father that belonged only to me. But it feels right.

"Wow, Mom. I wonder what they look like now?"

"I would imagine they're all decayed. Probably only the stone structures are even remotely intact. I guess. I don't even know when they built the dams."

The lake is always so peaceful. I love living on the water. It calms me. Everybody needs a calmer me.

"We're lucky to live here, aren't we, Mom?"

"Blessed is more like it." I examine his profile, remembering the days when the full curve of his cheek gave me no clue as to what the man would someday look like. Now many telltale signs occupy his superstructure. He'll have a strong, rounded, bullish jaw, not the bent, chiseled jaw of a model, but sturdy, dependable, and ready. His eyes will examine the world through their gray irises and recreate it in his own image. His nose will emerge below his forehead without indentation between the eyes. He seems to be hanging on to the fuller bottom lip.

I love staring at him. "Sometimes I wonder about who you'll be, and more to the point, what I'm doing now that will either stifle you or spur you to greatness."

He squeezes my shoulder. "You overthink this stuff, Mom."

"I don't know. I mean, maybe you'll want to be a simple man, a plumber like my father or a schoolteacher who grades all his papers during his free hours and comes home to work on his art."

"Maybe. I doubt it, but maybe. Although I would like to learn how to bend pipe. I could do some really cool stuff with that."

"But will I, the wife of a surgeon, the lady who lives in the big stone house on Loch Raven and vacations in places most people haven't heard of, will I be fine with that?"

He squeezes again. "Mom? You okay?"

"I guess. I'm just a little torn to pieces these days. I don't know where to set my feet anymore."

"Well, I'm here."

I turn to him, smile, and run the backs of my fingers down his cheek. "It's not your job to worry about me that way, bud."

"Hey, I worry about what I want to worry about!" He turns back to face the water. "So that Hotel place is really falling down?"

"It needs a lot of work."

He nods and shoves his hands deep into the pockets of his khakis. "I think I'm going to take a little walk." He steps away, walks toward the limestone kiln, then turns. "You know I don't need to live here, don't you? In this place?"

"Huh?"

He sweeps a wide arm. "All this. Don't hang on to anything for my sake, Mom."

And he walks away, hands in his pockets, posture loose and open. I call Laney again. She says, "You still sound troubled."

"I'm just remembering things."

"Like what?"

"When I was a little girl, my father used to take me to a peninsula on Loch Raven that turns into an island when the water is high. We'd pack up a blanket, some books, and a transistor radio. If an Orioles game was on, we'd follow along, picturing Al Bumbry and Brooks Robinson. Tippy Martinez in later years. If the O's weren't on, we'd listen to WLIF's easy listening music and read. Sometimes we'd read the same book, our heads close together on the blanket."

"You guys were close."

"Very. We read at the same speed. He would turn the page just when I was ready, and I never had to say a word. It was always me and Dad, Laney. I was glad to have my father all to myself. I was glad my mother had died after she left us."

"Your mother left you?"

"When I was really little. And then she died a couple of years later, and I never had to worry about trying to get her attention, getting her to love me, chasing after impossible dreams."

"Maybe sometimes, Heather, we just keep chasing the same dream over and over again."

So fine, then.

I stay up until 2:00 a.m., a booklet of stickers in hand as I start to categorize my belongings by placing a coordinating dot of color: red for less than five years old, blue for absolutely necessary—and my definition of necessary is pretty extreme—I mean really necessary, like settler on the prairie necessary. Blue like the ocean or the sky necessary. Yellow for sentimental value, a yellow glow, a yellow light in the window leading you home. Finally, green for unnecessary. Green for "go." *Good to go.* So far, having gone through the living room and dining room, I've used up two yellows and forty reds, twenty-seven greens and seven blues.

The next morning Jace, towel around his neck and pouring a cup of coffee, asks what's going on.

"Just a sort of inventory."

He shakes his head. "Care to explain, hon?"

"Nope."

He leaves for work ten minutes later.

If he can be slanty about his Bonnie thing, well, so can I about this.

Will's all over the idea. "I mean, how much stuff do three people really need, Mom?"

"Oh yeah, mister?" I rip off some sheets. "Go do your own room and we'll see how excited you are about it."

He grabs the stickers, the challenge in his eyes. "Just you wait and see."

ELEVEN

Nothing cheers up a Marylander like a crab cake. Lark, Will, and I finish up lunch at Bo Brooks Crab House. On the deck, the breeze off the river ruffles our hair and clothing; my blue and white sundress flutters. I like clothing that flutters. Will licks the last of the shrimp salad off his fork, and Lark scams the final onion ring, dipping it into the mixture of mayo and ketchup she always jumbles together.

My excitement returns while trying to relay to Lark the work going on at the Hotel. Lark says, "I don't think I've ever seen you this excited before, Heather."

"And I've got cake!"

"Lots of cake," Will says. "Lots and lots of cake."

We pull up to the Hotel thirty minutes later.

Will looks around him, eyes like planets. He has never been in a bad part of town. Fifteen years old and he has never been in a bad part of town.

I park around the side of the Hotel, smack up against a Dumpster that looks as if a stiff wind blew it end over end like a tumbleweed at least a decade ago, rust growing like copper mold around every crack in the army green paint.

Lark climbs out and shuts her door. Will and I follow suit, and my son and I just stand there, eyeing the decay, the garbage, and a pair of sun-dried underwear and three gray-white tube socks. I wonder if he saw the used condom. His round eyes lock on my own. Drat, he did.

Lark moves forward. "Oh, come on, you guys. Stop acting all scared."

"Like you can talk!"

"Hey, at least I know to get off the street."

Two young men run up the road, shouting just as we round the corner. A well-dressed man in a European-cut suit hurries toward us from the doorway of the Hotel. "Come inside quickly, folks. Those guys are bad news."

He's a beautiful pale mocha, and intense, glowing eyes catch the sun in their golden irises. Hair cut close to his skull enables us to see a scar running along the right side of his head above his ear. That must be a hundred-dollar tie too.

"Thanks," I say. "I'm not down here much."

Lark jabs me in the ribs with her elbow.

He smiles. A dimple in his left cheek too. What a charmer! I'll bet he's one of the local pastors. He opens the door. "Believe me, I've been around here too much. It can get a little rough."

Will says, "You obviously don't live in these parts anymore, though, right?"

"Will!" I say.

The gentleman waves a hand. "No worry, no worry. No, I moved away a few years ago, but I find myself around here more than enough. I'm a big fan of Sister Jerusha." He smiles sweetly, warm eyes casting a generous, welcoming net and pulling us in.

I sneak a glance at Lark, who's standing there looking like her brain has flown out of her head. *Lark? You attracted to this man?* I sure wouldn't blame her if she was.

"I am too," I say. "Sister Jerusha is amazing."

"No doubt, no doubt. She tries to do her best by people."

"You should know, Knoxie." Mo strides down the stairs like a milk chocolate Incredible Hulk.

Knox Dulaney? Ah, yes, Heather Curridge charmed by a drug dealer. Just perfect.

Knox turns to us. "Ladies, young man, have a fine day." He nods his head politely and leaves.

"Bad news, the man is bad news." Mo sits back down at his desk. "Well, hey, hey, Mrs. Curridge. Escorted by Knox Dulaney himself."

"Good memory, Mo, and it's just Heather, believe me."

"And who you got with you?"

"My friend Lark Summerville." Mo shakes her hand and she snaps out of her trance. "And my son, Will."

Mo shakes his hand as well. "Fine young man you got there!"

"Good to meet you." Will.

I lean forward. "That was really Knox Dulaney? The drug dealer? I thought he was a pastor or something."

Mo laughs himself into a coughing fit. "Oh, that was a good one, girl."

I don't tell him I wasn't kidding.

"You lookin' for Sister J?"

"Yes. If she's got the time. I've got some cake in the car too, for dessert tonight if you need it."

"Hang on, I'll buzz her. And we always need cake." He picks up the phone and presses a button. "Retha? Sister J upstairs with you? Tell her that lady whose husband was almost shot by Knoxie Dulaney's no-good cousin from Florida is down here to see her." He listens. "Thanks." Looks up at us. "She'll be down in about ten minutes. There's a social worker up there with some of the women, workin' things out. You know."

"No problem. Why don't we unload the cake?"

Mo calls one of the guys hanging around by the television set playing, of all things, *Martha Stewart Living*. "Sly! You wanna come give Mrs. Curridge a hand here? She brought cake."

Sly jumps to his feet. "There isn't much I wouldn't do for cake."

By the time we settle the boxes on the worktable in the kitchen, Sly has revealed he is twenty-eight days clean from crack.

He runs a hand over his shaved head. "I'm just, you know, tryin' to get my body strong first, and then I'm going back to work. My brother-in-law gets a lot of work bricklaying, and I'm a bricklayer too, been bricklaying since I was that boy's age. But . . . got to get this body strong first. One step at a time. You know."

Sister Jerusha pounds across the big room. "I saw the cakes. Terrific! Frish, but I've never seen such pretty food here at the Hotel.

You've given us a first, doll. And believe me, that takes some doing."

Will looks at me as if to say, *Frish?*

After I introduce Will and Lark, Sister J invites us back to her quarters for a cup of tea. So robust, so mythic, she hardly seems like a tea person, more like a whiskey person.

"What's your last name, Sister Jerusha?" I ask as she points to the small couch. We all crowd in as she sits on an old La-Z-Boy, the side upholstery held together with duct tape as promised. I think about the lounger in our family room. She needs one far more than we do, and I saw a wonderful chair online last week that would replace it. Or maybe I don't need to replace it. Maybe Will and I can run it down next week. Ah, and I can't forget to get the bed linens out of the back of the truck before I go. And the towels and plates.

Crucifixes of wood, silver, brass, ivory, and plastic hang all over the walls. Jesus, Jesus, Jesus. It's important He suffers down here. It's important these folk see what He did in obedience so He could not only redeem but understand.

"My full name is Jerusha Bridget Mary O'Neill. I grew up in the church, and I'll die in the church. I, my dolls, am a walking cliché."

"My mom's a cliché too," Will says. "So no worry there!"

"Will!" I turn to him. But I have to laugh. "If I was twenty pounds thinner, you'd be right on the mark." A lot of the physicians' wives I know, stay-at-home moms like me, are teeny-tiny little Botoxed, faux-buxomed beauties. It would bother me, but Jace assured me he'd be mortified to be married to someone so artificial. "Do you honestly think a guy wants to hug someone with a plastic chest, Heather?" Gotta love the guy.

Okay, thirty pounds thinner.

Lark has remained quiet since we arrived, taking everything in.

"Did you help with the cake?" Sister Jerusha asks.

Lark shakes her head no. "I'm just here to see what's going on. Heather hasn't been able to shut up about this place since the other night."

I nod. "It's true."

Sister Jerusha pulls out her hankie. "You either love us or

completely want to avoid us. I don't see much middle ground, that's for sure. Some folks actually dislike what we're doing as far as the downstairs set. Say it's enabling people to stay in poverty." She leans forward. "But God's been with me every step of the way." Sits back in her chair, once again starts fiddling with the simple linen square. "If it wasn't for that, well, I'd have thrown in the towel long ago. Plus, it isn't like I'm Mother Teresa or anything. Someday they sure as heck won't be talking about canonizing a St. Jerusha!" She laughs a great, loud "Humph!" then points to Will. "You like ice cream bars?"

"Oh yeah."

"Hang on, then." She rises to her feet, tucks the hankie into the waistband of her skirt, and disappears into the opposite room. A few seconds later she returns, Fudgsicle in hand. She hands it to Will. "Our secret. I never share these with the clients." She turns to us. "See? A saint I am not. But what can you do?"

The phone rings beside her. "Hold on a sec." She picks it up. "Yeah? You bet. Okay, tell her to wait just a couple of minutes and I'll be right out." She cradles the receiver once more. "Krista, remember her? She's back. I told you she'd be back, didn't I?"

An overwhelming sense of relief gushes through me.

"So I figure you're back here because you're feeling either guilty or blessed beyond belief, and maybe even a little called. What is it?"

Is that what I sound like when I speak my mind? No wonder everybody's worried! "I just thought Lark here might be able to help out the Hotel."

Sister J turns to Lark. "We can always use help. In what way?"

"I run the Charles Summerville Foundation."

"The one on the radio all the time?"

Lark nods. "Yes. I'm his daughter."

"No kidding."

"No. Heather says a lot of work needs to be done around here."

"Heck yeah. Always. I need new plumbing, part of the roof replaced, a couple of new machines for the Laundromat, a ceiling in the main room, and that's just to get you started. But what we really need around here"—she turns to me and points—"is more cake like that. Capiche?"

Capiche? I thought she was Irish!

Of course, Lark understood right away and tells me so on the way home when I ask what Sister Jerusha meant by the whole cake thing.

She sets the Christmas stocking she's embroidering on her lap. "She's saying there are always people like me to throw money at problems, and we're awfully good at it. It was no affront to me, believe me, and we're very necessary. But you brought cake, Heather, made in your own kitchen, with a lot of love and care, made with your own two hands, and Will's hands too. You can see the difference, right?"

Tears nick my eyes, and I force down the throaty emotion that rises like sea foam. "Do you think the foundation will be able to help them?"

"I'll make a recommendation. I don't see why we can't help fix up the Hotel. But it's more than that. Did you hear her talk about her dreams for a youth center, a health center, a job training place right there in the neighborhood?"

"I'd help tutor!" Will says from the backseat of the car. Gosh, I love that kid.

Lark reaches back and baps him on the arm. "Problem is, the Hotel lives on heightened alert 24-7. They're providing a lot of relief, and even some help in getting people on their feet, but I know she wants to do more than that. The rooms are pretty depressing. Can you imagine trying to make a life for yourself in a 10 x 10 with cracked walls?"

After dropping Lark off, I turn to Will, who immediately points back out the windshield to direct my attention where it belongs.

Okay, okay.

"I liked that man Sly, didn't you, bud? I've never met somebody that newly off drugs before."

"Me either, Mom. It's not really what you think, is it? I mean, Sly's a real person."

"Everybody there is a real person."

"Did you see that Chinese guy with the long hair who just sat there staring off into space?"

"Yeah. Hard to tell if he was stoned or just burned out."

" 'Cause we know all the signs of drug addiction."

"You got a point there."

We continue the drive north to my little windswept paradise on the cliff, far away from Sister Jerusha's Hotel.

Will considers the landscape flying by a little too deeply, silent.

He doesn't realize how lucky he is that these moments, these new experiences, can fall on him like a virgin rain shower; that he doesn't have children and a house and a life that muddy the ground upon which the raindrops fall.

TWELVE

I want to keep dotting my possessions, but centerpiece construction begins today. Only a few days remain until the freshman welcome dinner is yet another meaningless experience for all concerned. Will helps me gather up the craft supplies we're using.

"Do I really have to go, Mom?"

"I have no idea how many people will show up. Mrs. Peterson said she'd be there, and she's bringing Nicola."

"Mom, this dinner is so lame, and you know it. Do you really think everybody will get all buddy-buddy because of it?"

"No. But we're a part of this school, Will. And we'll do what it takes to serve."

There.

Will slams some pipe cleaners into a bag. "Well, if serving's the real issue, let's just drive this stuff down to Sister Jerusha and those kids upstairs on the transition floor. All this is going to get thrown into the trash by the time next week rolls around anyway."

And he's exactly right.

This stuff definitely deserves a big green dot of unnecessariness.

Laney grabs a seat next to me. Of course, nobody has shown up but them and us. Figures. "This reminds me of church," she says. "Everybody can find time for the actual activity, but the setup and the cleanup are left to the old faithfuls."

"You said it. The baby's adorable." A teeny little Brooke sleeps in her car seat.

"At least there's that." Then she smiles. "I do love my kids, Heather."

"I know."

"Good. Just making sure you knew." She grabs a hair elastic from around her wrist, and in the time it takes to sneeze, she commits fabulousness in the form of a tousled up do. But with Laney, you just don't mind.

Will and Nicola sit at their own table, mind you, taping foam blocks into bamboo baskets and glue-gunning moss over the top. After that we'll set in a tiki statue and finish it off with a circle of silk dendrobium in white and pink.

We sit in the cafeteria, a multi-windowed room decorated in shades of gray and maroon, the focus wall adorned with the school's crest. More boring than a khaki trench coat.

Mr. Maddock, the administrator, approaches. "Hello, Mrs. Curridge, Mrs. Peterson."

We greet him.

"Thanks for all your help here at St. Matthews."

"Sure," I say.

"No prob." Laney.

He peers down at the car seat and smiles. "Another future student, I see?"

"Uh-huh. We'll keep 'em coming!"

He excuses himself, back to the grind and all that.

I pull some moss from a cellophane bag, considering Will's dead-on observation. These things will definitely be food for the dump next trash day. "Don't you ever wonder what it's all for anyway?"

"What do you mean?"

"This school. This life. We just try to make things better and better for ourselves, don't we? You've got the doctorate in theology, Laney. Isn't it a little skewed?"

"Yes, frankly, it is. But I haven't figured out what to do about it."

"Maybe that's not the theologian's job."

She rearranges the blanket of her newborn. "But maybe it is. It all starts with our view of God, Heather, who we believe He is, what we believe He desires. Why do we think we can divorce our everyday decisions from the desires of His heart?"

Mr. Maddock pokes his head in the room. "Mrs. Curridge, can I talk to you privately for a moment? It won't take long."

Two minutes later he gestures to one of the chairs in front of his desk and sits down in the other. "I wanted to keep you updated on Ronnie Legermin."

"Oh, yes?"

"His father had no idea his son was behaving in such a way."

I'd find that hard to believe, but hey, my dad didn't know about me.

"He'd like to talk to you personally and in private."

"Does Ronnie know this came from Will?"

"No. I told him it was a grapevine affair. Do you mind if I give him your number?"

"Not at all." Oh, man!

Well, I survived the centerpiece gathering with only one deep scratch on my arm from a wire flower stem. I drop Will off at the club for practice for tomorrow's swim meet. Three hours to myself, and a list of things to do unravels like a falling hem. I need to sign Will up for fall art classes at the community college, pay bills, figure out if I've got all Will's immunizations ready for high school next year, and I haven't ordered his uniforms yet, but, well, the wanderlust in me triumphs again. I really need to drive.

I pull out onto Blenheim Road and travel north. I always seem to travel north past the horse farms and the farm farms, past the hilly woodlands, the wide bands of grass, the nurseries, the sensible ranchers on their three-acre plots; the mammoth new mansions-in-a-minute that border old farm property.

I call Jace. "Are you doing rounds?"

"Just about to. What's up?"

"I'm driving. Just driving."

"You okay?"

"Just thinking about how I always seem to end up where I went to school. It's odd to think that now a lot of kids who grew up in the Christian school movement have reached middle age and even odder to think we're no different statistically—divorce, alcoholism, our likelihood to have a TV—than the products of the public schools. When I first read that in *Christianity Today* or someplace like that, Jace, I practically freaked out. And now I begin to look around me and I think there must be something to this."

"How so?"

"The divorce rate among my own graduating class is off the charts, and I know of at least three extramarital affairs. So if we're not any morally different than the rest of the world, why do we think we're so great, why do we think we've got the answers, why do we act like such know-it-alls? Shouldn't our love for Jesus make a difference in our behavior?"

"I'd like to think so."

"As far as I'm concerned, all we have is hope. And if I'm honest, it's probably all we've ever had that's separated us from the rest of humanity. Isn't that right?"

"I don't know, hon. It sounds a little simplistic to me."

"I really didn't think so either. But I can't come up with any alternative theories at this stage of the game. All I know is I can't go on avoiding the questions any longer."

"I don't think you should. I think you should ask all the questions you'd like."

I turn off the air-conditioning and roll down the windows. "It seemed like all the answers were found in that Christian school in those days, or so I heard every week in chapel. But those suggestions sure as pie didn't do a bit of good for Gary and Mary Andrews, did they?"

"Who are Gary and Mary Andrews?"

"I've got to go. I'll keep a plate warm for you at dinner."

"Heather, who are Gary and Mary Andrews?"

"Another time, Jace. I can't talk about it yet."

If he can't tell me about what's going on with Bonnie, I don't feel the least bit guilty about not sharing Gary and Mary with him.

"Hon, are you sure you're okay?"

"Gotta go."

I park across the street at the veterinary office parking lot. I watch the little bungalow, hoping that maybe this time somebody will step out. It's got to happen sooner or later, doesn't it?

On the way to pick up Will, I call Lark. Leslie answers. "Hello, dear!"

"Hi, Mrs. Summerville. I called to talk to Lark. Is she home?"

"No, she took the bus to a meeting across town." The mystified disapproval rises like a fog out of the earpiece.

"Darn. It wasn't important, I guess."

"Will I do?"

"Well, it's like this. I was just thinking about Phillip Carmichael from high school. And I think I had a revelation."

"Tell me about it."

"When I was in ninth grade, I made it into concert choir at school. The alto section. Phillip Carmichael was this slightly effeminate tenor who was a junior the year I was a freshman. I have no idea where he is these days. And actually, I'm not really sure his last name was Carmichael. I don't really remember his last name, if you want to know the truth. I hadn't thought about him for years until the other day when I ordered blue cheese dressing to go with my wings."

"I love blue cheese."

"Me too. One day, on choir tour, we were sitting in a Shoney's somewhere in Tennessee, and I was in my chef salad phase. I ordered chef salad all the time during my early years of high school. Loved them! Phillip said, 'I hope you don't order blue cheese dressing again. That really makes your breath stink, Heather.' We traveled hours and hours by bus, so breath made a difference.

"So I ordered Thousand Island dressing. And you know, it wasn't half bad. With some extra pepper to counteract all that ketchup, I actually liked the way it went with the strips of provolone cheese, the salami, the ham, and wedges of hard-boiled egg."

"I love a good chef salad too."

"In fact, I ordered Thousand Island dressing for years, because heaven help us, someone told me I had bad breath. But over the years I ate less and less salad, and by the time I was twenty-five— *ten years later!*—I realized that blue cheese dressing was still my favorite and so were chef salads and how foolish to have let Phillip Whatever-His-Last-Name-Is deprive me of my favorite dressing for an entire decade."

"Yes, indeed, it was. It's important to eat what you like, because there's always somebody out there who doesn't like it and will tell you so, Heather, and if they tell you so, they're not appealing and kind."

"Pretty simple, right?"

"'Elementary,' as the old man said. I think I'll get Lloyd to make me a chef salad for dinner. You put me in the mood."

"Good."

"Heather, are you all right?"

"I don't know."

"Was this really about salad dressing?"

"Of course not."

"Are you the Phillip in the story, or are you you?"

"Both, I think. I think I'm Jace's Phillip and my own Phillip."

"Oh dear."

"Was there anybody like that in your life, Mrs. Summerville?"

"My Aunt Regalia."

"Regalia?"

"Ghastly name. Family name, of course, dear. One afternoon our housekeeper made biscuits and I slathered on the butter. She told me thin is more important than delicious and that I was looking more delicious than a girl should if she wants to look like a lady. I haven't had butter since."

"How old were you?"

"Twelve years old."

"Humans can be a rotten bunch, can't they?"

"Oh my, yes, dear. They certainly can."

"Would you do something for me? Would you go downstairs and tell Lloyd to make you some homemade biscuits with butter?"

"You know, Heather, I think I'll do exactly that. And grits too."

Lark called me back at eleven. I slipped out of the bedroom and downstairs into the kitchen ready to unload.

"So everywhere I went today I saw cake. First off, Safeway displayed posters advertising a buy-one-get-one-free cake sale in their bakery. In Strapazza's window a sign said 'Italian Wedding Cake Here!' And then, I swear, four people said 'piece of cake' to me during a conversation. Four people."

"Whoa, Heather."

"I think God's knocking on my brain, but I'm not telling a soul except you. They'd think I was nuts. Almonds, most likely—arranged on a fluffy bed of buttercream icing."

"Does Jace think you're nuts?"

"A little. But he's keeping his own secrets."

"Bad ones?"

"No. Good ones, ones he thinks I can't possibly understand."

"Are you hurt?"

"Yes. I have to admit it. I really am."

"Is his secrecy justified?"

Why does Lark always have to ask the hard questions?

"Probably. But I'm not ready to do what it takes to bring it all out into the open."

"Don't let your life pass you by because you're scared, Heather. I did that for years, and it was horrible."

"You raised Flannery, didn't you?"

"Not really. Sometimes I think she raised me."

Will finds me in the night gloom of my thoughts and sits down without a word. Stands back up. Makes us hot milk with just the right amount of honey and cinnamon.

"Mom?"

"Yeah, bud."

"I heard your conversation with Miss Lark. Mom, I'm not the most spiritually mature person in the world, but are you really that thick?"

I can't help but laugh. "Yeah. I guess I am."

"Dad and I started into Isaiah. God cares about those people down at the Hotel. And this"—he waves his arm around my belongings—"this is sleaze in comparison. So is my school. So is, well, just about everything in our lives right now."

So tell me how you really feel, Will.

"I think maybe you're crossing over the line, bud. Your dad has worked hard for all the stuff you're so readily disdaining."

"Sorry." He squeezes my arm. "This is all driving you a little nuts. Do you realize that? I'm kinda worried about you."

"There are things about me you don't know. Torments you have no knowledge of."

"Like what?"

Like a little gray house where two dirty kids lived, one of whom I betrayed. "I can't go there yet. And don't ask me to, Will."

"Okay." He stands up and kisses me atop the head. "I love you, Mom. I'm sorry if I was hard on you."

I grab his hand and kiss it. "Just go to bed, bud. It's very late."

"Okay. Hey, take a look in the garage before you go to bed. I've got some stuff for Goodwill. I couldn't believe how many green dots I had. It was pretty bad."

"And you've already got them boxed up and ready to go?"

"Well, yeah. I mean, what's the point in keeping it around?"

THIRTEEN

Tomorrow the freshman dinner descends like a giant spider. I'm so torn by Will's words. He's an idealist, yes, and always has been, but this school isn't bad. The parents are interested in their kids for the most part; the academics are excellent. So they want tiki centerpieces. So what?

Carmen, raven hair spiking up around her head, runs up to me as I hang up tropical floral swags in the cafeteria in preparation. Tablecloths go on next, and then the oh-so-glorious centerpieces.

"Oh, Heather, I'm glad I caught you. You'll never guess what happened."

I'm dying to know. Um. "What?"

"The Whittings can't do the cake. Her mother was rushed to the hospital last night with a massive heart attack or something. Can you make the cakes? Please?" Her lipstick is always so perfect.

"For tomorrow night? Ten cakes?"

"I'm so sorry, I just don't know what else to do." And she doesn't have those little jaggedy cracks around her lips sucking up the lip color either. How does she manage that?

Maybe it's a sign. Maybe God really wants me to make my cakes for the school. I mean, the Hotel is all the way downtown, and with my driving . . . "All right. But can you find someone to fill in for me tomorrow morning for folding programs and setting up the sound system?"

"Oh. Uh—hmm. Uh—well, let me see. It's kinda short notice."

"Try."

She looks up at me, sea-blue eyes suddenly gone round. "I'll do it. Sorry . . . Heather."

Immediately I flinch under that horrid remorse that comes bowling along whenever I blow it and act all snippy. Carmen works hard; she doesn't need a smart aleck like me, even if she is a clod sometimes. And make no mistake, that was definitely cloddish. "I'm sorry. I just can't do both. Not with that much cake. I'll be baking almost all night as it is."

She rubs my upper arm. "Sure. I don't know what I was thinking."

I shake my head. "It's always something, isn't it, Carmen?"

"You said it."

"Go ahead. You got lots to do."

"Good luck!"

Carmen really is a good person beneath her control freak, tanning bed persona. She just thinks her thing should be everyone's thing.

"Hey, Heather? I'm sorry about the powder room."

"Me too."

I watch her click to her car, cell phone already up to her ear.

Will slides into the family room on his dirty socks, laptop under his arm. "So, Mom, I hate to tell you, but I think the church bell thing your dad told you about Loch Raven is one of those myths."

I pat the sofa. Here I sit, watching my favorite cooking goddess, Nigella Lawson, who actually eats the food she cooks, looking like she's ready to swoon when she stuffs rare steak dipped in béarnaise sauce into her mouth; she's probably a size ten, which in Hollywood sensibilities relegates you to the category of sideshow freak. I click off the set.

"Okay, burst my bubble, then. Where did you find the info, Mr. Smarty-Pants?"

He sits down and opens his laptop. "Here on this site."

"How long have you had those socks on?"

He points to the screen. "There are several towns under water, but the biggest one was Warren, Maryland. There was a big mill there, and a school, and boys' and girls' gymnasiums, a church. Lots of stuff." He scrolls down. "You need to check this out. But let me just tell you, when the City of Baltimore bought the town from the Summerville family—hey, do you think they're related to Miss Lark?"

I shrug. "Beats me."

"Anyways, the city bought the town for a million dollars, and before the water filled up the valley, they disassembled the towns."

"Really?"

"Yeah. Sorry. I like the bell idea a lot more. But I don't think it's true. Bummer, huh?"

"Definitely. I've been listening for that darn bell ever since I can remember."

"I'll bet. You want me to leave the computer here?"

"Sure."

Fabulous, then. I'm so disappointed I actually want to cry. I read on. Sure enough, all the buildings came down, and the stone from Warren was used to build a shopping center down in Anneslie where Jace and I first lived. A shopping center! I'll bet I know the one too, stone buildings with a storybook appeal.

Will's right. My way was better.

I call Lark.

"I can't stand on the cliff anymore listening for a bell that just won't ring, can I?"

"If I knew what you were talking about, I might be able to answer that question."

"I don't understand it either, Lark."

"Heather, have you thought about therapy?"

"I don't need therapy, Lark. I need a frontal lobotomy."

Today I placed a hundred red and green dots, ten blue, and one yellow. Only one thing out of 111 possessions had any real meaning for me.

There hasn't been a day in my memory I've felt comfortable inside my own skin with anyone other than my father. And while I love the Hotel, I was just too busy with my cakes for school this morning when Lark called and asked if I wanted to accompany her this coming Monday. Besides, I have to be honest, the second time I went down there and actually saw all the homeless people, I just felt, well, awkward, really.

Uncomfortable.

I call Jace.

"Can't I just be a champagne socialist, a benevolent patroness of the Hotel? If it's good enough for Lark, isn't it good enough for me? What would those places be like without the monetary support of people God has blessed financially? I could plan a fund-raising dinner. Something nice at the club. Carmen could give me loads of good ideas right off the top of her spikey-haired little head. I'd rather spend money on this stuff than all the stuff I buy."

He sighs. "If you say so, Hezz."

"Okay, just checking. Bye."

"I mean, if you're so set on spending to make you feel better, I guess this is better."

"I said bye, Jace. Mercy!"

I hang up and survey the cakes on my island, ready to be iced. I outdid myself this time. Maybe I feel there's more to prove as second choice. I've constructed the vanilla cakes like giant tropical flowers; I'll decorate the chocolate cakes as edible jungle islands. Thank heavens the dinner is in the evening.

Once again I pull out all my decorating tools from the appropriate bin in the pantry and gloat a little. It never gets old. Like Will enjoys the mere sight of his paints and clay, the pristine expanse of white paper, the square gray lump ready to receive the crushing blow of his grasp, I love the sight of that sugary golden canvas in front of me—knowing what I do will actually give the partaker a burst of energy and, hopefully, a moment of joy when that moist, sugary confection touches their tongue and for a split second they forget their cares. Unless it's my rum cake—two pieces of that, and you can forget your worries for an hour at least.

I have to admit, though, that I don't feel comfortable even in this role—the sugar mama of St. Matthews Country Day School. Do people look at my thirty extra pounds—okay, forty—and say, "I'll bet she eats this stuff at home too!" And on the scale of importance, does cake rate very high when considered alongside the likes of teaching, preaching, playing in the church orchestra, and cleaning the facilities?

I call Jace back. But his voice mail picks up.

"Do we really just need to get back to church? Do you think that's what's at the base of all of this?"

I hang up.

Ah, but I do enjoy these things here in my hand, the decorating bags, the various tips, and the icing colors . . . the colors, how I love to mix the colors into vibrant hues, dusky hues, pastels—I love all the colors. Who knew what that little cake decorating class at the community college would do for me?

But there's still time for this, and surely I need more confectioner's sugar, don't I? It's only 8:00 a.m., see, and I have to get out of the house right now.

Back in my bus route days, it was just a dingy old bungalow on the outskirts of the town of Hickory. Back in those days, nearby St. Ignatius Catholic Church wasn't the thriving parish it has become. Back in those days, Hickory Elementary hadn't yet experienced the slightly postmodern do-over that it sports now. Back in those days housing developments hadn't filled in the gaps between houses and farms and businesses like the Tractor Supply Company or Bill's Deli or the Hickory Inn specializing in broasted chicken and charbroiled steaks.

I long to pick up my cell phone and call Jace or Lark, or even Leslie. But I can't. Too much at stake. How about Laney? Can I trust her?

I dial her number, and she answers in a whisper. "Oh, hey, Heather. The baby's asleep."

"Want me to call back?"

"No. Hang on a sec while I walk outside and slide under the deck."

"Under the deck?"

"They won't find me there. They never have yet."

I hear the sliding door open and the muffled sounds of her stooping over to walk beneath her shoulder-high deck. "Okay, I'm sitting down now."

"I always went to the linen closet in the guest bathroom."

"Did Will ever find you?"

"Eventually."

"So what's on your mind?"

"I have to tell you about where I went to school growing up."

"Having another spell?"

"Ah . . . yes. I guess you could call it that."

"Okay, shoot."

"Do you think I'm going crazy? The others do."

"No, I have this feeling you're probably saner than you've ever been."

"I feel that way, in some fashion. I hope you're right."

"Heather, when God speaks, it usually sounds like the light's not on in the attic, usually counterintuitive from mankind's boring ways of doing things. So go ahead and talk. I'm hearing you. I really am."

I fiddle with my Vera Bradley change purse as I talk. "I rode this bus route to a Christian school from third grade forward."

"I went to one."

"I felt a little silly wearing those fundamentalist Christian clothes that made up the dress code; hated the fact they paddled kids; hated even more that my fifth grade teacher had drilled holes in his paddle and painted 'Mr. Stinger' in bright red letters across its surface and then this bee with a big stinger coming from his butt."

"You've got to be kidding me!"

"No. Oddly enough, it seemed normal, in a harsh way, true, but nobody wondered how a grown man could keep a paddle like that up on the blackboard ledge. Nobody wondered if he was actually abusing children."

"Can you imagine that happening at St. Matthews?"

"No, thank God. I haven't thought about Mr. Stinger in years!

Wish I hadn't thought about him right now. Who says times haven't changed for the better?"

"I'm with you. So did you have chapel service once a week like we did?"

"Oh yeah. And what I heard there contrasted with Dad, who took me to his church for worship and youth group. He led a men's Bible study as well. Had a very vibrant inner faith."

"My dad's like that too."

"Dad took long walks around town by himself and called it his praying time. Sometimes I'd catch him on his knees by his bedside. But I never let on that I saw him. His body seemed to be strung in anguish at times like that."

"How did you end up at Christian school?"

"My aunt offered to send me, and he wanted to protect me from the sex education at public school. He was the single dad of a daughter, you know? I'm sure he was pretty scared about raising me right."

"Understandable."

"So I ended up on this bus to the Christian school where I heard so much talk about persecution and how the world was going to hell in a handbasket, how the 'godless left' plotted to steal away all our rights like a thief in the night, but I rarely heard much about love, about basic human kindness. It was all 'us versus them,' and believe me, the transition from 'us' to 'them' could be found in a single breath if someone found out you wore shorts or liked rock 'n' roll music."

"Sounds about right."

"Laney, nobody ever took me and my friends aside and said, 'What you're doing to Mary and Gary Andrews is abominable, horrendous, cruel behavior. What you're doing to those poor children is so terrible that if you ever come to some moral grounding you haven't been spoon-fed, you'll never be able to forgive yourself. If you ever become a decent human being who adheres to a code of kindness and the law of love, you'll look back on this time of your life and cringe at your own inherent depravity. You'll pray that God is merciful and your own children won't reap their mother's cruelty.' Nobody ever said that. And so I drive by their house a lot, Laney."

"How bad were you? I'm assuming you were horrible."

"Yeah. I don't think I can even get out the words to tell you. And now I wonder if Will suffers because of it. He's odd, and the type of group I ended up in would have had nothing to do with a talented, sweet guy like Will. I worked hard to get into that group because I was ridiculed myself until grade five because of my weight."

"How did you end up in the cool crowd?"

"Julia B. came to our school, fresh from New York City with a go-to-hell attitude, and she decided she liked me. I slimmed down over the summer due to a crazy growth spurt. We rode the same bus as the once-popular crowd that Julia B. dethroned and then asked into her court, and I rode her train to popularity."

"And Gary and Mary became the brunt on the bus?"

"Yes, and everywhere else too. Julia B. cornered the market on insulting superiority. She had a nose for the weak, descending upon them like a wild animal, the queen of our pack. She left after eighth grade."

"What happened to you?"

"A lot of them forgave me when I changed my tune in high school after Julia B. left. I assume she spent her time wreaking havoc at some other school in Pennsylvania where her father was relocated. But Mary and Gary were long gone by then."

"Can you find them, Heather? Do you know where they live?"

"I know where they used to live."

"Well, start there. Oh crud, I hear one of the twins. Hey, can Will come down later on? Nicola's jonesin' for him."

I inhale sharply. "She really does like him, then?"

"She's nutso. And she should be. For a while there she took a shine to that Legermin freak, but I nipped that in the bud."

"What did you say?"

"I told her that if she insisted on liking a cretin like him, she'd have to do the family's laundry for a year. That shut that down."

"Oh, Laney!"

We ring off. Laney doesn't think I'm crazy.

Find Gary and Mary. Is Laney right? I stare at the small house, as humble as the home in which my father raised me, played Monopoly with me in the evenings, readied me for church. But I live on the hill now. Away from them all. I live above. Away. Above. I live on waters that have swallowed towns whole.

I guess a new owner fixed up the Andrews's house. Putty-colored vinyl siding overlays the old siding; the door, diamond-shaped window pane still set into its surface, is painted a shiny hunter green, and new white picket fencing has replaced the former rusted chain link. I pull into the gravel drive, the wheels of my giant car crunching so loudly as to be violating.

What went on here, Heather?

For a person can fix a house so it appears fresh and without stain, cover up the grunginess, paint the surfaces that experienced the abuse and neglect of the once-inhabitants, but these acts are absorbed into the very fiber of the wallboards, the studs, the foundation blocks themselves. I feel that, just like at the Hotel.

I negotiate a sidewalk freshly invigorated with interlocking pavers before I can think further and rap my fist on the diamond door.

"Hang on a sec! I'll be right there."

Okay, so she must have smoked a thousand packs of cigarettes a year. For the past seventy-five years or so. Maybe I should go. This was a stupid idea. And it wasn't even my idea. *Thanks, Laney.*

The door opens.

Mercy!

So she isn't one hundred. Midsixties, perhaps. Her homemade hair color—a purply red; how did she get that shade?—is pulled back into a bow the size of a train case. I haven't seen one of those since the late '80s. I almost offer to give her a free cut and color right there. "Sorry. I had to sign off on my computer. What can I do for you?"

"I was looking for someone who used to live here. Gary and Mary Andrews?"

"Sure." She pulls wide the door. "Come on in. My allergies are killing me." As her reddened, tilted nose attests. She leads me down a narrow hallway into a small kitchen painted a sunny yellow at the back of the house. I feel sick. Are they still here at this place? "Mary?"

"Oh, good heavens, no! I'm old enough to be Mary's mother. She's long gone. I spent a fortune redoing this place, you know. Ultra-seal windows, state-of-the-art air purifying system." She turns on me suddenly. "You don't have cats, do you?"

I shake my head.

"Good. Have a seat." She points toward a dinette upon which sits an arrangement of faux sunflowers, a napkin holder with one napkin between its wooden sleeves, a shot glass with Splenda packets, and one bambooesque place mat. "Would you like a cold drink? Iced tea, water, or Tab?"

Tab? Who the heck drinks Tab anymore? Might as well see if it's as bad as I remember. "I'll take a Tab."

Her eyes light up. "Another Tab fan! Swell!"

She opens a harvest gold refrigerator and pulls out a can. "Ice?"

"No thanks. I'll take it straight from the can if you don't mind."

"You're my kinda gal, all right. I'll have one myself, I guess."

I take a sip. Mercy, it's just horrid. But the nostalgia factor is sweeter than hard candy, hearkening back to a time when you had a limited amount of choices. Boy, those days are gone!

She sits down. "So you want to know about the Andrews kids?"

"You know them?"

"I knew their grandmother years ago when I was a pharmacist in town. She worked the register. Was there long before I was."

"Is she still alive?"

"I don't know. I haven't seen her for, shoot, about thirty years, I guess. We worked together for eight, I guess."

"Do you know Gary and Mary?"

"Xavier's kids. Delores's grandkids. Well, sort of."

"What do you mean?"

"At least I did know them once. Every once in a while Delores brought them in. Xavier was a wild one. He was in high school when

I first started working with Delores. Oh, she'd complain about that boy all the time. But you couldn't help but like him, you know?"

I nod.

"So he was always one to win the ladies. Had that flash in his eye. Good lookin' he was, really foxy."

Foxy?

"He shacked up with this woman, Sandy something or other. Maybe Cindy. Mindy! Mindy was her name. Had these two kids, Gary and Mary, when she started dating Xavier after they met at the oyster supper over at the United Methodists. He used to work on the grounds crew at that church."

I remembered an old gray pickup truck parked near the house. A dumpling of a pickup, putty thicker than the makeup on a drag queen's face.

I sip on my Tab. There are worse things to drink. Offhand I can't think of what they are, but I'm sure they're out there somewhere.

"So this Mindy got her hooks into him, they got married, and he adopted those kids, I guess. Not two months later, she was gone!"

"As in left?"

"As in hit the road, Jack, and don't you come back gone. Gone, gone, gone. And she left Xavier with those kids. Now Delores tried to do her best by them to be sure, put them in that Christian school up a ways. They didn't like it after a while, though, and asked if they could just go back to the elementary school. Delores said sure, the tuition was a huge sacrifice for her. Actually brought in mayo and lettuce sandwiches for lunch just to make do."

Dear God in heaven.

"And then one day Xavier announced he was moving to Michigan and taking those kids with him."

"He got the kids when they were how old?"

"Elementary school age. Didn't quite know what to do with them, I guess. Delores was always getting on him, but he was lost. Sort of a wild one anyway, and then to be saddled down with those two. It isn't any wonder he couldn't take care of them."

She leaned forward.

"Delores once confided in me that he wasn't all that nice to them, really. She tried to make up for it all best she could, but she was only one woman, divorced years ago, and she was living hand to mouth as it was. And honestly, they weren't her grandchildren. But that was Delores for you. A kinder soul I've yet to meet."

"So they moved to Michigan, you say?"

"Years and years ago. Delores followed them soon after. Xavier needed her."

"Why didn't they just put them in foster care?"

"I don't know, really, only that Delores had a strong faith and probably figured God brought those kids to them for a reason. That's what Delores was always saying. 'These things happen for a reason.' It could be the most horrible situation, and Delores would say, 'This happened for a reason.' Me, I think she was a little overboard on all that stuff; I mean, I'm as God-fearing as the next person, but Delores never seemed to question one thing about God, as if He'd come down and give her a good shake or something if she did. Sometimes I'd ask her questions about why God allows this or that, and believe me, being a pharmacist, I saw a lot of pain, and she'd say, 'Oh, heaven help us, Peggy, it's not up to us to question.'"

I let out a laugh.

"Now what's so funny about that?" the lady I'm figuring is named Peggy asks.

"If that was the truth, I'd be going to hell in a handbasket." Speaking of hell and handbaskets.

"Me too."

"I always feel guilty about questioning God like I do."

"Me too. What's your name?"

"Heather Curridge."

"Peggy McCall."

Kindred spirits, obviously.

I drain my Tab. "I won't take up more of your time."

"Oh, I was just chatting up my grandson. He's all into the Internet these days. It's kinda fun."

A few minutes later I'm back on the road, headed toward home and some cake decorating.

Michigan. Thank heavens Delores had the sense to name her son something outlandish like Xavier. I mean, really, how many Xavier Andrewses can there be in Michigan?

And did I really just down a can of Tab?

FOURTEEN

Everybody raved about the cake, but as usual the food committee, translate Carmen, overestimated the amount needed, and Jace, who met me at school after work, helps me load the leftovers into the car. And five of the centerpieces that nobody even bothered to take as a door prize.

"You outdid yourself tonight, Hezzie. That was the best devil's food you've ever made. And those monkeys on the jungle cake were really cute."

Jace, a heart surgeon, is so proud of me and my cakes. Crazy, isn't it? I just adore the guy even if I don't get to see him as much as I'd like. Because it's like this: when he is around, he's really around. I mean, a lot of women tell me that they never feel connected, that as soon as their husband gets home from work, he's either on the computer, watching TV, or playing sports somewhere. Jace probably spends as much actual time with me as their husbands do, maybe even more.

"And the flower cake was really tasty too."

I hand him a box. "The red velvet?"

"Your best yet."

"You always say that."

"You just get better and better."

I'd gag if he wasn't so earnest.

"Did you actually try a piece of each one?"

He nods. "Of course. What are you going to do with this stuff?"

"I think I'll drive it down to the Hotel tomorrow."

Will bounds up. "Hey, can I drive home with you, Dad?"

"Sure."

If I asked my son to ride with me, he would. But I don't. Jace has a BMW.

And yes, we really are walking clichés.

So I slam down the hatchback, climb up into the behemoth, and start her up. Off I go, up the road from Timonium north to my cliff-hugging home.

But instead of taking the main thoroughfares, I decide to navigate the skinny way home across Merrymans Mill Road. No streetlights guard this byway that cuts close to Loch Raven west of where I live. Yet so much roils through my brain, it'll be nice to just drive.

My cell phone rings. And darn it!

"Yeah."

"Yeah? What kind of greeting is 'yeah'?"

"Hey, Lark."

"Hey, yourself. Where are you?"

"Merrymans Mill Road. What's up?"

"I'm heading down to the Hotel on Monday to talk to Sister J a little further, and I thought maybe you'd like to go."

"Nah. And you already asked me this. This answer is still no, Lark."

"Really? How come? I thought you loved that place."

No. No, no, no. Here I am, dotting my possessions, driving up to Gary and Mary's practically every day, buying white things, and making crazy phone calls to my friends. Everyone but Laney thinks I'm losing it, and my own husband doesn't even trust me with his dreams. I'm no more fit right now to put a ministry like that on my plate than I would be to pack up and be a missionary in Tibet, if they even allow them there. No, Lark.

"No. I just can't do everything, Lark, you know? I've got my responsibilities with Will's school, and Jace's surgical schedule is nuts. It's too much if I put that on my plate too."

"Oh, okay. No problem."

"Besides, I'm going down tomorrow to take this leftover cake from tonight's school dinner. I thought maybe they'd like that." Right? Doesn't that count for anything?

Lark doesn't say anything.

"You still there?"

"Uh-huh."

"What did I say?"

"Heather, take a piece of advice from me. Taking the rich folks' leftover cake may not be the best idea. Just a thought."

"You really think they'll be offended?"

"Wouldn't you?"

"I don't think so."

"But you don't know what it's like to be them, now, do you?"

"No, Lark, I don't. Mercy, you're awfully socially conscious tonight."

Lark laughs. "Tonight?"

Thank goodness she has dispelled the tension. "Okay, point taken. But honestly, I just can't come Monday. I can't take on one more thing."

"Suit yourself. Hey, though, let's have lunch here at the house soon. Mother's dying to see Will again. She just loves him. And my brother Newley's going to come next time. He wants to see this child Mother keeps raving about. Believe me, Mother never used to rave about anybody, really. She's changed, though, since I've moved in."

"Good. I'll call you tomorrow when I'm home to set up a time for lunch."

We ring off and I'm still driving in the darkness. Mercy, I was so gung ho on that old Hotel, and now, now I guess I'm worried I'll get too entangled in the place. And, well, I'll only admit this to myself, but the clients are odd. I have no idea how I'd even relate to smelly, mentally handicapped people.

No. Not this.

Not right now.

I don't have enough time. Maybe I need to get away for a few days, listen to the Holy Spirit or something.

I draw a mental picture of the Spirit rolling His eyes, shaking His head, and drawing His cloak more tightly about His broad shoulders. I hear the Spirit's words: "If you need to take special time to listen to me, you've got too much to do, Heather."

I see Will shove the pipe cleaners into the bags, angry at the waste of time and maybe even purpose, begging me to work down there; I see Krista pounding at the Hotel door; Sister Jerusha's veil blows in the city breeze; Knox Dulaney smiles and Mo waves a hand in disgust; the Asian man stares into space.

And I taste cake. Cake, cake, and more cake.

But I love my life, don't I? I'm here on the hill for a reason, surely. Perhaps I just don't know enough about Scripture, haven't studied enough to know God's will. I need to get to Greenleaf and find a good Bible study book. Lord knows, I haven't faithfully penciled in my Bible study fill-in-the-blanks for years now. That Becca Mills is such an anointed writer and teacher. That's what the women at my old church used to say, anyway. I need to get back to church.

And what's that hopping alongside the road?

Hopping?

Brown and furry, powerful hind legs.

A kangaroo?

A kangaroo!

And as I narrow the gap between us, still stunned at his presence here in Baltimore County, Maryland, USA, he darts into the road. I slam on my brakes, swerve, and careen into the ditch, leaves and branches thwacking my windshield while I pray the gully isn't deep and those darn cakes don't ruin the interior of my nice car.

Part Two

The Long and Winding Road

FIFTEEN

What in the world? Where . . . ? Here I am. Hands, yes, I see them, feel them. Yes, I can wiggle my fingers, bend my wrist—but ow! A spot higher up on the arm smarts. Feet—those move as well.

For real?

Or do I only think they're responding? I'm in a ditch apparently; I'm still alive apparently, and apparently, if the hand upon which the moonlight is falling is any indication, there's cake all over the place, all over me. The devil's food, apparently.

A tiki statue smiles at me from the passenger's seat.

Is this what death feels like, though? Do you not realize it, having never before experienced it, unless you once intersected with the "white light," which I haven't? I might actually believe I'm looking through my eyes, but they are really closed for good now, and I don't have the prior experience to realize what's actually going on. Will I float out of my body now? Hit the roof of the car and then somehow pass through like tomato juice through cheesecloth?

I shift in my seat. Okay, ow. Surely your spirit doesn't feel pain. And my head ripples with some discomfort, not a sledgehammer of pain, just that feeling that, "Yes, I have a head, and I know this because it hurts right now." I turn on the interior light, look out the side window, and see not a proper window view, but grass smashed up against the glass, some of it golden strawlike summer grass, other blades clinging to spring. And one now-beleaguered blossom of Queen Anne's lace.

125

The car interior is hideous. Cake chunks splattered against almost every surface.

I'm practically lying on my side against the door to my left, okay, a forty-five-degree angle, tops. I try to lift up my body, and a wave of pain courses again through my left arm.

I close my eyes and wait it out. *Oh, Lord,* I breathe. *Oh, Lord.*

I sit in the shadows wondering if the guys have made it home yet. Something warm slides down the side of my nose.

Am I bleeding? Don't think about that, Heather. You hate the sight of blood, remember?

Try to get up again.

Same thing.

Mercy!

I turn off the engine, relieved there wasn't some '70s boiling car explosion, and why is it cars explode on screen all the time but rarely in real life? Not that I mind right here right now. I knew my driving would get me into trouble. Did my guardian angel finally throw up her hands in despair?

The shade. The silence. Like I'm in a vast room with the door closed and locked, lights out, good night.

My breathing echoes inside my head and all around me.

I run a finger beside my nose and taste it. Yes, blood and cake. Never thought I'd taste that combination.

Injured in the dark seems an extremely solitary place, and how am I going to get out of this truck? And should I do that anyway? Are you supposed to wait until someone finds you, or call 911? Maybe there is some sort of accident etiquette to which I've never been privy, having never been in a real accident before, which, I'll grant, is a miracle akin to growing a leg back. Yes, there was that fender-bender. And the time I slipped on the ice and ran into the guardrail. And that trucker who ran me off the road. I forgot about that one.

It's going to take one of those primal yawps to sit up and twist into any kind of position that allows some leverage, and then I'm going to have to push open the passenger-side door that will be extremely heavy at this angle.

Or I could crawl through to the back and flip open the hatchback. Hopefully those air pump tube things aren't damaged.

More silence. More darkness. Not a car goes by, and a third option has yet to raise its hand.

Okay, then. The hatchback.

But in the meantime, I twist in the seat and shift onto my good arm, the injured arm sending blistering messages to my brain, and here's to no head injury, right? I mean, it hurts, but surely if I'd sustained real damage, I'd be unconscious right now.

That pretty much wore me out.

Okay, just for another minute I'll sit like this. Wonder where Jace is? Is he worried? Should I call 911?

No way. Not yet. Not with this cake all over me. I reach up. Big globs of it infest my hair. Ah, this'll be cute. Maybe I should just call the Three As. That's good. By the time they get here, I'll have wiped off at least some of this gunk.

Deep breath and I hoist myself onto my knees, sort of. And in a gangly, spidery, slipping-down course, I crawl to the back of the truck, smashing cake into the seats and surfaces wherever my hands and feet land. So much for these pants too.

But who was I kidding with these things? Pink and green?

More tiki gods smile upon me. Actually, I think they're laughing their little brown heads off.

I pull up on the handle.

Locked.

Oh, for the love of all that's decent, why me? And who tripped the child safety switch?

I swear, my arm is glowing with pain.

Back I go, more pain, more cake, and I push the switch, disengaging all the locks on the truck. Mercy, this is too much. I'm so glad I haven't called anybody yet. Some things a woman has to do on her own.

Still slipping, still glowing, I return to the back of the truck.

I yank on the handle again, and up the door rises, letting in fresh darkness and the smell of leaves and woods and strong skids of tar.

Finally.

And I forgot my purse with the cell phone inside.

Drat. I just have to keep moving forward. I can't go back again. I'll get it from outside after I rest.

Now just a quick climb out of this ditch. I claw at the grass with one hand, trying my best to keep my injured arm still. I doubt it's broken, but man, I wish that fabled "numbness" would settle in, for heaven's sake. Hey, I do have a bottle of ibuprofen in my purse.

No way. Forward, forward.

I crest the top and lie down on my back.

Merrymans Mill Road? What was I thinking? Why must I always take these drives? Why must I always take the long way home?

Ah, yes! That kangaroo.

What in the world was a kangaroo doing hopping down the road? Well, no sign of him now, but with my luck, he'll return to give me a good kick in the head with one of his giant feet.

I stretch my neck back, tendons as tight as metal strapping, and see a light farther off in the woods. Maybe I can reach it. Maybe they'll have a phone. Maybe they're criminals. Maybe I've lost my mind.

But heaven help me, I have to go to the bathroom. I've had to go since right after I left the house this evening. Okay, so if I hold my arm against my abdomen, it's a little better. No time like the present, Heather. Let's get going.

I roll over and up, the world astir, my head spinning a bit, and whoa! Okay, breathe in, get past all those carnival lights behind your eyes. Wait for the stars to fade.

Breathe. I breathe.

Now gain your feet and forward march and all that manly persistence jargon. Maybe someone like Jolly lives where that light is. Somebody lonely who could use an interruption from a warm soul like me. Or an old couple who just made a pot of tea for the evening— something herbal and light, although they'd probably just as soon have Lipton's Decaf. Maybe they'll make me a cup, and she'll gently suggest I call the Three As while handing me a phone with the wire still threaded into the wall.

Well, add thorn scrapes and a bleeding scalp wound to devil's food cake, and you've got the makings of a zombie fresh from the grave in *Night of the Living Dead*, and I have to admit, those movies crack me up, even if they do scare me more than I'd like to admit.

Through the trees I see some movement in the yard, hear an old woman's voice saying, "Hurry up and take a poo, Oatmeal. I was ready for bed an hour ago." The voice, soft, kind, and patient despite the words uttered, brings to mind Michael Learned on *The Waltons*, and I do believe if that character grew into old age, she'd sound like this.

I push aside some brush, and there she is, as old as Loch Raven, which I can see over her shoulder— older probably.

"Hello?" I try to speak as softly as I can without startling her but still letting her know of my presence. "I just had an accident."

She turns. "Oh!" And immediately starts walking my way. "Oh dear, are you all right? Look at the dirt!" She walks without impediment, sure on her miniature, old-style feet shod in brown loafers.

"It's cake. I had cake in the back of my car."

Concern pulls down her wrinkled features. She must be ninety if she's a day, which means she's lived through everything that's come to matter to us nowadays. Which means there isn't anything I could say or do that would shock her. Well, that's a relief.

"Your arm. Are you in pain?"

"Yes."

"And your head. It's bleeding."

"Yes. And I did go out for a couple of seconds, I think."

She reaches out a bent hand, arthritis swelling the knuckles. "Look there. There's a knot and an abrasion too. You may have a concussion."

Over her shoulder, the back of the house, modern yet warm, reclines in a bath of floodlight. Walls of windows set in fawn-colored frames, stacks of river rock, and expanses of stained cedar create a lived-in sculpture. A wide chimney pokes through the flat roof to stand darkened against the stars. Will would love this.

"I feel pretty clear-headed, other than I forgot to check for the lock on the car door before I climbed to the back to get out. And my purse is still up by the front seat with my cell phone, and the keys are still in the ignition." Did I say I was clear-headed? Mercy!

"I'm sure everything will be fine. Most people don't travel down this road at night unless they have to. Let's get you inside and you can call home. Careful now. Oatmeal probably did her business, and while she takes her time choosing her spot, she does tend to leave it out in the open."

"Thank you."

Her close-cropped white hair hugs her head, and the porch light attached to an overhang at the side of the house illumines the rosy scalp beneath. A sweater covers her bones on this cool June night.

She yanks open the sliding glass door at the back of the house. "Liza! We've got company!"

Taking my good arm, this angel-lady guides me into a den, past some old modern couches, two bentwood rockers, and a stone wall with a darkened fireplace, and into a cheerfully lit kitchen. The plain wooden cabinets soar to the ceiling, and the gold counters provide a space for copper canisters, a white Sunbeam stand mixer like my grandmother had, and a carved wooden fruit bowl. In the center of the room, a simple, round wooden pedestal table supports a bouquet of peonies in a glass bowl.

"My sister and her late husband built this house over sixty years ago. He was an architect." She speaks with apology.

"I like modern."

"I don't necessarily prefer it. But there's no accounting for taste, is there? Liza's always been the artistic type, or at least she found herself in that colorful kind of company. Even after Alva passed away, which was years and years ago, poor thing, she still found herself at all the gallery openings and exhibits and such." She leans forward. "My sister's very active, very bold. Of course she's five years younger than I am, which might explain it."

As if that matters by the time you've reached this age. This lady is so adorable.

"How's that arm? Let me take a look at it now that the lighting's better."

She lifts my arm and presses spots here and there, asks me all the right questions. I try not to grimace.

"Well, it isn't broken."

"Are you a nurse?"

"Doctor."

"Sorry to assume. My husband's a doctor."

"Cut my medical teeth in the Korean War." She turns. "Liza, honey! Oh, I don't know where she is. But let me run and get an old sheet for your arm. I'll make up a quick sling, and then would you like something to drink? And you'll need the phone."

"I'm coming, Anna!" an elderly voice calls from somewhere down the hallway. "I'll be there in two shakes of a lamb's tail!"

"I'd love something to drink. Maybe a cup of tea?"

"Surely. And the phone is right over there." She points to a bone-colored plastic phone attached to the wall. "I'll be back in a jiffy."

I still have to go to the bathroom, but I'd better call Jace. I lift up the receiver and dial Jace's cell.

"Jace, it's me."

"Hey, babe," he whispers. "Will and I decided to go to the movies. I kept trying to call you on your cell phone but wasn't getting an answer."

"You're not going to believe this." I tell him about the kangaroo.

"I'll be right there."

"Whenever you get here is fine. Finish the movie. I'm at someone's house. I probably should have called the Three As, but I saw a light in the woods and walked here. The lady who lives here is a doctor. She said my arm isn't broken, and she's off to get an old sheet for a sling."

"I'll come pick you up."

"Take your time, Jace, really. I'm fine. She's making me a cup of tea, and I just need to sit for a minute. Can I give you a call as soon as I collect myself?"

"Absolutely. We'll be on our way. Did you hit your head?"

"Yeah. It doesn't hurt that much though. I need to wash up. I've got cake all over me."

"Well, it sounds like you're in good hands, but I don't like the idea of that head, Hezz. Listen, we'll be there in about forty minutes. We're at the Senator. Some indie film Will wanted to see."

"Okay."

Gosh, I feel more frayed than a forty-year-old coat!

"What happened to the truck? Not that it really matters, but I thought I'd ask."

"Well, there's cake all over the interior."

"That's all right. They'll be able to clean it up."

"I hate that truck, Jace."

"We'll talk about that later."

"I don't know why I had to have it. It looked as big and stupid there in that ditch as it looked shiny and promising in the showroom. We only have one kid."

"We'll be there as quick as we can."

"Do I sound that bad?"

"Just a little out of your head. Let me talk to the doctor."

"Anna!"

She hurries in. "Yes, dear."

I hand over the phone. "My husband wants to talk to you."

"Of course." She holds the phone up to her ear as if both are made of glass, the way old folks tend to do. For half a minute they speak in the medical jargon I've learned to tune out, then talk about getting the car towed, and apparently I'm all taken care of. She hands me the receiver and zips back down the hallway.

Jace says, "Good, hon. Sounds like you're in good hands. Anna told me where you all are. I'll call the wrecker to meet me."

"All right."

We hang up and I head into the powder room, thankfully, right by the phone.

Liza, I assume, clips into the kitchen where I stand, cake still over-laying my person. "So you're Anna's patient."

"Yes, I guess so."

"Now a cup of tea is what you need. And don't ask for coffee. I ran out this morning and forgot to stop at the store."

"Okay."

"Right, then. First the kettle, and you need to go sit in the den there. The couch on the right is truthfully the most comfortable. Feel free to put your feet up on the coffee table. I'm sure the Eameses wouldn't mind."

The Eameses?

"Go on. Tea will be ready in two shakes of a lamb's tail."

"Thank you."

"My pleasure."

I haul my wounded arm into the den. My goodness, what a gal! As spicy as her sister is sweet, she exudes that artsy confidence of, say, a gallery owner or a museum curator. Her hair, a shining silver, is pulled back into a tight, chic bun at the nape of her neck. I'll bet she has worn it like that for years. And her skirt, black and slender, hugs her sapling frame. Only the flat silver house shoes attest to her age.

So she married her an architect. Seems fitting.

I can't sit! I'll ruin the couch with this cake.

Purposeful clankings sound from the kitchen as Anna returns holding a strip of snowy sheet with pink rosebuds scattered about its folds. "Let's get that arm stabilized. And I'm sure you could use some painkiller. I'll get you a glass of water too. Wait, you might like to clean up before I put this on. How did you get all that dirt all over you?"

"It's cake."

"Oh my, yes. I forgot already." The aquamarine eyes sink deeper in the smiling flesh. "It seems when I turned ninety it all started going downhill. Liza! Could you get a pair of Maria's lounge pants? And a shirt? This woman has cake all over her!"

"That's not dirt?"

"Apparently not."

"It's devil's food!" I yell.

"What's your name, honey?" Anna asks.

"Heather Curridge."

"I'm Anna, and that's my sister, Liza, in there. Let me show you to the bathroom, where you can take a shower. Your husband is delightful."

"Who's Maria?"

"Our great-niece who comes to visit occasionally." She turns the faucet inside a built-in tile shower and then faces me with an impish smile. "She only comes around because Liza's loaded!"

So a bit of cayenne mixes with that sugar.

"The water will be warm in a jiffy. Yell if you need me."

Liza sets a cup of tea on the kitchen table. "Right, then. Here you go. You must feel much improved sans all that cake."

"Definitely."

Anna bustles in. "The guest room is ready. My, this is a bit of excitement for us two biddies, isn't it, Liza?"

"Speak for yourself. I refuse to be a biddy."

Their eyes meet. Sisters.

Liza picks up my teacup. "Let's take this to the guest room and you can rest there in comfort until your husband comes. You've been through enough already without having to listen to our inane conversation."

"Speak for yourself, Liza. I refuse to be inane." Anna scrunches up her nose.

Maria's sweatpants are as soft and broken in as crushed rose petals, and as Anna ushers me into the velvety beige guest room, the down counterpane pulled down, exposing cocoa sheets, nothing but this arm impedes a comfortable rest. I won't complain about the Percocet either.

"Just rest."

I love being taken care of like this. I feel cozy, a scuffed fairy-tale princess finding refuge at a hidden cottage.

"Thanks for taking me in."

"Oh, honey, it's a pleasure. Would you like me to turn off the light?"

"No thanks. I'll drink my tea and maybe just read." I pick up a book on the nightstand.

She smirks. "That one will put anybody to sleep. But it's one of my favorites."

And she shuts the door quietly. *Pacificism and Biblical Non-Resistance.* Also on the nightstand, *Cyrus Pringle's Diary.*

What? She's right. This looks drier than my skin in February. And I'm tired.

SIXTEEN

Upon opening my eyes, I know the morning settled in awhile ago. What happened to Jace? The warmed air has burned away the night. The sunlight, welcomed by the wall of windows, gilds the room. Everyone should have a wall of windows, I've decided lying here.

Peace has come upon this place, and I'd love to know why. And how. And can I take some home with me?

I roll onto my side to sit up. Pain darts through my arm. "Ow!" I can't help but cry out.

A quick bunny knock vibrates the flat door. "Heather, honey, are you all right?" Anna.

"I just forgot about my arm and rolled onto it. Come on in!"

She enters without hesitation. "Let me look."

"Actually, it feels a lot better than it did last night." I lift it up by the shoulder, bend it at the elbow, then the wrist. "It's stiff, but that's all."

"You'll still want to keep it in that sling today, and an X-ray would be a good idea." She sits down on the bed. "So your husband came by last night. I told him just to meet the wrecker and check on you while you slept. We both agreed it was best to let you go on sleeping. Jace. Is that his real name?"

"Yes."

"I like it. Very different. Very 'cool,' as the younger set would say."

I smile at her. She's dressed in a pair of khaki serge pants and a short-sleeve pullover top in heather gray. Small pearl drops weigh down her delicate earlobes.

"He's a good guy."

"Yes. Used to work on a hospital ship, he said. I have a thing for men who care about others."

"Did you have glasses on last night, Anna?" Mildly hip rimless spectacles rest on the bridge of her nose.

"I still had my contacts in."

It's all I can do not to giggle. She's so old, so cute. And yet she's a doctor. Talk about un-cliché! Nothing like us Curridges.

She pats my leg. "I'm going to bring you in a nice pot of tea and a roll. Liza's helping me get ready for a meeting for clearness out in the den, so if you want to stay in here and rest, that's fine. Jace called early and said he'd be by, but I told him you were still asleep. He'll be here around one because of Will's swim meet, which he was going to 'blow off,' as they say, but I told him to go on ahead." She stands to her feet. "So you still have a few hours to rest."

"What's a meeting for clearness, Anna?"

"Oh, I belong to the Society of Friends. Quakers. A meeting for clearness is when an individual has a decision to make and seeks counsel from his fellow Friends. In this case, it's Adam, who's wondering which college he should attend this fall. He's been accepted to two, but he just can't seem to make up his mind. Nice young man."

"Is Liza a Quaker?"

"Not really." She laughs. "Depends on what day you ask. Liza could never be a wholehearted anything when it comes to organized religion. She takes Christ by the hand and hits the ground running each day. She dabbles in all sorts of denominations and ways to serve, and she certainly wouldn't get herself arrested for peace or anything like that, but she does the work of the cross."

"And you'd get arrested?" I couldn't imagine this sweet old lady being taken away in handcuffs.

"I've been arrested more times than I can count!" She waves a hand. "I know! Surely it's the last thing you'd expect. Why don't you sit outside? I'll bring your tea there and you can look at the water. I so love looking at the water."

I throw back the covers and pad to the adjoining bathroom. Over a simple dresser hangs a saying in calligraphy.

The Friends Peace Testimony
"We utterly deny all outward wars and strife and fightings with outward weapons, for any end or under any pretence whatsoever. And this is our testimony to the whole world."
From "A Declaration to Charles II," 1660

So she really believes all this? Wow. I don't know anybody, not one single person, who would get arrested for their beliefs, including me. I've never even written my legislators.

On the dresser, my clothes are laundered and folded.

Five minutes later I'm sitting out on the slate veranda that anchors the back of the house and extends around to the side I didn't see last night. I believe there's a pool around there because I smell chlorine, and a wringing wet Oatmeal just came running from that direction. A wooden deck peeks from behind the other side of the house.

The dog plops down next to me on the warmed stone as I sip my tea in the morning sunlight. The lake lies placid this morning, so deep, so calm and mysterious.

And so devoid of underwater church bells.

I'm still disappointed.

Ah, but what perfect tea, rounded and smooth with a large dollop of honey and a smidgen of milk that removes any rough edges whatsoever, if there were any to begin with, which I doubt. These women seem to hide all the secrets of life inside deep magical pockets that hold things much too large for their dimensions. Living ancient like this never appealed to me, but if I resemble these sisters, may my trunk grow thick and my roots grow deep.

The open sliders usher the morning breeze into the den; screen doors banish the bugs. The group speaks every so often, asking questions, I presume. Mostly they sit in silence. I suppose they are praying. I heard someone mutter something about discerning the will of God and the leading of the Spirit.

"I only desire the will of God. But I can't discern God's from mine." The young man's voice sounds so earnest. And he begins to summarize before the small group of what, I surmise, are very trusted people who've invested in him his entire life.

I shouldn't be listening.

Cradling my arm, I heft myself off the lounger and head down the steps toward the lake. Oatmeal follows me, prancing in the grass like a dancing wet mop.

The group stops speaking as I pass by. They appear normal enough. Nothing like the Quaker Oats guy.

Oatmeal!

I get it.

I lean down and touch the dog's wet head, and she wags her stump of a tail. I have no idea what breed she is, but maybe some Lhasa Apso loiters somewhere in her assemblage. My grandmother had a Lhasa.

So I sit cross-legged on the grass and stare at the water, longing for the bells and wondering if just maybe one of them escaped the wrecking ball.

"We've got cake!" Anna laughs. She's found me.

"I don't think I could possibly eat a bite of cake, having worn so much of it."

"Do come in, dear. Liza made it." She looks over her shoulder and whispers, "It looks horrible. But it's got more chocolate than Willy Wonka inside of it." She waves a hand, proud of her own joke. "Come."

"I really don't want to disrupt what's going on. It sounds rather serious."

"Well, then. I'll sit here for a while if you don't mind. Clearness committees are always exhausting."

She bends down, slowly lowering herself beside me. "I may need a committee to tell me how I'm supposed to get back up."

"I'll help you."

"With that arm?"

We laugh. "You're good for my soul, Anna."

"Thank you. I surely appreciate the compliment." She looks out over the lake.

"It's beautiful here."

"Jace told me you live on the lake too. Not many of us, are there?"

"No. We're quite the club."

"Oh, goodness, yes." She smiles, suddenly far away.

Her face lifts to the sunshine, gravity pulling away some of the creases atop her features. She was an interesting-looking woman in her day, I'll bet.

And why do I always try to find the young woman buried beneath the aging landscape? Aren't Anna, and Peggy McCall at the Andrews's house, and Sister Jerusha beautiful enough all on their own?

I don't know how much later, Anna opens her eyes. "I'll bet they're gone now. How about that cake?"

"All right."

"How about that hand?"

I help her to her feet. She chuckles at her own creakings and groanings. "Oh, goodness, I don't know if a body's supposed to go on this long." And she tucks her arm through mine. "I'm glad you've come, Heather."

She didn't say it, but I felt her next thought. *You are a troubled soul, dear, and maybe somehow, here at our house, you will find a measure of peace and light.*

Liza crosses her arms and looks at me as I take my first bite, and I know the feeling.

"Fabulous!" I pronounce.

"Right, then." She turns on her heel. "Anna, I'm going now!" she calls, grabbing her purse off a hook near the phone. "You be careful, Heather. I'm glad that husband of yours is coming to get you. Truthfully, I'm still not sure if you're all right."

"He'll give me a good once-over."

"Yes, Anna told me he's a physician too."

"Yes."

"Right, then. I'm off."

She's wearing jeans—yes, jeans—and a green blouse. Sensible shoes too. I didn't notice it last night, but she has a sort of Julia Child curve to her back. "Do you mind if I ask where you're going?"

"To the halfway house in Cockeysville."

"Halfway house?"

"For alcoholic men. I help the men clean on Saturdays. My late husband was a drinker like you wouldn't believe. He died young."

Mercy! Such candor.

"I'm sorry."

"Alva enjoyed life even if he did live it with such intensity. Anyway, that's neither here nor there after half a century. Needless to say, I've learned to live without him."

I can't help it. I bark out a laugh.

Liza smiles. "Bye now. And don't be a stranger."

And she walks away, so very different from the rest of the world, but somehow fitting right in. I'm seeing firsthand what it means to be in the world but not of it.

"Anna? Has she always been like this?"

Anna shakes her head. "The Lord came to her one day. That's all she'll say. I don't know what form He took, but I do know she recognized Him for who He was."

SEVENTEEN

Jace shuts my door and swings around to his side of the car. "Seriously, aren't those the coolest ladies you've ever seen?"

"Definitely. They were wonderful."

He shakes his head and puts the car in drive, and we head off into the woods that front their acreage. "Man, I'm glad you're okay. Your arm should be fine. It's heavily bruised, but if you want to see an orthopedist, I can arrange that. You've got good movement, but maybe we should get an X-ray."

"Let me just give it a couple of days."

He pulls out onto Merrymans Mill Road. "I knew you'd say that."

"Will okay?"

"Absolutely. He wanted to come, but I thought you'd be a little overwhelmed. His enthusiasm can be a little suffocating."

"I'm feeling a little overwhelmed in general these days."

"I could tell. Laney's husband, Cade, got him from swim practice. He's spending the day with them. You want to get some lunch? Just the two of us?"

"Definitely." Maybe he'll open up about Bonnie's request, whatever it was.

Jace chitchats about his new patient—an old blind minister named Carl whose daughter is actually married to the brother of Snap, the lead singer of Great Guns. "Remember them, Hezz?"

"We listened to them all the time in high school."

"So did we. Anyway, my patient's a wonderful man, second time for open heart. He's grieving the death of his youngest daughter from an accident a little while ago. He said, 'If you could mend that big tear right down the middle of my heart while you're in there working on those valves, I'd appreciate it.' I wanted to cry."

"What did you say to him?"

"I said I'd do my best, but only one person can heal a wound like that."

"How do people get through things like that?"

"I don't know. I pray to God we never have to find out."

"Still. I wonder if my faith would hold."

"As do we all. What would happen to our faith if it was tested, really and truly?"

"I don't know." I whisper the words.

And now we sit at a table for two at the Nautilus Diner in Timonium. After Liza's cake and my general cake garment of the night before, I will most certainly skip dessert.

"I'll take the moussaka, light on the tomato sauce." The waitress writes down the selection.

Jace orders the grilled salmon.

I guess when you see hearts literally encased in globby yellow fat, it's got to affect you somewhat.

The waitress asks if I want all the peripherals. Salad, soup, bread. No thanks.

For the first time in my life, I'm not really all that hungry.

I lean into the table after she leaves. "Something's very wrong with me, and all the long drives in the world won't fill the emptiness or shine a light or whatever it is I need. I realize that now."

"I've been thinking about things, Hezzie. Do you think you might want to try some medication?"

"For what?"

"Anti-anxiety, perhaps?"

"What will that do?"

"It will dull those scared feelings you're experiencing."

"Who says I'm scared?"

"You have. Not in so many words, but you have."

"I'm wide-awake for the first time in my life, Jace. I don't want to dull anything."

"Tell me what you mean by wide-awake."

"I'm comparing myself to three old women. Sister Jerusha in that rundown hotel, and then Anna, who actually gets arrested for her beliefs, and her sister Liza, who right now is cooking at a halfway house." Maybe dessert would be a good idea.

"Is this comparison a good thing?"

"I don't know."

"But maybe some medication will help you see things more clearly if the fear's gone."

"Who said fear is always a bad thing, Jace?"

He stares at me for a moment, then takes a sip of his water. "What can I do to help you see your way through?"

"I don't know. I love it there at the sisters' house. They told me to come back if I needed to. I think I might need to. I've been driving too fast, thinking too much, saying more than I should to anybody who will listen. I can't even begin to hear God speaking, Jace. And I have no idea what He'd say if He did."

"My parents have been wanting to take Will for a couple of weeks. I've got that seminar in Chicago the week after next, so I wouldn't mind the quiet in the evenings to prepare. I'll probably spend some time at the library too. Maybe you should take them up on their offer?"

"Are you sure?"

"Give them a call and see what they say."

Already I feel a little better. Not much, but any break from the routine that has become my life sounds like a good idea.

"So what's happening in Chicago?"

"Just a seminar for cardiologists."

As we listen to music on the way to the Curridges' vacation house, the recumbent farms of Delaware whizzing by, Will asks questions about the Sermon on the Mount. He's been reading the book of Matthew since school ended. He has too many questions.

We listen as he asks them, and I think about my life when weighed in the balance of the truth of Christ, drowning in the hard sayings of Jesus, and I think I'd just as soon keep my mouth shut.

"What does hoarding treasure really mean, Dad?

"What would it look like if we really didn't judge?

"Aren't preachers always asking people to make vows? To sign little pledge cards, although that's in direct opposition to the teachings of Christ? Or is it? Was that what He was talking about?

"How do we know what to throw out and what to keep? I mean, if we only pay lip service to His teachings anyway and they have no real showing in our actions, haven't we cast them, in all reality, into the dustbin?"

"The dustbin? Where did that word come from, Will? I haven't heard anybody use it for years. Other than my grandmother."

"I have no idea, Mom."

Jace grips the wheel, and I know his thoughts. All Christian parents pray for their children to be interested in the things of God . . . but fifteen and asking these questions? Will it do more harm than good?

And then the inevitable question I ask myself: "What kind of trust in God is *that*, Heather?"

"Love your enemies? If Jesus let His enemies crucify Him, what does that mean for us, Dad?"

" 'Take up your cross and follow me,' Will."

I can't stay silent. "That's impossible."

Jace frowns. "He wouldn't have said it if it was."

"I know. But it still seems impossible."

Will leans forward. He always sits in the middle of the backseat. "But we have this book that shows us what God would do if He was human; what God *did* when He was human. Doesn't that count for something?"

"Then why does living as a Christian seem like such a mystery?

More books than I can remember on how to do this very thing have been passed around in churches."

And yet the very example we have, we pooh-pooh, saying, *Well, He was God. Of course He could do that.*

Jace breaks for a stoplight. "Maybe we don't live *for* Christ because we don't live *like* Christ."

"Right, Dad. And maybe I don't live like Christ because I've taken the Man out of Him, made what He did here so mysterious and unreachable that I've taken away any possibility of success in imitating Him."

Jace steps on the accelerator. "He wouldn't have told us to be like Him if it was impossible."

"You really believe that, don't you?" I ask.

"With all my heart. Although most days, I wish to God I didn't, Heather."

Sandals, a robe, a cloak.
 No place to rest His head.
 Friends, disciples. Followers.
 "I proclaim good news to the poor."
 Twisted and broken on a cross.
 "Father, forgive them."
 He could have called ten thousand angels, but He didn't. He lifted his face to the corruption, the power plays, the violence of His own creation and opened not His mouth.

I write these words on the back of an envelope from my purse and turn to Jace as we drive home from dropping Will off at the Curridges'.

"Can we do it, Jace? Can we really follow His teachings?" I have a feeling I'll be asking this question over and over for as long as I breathe.

"I believe we can, hon. We won't do it perfectly like He did, but that's where the grace comes in."

"Yeah, but I can really abuse grace."

"From your perspective, sure. But if there's an unlimited supply, how can you use up too much?"

"Still, a lot has been left undone in the name of grace."

He's quiet for a little while. Then, "It's a fine line, isn't it? I guess, for me, I'd rather use more grace for having tried and gotten it wrong than for not having tried at all."

That's it. That's it exactly.

"Hezzie?"

"What?"

"Nothing. Never mind."

The sisters are delighted I called. Anna answered the phone, and Liza picked up the extension in the kitchen and said they weren't surprised to hear from me and were glad to help in any way.

"In fact," Anna says, "I bought more of that cranberry tea you liked so much as an unspoken prayer."

Ah, I love that woman.

But before Jace drops me off, I hop on the Internet to locate the whereabouts of Xavier Andrews in Michigan. Okay, people search or something.

I hate this stuff. I'm just no good at it. I should have done this before Will left for the shore. He's a whiz at this sort of thing. But then again, I can't tell him what I'm doing, admit I was once Ronnie Legermin. Not after what he goes through.

I'd still like to take him out of that school, by the way. But no go! Especially not with Nicola in the works.

After thirty minutes of pointing and clicking, I find nothing on Xavier himself, but his mother, Peggy's coworker Delores, died in 1982, the year Gary would have been a senior. I locate the town, look up the local high school, and his name appears on the list of the 1982 graduates.

The name, so real in the black cyber-ink on my monitor, shoots a jolt up my spine. I quickly bookmark the site, shut down the computer, close the door to the office, and tell Jace it's time to go.

On the car ride over, I offer him one more chance to come clean on Bonnie. But again my husband will not trust me with his heart. Probably because he has already given it to me so thoroughly he can't ask anything of me anymore. I deserve this.

"Hon? What are the dots all about?"

I tell him the plan and the code.

"Oh, wow. We have that many meaningless items around?"

"Yeah. It's worse than even you thought, Jace. And don't say 'I told you so.' Please."

He places a hand on my thigh. "You going to get rid of any of it or just be thankful for what you have?"

I don't know.

What would Jace think of an all-white house?

EIGHTEEN

Anna leans over the railing, looking down at the creek. It rained last night, and the water, smelling of leaves and ozone, rushes beneath our feet, hurrying to join with the bay. We've stopped on our way to visit a friend of hers at the VA hospital in Havre de Grace. "And the other men too," she says. "A lot of the boys are there."

"Do you know them?"

"I do now. I just go to let them know somebody hasn't forgotten."

"But you hate war, don't you?"

"Yes. But I love people. I put many a man back together out on the battlefield, Heather. I've more than earned the right to hate war and still love our soldiers. It is possible to do both, dear." She turns to me. "Heather, why are you here?"

"I'm not sure," I whisper. "I think everybody thinks I'm going a little crazy."

She nods. And gazes back at the water. "Do *you*, dear?"

"A little."

"Is it a good thing or a bad thing?"

"God's speaking to me, Anna. I just don't know what it is He's saying. But I hear Him, like I hear the wind in the trees or that running water beneath our feet."

"Most likely you know it deep down already. No matter. God has plenty of time. It's one thing He's never short of."

"But I feel so muddled."

"Through the ages people who listen to the promptings of God have always been thought more than a little goofy."

And she begins to tell me story after story of saints who make my meanderings, my dots, my white items, my conversations, seem like a walk in the park.

Okay, so I thought the Hotel felt depressing. This VA hospital is the singularly most disheartening place I've ever entered in my entire life, and that includes airport bars, casinos, and beach bathrooms, not to mention bus stations, pawn shops, and the health department. Anna whirls from patient to patient like love potion in a misery cocktail, greeting each of them by name, a peaceful sweetness accompanying her simple act of knowing them: their names, their conditions, their birthdays. She hands out several cards.

Ah, Lord Jesus, all the suffering in the world. More walls of sadness. How have I lived so long without coming face-to-face with this? Have I purposely anesthetized myself, or was I programmed years ago to avoid the living tragedy? And does it matter now that my nerve endings have begun to awaken and my taste buds have matured to include the flavors of despair and responsibility?

Anna curls her arm through mine. "Come see my dear friend Bobby." She leans her head toward me and whispers, "I had a thing for him years ago. He was much too young for me, though."

She leads me down a hallway, still greeting each man who sits in a wheelchair along the path, introducing me like I'm Sophia Loren or something. I've never seen so many lost limbs or burn scars in one place. I'm grateful, believe me, but the heartache that petrifies my insides at what man does to man weighs down my footfalls. I walk more heavily. I feel my shoulders droop under the knowledge of their anguish, their lives lost yet still going on, these forgotten men.

Anna pats my arm, then swings me through a door.

"Bobby Stewart! You old rascal!"

"Anna Banana!"

Bobby lies in a bed. I assume he's paralyzed, but I'll have to ask later. His cumulonimbus hair is obviously the true testament to his personality.

"Bobby and I were in the same unit in Korea. He's a doctor as well."

"Used to be." Bobby raises his arms. No hands. "Left them somewhere in Vietnam and somehow can't finagle the time in my busy social schedule to go back and find them."

"He only wears his prosthetics for special occasions." Anna. "I'm old hat, obviously."

"Well, you wouldn't be. I keep asking you to marry me, Anna, and you keep refusing."

"Not to mention I'm twenty years older than you are." She laughs. "He was a real Lothario back in the old days, dear. Much too wild for my poor blood."

He jabs a stump in my direction. "So she roped you into coming along on one of her do-gooder rounds, did she?"

"I'm afraid so, Dr. Stewart."

Anna. "Heather's husband's a medical man too, you know."

"Oh yeah? What field?"

"He's a cardiac surgeon." Each word makes me feel like I'm dangling a luscious plum in front of a person with no teeth.

"Remarkable strides they've made in cardiology since my day." Bobby.

Anna sits on the edge of the bed. "Oh my, yes. Bobby still keeps up on the medical journals. He puts me to shame."

"Have to keep myself busy mentally. In between visits from old Anna here."

"You know you count the minutes until my arrival, Bobby."

He winks. "Pronounce me guilty."

"I talked with the Department of Veterans Affairs, and they said they'll look into your benefits, see if you can get into a different facility, but for now, I'm afraid you're still stuck here."

"I feel like I'm in prison."

"You are," she said. And she changed the subject, talking about happier times after the Korean War when they met downtown and danced the night away. "Of course, Bobby picked up a more willing partner, and I went home to Mother. Hardly fair."

Bobby only replied, "It depends on what your definition of fair is."

On the way home, I asked Anna, "Doesn't Bobby have family that can help him?"

"Not to the extent he needs, Heather. He never married, so he has no children. That we know of, anyway." Her laugh sparkles like a sequined scarf. "His only sister had a couple of kids, but they don't know him. She lives on the West Coast. He's most surely a forgotten man."

"Mercy."

"Terrible, isn't it?"

"How come you're doing all that stuff for him, though? He seems more than competent."

"Can you imagine the depression that has overtaken him? He's quite debilitated that way. Turn down that road there on the left, dear. Anyway, there's more than one way to support the troops, isn't there?"

"I guess it's pretty easy to wave a flag and mutter some words, isn't it?" I thought of my car flags when the war in Iraq broke out. But men like Bobby were totally off my radar. In some ways I wish he still was.

"We can cheer them when they go away to die for us, but most of us don't want to think about them when they come back and suffer the rest of their lives for us, do we?"

"I guess not."

"I've exposed myself to what happens on the back end the way not many other people do." She looks out the window, then turns to me. "And I've seen them die and suffer on the front end too. I appreciate their sacrifice for me, but I can't help but believe there's a better way to shore up our freedom. That we don't have to rely on the deaths of these precious men and women to do it."

I've never heard talk like this before. I don't even know what to think, really. But we don't have to agree on everything to appreciate one another, do we? I mean, my father was a Marine when he was young. "But God used death all the time to get His will done."

"Jesus didn't. And He's really all we have to go on, isn't He?"

Ah, my goodness, there it is, more of that vein Will has been thinking about. I don't know if I can handle all this deep thought. Lord, I came to get direction, not to become even more confused.

I continue on down the road, our speed consuming the fields and fences of Harford County. "Are you hungry?"

"Oh yes! I always eat a little lunch on the way home. Would you like to stop in Bel Air?"

"Okay. Do you have any place in mind?"

"There's a little tearoom called Tea by Two. I love their scones and watercress sandwiches."

"Definitely."

Anna tells me about her parents. Her father was a doctor at Johns Hopkins who specialized in pediatrics; her mother ran a local chain of supermarkets with *her* father. Anna and Liza grew up downtown in well-to-do Mount Vernon, went to all the best schools, had the greatest advantages children could have. "But always with a great attention to love and responsibility. My mother didn't always make life easy for us! Oh goodness, no. I was doing my own ironing by the time I was eight, and Liza and I volunteered at the hospital all the time or stocked shelves at the store. Mother was quite the woman."

We enter the tearoom and are seated at a table draped in white damask, a china sugar bowl and creamer holding down the center.

After ordering, I ask, "Did you grow up Quaker?"

"No. My father was an agnostic and Mother was too busy."

"How did you find Christ?"

"In a still, small voice."

And I can tell by her tone that's as much of the tale as she is willing to tell.

"I've never met anyone like you before, Anna."

"Well, you'll find if you open yourself up to the possibility that

God is found in locales you've never imagined; you'll meet Him in all sorts of faces and places you never thought possible."

"How do you know when you've heard the Spirit speak?"

The waitress delivers a serving tray loaded with three plates: sandwiches, scones, and cookies.

"My way of hearing may be different than yours, Heather. So it isn't for me to say. I don't want to put my fences around you."

"This isn't helping me any."

She raises her brows and lifts a tiny sandwich to her mouth. "On the contrary. One day you'll look back and see I did you the greatest favor I possibly could by keeping my mouth shut." She bites down into the soft white bread.

NINETEEN

I've settled into the same earthy, restful room. Peace. They talk about it around here, and I sense it in these walls and long to feel it inside of myself. How do they make it seem so easy? And is it easy? Can you truly feel at peace?

And is freedom the result of peace? Or is peace the result of freedom? I look around me and shake my head. I've always believed the latter. But now I'm not so sure. I want to be free. I want to be at peace. At present I am neither.

Then again, the sisters are in their nineties, and their peace arrived with a hefty price tag. The late afternoon sunshine casts the shadows of the hills onto the loch, deepening the waters, blocking the reflection of the sky. I can gaze out into the nature scene from where I sit on my bed. It's easy to feel peaceful here, really. Maybe that's their secret.

Ah, yes. I have much the same view from my bedroom at home, don't I?

But then, the answer couldn't have been that easy.

I slip my Bible from my suitcase and turn to Matthew, remembering what Anna said, what Jace and I talked about. Jesus is all we have to go on, really, as far as who we imitate, as far as what God looks like as a human being, and we're supposed to be like God, right? I'll start with Jesus. And I'll pay great attention to the red letters.

Teach me, Lord.

I don't pray these words through a great holiness. I pray them through a clawing sense of desperation. I don't want to run away anymore. I want to find my way right here, inside my skin, the skin of those I love so much, and the skin of those who have gone and are going before me.

Laney picks up on the sixth ring.

"Can I ramble?" I ask.

"Sure."

"I've spent most of my life in service to my family; first to Jace and his medical degree and then to Will. I don't regret that."

"But . . ."

"But I could have listened to the Lord more, Laney. I let my service to others drown out His voice. We can do both, right? Listen to His voice and serve our families."

"Yes. But usually we sacrifice one for the other when they're supposed to go hand in hand."

"What does it look like when a woman does both?"

"Well, don't look at me for the answers, Heather. My life is about as balanced as the federal budget."

Next I call Jace. "How's the prep work going for the Chicago trip?"

"Good. So how are you doing at the sisters'?"

Next I call Lark. I tell her about Jace. "I'm hurt. Should I be?"

"Maybe. But can you blame him? Really, Heather, have you thought of what that tennis court you're planning must feel like to him? You might as well put jail doors on the entryway and lock him inside."

Liza, dressed in midnight blue crushed velvet lounge pants and an ivory satin blouse, sets a record upon the turntable of the old stereo in the corner of the family room. The sounds of the Glenn Miller Orchestra and "Little Brown Jug" enliven the space, the piano's bass launching the piece, the throaty trombones grabbing the melody, the trumpets lying down on top for the breezy ride.

"I loved the way he sometimes played big band with a different equation, the trombones playing the melody so much." Liza claps in time with the song. "It's why you can always tell it's Glenn Miller."

Really? They did that?

I just nod, and she reaches out her be-ringed hands toward Anna, who walks into the room with a tray, our coffee mugs steaming on its teak surface.

"Come on, Anna, let's dance a little!" She wiggles her fingers.

Anna doesn't hesitate. She sets the tray onto the blond coffee table and snaps up her sister's hands, and they slide into a thrifty jitterbug, right through "In the Mood" and onto the depot in "Kalamazoo."

Their blue eyes sparkle, the notes settling upon their features like dew, their smiles stretching their faces young. Anna's short hair feathers in the wake of their movement, moving in the same direction as the hem of Liza's velvet pants.

I want to weep in the presence of these lives well lived. I'm witnessing the most beautiful thing I've ever seen, and I know it.

When "Pennsylvania 6-5000" disconnects, Anna sits down and takes a sip of her coffee. Black coffee. "So do you know how to knit, Heather?"

Okay, then.

"No, I don't."

"Then let's get started right away."

Liza lowers herself onto a rocker and draws out a crochet hook attached to a length of work about a foot wide and thirty or so inches long.

"A scarf?" I ask.

"How did you ever guess?"

Anna. "Oh, Liza!"

Thank goodness Anna is a patient teacher, because clearly knitting is as natural to me as American cheese. I've already knotted up the yarn a dozen times, knitted when I should have purled, and how can anyone possibly find this soothing?

"I think I'd better go to bed."

"I don't blame you." Liza.

"Liza! She's done a wonderful job for her first try!"

Liza winds the free length of yarn around the ball. "Tomorrow I'll teach you how to crochet. You may find that easier."

"Who said easy is the best way?" Anna.

Ah, a sisterly fight.

Now this is more like it.

"Please, Anna. People are either crocheters or knitters. It's that simple."

But Anna shakes her head. "You can do both, dear. I know it."

I hug them and head into my room for more Matthew, more Jesus, and hopefully a little more light.

"You do both, Liza. You just happened to pick crocheting tonight."

I smile.

And the kingdom of heaven is like a mustard seed, a net, a hidden treasure. She who has ears to hear, let her hear.

TWENTY

"Mary! Mary! Dirty Mary!"

The children sing softly so the bus driver won't hear.

Mary sits in front of us, dirty blonde hair waving in clownish, kinky, matted chunks that jump up and down in the stream of air from the open bus windows.

It's always warm in my school memories. The bus windows always clicked open. The children always boisterous and yelling like police sirens.

Donald pulls a straw out of his pants pocket, wads up a bit of notebook paper, and places it in his mouth. He chews on it, letting the saliva soak into the very core.

He positions his lips around the straw, loads the spitball with his tongue, aims it at the back of Mary's hair, and blows with all the force he can push from his lungs.

The projectile whizzes out, lodging in the hair just above her shoulders. She doesn't move. She doesn't turn around or yell at us or even remove the spitty wad from her hair. Maybe she's learned that no matter what she does, we'll make her life miserable, and that in the end, we will always win. People like us always win.

I reach forward and push her head with my hand. "You're so gross, Mary. You're a disgusting, filthy little piece of nothing. You're nothing now; you'll be nothing tomorrow and clear into the rest of your life."

I stare up at the ceiling from the womb of my bed, breathing heavily, the dark air breezing off the loch and into my window.

I'm sorry, I'm so sorry.

I call Lark. It's 1:00 a.m.

"Hi, Heather."

"Do you have caller ID?"

"No. It was either you or Flannery, and Flannery's out of town at a gallery showing, so I figured it wasn't her."

"Were you up?"

"Uh-huh. Working on a proposal for some renovation supplies for the Hotel."

"You don't have someone to do that for you?"

"This is my backyard, Heather. So what's up?"

"I had a horrible dream. Something's happening to me, and I can't figure it out."

"Oooh, what a surprise."

"Let me wipe my chin a sec. A huge drop of sarcasm dripped out of the phone."

Lark laughs. "Just spill it. I'm wide-awake anyway."

"How come?"

"Mother had a terrible night last night, and I ended up sleeping until two this afternoon. My sleep schedule is all screwed up."

"Is she okay?"

"I think she's slipping. I won't be surprised if they find even more cancer."

"Will she go on chemo again?"

"I doubt it."

"You want to talk about it?"

"No way. Not at 1:00 a.m. I doubt I can process anything yet, and her doctor appointment isn't until next week, so I'd just be obsessing about something I don't even know is the case. So tell me about the dream."

I tell her the dream as well as other episodes of tormenting Gary and Mary. The way one of us would crawl up underneath the bus seats and slip something out of her book bag and throw it out the window. Or grab her lunch. Or cut a hole in her tights. The songs we made up, the many notes that said, "Take a bath" or "Brush your hair." The drawings of her, buckteeth sticking out with mile markers along them, or mice and bugs living inside her hair, dialogue bubbles saying, "Help! I'm stuck in here!"

"And that much would happen in a week! It was constant, Lark."

"Oh, Heather. You really did all that?"

"Yeah." And that wasn't the worst of it. But I can't even think about it yet, much less confess it to anyone.

"Wow."

"Were you ever made fun of, Lark?"

"A little, by the stupid kids. Never had all-out war declared on me, though."

War. Interesting metaphor.

"So why do you think I'm recalling all this now? I went for years without this bothering me so much. I mean, I always felt bad, but now . . . it's plaguing me."

"I don't know. Just sounds like God's doing a number on you in general. Cleaning you up inside and out, maybe."

And I always thought I was so squeaky clean. "Yeah, maybe."

"Get some sleep, Heather. Call me in the morning."

"Okay."

Squeaky clean or whitewashed tomb? I mean, honestly? No, I don't murder or steal or commit adultery, but inside, God knows I'm filled with unconfessed sin. Pride. A lot of pride.

A light knock.

"Come in."

Anna opens the door. "Are you all right, honey?"

"I'm sorry. I had a terrible dream and called my friend to talk about it."

"Oh, then. I was hoping everything was all right. It is all right, isn't it?"

"I'm having a crisis of guilt, if you want to know the truth."

"I always want to know the truth."

I believe her.

"I'll tell you about it over breakfast tomorrow." I'm sure she's tired, and it's so late.

"All right. If you change your mind, that's fine as well."

She sure knows how to take the pressure off.

"Thanks, Anna."

"My honor, friend."

"Anna? Did your pacifism lead you to being a Quaker, or was it the other way around?"

Anna leans against the doorjamb. "Quaker is actually a nickname, Heather. We are the Society of Friends. And even that is shortened. It was originally the Society of the Friends of Truth. Truth being Jesus. I met Jesus first."

"I thought I met Jesus, but now I'm not so sure."

She rests her hand on the doorknob. "Jesus comes to us in many ways, Heather. Don't discount your journey so far. He may be leading you down different paths now, but that doesn't mean your previous paths were rabbit trails, does it?"

"I guess not."

"God knows you, Heather. Every little part of you. Good night, my dear."

I check my cell phone for the time. A message came in earlier. I'll get it tomorrow.

Liza shakes her head. "My golly, you were awful, Heather."

Anna. "Liza!"

"Well, it's true! What did that poor girl ever do to any of you?"

"She obviously feels bad about it or she wouldn't be bringing it up."

"You're right." Liza lays her hands flat on the kitchen table. "Sorry. I'm not nearly as sweet as my sister."

I grip my coffee mug with both hands. "I've been trying to find them. So far, I'm up to 1982 in Michigan where Gary graduated from high school. But I'm wondering if I'm doing the right thing."

Anna. "Well, only you can say. Why do you want to find them?"

"I want to apologize, I guess. I want to see if they're okay, if my treatment of them, especially Mary, affected their lives for the worse."

Liza. "And if it did?"

"Then I want to try and make it up to them."

Anna puts her hand over mine and squeezes. "I guess all we can do is pray that what you're doing is coming from the Spirit."

"And if it's not, that you'll meet a door you just can't open and that'll be that." Liza.

That'll be that.

I wish.

But I'll move forward. I believe I must.

Anna stands up, scraping her chair backwards. "Just try to make sure you're not doing this for yourself, to assuage your own guilt and feel better. If that's the case, Heather, then you don't want to drag Mary through the pain again."

Heaven help me, but how Mary might feel never entered my mind. I guess I really haven't changed all that much, have I?

They've nurtured me for the past five days. We've knitted and crocheted, depending on which sister got to me first. And I'm not too bad at either of them now, after a great deal of practice. We listen to the breeze outside and not much else.

When Liza cooked, we ate classic French food like coq au vin or cassoulet or something exotic yet simple like Cornish game hen with truffles. Anna usually set out homemade bread and cheese with some fruit to round things out. Or perhaps a piece of fish and a steamed vegetable. Every morning, steaming oatmeal topped with sliced banana, laced with brown sugar, and surrounded by milk. Strong black coffee.

We walk sometimes and we sit and read, one sister beginning to hum, and the other joining in, and always they seem to stop at the very same place.

Blue moon, you saw me standing alone.

L is for the way you look at me, O is for the only one I see. V hmm, hmm, hmm, hmm, hmm.

I can only give you love that lasts forever.

And we work, scouring one room each day, gardening, raking, and canning food.

The humming is almost always off key but always exactly on the beat.

Will calls with a stockpile of information on the ecosystem of the Chesapeake Bay and "Mom, Grandma and Grandpa actually took me for a sail on a real skipjack. I got some great photos with the unbirth-day camera you left for me in the suitcase. Thanks."

We chitchat, and I decide to tell him, "Sometimes I wonder if I've taken the right tack with the kids who've made fun of you in school. Well, maybe that's not completely true. I regret that I haven't found the right plan."

"You tried, Mom."

"I've tried everything I could think of, bud. I talked to teachers, the administration, the janitor. I talked to anyone who would listen. I also encouraged you to take it silently, and when that didn't work, to fight back, and when you came home with your blazer ripped, I knew that wasn't the answer either."

"I could have told you it was a bad idea."

"Why didn't you?"

"You're my mother. I figured you'd have an inside scoop on the perfect response."

Mercy.

"And I don't know why I didn't look harder for an answer some-where else. Should I have homeschooled you? Should I have just sent you over to the public school? It couldn't have been any worse there, right?"

"Mom, I didn't want to go anywhere else. Don't get all revisionist on me. I was the one who asked to stay. And another thing—those guys are mean, but I've made other friends."

"But those kids are so popular. Don't you ever—?"

"Want to be popular? Sheesh, Mom. Those kids are the long-haul dorks. They'll get to be your age and they'll be insurance agents over the phone and they'll wonder what happened to all that popularity. They'll have done nothing special to speak of with their own lives."

Does he realize he could be talking about me?

"But what if that doesn't happen?"

"Mom, what goes around comes around. Nerds rule the world. Not the cool people. You know that. I mean, think Bill Gates, think Warren Buffet. Shoot, I'll bet J. K. Rowling was an utter geek in high school."

"Have you been talking about this stuff with your father?"

"Most definitely. Dad's helped me big-time to accept these things. I don't know why you think you have to wave a wand and make it all go away. Life is never perfect."

Lord, oh Lord. What do you have planned for this kid? And should I buy myself protective armor just in case?

How will he take it when I tell him I'm trying to find the Andrews kids and when I tell him why?

TWENTY-ONE

Liza's driving diverges from her personality as fully as Gloria Steinem's face from her political views. She crammed a fifteen-minute drive into forty, the queen bee leading an angry swarm of motorists down Paper Mill Road.

I am thirteen again, sitting in the front seat of our Barracuda as Dad drives to my grandparents' on the other side of town, or to church, or out to Loch Raven. His slowpoke ways, especially on the beltway, especially in a car that could blow the doors off most of the other vehicles on the road, made me more embarrassed than a woman caught gossiping in the church bathroom.

I can feel my own scalp.

Liza doesn't notice a thing. "So you must be fairly discontent with your life if you feel the need to get away from it all and stay with us ancients."

So tell me what you really think, Liza.

"Guilty."

"I see. Is it helping?"

"I don't know. We'll have to see."

"What's so unacceptable about your life as is? Your husband seems awfully nice, and you haven't mentioned your son in such a way as leads me to believe he's giving you trouble."

"No. Will's my buddy, and Jace is a good husband. Works a lot, but he's a good man. I'm not under the delusion that I can have it all."

"Really? Most people are, I've found."

I shrug. "Part of me is beginning to think of all my stuff like

166

weights, not anything that lifts me up. There's a part of me that would like to throw everything out and start over. Buy simple white plates and plain cutlery. Seven outfits. One church dress." I'm not about to tell her the process has begun.

"Why don't you do that? Just pare down to those things."

"I said there's a part of me that wants that. But having the trappings comforts me. I hate to admit it."

She takes the next curve with all the recklessness of a tuna salad sandwich on Wonder Bread. "That's why I've always loved my house. It was all created to work together without the need for more, more, more."

"Your husband designed it?"

"Yes, he did. Including the dinnerware and the textiles. Was quite the visionary." She turns to me, and I'm tempted to point out the window like Will does. "And he designed wonderful, affordable houses for the simple working man. Modern, of course. Functional. Inexpensive to heat. The neighborhood is down in Glen Burnie."

"Did you have children?"

"One. He's gone, though. I don't talk about him. His very death defames him, and I said I'd never do that."

"I'm sorry."

"We weren't talking about me. I'm not the type to let people off their hooks, Heather."

"I believe that."

"So what about church? You haven't said much about it, and I saw your Bible when I dusted your bedroom."

"We left regular church attendance last year, and I don't know whether it's my fault or the church's."

"Why does it have to be anybody's fault?"

"I don't know. Shouldn't it?"

"Maybe it's not about casting blame, Heather. Maybe you've got a different testimony to live out."

"Testimony?"

We turn into the parking lot of a newer building with a sanitary residentiality about it that screams, "Not a real home, but we're trying!"

She crawls into a space, shuts off the engine, and looks at me. "It's one of Anna's Friends things. I always thought of testimony as our story. How God came to us and how we recognized Him and decided to follow."

"Me too."

"But for the Quaker it's about the inward *and* the outward journey. For some reason, I always found it easy to fall into the trap that our testimony signifies all that we abstain from. I don't smoke, or get drunk, or fool around, so my testimony is good. But Anna speaks of her testimony as something more—her good works, her commitment to the community, to the least of these—like her friend Bobby. That all of this bespeaks a commitment to the light of the Spirit that lives inside her."

"She's a good friend."

"Certainly. So did your church encourage you all to move outward, or was it inwardly focused?"

"Mostly inward. I did much more for my church members than I did for my neighbors, if that's what you mean."

She places her hand on the doorknob. "Maybe God's simply flipping the equation."

"Putting the trombones on melody?" I ask, remembering Glenn Miller.

"Who knows? Might just be something to think about."

Liza seems more comfortable at offering concrete theories than Anna.

"And," she continues, "if God sent you here to be with us, He's obviously got some sort of plan. Of course, Anna's more cerebral and ethereal and mystical about all of it than I am, so she might disagree."

"You think?"

She leads me into the home for alcoholic men. The foyer is bright and clean, painted white with mass production artwork hanging on the walls; mostly Thomas Kinkade's unattainable regurgitations, and wouldn't Will the artiste have a fit? To the right, a set of steps, tan runner cascading down, leads to the upper floor.

We continue on through to a kitchen in the back. No one greets us.

"Is the place empty?"

"Yes. Everybody works outside the home during the day. Unless, of course, somebody's sick, which isn't out of the question. Here." She reaches up, grabs an apron on a hook by the pantry, and hands it to me. "Get one of those big pots out and fill it with water. Set it on the stove to boil. I'm going to make pasta primavera."

"Do you have much contact with the men?"

"Depends. Not on Fridays. I just cook and put it in the fridge to be warmed up by whoever has KP tonight."

"Do they cook for themselves?"

"Usually. But Friday is a big night for them. Family can visit. I do this so they can eat, clean up, and spend time with their loved ones."

She turns on a radio, and we listen to classical music from the local NPR station, working in silence, working in peace; chopping broccoli and carrots, browning onion and garlic, grating cheese.

An hour later, a man in a mechanic's jumpsuit walks into the kitchen. "Miss Liza."

"Howie!" She turns, and I see a different woman. She rushes over and hugs him. "How are you? I haven't seen you in weeks!"

"Been workin' hard. Just came in to get my insurance card. Got a doctor appointment."

Howie possesses the lean frame of a whippet and the eyes of a basset hound.

"Are you all right, lovey?"

"Just a checkup. Been dry six months now." Satisfaction turns down the corners of his mouth. Ah, and there's the bulldog side of him.

"Good for you. Listen, I'll make you a sandwich in two shakes of a lamb's tail while you go get your card."

Howie retreats down the hallway toward the steps.

"I just love that man. If anybody deserved to drink, it was Howie."

But she offers nothing more, and I don't feel it's my place to know his story.

She hums Glenn Miller as she assembles a peanut butter and strawberry jam sandwich, her features younger and softer. This woman who buried a husband, buried a son. Her only son. My, but humans are resilient.

My cell phone rings, and darn it, but I'm right next to it. I really don't feel like talking to anybody. It's so lovely sitting here by the pool.

Legermin, Ronald.

I push the talk button. "Hello?"

"Is this Mrs. Curridge?"

"Yes."

I'm going to make him work for it.

"This is Ron Legermin. My son, Ronnie, is in your son's class. As I'm sure you're already frighteningly aware of."

"Yes. It's nice of you to call."

"Thanks for allowing me to. Mrs. Curridge—"

"Heather."

"Thanks. Heather, I just wanted to call and apologize for my son's behavior this year."

"It's been years, actually."

"I figured." He sighs. "I want Ronnie to apologize to your son."

"But then he'll know Will had something to do with it, Ron."

"I know. But I honestly don't think he'll repeat the behavior."

"Really?"

"Yes. Believe me, he's not having a great summer because of it. I'm so sorry. I had no idea. I've always thought parents oblivious to their kid's faults had no excuse. And I'm right."

"Why don't we just see how it goes at the beginning of the year?"

"Will you promise to keep me posted?"

"I will."

"I can't help my son if I don't know what's going on."

"I know. And I accept your apology, Ron."

"Thanks."

After saying good-bye, I look out over the chlorine waters of the pool. Just great. Now I'll have to wait until September to see how this is all going to shake out. But Will would rather be hung by his hair than have to endure a false apology from Ronnie Legermin.

***

Anna slides open the top drawer of the built-in buffet in the dining room. "It's all laid out in here."

It will take me all weekend to polish this silver. But ah, it's fabulous. Smooth and cool and sleek—artwork, really.

"Thank you, Heather. Our hands just aren't what they used to be."

"I really don't mind."

"I'm heading out for a bit, down to the market. I'm cooking tonight and I just feel like fried pork chops. Do you like fried pork chops?"

"Definitely."

"I realize this goes without saying, but help yourself to anything you need. All we have is yours."

"Thank you." I pull out the first fork. "These will go nicely with my china."

She holds a hand up to her mouth and giggles. "Oh, Heather. You crack me up, as the younger set says."

I watch her leave the room. I hear her gather her purse and keys. Listen to the front door open and shut, the car start, the wheels roll down the drive. I love Anna.

Liza's taking Oatmeal for a little stroll, so I put my cell phone on speaker and call Will down at his grandparents' house. He practically shoots electrical sparks through the airwaves, he's so filled with excitement.

"Mom, I did the coolest collage out of watercolor paper. Very abstract, but you can tell it's the bay right around here."

Jace's parents bought a vacation home right on the Chesapeake Bay years ago, and now they live there all summer long. I don't blame them one bit. It's my favorite spot in the whole world. Who can blame anyone for wanting to live on the water?

Will has plans for more, however. Make it a series about the needy, and he's going to show people from the Hotel drowning in the bay in front of vacation houses, and oh yeah, Grandma bought an Xbox for the place.

I don't comment on the irony.

He also thinks about things and feels and black is black and white is white. He's like Liza. He doesn't let people off their hooks either.

Will asks me about the Hotel. "Mom, have you thought more about it? Really?"

"A little." A lot.

"I mean, a kangaroo? You've got to see that as some sort of a sign."

"And what would that sign be?"

"How should I know? I'm not the one who crashed her car because of it."

"You crack me up." As the younger set says.

Jace next.

"Hi, hon."

"Where are you?"

"In my car on the way to lunch. Where are you?"

"In the dining room polishing silver."

"Is that right? How's that going?"

"Fabulous. I imagine it'll be very therapeutic."

"Did Anna talk you into it?" Jace has heard updates every day. He feels like he knows the sisters.

"How'd you guess?"

"I must be psychic."

I pick up the silver polishing cloth. "Hey, while you're there, I want you to do me a favor. Read Matthew 25 for me."

"Sure. Did Will tell you about his collage?"

"Yes."

"It could be Loch Raven and our house, you know?"

"Big-time."

"What about the sisters? How do they deal with living here in this area?"

"Shoot, Jace. Their house probably cost about $15K to build and has been paid off forever."

"Seriously. Ouch."

"Uh-huh."

"Why did Jesus have to raise the bar so high?" he asks.

"And how did you and I get so far off track?"

Jace clears his throat. "There are a lot of people who disagree with you about what you're thinking these days, Heather. They think the more you have, the more you must be doing something right because God's looking upon you with favor. That Christianity should be about safety for their families, a place to stay holy and pure."

I pick up a knife and wrap the polishing cloth around it. "I guess it's my definition of holiness that's changing, then."

"I'd better go. I'm at the restaurant."

I say good-bye and settle into the silence and smoothness of my task. Here I am, polishing expensive silver. Somehow these ladies know how to handle material possessions and social responsibility.

Still, I bet they haven't bought anything new for this house in decades. Liza loves the things she has. Maybe there's a key in there, loving the things you have, not the things you don't have. And I suspect she'd give it away if someone asked for it.

Of course, I do that too. Only to trade up. Lock Jace in more. And more. And more.

Am I punishing him for the decision I made to live my life for his? Is this a retribution of sorts?

I make another call to the contractor who's scheduled to build our tennis court next month. I cancel the plans. Maybe it's in the cards someday. But that day is not today.

Another message on the phone. I listen to Carmen asking me if I can host the new mothers' tea this fall and why didn't I answer the last call?

I open my Bible to Matthew 25.

When I was hungry, you gave Me something to eat. Thirsty, you gave Me something to drink. Naked and clothed Me. Sick and in prison and you came to Me. If you've done it to the least of My brothers, you've done it to Me.

Jesus said that.

Oh, Jace.

I call him though it's midnight, but the phone just rings and rings, and his cell phone switches right to voice mail.

TWENTY-TWO

Anna explains as we enter the building. "It was a Full Gospel church once upon a time, but as you'll see, we rearranged the pews and conduct our meetings much differently than the Gospels did. First, though, we'll go to Sunday school."

Good! Sunday school. That sounds normal.

We thread our way through the hallway and into the library. Mismatched furniture circles the room, and I sit next to Anna. As the group assembles, people choose the hard, uncomfortable chairs first, the couch and lounge chair the last to be taken. Interesting.

I've never seen this many pairs of sensible shoes in my entire life, and the man sitting next to me, hair sprouting from ears and nostrils, has the worst case of nail fungus imaginable. I can't stop staring at his hand curled atop his cane. Do I appear rude, un-Quakerish, an individualistic, hedonistic, warmongering person who doesn't care about the environment?

Mercy, just relax, Heather. You're staring at somebody's hands, that's all.

I expected a Bible study like regular Sunday school, but they talk about initiatives the Friends Committee of National Legislation should focus on for the next two years. The man leading the group reminds me of a friendly, silver-haired lion. Campaign finance reform, clean and verifiable voting procedures, global warming and fossil fuel dependency, opposition of the doctrine of preventative war, immigration, living wages, and poor working conditions. Defense of the rule of law by limits on executive power?

Health care.

AIDS here and abroad.

National security: diplomatic versus military solutions.

What next, abortion rights?

Apparently not. Nobody mentions reproduction.

This is the craziest Sunday school I've ever seen. But I like these people anyway with their simple clothing, dye-free hair, pristine beards. They've even brought in their own breakfasts, which don't include a bag with golden arches but rather consist of yogurt, a bran muffin, some fruit. No wonder most of them have a granola glow. By my count, seven elderly people, two in their twenties, one in his thirties, and four in their forties or fifties circle the room.

I wonder if they have youth group?

Of course my nose has started to run, and every sniff sounds like the winds of a hurricane here in the silent gathering. Most sit with their eyes closed, expecting a thought from God or waiting for someone else to stand and deliver the Spirit's message. At least that's what their literature says they're doing. Me, I'm just looking around, breathing foreign air, and wondering what they'd do if I stood up and shouted, "Praise the Lord and pass the ammunition!"

My shoulders start to shake with laughter.

Anna grabs my hand and squeezes. I just cannot stop. The harder I try, the more heat builds in my face, providing a greenhouse for the tickles. *Please, God, let me stop!* But it's not going to happen. Maybe if I just relax.

Okay, yes. Yes. Good.

Think of tragedy. All sorts of tragedy. I think of my dad. But he would have been chuckling too.

Yes, just let your mind drift away. Perfect. How about Carmen? Nothing funny there.

And then—

Anna's shoulders start shaking too. In fact, the entire pew is vibrating underneath our giggles. I'm ten again and I'm sitting next to Dad during the Eucharist and he's squeezing my hand, trying not to smile.

Finally we stop, just waiting for the beast to bite again, when a man stands up and says something about summer and the newness of life in his vegetable garden, comparing it to peace, its hopes, its dreams, its ability to work miracles, widespread and worldwide. My underarms and back are slick and my heart is happy. I don't know if I found God here, but I watched other people find God. I do know that.

All at once several people stand. It is over.

"I don't know, Anna," I say on the car ride home. "I think it would drive me crazy week after week."

"It's all right, honey. Obviously, it isn't everyone's cup of tea. Speaking of tea, how about a cup of that cranberry tea when we get home?"

And that is that. I know Anna won't ask me to attend with her. She'll leave it up to me.

Anna picks up a fork. "How nice to eat off of polished silver."

"Certainly is. Thank you, Heather. And the potato salad looks divine." Liza hands us all a napkin.

Sunday dinner today is my contribution to the culinary life of the house. Food is so essential here, so holy. I made up the potato salad last night because it's always better the second day. Before church I put a brisket in the oven swimming in the makings of a barbecue sauce with a teriyaki slant. We picked up fresh rolls on the way home from the service, and now an easy peach cobbler is baking to a bubbling ecstasy in the oven.

Yes, I love food. Sweets best if forced to make a choice.

The women eat with such daintiness. Honestly, I do feel a bit, well, oxish. Each generation seems to eclipse the one before it in size somewhat, and the sisters were small in their own day, I'm sure.

So I help myself to a skosh more potato salad to even out the meat on my plate. I do need to make sure it all ends up evenly for some reason. I always have. The problem is, the more you have, the more that needs evening up.

"So how do you know when it's the Spirit speaking to you?" I ask Anna. Again. Maybe I can browbeat an answer out of her, like the insistent neighbor Jesus talked about, knocking and knocking and knocking.

She wipes her mouth. "I'm sure Liza would answer differently. But for me, it's the Spirit if it leads you closer to God."

Liza nods. "If it leads you to act more like Jesus is how I might put it."

It's funny how these two women have such a drastically different slant on the same God. Anna relies on the Spirit, has such a gentle, ethereal faith that works itself out in the sadness of others. Liza has jumped in Jesus's arms and said, "Let's go, good buddy!" And they gallop off together in search of the most awful places where their presence will make the most difference.

Doing justice, loving mercy, walking humbly with God. That's the sisters. And isn't that in the Bible somewhere?

Can I be a little of both someday, Lord? Someday when I grow up? A little of Anna, a little of Liza—and a little of my dad. I want to be like my dad too.

Eleven days. Only three more left here at Alva's home, and the trill of panic vibrates inside. It will be good to see Will, good to see Jace, but if I could meet them in some new life where we walk into that small house with those white walls and just the clothes on our backs, I'd be the happiest woman in the world. I've been drilling Liza about modern architecture and its values, and I've got plans in my mind, a small house with built-ins for storage, but with a homey aesthetic that I find a little more appealing.

And no cause for dotting.

The silver is polished, and when I hold up a spoon, I'm greeted by a convex portrait of myself, large wide nose and mouth, little eyes, and a forehead sloping back like in the drawing of Cro-Magnon man. But the smile is wide because I'm proud of myself.

I took it upon myself to wash all the table linens and iron them as well. The sisters were delighted.

I call Lark from my bedroom. "I feel another string of thoughts coming on."

"Go on, crazy lady."

"After trailing around with the sisters to all their meetings and workings, I honestly don't know how they stay sane. I've always thought the people who I've journeyed with so long ignore the down-trodden portion of humanity because we're too busy with everything else, too tired, too preoccupied with our own families and our churches."

"You think?"

"And yeah, I have to be honest with myself and say I fall into that camp. When was the last time, before taking the cake to the Hotel, that I did anything for anybody who couldn't possibly do anything in return? But I think there's more to it. Maybe we're frightened that we'll bend beneath the pain we'll feel for others, that maybe we'll buckle under the atrocities some of God's creatures are forced to endure."

"And there are many," Lark says.

"And will the God we've worshiped blindly from our cushioned lives hold up under the stress of a world that's bloody and bruised, blind and broken with absolutely no hope this side of heaven, sitting literally before our eyes? Will we trust Him ourselves when it seems that others, with their lost limbs, children, sight, and families, seemingly can't?"

"I can't answer that for you. The question isn't 'we,' Heather. A lot of faithful people serve like that. The question is 'I.' Will *your* faith hold under that sort of pressure?"

"I don't know. Would I be so quick to shout 'Hallelujah' if my infant son just had his arms hacked off with a machete by a cruel soldier or Jace died because I didn't have the money for a doctor?"

"I don't know. I don't think I'd be doing any shouting. Have you been on the Internet again?"

I'm not ready to be sidetracked. I'm Liza. I'm Will. "We pray we never have to really answer these questions for ourselves, don't we? Because in those moments when we give honesty its rightful place, we don't know if our faith will survive."

"Is that all God is to you, Heather? The Bob Vila of this decrepit world?"

"Sometimes, yes."

"I've noticed something. It's people like us who think these thoughts, because we have the white-bread luxury to think them. Those who've experienced horror, deprivation, and loneliness tend to see God in ways we never could. And that, my friend, is something worth considering."

"Why?"

"Did you ever think that these people may actually have something to teach you? That it's not just about you going into the uttermost parts and being the big savior? That they have wisdom and grace to share that you'll know nothing about until you sit yourself down in front of them and get to know them?"

"Of course I haven't, Lark. I've already confessed I'm bereft about these matters."

"Okay. Well, think about it. God's like a grandmother who grew up in the Depression. He saves every little scrap of food, of tinfoil, of plastic wrap, and He uses it again and again for different people. I'm sure there's a ream of faithful wisdom you can gather from those you're running away from."

"In other words, it cuts both ways."

"Yes! You'll gain far more than you'll ever give. And it's okay to be selfish about it like that. Suck out all the juice life has to offer, Heather. I think God wants us to, don't you?"

"I do."

"Then why are you making yourself so miserable about your calling?"

"I've got a calling?"

"Oh my gosh, Heather. You actually had a kangaroo cross your path. What more do you need?"

"A notarized letter?"

TWENTY-THREE

I find her on a boulder at the bottom of the steep incline leading down to the lake. Liza sits with her back to the breeze looking west toward the Dulaney Valley Road bridge. Does she somehow hear church bells beneath the waters? No, Liza knows the truth.

I start down the hill.

Her profile speaks of granite and statues, things unforgiving and bald. The noonday sun bleaches her features to a flat mask. The high wind diminishes her.

When I'm not with Liza, my mind-vision of her is of a much younger woman. I remember her with darker eyes and dark hair and gauzy movements. And when she walks into the room, I'm always surprised by her age and her well-planted feet.

She hears me approach and turns. She doesn't welcome me. "It's my day, Heather."

"Anna said." I stop halfway down, holding on to a sapling to keep from tumbling forward.

"I'd prefer to be by myself."

"You don't like to talk about him."

"No."

"You'd rather keep him to yourself."

She looks back to the waters. "Yes. It's easier."

Liza's only son died fifty years ago at the age of fifteen, Will's age. It was one of those stupid things, Anna said, that could have been easily avoided. Lou had always been a good swimmer, and why he chose to go out that night into Loch Raven nobody knew. The lake wasn't for swimming, and he knew that. Anna said that Liza only once admitted to finding a bottle of gin at the edge of the yard. Alva died only a year later.

Somebody's burning leaves somewhere, and the smell of autumn veils the summer day, anchors it for the grief-filled memorial.

Sometimes telling somebody you'll pray for them seems almost disrespectful, like saying, "This is a mountain you can climb." Sometimes some mountains are too high to ever get over, so I slide down the rest of the path, lay a hand on her shoulder, squeeze, kiss the silver smoothness of her head, and climb my way back to the house.

Anna and I sit on the couch together, holding hands and praying silently for Liza.

The sunbeam falling through the sliding glass doors lies on us warm and uncomfortable like a quilt from the dryer; the clock on the mantel holds a microphone inside. All is thorny and itchy, woolen and flax. But she keeps her hand in mine. Warm hand. Our perspiration mingles, and she holds tight. Doesn't she know the rule of prayer hand-holding? When you start to get uncomfortable in the grip, you either squeeze lightly twice or wiggle your fingers a bit. And then the other person is supposed to let go. Vice versa: if you feel this being done to you, you let go right away.

I've done this several times, and she's either ignoring me or too deep in prayer to notice.

Ah, Lord, I wish I could lose myself in prayer like that.

I close my eyes.

Two hours later, I awaken. And Anna still prays for her sister.

She opens her eyes.

"When will she come in, Anna?"

"After dark. We'll be long in bed. I'm glad it's not raining today. I always pray the weather will be mild for her."

The day progresses as we move about under the weight of remembrance, cooking our meals, washing our sheets, doing the crossword puzzle, and finally, watching *Jeopardy!*

"You think she's all right, Anna?"

"No. She will never be all right. And hasn't been all right for fifty years, Heather. But then, none of us are really *all* right, are we?"

No, I guess we're not.

This morning Liza and I traveled downtown—I begged her to let me drive, and she did—to the Church of Holy Peace near Essex. First of all, we were two of four white faces in the mix. Second of all, I've never seen people actually running around the sanctuary. I usually feel a little strange when I want to lift up a hand to worship, but folks were actually running around the sanctuary. Needless to say, I lifted both hands and wasn't the least bit embarrassed. It liberated.

The pastor, who hopped on her high heels, danced about and sang in a sing-song, "The Lord is good. Let me hear you sing it with me. The Lord is *good*."

And the congregation joined in as the band encouraged them with the one-two gospel beat. "The Lord is good. The Lord is good."

"Sing it out, y'all!"

Oh, Lord, she was beautiful in her violet two-piece dress with just a hint of sparkle up top.

"The Lord is good," I sang, looking around me. But lost in their own praise, nobody noticed me.

Liza simply sat with her eyes closed, drinking it in like a desert flower. And in that crowd of Christians, even that was understood.

On the drive home I asked her how she'd found the place.

"I'm a nomad Christian, Heather."

"But what about finding a church home?"

"I have a church home, with the men at the halfway house."

"Is it the same?"

"We are all God's people, Heather. My church is *the* Church. I don't have many years left and want to be with as many of God's people as I can."

Jace and I sit on the patio outside the family room. The sisters putter about the kitchen, tickled to have a dinner guest of the male persuasion, and isn't that sweet? Earlier during breakfast before church, Liza patted the corner of her mouth with a napkin. "Now, Anna, men like beef. We'll have a rib roast, twice-baked potatoes, and a green salad."

"Then I'll do the dessert. Apple pie with butter crumb topping à la mode."

"Right, then. I'll throw the roast into the oven before we leave."

I almost spit out my coffee. No argument? Mercy!

Jace shoves his hands in his pocket. "So here's the deal, Hezz. Will wants to stay with my parents for another week. I think it might be good for you, if the sisters don't mind, to stay here until he's back. I think rattling around at our house, with what you're going through, will be the worst thing for you. My surgical schedule is crazy tomorrow and Tuesday, and Wednesday through Sunday I'll be at that conference in Chicago. Believe me, though, it'll be better after that."

Will it?

"What's the conference about again?"

"Just a surgical thing."

"Can't you be a little more specific?"

"It's pretty generalized, hon."

"Then why a conference on it? Aren't they usually pretty specific?"

"Not always."

Man, Jace! Fess up, okay?

But another week with the sisters? Like I even have to think. "Let me ask Anna and Liza."

"I already did. They said it was fine."

So what's all this about? Does he want to get rid of me for the week, or keep me with the sisters because they're a good influence on me, or is this something he thinks I need? For such a nice guy, he's driving me nuts right now.

And it stings a little. He has never kept a secret from me before. That I know of.

Mercy.

"Wanna walk down to the water?" I stand up.

"Good idea. By the way, Carmen's trying to get in touch with you. She's called the house a bunch of times."

"I know. I just can't go there right now."

We slip and slide our way down the embankment and settle on Liza's rock. We don't say too much. Who says much when the ship you're on begins to pull away from the dock and out into the harbor?

"Do you miss the hospital ship, Jace?"

"More than I can say."

"I canceled the tennis court."

"No kidding!"

"Nope."

When I kissed him good-bye an hour later, still no confession about Bonnie.

I tell Anna. "Is this a problem?"

"Oh dear. The fact that you can't come out and ask him speaks to something far deeper."

TWENTY-FOUR

We picked our own. Now that really does make sense after having been with these women, nonstop, for the past two weeks. It's really not quite the same to climb in the car, drive down to Klein's or Safeway, and pick up a flat of strawberries from California or South America or some exotic place with a strange-sounding name, far away over the sea.

The farmer, Dave Bittner, helped us pick the berries as we zig-zagged down the rows. Young, energetic, and somehow drawn to the sisters just like I was, he chattered about his kids, his crops, and all the plans he had. He talked about land and soil and rain, about roots and seeds and leaves, all these things God makes. And this is his life. Not ideas that remain ideas. Not postulations or prose. Dave Bittner must scrape the very planet from beneath his fingernails each night before he picks up an ear of corn and bites down with his calcium teeth.

Yeah, that sure beats the Safeway.

And now clear running water thrums into the stainless steel kitchen sink. Liza gently places the berries in to soak, although, you guessed it, they were grown without pesticides. Still, dirt, no matter how clean, isn't something most people want to eat.

Okay, yes, there's that odd man who pops up on TV shows every once in a while who eats dirt. But he only proves my point.

I begin cutting off the tops. We're making jam for all the min-istries the sisters support: the home for marginalized women down in Randallstown—unwed mothers, battered women, undereducated women, pretty much anyone with girl organs who needs a hand and wants to get on with her life. The alcoholics' home, of course. And I'm sure Anna will take some to her Quakers and the Vets. I ask if I can make some for the Hotel, and they are delighted by the suggestion.

I bask in the holiness of these berries. I eat one, worshiping in a very taste-filled, texture-filled way as it slides down my throat, the natural sugars defining the moment, the sweetness a gift from heaven.

Liza pops one in her mouth too. "The best part. Sneaking tastes."

"I agree."

Anna told me not to ask Liza about Lou, and though I'm eager to know how she's doing, I refrain. Anna so very seldom gives concrete suggestions, I know this must be something I'd be wise to listen to.

"Liza, how do you keep going with all this? Don't you ever feel raw from dealing with so much heartache?"

"Well, Heather, if it was about me, I suppose I would."

"Even so. A person can only take in so much."

She starts to mash the berries in a pot over low heat. "Now there's your mistake."

Anna would never say something like that. I like it. "How so?"

"It's like this. I don't just take in, dear. More comes out of me than goes in. It's why I give, have really made a life work out of it. When you take so much in, it can fester inside of you, knotting up your muscles, your psyche, your stomach, your nerves, even your soul. You've got to find some way to get it out. So when I give some jam, or make a meal, or talk with the men down at the home, I'm giving away some of my doubts, my fears, my own sin, and the sin of others that I know about."

"I don't get how that helps."

"As long as good is happening, God is there."

"But isn't He in the pain too?"

"Yes. But in the pain I lean on Him. In the good, somehow, I participate with Him in a way that binds me to Him and Him to me in a different way. He allows me to partner with Him during those times, and I find that to be the highest honor He could ever bestow upon an old sinner like me."

I pick up another berry. "And then become like Christ Himself, who wasn't content just to say things, but to touch people, heal them, eat with them."

"Be with them. Jesus showed up, Heather, at the weddings, the funerals, the meals, the stonings, the healings, the crucifixions. We tend to forget how straightforward it can really be."

"Liza? Do you ever wonder if you would have remained with Him in Gethsemane, along Calvary road, and at the foot of the cross?"

"All the time."

"I do too."

"The only answer I can give to it is to ask a question. Am I there now? Right now with Jesus? Am I walking the road, praying in the garden, taking up my cross? If I can't say yes to that right now, how can I begin to answer the other question? Do I have the right to even ask it?"

"I often wonder how Jesus actually saw this world as worth dying for."

Her brows raise. "Oh my! Wouldn't you die for your son?"

"Of course."

It's all so simple with Liza.

She measures out sugar. "But most of us are only called to live for God, His world, our children, His children, aren't we?"

I raise my brows. Oh, so that's all it takes?

She smiles her saucy smile. "Easier said than done, I know. But honestly easier done, in the long run, than undone."

Lark picks up on the first ring. "Hey, Heather."

"How do you do it? You always pick up right away." I take a sip from my nighttime cup of tea.

"I'm scared I'm going to miss something important, maybe even life-threatening for somebody else, all because I didn't get to the phone in time. I used to have a toll-free line, 1-800-I-Pray-4-U, and I've been paranoid ever since."

Honestly, she's a bit wacky, which is why I love her.

"So what's up?" she asks.

"Did your father set up his foundation before or after he came to faith?"

"Before."

"Why?"

"He loved all the folks. The people in his factory, the people he met on his travels. He saw them as real people, with hearts and minds and lives to live. After he found Christ, he spent a lot of time in the Prophets, Heather. Particularly Isaiah. His life verses were Isaiah 58:6–8."

"Isaiah 58, you said?" I fish for a pencil in the nightstand.

"Yep."

"Thanks."

"Try Micah 6:8 while you're at it. It's the do justice, love mercy, walk humbly with thy God thingee."

"You're a veritable font of Scripture knowledge tonight, Lark."

"Well, I had to make sure I wasn't doing all this stuff for nothing. A lot of Christians play down good works like it's some smelly thing that only people from mainline denominations rely on to work their way into heaven. People who aren't really close to God in the personal devotion-slash-refrain-from-sin type of stuff."

"I know. Which is one of the struggles I'm having."

"People's souls may go on forever, but I think God wants us to help their bodies and spirits here right now too. And not just Christian people."

"Thanks. I'll look this stuff up."

"I mean, it's hardly an either/or situation, now, is it?"

"Not if you say so." Whoa, Lark.

"Okay. Go to bed, Heather."

I decide to check my messages. Oh my goodness, two more from Carmen. The new mothers' tea. The new mothers' tea. Does she never give up?

TWENTY-FIVE

Of course it takes us twice as long to get to the Hotel with Liza driving, but we left in plenty of time. Anna waved us off, clutching her own purse to head out to the Veterans hospital. Five jars of strawberry jam rest in a basket on my lap.

Though Liza may have lost her road speed, she should get a medal for her parallel parking. With two cake boxes in my hands, one in hers, we clop our way down the broken sidewalk alongside the Hotel. The jam hangs in a basket from the crook of my arm.

Mo sees us after we round the corner and walk past the plate glass window near his desk. He gains his feet and slips over to the door, flipping it open wide. "Well, here she is, and with some more of that cake!"

"Hey, Mo."

"And you brought along a friend, I see."

"This is Liza Stephens."

Mo takes her cake and sets it on a nearby table. The small, gentle movements of this mammoth man fascinate me. "Krista," he calls. "You mind helping these ladies get these cakes to the kitchen?"

She stands up without a word and walks toward us. It's the young woman who was locked out a few weeks ago. Grabbing Liza's boxes, she jerks her head toward the door at the back of the room. "Come on this way, y'all."

She doesn't seem too happy about this, but it gives me time to examine her from the back. Her black hair is piled into some intricate, wavy do, and two large hoops dangle from her ears. A tattoo screams "Playgirl" across the back of her neck. Ah, her creamy skin looks like soft velvet beneath those words.

She's no longer pregnant. I wonder where her baby is.

"How's the baby?" I ask.

She pushes through the swinging door and into the kitchen. "You can set them right here on the table. And how do you know about my baby?"

"I was here the night Sister Jerusha wouldn't let you in because it was after nine."

She shakes her head. "That woman can be a witch."

"We all can," Liza says. "I've never seen a bigger one than myself."

I laugh.

Krista tilts her head to the side. "I guess that's true of me too."

I nod. "Me too."

"So my baby been taken away. She in foster care and here I am. Just tryin' to figure some things out. Anyway, you wanna see Sister J? She back in the office."

"If she's got time."

She leads us through the kitchen to the back hallway and knocks on the door to Sister Jerusha's quarters. "Sister J! It's that cake lady and a friend of hers."

"Come on in!"

She sits with that suave, well-dressed man, whose sculpted face, exquisite and fine, breaks into a smile. "This is my godson, Knox."

He nods at me. The drug dealer strikes again. And that smile. What an intoxicating smile.

"Knoxie, this is Heather Curridge and—"

Liza puts out her hand and Knox takes it. "Liza Stephens."

"Pleasure to meet you." He turns to me. "Pleasure to see you again, Mrs. Curridge."

"Heather. Please."

"Of course."

He kisses Sister J on her cheek. "Better go, Aunt Jerusha. Don't you be too hard on these ladies. You know how you can get."

Sister J beams.

Mo would be scowling right now if he saw this, I can tell you that.

Once again Sister J gives the tour. She loves giving the tour, it's evident; cheeks flush, voice rises in excitement. And as you can imagine, Liza and Sister Jerusha are like oil and vinegar. Not really mixing, both too strong and too different, but really, made to go together in a way that would make whatever they would land on just that much better.

After about an hour of hearing them talk about the missions they've worked in, mutual friends, and how on this green earth they've never met up before this, I head out to the big room to watch TV with Krista.

"You like this show?"

She nods. "Martha Stewart—the woman understand more than anybody know. Especially now that she been to prison."

"You been to prison, Krista?"

"Spent a few sleepless nights in jail. Back in the day when I walked the streets. Then I got pregnant with Kenya and took off. I'm from Chicago. Moved down here to live with my aunt. Just got through a week of rehab. Three more to go, and Sister J gonna work on getting Kenya back."

"Did you graduate from high school?"

"No. I like to get my GED. But I got to get me a job. But I can't get a job without my GED. Not a good one, anyway."

"How old are you?"

"Seventeen."

I turn back toward the screen. "Now I'd like to be able to cut up a chicken so easily."

Krista waves a hand. "Oh, that ain't nothin'. I can do that with my eyes closed. My grandmom taught me all sorts of things about cooking."

"Well, that's a skill right there."

"I got bigger dreams than that, ma'am."

"My name's Heather, by the way."

"People tend to think people like me don't have big dreams."

Mo calls over. "Krista! The van's here."

"Gotta go. Three more weeks and then maybe I can figure out what's next."

And the horrible, privileged part of me doubts she ever will. I hate this creature, arms crossed and head down, that lives inside me, this part that knows nothing about the Kristas of this world and wishes she would, by golly, just pull herself up by her bootstraps and make something of herself. Enough people from the "hood" have done that very thing, right?

Lord, I believe. Help Thou my unbelief.

Five days remain, and I need another project. The sisters' deck could definitely use a fresh coat of paint. So I ask them at breakfast about taking on the task.

Anna sets down her toast. "Why, I think that's lovely, Heather. Are you sure you want to do something so ambitious?"

"I enjoy that kind of work."

"I like the idea." Liza.

"I can get the paint and start this morning. Did you have a color in mind?"

"No. Why don't you pick?" Anna.

"Any color I want, Anna?"

"Any color you want." She places a firm hand over her sister's.

Liza raises an eyebrow.

So now I'm standing in line at the paint store with a tub of primer and a five-gallon container of cobalt blue paint—high gloss. I don't know why I'm choosing this color. Maybe to see if they really mean what they say, if these women really are who they say they are when it comes to their own things.

I mean, a lot of people do things for others, but it's hands off when it comes to their own space, their own property. And I can't blame them.

But these sisters? Time and a lot of blue paint will tell. I call Laney and tell her what I'm doing, and she laughs for at least five minutes.

Okay, one minute.

"Heather, you are such a brat!"

I call Will, who asked all about my trip down to the Hotel. "I'm telling you, Mom. This is it. You've got to volunteer there."

"How can you be so sure?"

"I just feel it."

"What about all the stuff I do at your school?"

"They'll find other people to help. There are lots of moms who don't lift a finger. They work all day, right?"

"Uh-huh. But what if I like doing all that?"

He laughs himself silly. First Laney, now Will.

Mercy, of all the possible kids, I had to get one like this! I don't know if I can take his pressure much longer. Changing the subject, I find out he's been fishing with that skipjack crew and making ten bucks an hour. Mrs. Curridge comes on the line and says, "He's as brown as a berry, Heather."

Another message comes in from Carmen as I talk. I've got to, got to, got to call her back. Tomorrow.

Jace left for Chicago and his nebulous "conference."

The Towson Library is always a good place to do a little research. Maybe I can find Xavier Andrews before heading back to the sisters.

The young woman at the research desk eagerly accepts the assignment. Which is a nice change. She's new, looks fresh out of college. "I like a challenge every once in a while. And we have plenty of directories available."

"Somebody told me he relocated to Michigan, and that's the last place I have."

With her height and long cinnamon hair, she really should be a model, not stuck here in some library in Maryland.

"Michigan? Let's see." She turns to her computer terminal and starts clicking away despite long shell-pink nails.

"I've already been on the Internet."

"No offense, but I'm really good at finding things on the Internet." I smile and raise my hands. "Don't let me slow you down."

The building remains familiar. "I remember coming to this place as a child. Saturday nights, just my dad and me. We'd park in the lot out back that's the parking garage now, and then wind our way up the ramp walkway." The giant concrete cylinder of a lobby caused quite the design controversy when it was built. The librarian says nothing. "My dad would drop the books off at the circulation desk: a Zane Grey or Louis L'Amour and perhaps some photographic essays of the West, maybe some local history book; and my Little House or Nancy Drew books. Ah, I loved that Nancy Drew. Did you?"

"Uh-huh."

"She had it all together, didn't she? Her own car, a hairstyle, and a best friend."

"Actually, I was a Goosebumps fan."

Mercy. "Sorry. I'll stop babbling."

"No prob."

I try not to think about the fact that I miss my father like he died yesterday, and normally I can go on, but today, here at the library where we spent so much time, I feel it rush me down into a vortex. After he died, Jace and I moved into the big house on Loch Raven, the big house needing so much to fill it. So much time to spend picking out drapery and upholstery fabric, landscaping options, a new driveway.

She raises her hand off the mouse. "Aha! Here he is. Xavier Andrews, Grand Rapids, Michigan. Tax records. Owns the house, apparently. At least he did in 1993. It's the latest documentation I can find. So far."

She swivels her chair a bit and writes down the address and phone number. "You want me to keep looking?"

"No thanks. I'll take it from here and see what happens."

"If you don't mind my asking, why do you want to find him?"

Wow, that was a librarian faux pas. I like it. "To apologize."

"That's refreshing."

Just for old time's sake I check out a coffee-table book of the photographs of Ansel Adams. My dad would be glad for it.

"I've got it, I've got it, I've got it!" I step lightly into the house. Anna is on her hands and knees wiping the baseboards in the foyer.

She sits back on her heels. "My, you look happy!"

"I found Xavier Andrews's phone number. In Michigan."

"And did you get the paint?"

"Yes."

"So when will you call?"

"I don't know. Soon. I guess. I'm still sitting on your question as to my motivation."

"The answer will come, Heather."

"How can you be so sure?"

"I'm ninety-two years old, honey. Some things you just pick up along the way."

TWENTY-SIX

Liza's shadow falls across the deck planking. "Oh my! That's quite the blue color, isn't it?"

I've painted only two boards. "I thought the cobalt would be pretty with the green of the trees."

Liza looks upward and nods once. "And it adds a postmodern flair to the modern. Just a tad. I think my Alva would approve. He wasn't a man who got something stuck in his craw ad infinitum, you see."

"That's a good thing."

"Certainly. Alva had vision. Shame he couldn't get through the day without a drink."

"I had an uncle who was an alcoholic. Nicest guy, though."

"There wasn't a better man than Alva Stephens. He wasn't a mean drunk, either, and always handed me the keys. But it got to his liver anyway. We just didn't know things in those days like we do now."

"That's for sure."

"And there are plenty of mean drunks too."

"I know. My aunt was a closet drinker, but we all knew when she'd tied one on, no matter how much she brushed her teeth and sucked on breath mints. I hated Thanksgivings at her house."

"Right, then. I'm off to go pick up Anna."

"I thought she took her car."

"Yes, she did. But I need to post bail."

I set the brush on the paint can. "Post bail?"

Liza sighs and places her hands on her hips. "She went and got herself arrested again. That makes fifty-two times." She shakes her head.

"I think she gets a kick out of it, if you want to know the truth. Which makes me wonder if she's getting any brownie points at all!"

"I was wondering where she went to. She was gone before I woke up. I'll just stay and keep working."

"Oh, please do. Truthfully, it's not like this is a big deal anymore. But what is she going to do when baby sister's not around to bail her out? That's what I'd like to know."

I don't want to think about the world without either of these two women binding its wounds.

"Was she demonstrating against the war?"

"What else? When I heard on the news a few years ago the president declared war, all I could think was, *I'll be running hither and yon after Anna now!* And now I have to drive all the way down to DC."

Which could take days, if I know Liza.

The clock on the piano in the living room chimes noon. They'll be home by dinnertime, I'll bet. I root through the refrigerator and find a roaster and, glory be, some asparagus and pearl onions. Ah, I can already smell the meal. Chicken slow roasted with herbs and garlic and pearl onions. Steamed asparagus.

I check the pantry.

Yep, egg noodles. Buttered egg noodles with fresh parsley; a nice hearty dinner after the jailhouse.

Mercy!

They return around five thirty. Anna has a sheepish glow; Liza looks like she's whiled away the day in a hornet's nest, hair frizzing out of its normally sleek bun.

"That I-95 is going to be the death of me!"

"You and everybody else on the road around you," Anna quips.

Well, Anna!

"Not a particularly peaceful response from someone who just got herself arrested in an antiwar demonstration, Anna."

Anna winks in my direction. "Liza's driving would make even the president go to combat just to get away from her."

"Well, come have a glass of wine. Dinner is almost done. I chilled up your favorite Chablis, Anna."

"I'll take a martini." Liza. "I'll fix it myself."

She walks through the foyer and back into the family room to a small liquor cabinet next to the sliding doors.

"You want ice?" I call from the kitchen.

"Thank you, no."

I pour Anna a glass of wine, and she sits down. "I hope you don't mind if I just rest here while you finish up. I'm exhausted."

"Were you treated all right?"

"This time. DC police are used to us, honey."

I pull the chicken out of the oven to let it sit before carving. "Why do you do it, Anna? Aren't we as Christians supposed to obey our rulers, Romans 13 and all of that?"

"Not when they are going against God."

"You believe we are?"

"With all my heart."

"I just don't know about any of this anymore." I set a pan of shallow water on the cooktop to steam the asparagus.

"Well, that's good. It's when we believe we have all the answers that we find ourselves in trouble." Anna's voice curves with humility. I never knew people like her really existed.

"Besides, my father was a Marine."

She smiles into my eyes. "I'm sure he was a fine soldier, Heather. A fine man."

"Anna, have you ever seen a kangaroo in these parts?"

"No, dear. Why do you ask?"

"One hopped across the road the night I found you all. He was the reason for my accident."

"Oh my! Lucky for Liza and I, he did just that."

"Lucky for you?"

"Yes, dear. You're teaching us many things."

The onions. I scoop them into a serving bowl. Ah, browned and caramelized. I could pop one into my mouth right now if no one was looking.

I'm afraid to ask exactly what it is they're learning from befuddled Heather Curridge. "Like how a deck looks when it's painted blue?"

She pauses and looks me in the eyes. "Yes, Heather. Exactly that."

"What would you think about yellow railings?"

She takes a sip of wine. "Now that, my dear friend, would be going a little too far."

"Yeah, I figured."

Liza strides through the kitchen and pours her drink down the sink. "Sometimes I forget we're not too old to be stupid." She looks up. "Right, Alva?"

She sits next to Anna and watches as I carve the roaster, then bowl the asparagus and the noodles. I serve them their meals, and this is my privilege.

TWENTY-SEVEN

My clothes, freshly laundered and folded in tidy stacks at the bottom of the bed, smell of the dried lavender Anna tucked between them. I lift my suitcase out of the closet.

They'll arrive soon, my family. All will be layered inside this brown leather case. But more than clothing, shoes, and toiletries will accompany me back home.

I tread over to the window, pull aside the curtain, and look out over Loch Raven. I swear I hear a bell chiming. An airy ring of promise, a signal saying, *Come and worship*.

Oatmeal sleeps on my bed. She's been sleeping with me for a week now. She's a young dog, and I cringe at the thought, but someday she'll need another home.

Liza enters the room. "Ready to go?"

"Just finishing up."

"Mind if I sit with you?"

"Not at all."

She lowers herself into a chair formed of black leather straps and chrome piping. "Ah, Breuer. Now he could design a chair."

"I have to admit, it's unexpectedly comfortable."

"We're sad to see you go."

"I'm sad to leave."

"And happy?" She crosses her legs, ankles bare beneath the hem of her moss green pants.

I scoop up the stack of shirts and shorts. "I've missed my family."

"Naturally. We'll miss you, Heather. You've been a delight to us old gals."

Next the nightshirts and unmentionables. "Ah, yes. I keep forgetting you're old."

She waves a hand. "So do we. That's why you've fit in so well. What will you do once you get home? Other than taking care of your family, of course."

I place my work tennies along the back of the bag. "I have no idea. I'm a little frightened. I'm not sure I'm the same person I was when I left."

"Certainly you are. You just have some extra bits now."

I sit on the bed across from her chair and fold my hands in my lap.

She reaches out and jostles my knee. "You really are worried, aren't you?"

"Yeah."

Liza arises, sits next to me, and places an arm around my shoulders. "Heather, you're facing new things about yourself and the world around you. You're choosing to no longer ignore what's been staring you in the face all along. That's a courageous act, my dear. One not a lot of people are capable of handling."

"I don't know if I can see it through to the end."

"And what might that end be?"

"I have no idea."

She takes my hand with her free hand. "Right. For once I'm with my sister on the obscurity angle. You only have to commit yourself to tomorrow; you can decide about the next day when it comes."

"I don't know if I can live like that."

"Oh, Heather. We're always living like that. Each day we choose to go on, whether we realize it or not."

"There's truth in that."

"Of course there is. And you will go on and go forward. I have every confidence in you."

I shake my head. "But how can you? I'm a mess."

"God took you aside, Heather. He was here with you, don't you think?"

"Yeah, I do."

"Do you have any reason to believe He won't go with you from here on out?"

"No good reason."

"God won't fail you." She squeezes my shoulder and kisses my face, her lips so soft and fragile. I feel the warmth of it travel from my cheek down through my limbs. "You have our prayers, for what they're worth, as well."

"They're worth a great deal. More than you'll ever know."

She stands to her feet. "I know a lot about the meaning of prayer, dear. More than I ever hoped I would." She places her hands atop my head and kisses it, blesses it. "And you're hardly a mess."

She leaves the bedroom, her pain tucked somewhere inside, her love shimmering on the surface like water beads after a summertime rain. A soft hint of her perfume lingers in the air around me. I press it down into my clothing.

The grille of the Suburban glints in the sunlight as the car turns into the parking pad. Two seconds later, Will jumps out of the back and runs to me, slamming himself into my arms, burrowing his head into the base of my neck.

I'm still in love.

Jace next, hands in pockets, sidles up. He hugs me with that fleecy warmth, a calm, still hug that he holds until he steps back and says, "Wow, it's good to see you. I missed you so much."

The sisters stand on the steps by the front door and welcome my guys. Anna shows Jace the suitcase sitting in the foyer, and he loads it into the car. Oatmeal skitters around Will's legs, and he scratches her ears.

Liza pats an imaginary errant hair back in place. "We hate to lose her. But I'm sure you'll be glad to have her back."

"Oh yeah!" Will.

"Absolutely." Jace. "Thank you for taking such good care of her."

Anna smiles. "Nonsense. She took good care of us."

Jace takes my hand. "She's got that way about her, doesn't she?"

Liza points to Will. "Now how old are you, young man?"

"Fifteen."

She looks at me. "You take good care of him, Heather, you hear me?"

I hug them as quickly as I can to get it over with. I want to go home, but I don't want to leave them. "Why don't you come live with us?" I ask.

"Can you imagine?" Liza. "Us two? Always bickering."

Will. "Oh, we don't mind."

Anna lays a hand on Will's shoulder. "Well, you never know, then, do you?"

We climb up into the truck.

Liza shuts my door and I roll down the window. "My, this is a big vehicle. You drive this thing?"

"Yes."

"Goodness. How brave."

Jace starts the engine, then backs up.

We all yell good-bye as we head toward the street.

"Go in peace!" Anna cries, picking up the dog and cradling her in her left arm.

And Liza reaches for her sister's free hand.

They stand there, linked together, waving fragile hands, wishing goodness for me and my family from their stalwart, ocean-sized hearts.

I lie on the couch. Say what you will, but overstuffed furniture, while not sleek and clean like modern, just feels good. I'm going to switch the blue dots from the living room set to this one. Jace sits down and hands me a cup of tea.

I shift to a sitting position. "Thanks for dinner. It was really good."

"Grilled hamburgers are a real culinary feat."

"Yours are." I sip my tea. "How's Jolly? Have you seen him?"

"Yes. He looks a little rough. How old do you think he is, hon?"

"I don't know. Seventy? Seventy-five? It's hard to tell with African-American men. No offense, Jace, but they age better."

"I'm a little worried. I tried to talk him into an appointment with Brad, but he balked. Maybe you can talk to him."

Brad is one of Jace's friends from med school.

"Maybe he's just not eating like he should. But I'll give it a shot."

"Right. Even for just a checkup. Now finish that tea, and I'll give you a back rub."

A back rub? How can I refuse?

A few minutes later he's massaging my shoulders. "Jace, we've got to talk about Chicago."

"Hold on, I didn't tell you. I had two procedures on people from the Hotel last Monday. Can you believe that? Sister J visited one of them while I was there. She said she figures I've done several surgeries on her clients. I guess our paths never crossed."

"No kidding."

"Right. I just found that a little eerie."

"Me too."

"So you had a good time with the sisters, huh?"

"Chicago, Jace. What were you really doing there?"

"Why are you so interested in Chicago?"

I blow a stream of frustration from between my lips. "Urrrrrr! I overheard your phone call with Bonnie, okay?"

He stops the massage. "Oh."

I'm trying to think of something to say. Nothing comes.

Then he lays his hands back on my back. "Does that have something to do with the tennis court being canceled?"

"Yes." I sit up.

"Oh, hon." He puts his arms around me, but I'm not having that. I move away from him.

"Why did you keep this all a secret? Don't I deserve to know what you're thinking?"

He reddens. "You're spending my paycheck as fast as I can make it, and I don't know how I can keep it all going and still do mission work on the ship."

"Is that what you want to do?"

"It's what the conference was about. In a year they're losing their cardiac surgeon. But there's no way I can take a year and do that, now, can I?"

"What about Will and I?"

"You all can go with me. We'd be a little cramped, but can you imagine the experience it would be for Will?"

"What about the Hotel?"

Confusion lowers his lids. "I don't understand."

"I think I'm supposed to be there, Jace. But if you say it's the ship . . ."

He takes both of my hands in his. "We've got a year, hon. Let's see what kind of miracle God's got in store before we worry about how things are supposed to be in the future."

I lay my forehead against his chest. "I'm sorry for chaining you like I've done. I never realized what all those purchases were doing to you. I just thought you loved your job, and the money was good, so where was the problem?"

"I do love my job. Just not where I do it."

"I'll put a buying moratorium on myself."

"I can't tell you what a relief that would be. It was really starting to affect how I felt about you."

"Really?"

"Yes, because it seemed that all my hours working myself to exhaustion were taken completely for granted. Every new thing we didn't need felt like a slap in the face. But yet I wanted you to be happy. I don't know how to even explain it, hon."

So I sit back against the couch and tell him about my dream. Mr. Purpose and the little white house. How the dots fit in. A small, practical little home for the three of us. Will's permission to leave this hill. This time, though the hour is late and all I can hear is the thrum of the air-conditioning unit and my own voice, Jace doesn't fall asleep.

"You're not just saying what you think I want to hear, are you,

Hezz?"

"Nope. This is all me."

After he goes to bed, I walk to the banks of Loch Raven and weep for my father and let him go a little more, my memories flung over the dark waters to come back healthier and dressed in smoother raiment, white and neat and with no extra yardage.

Yes, it's time.

I hurry back inside, pull down the attic door, open up the box, and place my hands around the urn. *Okay, Dad, you ready?*

In the darkness I slip down to the water. He must have been scared having to raise a daughter on his own. He must have wondered why such a load was placed upon his shoulders. And yet he never flinched. Never once. He loved me.

Oh God, how my father loved me.

I don't fling the ashes, but, crouching low like a little mouse, I tap them from the container and into the night-blackened waters. Just him and me.

TWENTY-EIGHT

On my nightstand a note from Jace says, "Carmen called.

"Carmen called again.

"Again.

"Again.

"Again."

Oh great. I never did call.

I unpack my suitcase and lay the lavender on my dressing table. I feel something thin and cold at the bottom. Pulling it out, I smile at the sight of the sisters' silver fork. Around it a ribbon is tied, and attached to it, a note.

You are our dear friend. We will miss you. Thanks for brightening our days.

Love, Liza and Anna (and Oatmeal)

I drop Will off at swim team practice and swear to myself I'll call Carmen on the way home. But to my dismay, she comes charging over to the car. "Heather!"

"Hi, Carmen. I am so sorry—"

"I've been trying to get in touch with you for weeks."

"I know. I was away."

"Lucky for you. Do you realize I've put you in charge of the new mothers' tea?"

"Well, I didn't think I'd agreed."

"Oh great! Now I've got to find somebody else."

"I'm sorry."

"I heard you were staying with those two old biddies over on Merrymans Mill Road."

"Well, they normally refuse to be called biddies, but yes, Liza and Anna let me stay with them."

"Life goes on, Heather. I've been picking up your slack."

"There are other women in the school, Carmen."

"Oh please. They're worthless."

"I can't do the tea. I've got other volunteer opportunities."

"Such as?"

"A homeless shelter downtown needs help right now."

"But what about your own son?"

"Will isn't exactly a baby anymore."

She crosses her arms. "You know the school does so well because of its volunteers."

"Yes. I didn't say I wouldn't ever volunteer for St. Matthews. I just can't take on so much this year."

"Then I've got my work cut out for me. I've got to go."

I watch her walk to her car, cell phone once again plastered to the side of her head, her other hand whirling about in angry circles as she talks.

The light has changed. The afternoon has obviously waned. Golden blinds block the low sunrays. What a lovely nap that was!

I pick up my Bible, and there it is, tucked in between the pages of Galatians, Xavier Andrews's phone number in Michigan.

Sunday afternoon is a good time to call, so I pluck the phone on the nightstand and dial the number before I can change my mind.

A cracked voice, churlish and clipped, answers. "Yeah."

Okay, then. I can do this.

"I'm looking for Xavier Andrews?"

"He hasn't lived here for a few years."

"Do you know—"

"Yeah. Used to work for him. What do you want with X?"

"I've been looking for him. I've got something I need to discuss with him regarding his wards. Do you know where he lives?"

"He doesn't have a phone. Went and bought some land in the most god-awful place in Minnesota you ever saw. Cold. Lonely. Nothin' out there but this crazy old lodge. We all thought he was crazy."

"Can you give me the name of the nearest town?"

"No, but I know he's somewhere near the Boundary Waters."

"Thanks."

I hang up on him before he can hang up on me.

I write the words *Boundary Waters* on a slip of paper. Fabulous—Minnesota. Remote Minnesota. It might as well be Guatemala.

"How's your mom?"

"She's in bed today. Very tired."

"I'm sorry."

"She'd love a visit."

"I'll bring Will down tomorrow morning."

"Great. Come early for breakfast."

Lark and I are eating a cell phone lunch together; she's out on the patio at the Medieval Monstrosity, and I'm sitting at the picnic table by the pool. I tell her about further locating Xavier and that I'm thinking about making the trip to northern Minnesota.

"Better you than me," she says. "Let me ask you a question, because I've been thinking about it a lot. Did you ever once do anything nice for Mary, or even act nice or something?"

"Only one time did I ever treat Mary Andrews as a human being loved by God."

"What happened?"

"My dad, for some reason, agreed to drive Mary home from the big Christmas basketball game, alumni versus the varsity team. I don't know how it happened, and I wasn't all that curious back then.

"So I slid in the front seat and Mary sat in the back, and Dad asked her all sorts of questions, and Mary answered with 'Yes, sir,' and 'No, sir.' I said nothing. It was easy to see Dad liked Mary, and as he continued his questioning, I found out that her mother had grown up not two blocks from Dad. He actually knew her when she was a little kid, and had babysat her a couple of times.

"When she got out of the car to go into her house, I smiled at her and she smiled back.

"And then, when January second rolled around and she climbed on the bus after Christmas break, she looked at me with hopeful eyes. I turned away.

"I made myself greater than God."

"It's easy to do."

"I haven't told you the worst of it."

"Darn. I was hoping we could put this all to bed, that I could shake some sense into your head. What happened, if you're willing to say?"

I've got to start over. I've got to throw myself into a place where there's nothing but an empty me, a full God, and a lot of people who need Him in a way I never have. Maybe this is a good first step.

Easier said than done, right? But as Liza says, easier done than undone.

"Okay, the fact that my dad babysat her mother, that they grew up together, was information I could not afford to get around school."

"So you were just as socially unsure then as you are now?"

Ouch. "Mercy, Lark. Can I finish?"

And I told Lark about the scheme. How my friend Rich, and Julia B. of course, cooked it up one morning on the bus. I sidled up to Mary and told her Rich liked her, and did she like him too?

Mary nodded, looking almost pretty. I knew if I had said that about any of the boys, Mary would have nodded. Just the thought of being liked by any boy would render her completely in love with him. Step one was out of the way. Rich hung out with Mary on the playground for a couple of days before the big math exam that would finish out second semester, just before Christmas.

Now Mary didn't get great grades, except for math. Rich convinced her to let him cheat off of her. She would have done anything for Rich. And Julia B. and I were acting all buddy-buddy, even inviting her to sit with us at lunch.

During the exam, Mary was supposed to look over at Rich's paper, see which answers he got wrong, and pencil in the answer on her scratch paper. It had to be this way so it looked like she was hell-bent on looking off his paper. I slipped out of my desk and walked up to the teacher and whispered, "I think Mary's cheating off of Rich." Then I just as quietly made my way back to my seat.

Five minutes later, the teacher stood over Mary's desk. She was taken to the principal's office and suspended for three days. She gathered her books to sit in the library until school let out, and she looked at me like she knew. I felt like Simon Peter when the cock crowed, but really I was Judas. On the bus ride home, I hissed in her ear, "If you *ever* let on that our parents grew up together, you'll get more of this."

"Wow, Heather."

"And she got a zero on the exam, and the only A she had went down to a C. Three days later after she served her suspension and came back to school, she got on the bus with a bruised cheek and marks around her forearm from what looked like someone gripping her hard. She was terribly uncomfortable in her seat."

"You think her dad beat her?"

"Yes. I never wanted to admit that before. She was beaten for cheating she didn't even do. And I just laid on some more blows. I knew it, Lark. I knew it then. Looking back as an adult, it's even more clear."

"You should find her, then."

TWENTY-NINE

Before I gave birth, my periods lasted nine days, and my cramps felt like a giant snake snuck up behind me, sank its teeth into my backbone, and tried to suck my uterus through it—and now my periods are a light five days with no cramps. Before I gave birth, I'd get the worst canker sores about two weeks after my period; now I only get them when the toothbrush slips and goes crashing into my gums. Before I gave birth, I had mousy brown hair. Now it's a rich dark brown, a dark baking chocolate brown, not that anybody'd ever know it after my buck fifty trips to the salon.

As payment, I lost my waistline, my smooth thighs, and the ability to drink large glasses of orange juice without calculating the calories.

It's worth it, I guess.

Usually. But I stand in front of the bathroom mirror as I slip on my nightgown and want to cry.

And Jace is so looking forward to this?

What is wrong with the man?

Music starts to play in the bedroom. A little Barry White.

I laugh. Barry White? The man is too much. Well, if we can't make it sexy, maybe we can make it fun.

I lost my sexual desire years ago, and I've looked for it everywhere. Remember that miracle cream someone touted on *Oprah* a few years back? That did absolutely nothing. Supplements? Nope.

It's not like I don't try or anything. I want more than anything to desire lovemaking.

Afterwards, Jace reaches over to the bedside table and takes a sip of water. "Would you like to head down to the Hotel with me tomorrow? I told Sister J I'd stop by and check up on those patients."

"I'm on it."

"You really ready, Hezzie?"

Yep, I really am. "I'll tell Sister Jerusha tomorrow."

Mo swings an arm like one of the *Price Is Right* girls. "And look at this. Those Summerville people did it right! We've got carpet, we've got paint and plaster, we've got new ceiling tile. Now all we got to do is round up the volunteers to install it, and we'll be sittin' pretty."

Two large rolls of carpet, cases of ceiling tile, and paint cans assemble nearby with little thought to arrangement. Behind the serving table parks a heinously ugly roll of padding that looks like a thousand sponges got in a tear-'em-up fight in front of a steamroller.

"Fabulous!"

"I can hardly imagine this place fixed up." Will.

"I know that's right. Hey, you all here to see Sister J?"

Jace nods. "I'm here to check up on a couple of patients."

"Uh-huh, that's right. I'll call 'em down."

I step forward. "Is Sister Jerusha in?"

"Naw, she gone to some seminary somewhere for some downtime. Some crazy Catholic-silence thing. Be back tomorrow."

Drat. I'll have to call her on the phone and tell her I'm all hers.

"What about Krista? Is she around?"

"She sure is. I'll call her down."

Mo starts making his calls. Jace looks around. "Maybe we can help find some volunteers. Your friend Laney at school, Hezz. Doesn't her husband lay carpet?"

"Yeah."

"Maybe me and the guys from the old food-basket ministry at church can replace the ceiling tiles and lay the carpet. Redo the plaster too."

"I'll bet Carmen and I could round up a group of ladies from Will's class to help. If she'd even take a call from me."

Jace puts an arm around me.

"I hate it when I burn bridges like that."

Krista walks down the stairs. "Miss Heather!"

"Dang, you look good!"

She turns. "I got it all cut off! You like it?"

"I do."

Her hair is shorn close to her head. She looks so sleek.

"Jace, remember Krista?"

"Absolutely. How are you?"

"I'm good. Good."

"Great."

"Dr. Curridge! Your patients are on their way down." Mo.

Jace turns on the kind professionalism even as he turns toward the first patient walking down the stairs.

As long as he's turning, I turn toward Krista. "How about we go get something to drink?"

"Okay."

Will looks at Mo. "Can I stay here with you?"

"If it's all right with your mother."

I shrug. "Sure, if you don't mind."

"Wanna play dominoes?" Mo asks Will.

"You'll have to teach me."

"Sit down, sit down, sit down." He drags a chair to the desk. "And learn from the master."

A few minutes later Krista and I sit on a bench on North Avenue, right near the Great Blacks in Wax Museum. The row houses along this stretch, some of them four stories high, sat pretty and proud back in the day, I'll bet. Beautiful woodwork probably hides behind drywall or heavy layers of paint inside those homes.

"So what's the news? Are you still going to rehab?"

"I'm just going to regular meetings now."

"Are you hopeful?"

"I guess so. It's hard, though, you know? Living there at the

Hotel. If I could just find me a place, just a little place with my own refrigerator and a stove where I could make up a stew or some beets—I love buttered beets—a little room with a pullout couch and room for a crib."

"An efficiency apartment?"

"Yes, ma'am. Nothin' much, just a place I can make my own. There's women at the Hotel acting like they know all that and more, and if they do, what they doin' there? No, ma'am. I just want to have a little place to call my own and still be accountable to somebody. I got to have that. I know I can't figure this all out by myself, but I'm about to go crazy there!"

"I don't know of any place like that."

"Me either."

It's amazing how different Krista is now that she's clean. I grieve to imagine her heading in again and losing all hope of getting Kenya back.

I reach into my purse and pull out a little calling card I had printed up when we moved into the house on the hill. "You know what, if you ever need anything, just call me. I'll drop everything."

She takes the card and doesn't say anything.

I want to fill in the gap and expound on my offer, but something tells me to let it be.

Mo trounced Will in several games of dominoes, and Will is determined to best him next time.

Jace examined some extra patients who heard there was a doctor in the house.

I actually had a conversation with Knox Dulaney just as I slipped back inside the Hotel. Krista took one look at him and hurried up the steps.

So here's the crazy thing. I've never before communicated at length with a criminal, but he's so cordial. I can't understand that, but I do understand how Sister J can't forsake him. He's lost. So very lost, and a piece inside him knows it.

"Sister Jerusha told me about my man giving your husband trouble awhile ago. I just wanted to apologize."

What do I say? It's okay? I mean, this isn't your standard situation. Oh, sure. It's okay if your enforcer or whatever they call these guys was ready to rough up my husband. No prob.

He smiled. "It's awkward. It's okay. Listen, when I walk in here, I lay everything else aside."

I nod. "Okay."

"Will you be coming back?"

"Yes. I wanted to talk to Sister J about that today."

"Well, do me a favor. You keep an eye on her, won't you? She burns the candle at all three ends."

"I will."

And then he left. And I swear, when he walked out that door, the delicate planes of his face hardened into walls of concrete. He slipped into the backseat of a black BMW, and it sped off as he closed the door.

Even now, I can't believe I interacted with a drug dealer. How can he come into that place knowing he's the reason a lot of those people are there in the first place, hooked on his drugs, scared to be anywhere else?

First of all, I don't buy that he casts aside his criminal persona. His presence intimidates people. When I asked Sister J about this a few weeks ago, she said, "He's Jesus too, Heather. As far as I can tell, Jesus didn't tell me who and who not to love. He told me to love them all."

She's a better person than I am, that's all I can say.

Jace climbs into bed that evening. "I think I'm going to go to the Hotel every other week. Maybe take JoAnne from work. The problem is, a lot of the residents there don't have time to get to the health department. One man I looked at is working three jobs. But I think I'll go in during the evening next time, after people are done working."

"What about prescriptions? How are they going to pay for what you write out?"

"Leave it to me. I've got some ideas."

I slide my Bible off my nightstand. "I think we both need to read Isaiah 58 every night for the rest of the summer, Jace."

"Go ahead and read out loud. I'll listen from here."

And I begin shading in a life that, up to this point, has felt very much like a line drawing.

I'm certainly going to look up real estate prices there on North Avenue. Surely one of those houses, or several of them together, could be made into a community home for women with living spaces just like Krista longs for. Privacy and some accountability both available. And cakes. Cakes are always good.

During the middle of the night I sit up straight. I dreamed Jesus came and led me out of the basement of an old stone church on fire, up through a rubble-strewn sanctuary. We climbed upon hewn stone blocks, up through rugged beams, sun beaming in strips through the latticed roof, leaving all the smoke and ash behind. And the rubble. And the debris.

And He never let go of my hand during the climb.

Then He left me, covered in the warmth of His breath.

THIRTY

I went and sat with the sisters for another shot of wisdom yesterday. For three hours we sat, each of them asking a question for clarification every so often. When will you volunteer? How will this affect your family? Mostly we sat in silence and I looked at them, Anna sitting with her hands lying like gloves in her lap, Liza with her arms crossed, staring at the copy of a Calder mobile over the dining room table.

Inside, a question erupted. *Will this hurt Will?*

And another question skidded up beside it, wanting a fair shake. *But what would hurt my son more?*

Meanwhile, the sisters sat in silence.

Do I want him to be raised to seek his own comfort and well-being, both physically and spiritually, or do I want him to be raised to seek the physical and spiritual well-being of others, especially those toward whom God feels such a tenderness?

Children learn best by example.

The sisters still said nothing.

And in the giving, my son would receive more than a ho-hum church life could ever offer.

The decision was finally made for good.

It is time for Jace and me to follow the desires God has placed in our hearts. In our hearts, both of our hearts. At the same time. This stunning display of God's love is something I don't deserve. We move forward, hand in hand, steps in unison. How beautiful is this?

So now it's time. Time to set my husband loose like a rock in a sling-shot toward that ship. Time for me to follow Sister J around for a while to figure out just what it means to really care.

Something happened in the silence. I don't like to call it a vision, really, but I saw my house on the hill glister before my eyes in a flashcube moment, the hill in negative, house crumbling and par-tially hidden by ivy.

Deep in my heart, I know my days on the loch are numbered. And they are numbered for all of us. In this, I grieve. Yet I know riches come in many forms, and God, who works in paradox and always has, will give us something far greater than a new tennis court in return.

But first I need to show up.

So with the first scent of a waning season in the air, I call Sister J from the bright blue deck of the sisters' house.

"Hi, doll. What's up?"

"I want to be a regular volunteer at the Hotel. As soon as Will goes back to school."

"You bet. Is cake part of the bargain?"

"Absolutely. What days would be good for me to come?"

"Any day. You pick. We aren't choosy."

"I was thinking Tuesdays and Thursdays. Will goes back the first Tuesday after Labor Day."

"Sounds like a plan. What do you want to do here?"

"Whatever you want."

"Doll, don't ever say that to a mission director. You don't know where you'll end up."

"I'll bring some cake down sooner."

"Good. Everybody loves your cake."

So that's that. I'm locked in. But there are some things to take care of first, I think.

Everybody loves my cake. How nice.

While I'm paying the stack of bills that accumulated, the doorbell rings.

I peer through my living room window curtains onto the entry porch. Ah, yes, it's Carmen. Fabulous. Probably come to ream me out for the other day. Should I pretend I'm not home?

I mean, really, we do that sort of thing all the time in one way or another. Maybe not literally, but the incessant answer of "I'm busy" to the perennial question of "How are you?" is pretty much saying, "No, I can't do another thing, so don't ask."

A pot of coffee is brewing, though, in preparation for a nice, cozy, sofa-sitting surf of REALTOR.com. Must be a sign. Besides, I left the garage door open.

I walk to the door and open it. "Carmen! This is a surprise!"

She rearranges the shoulder strap on her purse. "I'm sorry I'm just dropping in like this. I'm on my way to the doctor's office and I could have called, but, well, it's been awhile since we've really connected."

"Come on in. I just put on a pot of coffee a few minutes ago. It'll be ready in just a sec."

"I've only got a little bit of time. I promise I won't ruin your schedule."

I see it all!

Carmen is scared! This incredible responsibility rapes her calendar, gnaws her soul. It's stealing her life. Meetings and groups and events to arrange in such a way that parents will love it, feel appreciative for the school, give money, and keep the cogs a-greased.

But who appreciates Carmen?

She's frozen in the headlights, people!

But she has superglued the Happy Christian mask to her face. Even though I don't know if she's a Christian or not, I'd recognize that mask anywhere.

Poor Carmen.

"Have you had lunch?" I escort her back to the kitchen.

"No. I meant to make a sandwich before I left, but you know how that goes."

Not really. I always carve out enough time to eat, unfortunately. "How much time do you have before you have to leave?"

She checks her watch. "Twenty-five minutes."

"Have a seat." I slide out one of the counter stools by my island. Then I pour her a cup of coffee and fix it just the way she likes it, barely sweet, lots of half 'n' half, and I know that because I know these things about the people I'm involved with. I've always prided myself in knowing these things.

She sips. And sighs. Sips and sighs.

I dig through the snack drawer in the fridge. The Snack Drawer. Haven't yet figured that one out. So I use it for lunch meats and cheese. And tortillas.

"I'm going to make you a wrap, Carmen. Roast beef, Havarti, tomato, and horseradish sauce sound good?"

"Are you kidding? Can I have two?"

"Definitely."

I gather the cellophane bags holding these, truly, wonders of the world, and Boar's Head knows how to do roast beef, don't they? Cream Havarti too. The crimson tomato, compliments of Jolly, bursts as I drive the knife into its juicy flesh.

Ah, I love summertime. I slather the piquant white sauce on the tortillas.

Carmen sets down her cup. She does everything with a crisp thrift. Love her baby tee. Pale pink with pansies across the bosom. Matching lips too. "I'm getting together room mothers for the fall, and I was wondering if I could count on you this year, just to arrange the babysitting for parties and such."

It's an olive branch. I know it. I long to take it, but who am I trying to fool? I'd just be prolonging the inevitable. I lay on the cheese. "I don't know, Carmen. My schedule is filling up."

"It would only be one morning a week at the most."

The roast beef, the tomato. "Some lettuce?"

She nods. "So, will you?"

Roll up the sandwiches and slide the plate to her. "I don't know if it's a matter of *will*, per se, Carmen. It's more like *can*."

She picks up a sandwich. "Oh?"

"I'm going to volunteer downtown a couple of days a week while Will is in school."

"You mentioned some homeless thing." She puts down the sandwich. "Where downtown?"

"Near North Avenue. It's called the Hotel."

"Is it a Quaker thing?"

I shake my head. "No."

"'Cause those crazy sisters are Quakers, you know."

"Sister Jerusha who runs the place is Catholic."

She winces. "You're going to work for the Catholics?"

"They're doing good things down there, Carmen."

"Still." She takes a staunch, Protestant bite of her sandwich. "I grew up Catholic. It did nothing for me."

I'm going to let that slide. Not because I feel superior in my ecumenism, but because I believe her. I shrug. "I grew up Lutheran. Want some chips?"

"Sure. Thank you. And here we are with our children at an Episcopal school."

I make my own sandwich in silence. On the CD player in the living room, Will plays some obscure band called the Psalters. Crazy Jesus music. He's out there reading a cookbook on Texas grilling. Someday he's going to start investigating the meat industry, and we'll all suffer.

"So are you going to spend all your time downtown, then?" Carmen asks.

"Most of my volunteer time, yes."

"So, then, the school can just take a backseat now?"

I wince. "I'm just trying to figure things out."

"St. Matthews has always been the place for rational, well-educated people and their children. Maybe it's not the place for your type to begin with."

"That was pretty nasty, Carmen."

"Well, neither of us is one to mince words."

She puts a chip in her mouth, chews, and takes another bite of sandwich. I turn my back and pretend I'm going to the fridge for something, anything to give her some thinking space. Surely something looks promising. Ah, there. Pickles. That's convincing. I grab the jar.

And I do love sweet pickles.

She lays down her sandwich. "I'm sorry. That was over the line. Why now, Heather? Why all this all of a sudden?"

"I don't know. I feel like I'm being called out, Carmen."

"I don't even know what that means. Are we that horrible to you?"

Horrible?

I walk around the island and sit on the stool next to her. "Is all this . . . well, I don't know what to call it other than drama . . . because of me personally or because you'll have to find someone else to help out with school?"

Her eyes grow round. "I haven't really analyzed it. I thought maybe we were friends. Sort of."

Mercy! Friends? Carmen and I?

"Carmen, have you ever once called me and suggested that we go out for coffee or something?"

"Well, no. But neither have you, Heather."

"I know. I'm just a little floored by the friendship thing. You seem too busy for friends."

"Yes. I hate that about myself. I've been trying to work my way into favor with people my entire life, and all I do is end up pushing them away."

"You haven't made one real friend at St. Matthews?"

"No. Have you?"

"Laney Peterson. She's a good lady."

She finishes up her sandwiches, and we chat about safer topics like the new diner in Cockeysville, and isn't it great at Curves?

I walk her to the door. "I'm sorry I can't help out this year."

"I'll just call somebody who's more interested."

I wince again. So unfair, Carmen. "I gave my life to this school for years, and if I got ten thank-yous in that time, I'd be shocked."

She bends. "I'm sorry. I'm overcommitted and overextended and

I've got to find people. I don't know how it's all going to survive this year if more people don't step up to the plate."

"I'm sorry too."

"I don't know why I took the position as volunteer coordinator. Stupid." She rubs the bridge of her nose. "Well, I hope it goes well downtown for you, Heather. I really do."

I don't believe her.

And then she looks up into my eyes, her brown eyes peering out of prison bars. "I really, really do," she whispers.

I hug her. She hugs me in return.

"I'm sorry, Carmen. I just need a little time. That's all I'm asking."

"Okay. You got it. But if we need cake?"

"I'm still your gal."

THIRTY-ONE

I once heard someone say that we only change when staying the same becomes even more frightening. Well, I don't know if that has anything to do with this car; I only know I can get rid of it. I've come to hate it so much. The Suburban. Irony at its finest. First of all, it's not a suburban vehicle at all; it's a country vehicle. Got a farm? Get a Suburban. They should have called it the Countryboy or the Ranchhand.

It deserves at least a thousand green dots on it.

So here I stand in the car lot. I just want a wagon. A station wagon. Like a 1960s mom. This is cute, a streamlined white Saturn wagon. Oh, it'll be the talk of the country club and not in a good way. They'll be wondering if we took a hit on the stock market or stood on the wrong end of a business deal. Actually, it'll be kind of fun to see what happens.

Actually, we might want to quit that darn thing. Jace doesn't even play golf, and it sure is an expensive way for Will to swim. More green dots.

I page Jace, who calls back during the test drive. "I'd like to trade in the Suburban. Right now."

"Where are you?"

"At the Saturn dealer. Well, actually, I'm on Warren Road, test-driving a wagon."

"Aren't they kind of small?"

"It's the midsize. I want to trade in the truck, Jace. Right now."

"See how much they'll give you on the trade. You may actually walk away with some money in your pocket. But yes, I think it's a good idea." The relief he must feel shakes his voice a little, or is it skepticism? Is there truly a light at the end of this tunnel labeled *more-more-more*?

Of course there is. Because I say so.

I didn't walk away with money in my pocket, but it was almost an even trade. They gave me a zippy little wagon for that big old truck. I'd say I came out on the top end of the deal.

And it's a stick shift. I haven't driven a stick shift since my days in beauty school. I drive by Robert Paul Academy where I trained. The best cosmetology school in Baltimore by far. I stroll by the windows, watching the students work on their mannequins, looping and pinning fancy up dos. I smile and wave at a pretty, petite young woman bobby-pinning a curl in place. She finishes her task, smiles, and waves back.

I was you a long time ago, I want to say to her. Right now, I don't feel as far away from that as I used to.

On the way home I drive up Merrymans Mill Road and slow down in front of the sisters' drive. In the corner of my eye, a patch of yellow catches my gaze. A maple tree just begins to shrug off its slicker of green. My father once said as we stood on the banks of Loch Raven right before school began, "Heather, it's my sign, that first patch of yellow. My sign that summer is ending."

Thank you, ladies.

I do not turn into their drive, but continue on, back to Will, to Jace, to a promise that something golden will spring up from the lovely green garden my life has suddenly become, a garden planted in fertile soil, ready to nourish a greater purpose.

Mr. Purpose has offered his hand, I've placed mine in his, and we're riding along to someplace I've probably never dreamed of.

I laugh at myself. Sentimental, optimistic little fool that I am.

Part Three

I'll Follow the Sun

THIRTY-TWO

I'm whizzing down I-83 in my little wagon, past the numerous apartment complexes, the defunct mills now transformed into upscale lofts, the old London Fog factory, Stieff Silversmiths. The windows open, my hair is twice its normal size, and will God keep me out of the police radar since I'm headed down to do good works?

Ah, no.

At least that's what I'd bet if I had to.

Will's off to school, steps airy and expectant and ready to make tracks in Nicola's direction. The summer of Nicola. Let's hope it lasts throughout the year.

Of course, I'm waiting to hear how Ronnie Legermin behaves.

I've already called Lark, who cheered me on in her Larky way.

Will said, "Go get 'em, Mom! Was I right or was I right?"

Jace packed me a lunch complete with a Ho Ho and a carton of chocolate milk, obviously throwing his medical knowledge out the door. "You're going to do great, hon."

But for now, Unsearchable Riches, my favorite Baltimore Jesus band, sparkles at sixty miles per hour, their happy honky-tonk rock on my car stereo providing a spot-on soundtrack for the wind, the sun, and the speed of my wheels. And I want to throw back my head and laugh because I'm free at this very moment.

I love Mo. I realize this as I push my way through the door, so excited to see him. I also realize I don't know Mo's story, and just how he came to be sitting at this desk.

"Mo!"

"Heather! Yo, girl!"

"How are you today?"

"Good. You're one brave lady, that's all I got to say."

"Yeah?"

He shakes his two-ton head. "You got any grubbies with you?"

"Just what I'm wearing."

He examines my garb. "Can they be replaced?"

"There's not too much that can't be replaced. Well, if it's inanimate, that is."

He jerks his head toward the kitchen. "Health department cited us. That kitchen needs to be scrubbed top to bottom."

My stomach sinks. Yeah, I admit it. I had visions of chopping veggies, opening cans, skipping from big pot to bigger pot like a pixie, waving my magic spoon, creating fabulous meals from whatever anybody happened to bring by.

Drat.

"Point me at it."

"No need. You already know where the kitchen is."

I smile at him, and he knows.

He pats my arm. "Baptism by fire, girl."

"You said it."

I hoist my purse up on my arm. "Okay, then, wish me luck."

He raises his brows. "Oh, you need more than luck."

I gather as much air into my lungs as possible and move forward. One step. Then another. And then another.

Sister J's office door is open. I peek my head in. "Sister J?"

"Hi, doll. Come on in. Ready to work?"

"Yep. Mo filled me in."

She laughs, that grating hack. "I'll bet he did! You sure as heck can't clean in those. Go back to the clothes closet and pick out some of the used duds. No sense in ruining your good stuff."

I bristle. "No, no, no. I really don't mind."

"I insist." She looks at me, no-nonsense eyes. "Go pick something out. Doesn't matter what."

"But—"

"Now!"

Okay, okay. What is this? Some sort of bait and switch? The crusty yet nice nun turns into a hard-nosed mother superior?

Remember, Heather. Remember why and remember Who and who. There, that nice, righteous-sounding thought should see me through, right?

I head back out into the kitchen, into the main room, and over to the clothing room. They're all free, these clothes. But those who come for them can take only five at a time. I've heard Sister J's spiel three times now, so I know. The room sits devoid of clients. Ceiling high, windows grimy. I breathe in.

Oh, Lord, I've never put on someone else's clothing in my entire life! Other than my cousins' hand-me-downs or good friends' clothes. I don't know where these have been. Have they been washed? I pick up a pair of jeans.

Did someone urinate in them at one time? I close my eyes and sniff. They smell clean. But . . . how many people have slid their legs into these, and who were they?

I bow my head.

Help me.

I look up. Maybe a shirt would be a better first pick.

Sweaty underarms. Unseen dribble from a slack mouth down the placket, perhaps? Looking around, I see the ghosts of bodily secretions in neon colors on every garment. I see dirty people and poor people.

I see black people.

Oh God!

And my own prejudice confronts me in this garment I hold in my hand. All the thoughts I never allowed front and center, all the fears that never found their place.

Help me, God. Please help me. I don't want to be like this.

I stand. Frozen in the frigid pool of my own sinfulness.

A hand squeezes my shoulder. "Miss Heather?"

I turn. Krista. I hold out the jeans, speechless.

In her eyes I see time and pain and understanding, though heaven knows, I don't how or why she should, or would.

"Can I help pick you something out?"

I nod.

"What size?"

"Fourteen."

She starts at the pants table. "Mo told me you gon' be scrubbing the kitchen today so you want to be comfortable." She lifts up a pair of painter pants. "Here. Sturdy too."

I receive them from her.

She walks to the shirt rack. "I know color don't matter cleaning the kitchen, but we have to look good, all right? I think blue is your color."

"Why are you doing this?" The words slip out.

"You need me to."

"I do." I whisper the words.

She pulls out a blue blouse, blue the color of the Aegean in a travel poster for Greece. "Now that will go with your eyes. You go change in the bathroom."

She hands me the shirt and leads me out of the room, into the main room. "The bathroom is right before Sister J's door."

"Thank you, Krista."

Krista shrugs. Then she smiles. And she sees me for exactly who I am, a do-gooder white lady come to save the world.

Only she's the one who's going to save me. But I don't think she knows that yet.

Maybe Jace was right about medication. I cry in the bathroom. Who do I really think I am?

Sister J peers at me as I walk into her office. "Good choice."

"Krista saved me."

"She's got that in her. It's why I'm so hard on her. Okay"—she hoists herself to her feet—"come on in and meet Jimmy, our cook."

"There wasn't anybody in the kitchen."

"He's probably having a smoke outside."

Sure enough, Jimmy sits on the alley stoop, smoking a cigarette. He wears one of those caps that look like somebody cut the legs off a pair of pantyhose. His height makes me feel like I'm eight again.

"Jimmy, this is Heather. She's going to help on Tuesdays and Thursdays. Said she'd clean your kitchen for you. Wanna show her the supplies?"

"If you say so."

He takes one more draw, crushes the smoke beneath his sneaker, and rises to his feet. He walks by without looking at me, shows me the closet crammed with half-full bottles of every kind of cleaner known to broom closets. "There you go."

"Thanks."

Sister J heads back to her office. "If you need me, just holler. Jimmy, what's for lunch?"

"Soup!"

She rolls her eyes, shakes her head, and flies away, her black veil last to leave the room.

Jimmy turns away from me, and I grab a bucket and some rags. And Mr. Clean. I need a guy like Mr. Clean right now.

He points to the far wall. "Utility sink's over there." And he disappears.

I feel so otherworldly. So out of place.

But I fill the bucket and begin to scrub the baseboards.

Four hours later, I'm only halfway through the kitchen. I've seen

more roaches and roach carcasses, more grease, more primal yucki-
ness than ever before.

I change my clothes. Mo isn't at the door.

I leave.

My trip home is quiet. Windows up.

It wasn't what I thought it would be.

Not even close.

THIRTY-THREE

Sitting on the edge of his seat, Will listens and shovels in mac 'n' cheese without even chewing. I don't know how he does that. It makes my throat close into that gagging feeling just watching him. But there is something cool about it in that "boy" way. He keeps looking up at me, saying, "Sweet," every few seconds as I tell him about my day. Jace isn't home.

I almost want to turn on him and say, "Don't you get it, Will? I had a lousy time. Jimmy was rude and I spent a disgusting day scrubbing a bunch of disgusting surfaces and didn't even finish the disgusting job. A ministry of presence? Yeah, right, Jerusha."

He caught the demeanor of the thoughts in my expression.

"Didn't you have fun, Mom? You did, didn't you?"

How can I do this?

"No. It was the most humiliating experience of my life. I hated almost every minute of it."

Will bows his head. He's trying to hide the tears that always gather when he's had a horrible day at school or disappointment strikes like the clapper of a bell.

"But I'll go back Thursday."

Will looks back up. "Really?" He sniffs. "After all that?"

"Yeah. I've got to. If I don't finish that kitchen, they'll shut the place down."

A voice inside me says, *Those people will survive without you.*

"But life is about more than surviving."

"What did you say, Mom? Never mind, I heard you."

"It's that voice inside me telling me I don't have to go back, bud. That those people have it better than a lot of people in the world."

"Better than us?"

"Yeah, I get it."

He shoves a forkful of macaroni between his lips and grins a noodly grin.

"Gross."

I load up my own fork and we talk about his day at school. Ronnie Legermin broke his legs in a freak hang-gliding accident the day before school started and won't be back until at least Halloween.

Loser that I am, I actually high-five him on this. Poor Ronnie, right? I wonder how Ron's dealing with it? Maybe I have a lot to learn about compassion after all.

I put the positive spin on the day with Jace. He looked so tired when he pulled in around ten, I couldn't bear to burden him further. Besides, it'll get better, right?

Mo's eyebrows rise up so high I wouldn't hesitate to call it a wonder of the world.

"So you want to hear my story, huh?" And he laughs and laughs and laughs. He laughs so hard I think he's going to fall out of that chair, which has definitely lost the tone along its spine.

Pulling out a handkerchief, he actually wipes his brow.

"Never mind," I say.

"Good girl!"

I walk toward the kitchen, and he says, "Hey!"

I turn. "Yeah?"

"You all right, Heather. I can't believe you back here today."

"Don't give me too much credit, Mo. There's always next week."

And he starts laughing again.

The big room is filled with folks. Panera sent over a huge trash bag full of bread, bagels, and pastries clients are picking through. Neighbors too, I think. And there's some pretty good stuff in there—croissants too! I wonder if anybody'd mind if—

Heather!

We all love a good find, don't we?

I came prepared today. Tuesday's outfit is laundered and ready to return to the rack. I dressed in an old pair of jeans and a T-shirt from Ron Jon Surf Shop. Yeah, did I mention I tend to keep stuff?

"Hi, Jimmy." Jimmy's arranging a tray of cling-wrapped, day-old blondies and muffins that have a decidedly Starbuckian look to them.

He looks at me and nods. Turns back to his work.

"Sister J in?"

"Nope."

I stand there and wait for a possible explanation.

Nope.

Right, as Jace would say.

I pull out Tuesday's bucket, the colonial blue Rubbermaid with the plastic tube missing from the handle. Luckily I don't have to drag it far, or bye-bye, circulation in my fingers.

Mr. Clean again, and just for kicks, I add a couple of caps of Pine-Sol, mix it up a little, make it interesting. The water falls warm into the bucket, sudsing up the cleanser, and I place my hand beneath the stream. I close my eyes and feel the comfort of the hot wetness.

Okay. I can do this today. I made it through last time; I can do it again.

"I think I'll tackle the stove today."

Jimmy rummages through the large glass-front refrigerator, then snatches up some oranges in a red net bag and places them on the worktable. He looks at me and turns up the radio. I have no idea who the artist is. It's rap. I know nothing.

Well. Good, then. Maybe at least the tempo will keep me moving.

I pry the iron grates off the gas burners and throw them in the utility sink, stopper it up, and pour in plenty of dish detergent. The hot water flows again. It will take several hours to soak off that grease, and Jimmy will be making the soup soon.

We'll see what happens.

And the scrubbing begins. Wouldn't you know it? I forgot my rubber gloves. "Jimmy? Are there any kitchen gloves?"

He turns up the radio, and something the artist is doing sounds like a fly buzzing around.

I can't take him personally. He doesn't know me, right?

Or does he? More than I even know myself? Surely women like me have come and gone.

Time will tell. He's got to be thinking that.

But he heads around the corner to the pantry shelves and returns with a box full of tuna cans and several loaves of bread. "We'll have us a cold lunch." He starts opening cans with the industrial can opener attached to the worktable.

Krista walks into the kitchen with the creamer and sugar bowls in her hands. "These are all out."

"Creamer's gone." Jimmy.

She shakes her head.

Jimmy turns to me. "Folks bring by ramen noodles, green beans, white beans, black beans, pinto beans, kidney beans. They bring by canned soup and day-old bread. But you know what? We really, really need us some creamer."

It's nine o'clock, and I am exhausted. Finally the stove glistens. So do the refrigerator and the sinks and every corner of that downcast kitchen. Bring it on, health department.

Sister J came through, said hi and chatted for a bit, and spent the rest of the day in meetings.

I had a different picture of all this.

Surely there's some good I can do near home? Maybe visit a nursing home, read to the blind, grow a garden and take the produce to the elderly somewhere?

At least they'd appreciate me. Wouldn't they?

And I feel so white, rhythmless, and uncool. Sort of like a bleached whale whose only trick is to roll over and wave with her fin in the midst of dolphins that jump high into the air and turn somersaults. Floating ungainly, out of her element, while the dolphins ignore her existence and scornfully gaze upon her mass.

On the way home I stop at Costco and pick up a case of creamer.

I also noticed Jimmy has to cook with very little oil. I put a huge jug of olive oil and one of safflower oil next to the creamer, pay the cashier, and head on home.

So Will loves Pink. I know. A little girly for a boy, but I'm glad he ventures out from Led Zeppelin every once in a while.

Yeah, yeah, yeah. While Pink will never win the Brio award for good Christian girls, she doesn't compromise her standards—whether or not you think her standards are proper, she does stick to them! I like that about Pink.

I like her music too. Spunky, hip, full of groove.

I know all the lyrics to her album *Missundaztood*. It was in my car CD player for two years.

"Doctor, doctor, won't you please prescribe me somethin', a day in the life of someone else, 'cuz I'm a hazard to myself."

I am so there.

So when "Get This Party Started" blares from Jimmy's transistor on Tuesday, I can't contain myself. And it isn't like he's in the kitchen anyway.

I boogie my way around the stove, a mess again after the weekend, wiping, flicking my rag, wiggling my behind in time to the music. Singing as loud as I dare, but not close to as loud as I can, "'I got lotsa style with my gold diamond rings. I can go for—'"

"Aww! Caught you! Caught you singin'. And dancin'! Ha, haaah!"

I whip around, feeling like somebody opened the door to the restroom stall by accident.

Jimmy stands in the doorway, shaking his head, his face rent by a smile.

"You caught the rhythmless white girl. I'll try not to scare you like that again."

"That Pink. She my *girl!*" He claps his hands, bends double, and laughs some more, swinging his head from side to side. "You all right, Heather."

He disappears out to the stoop to smoke a cigarette.

Something happened after that. Jimmy talked to me. Told me about his cocaine addiction, his association with a famous dead rapper, how he came to be cook at the Hotel because Mo caught him sneaking in to sleep in the storage room and offered him work. A few years ago he led a Bible study in the home for alcoholics he stayed in, and he'd love a good study Bible. I'll bring him one next Tuesday.

And when I cut away the rot from a case of oozing tomatoes that came from only heaven knows where, I experienced euphoria like I'd never known. I knew that at that moment I was doing the holy will of God. I was exactly where I was supposed to be; it was holy and good and just. Merciful—to me, the chief of sinners—and humbling. I shouldn't have been privy to such blessing, such favor from God as to serve right there, right then. He called me out to do this, and I deserved none of it. I could have been in my house at this moment, sitting on my plush couch with a cup of warm tea, a Bible in my lap, and a study book beside me begging God to make me whole while doing none of His dirty work. But no. I cut rot off tomatoes in a roach-infested kitchen off of North Avenue.

It didn't get any better than this.

Sister J walked into the kitchen just then. "What are you so happy about?"

"I can't believe I get to be here."

She rolled her eyes. "Believe me, you'll get over it." And disappeared. But I saw a hint of a smile before she turned away.

I loved where I stood. I loved the sink. I loved the stove. I loved Jimmy and Krista and Mo. I loved.

I loved.

I love. In a bigger, broader way than I ever have before. I realized Lark was right. God wants us to care for the poor and the lonely and the sick, not just for their sake, but for ours. Because in this, we become like Him, growing a bigger heart than we ever thought possible.

It wanted to burst from my body.

I wanted to tell everybody. I wanted to shout it from the house-tops. God makes it all work together, folks! It's redemption time, and will you come to the well and drink deep? You'll get far more than you could ever give. Don't die in the desert of your Christian radio, Pottery Barn lives.

A cop pulled me over on the way home, and I swear he thought I was drunk, the way I was smiling.

"Do you know how many times you swerved over the lines, ma'am?"

"No."

"Five times to the right, four to the left. I thought you were drunk."

"I'm on my way home from volunteering at the homeless shel-ter." Would that extend me a warning and not a ticket?

He shifted his feet. "It's obvious you're not intoxicated, ma'am, but I must say, your driving is atrocious."

Well, I could have told him that!

I couldn't wait to tell Jimmy about it. And Mo. Oh yeah, he'd get a good laugh.

THIRTY-FOUR

Jolly has been delivering something from his autumn garden or his orchard every day. He's trying so hard to get over Helen, or at least to find a place to set his feet between the time they hit the floor in the morning and rise above it at night. He and Will are establishing a poetic friendship. An old man, a child, and so much to figure out on both of their parts.

I actually found time last night to read some Dylan Thomas.

Sister J thinks Jolly grows the best peppers she's ever tasted. I told him folks at the Hotel don't get enough produce, and Jolly scratched his cheek and said, "That so? Well, I believe I can help out a bit there." He's already planning a vegetable garden twice the size next year.

Jace fell in bed last night and said, "Well, Bonnie's ecstatic we're even thinking about it."

"What did she say about Will and me?"

"Not a problem as long as she can put you to work too."

"That's Bonnie all right. Nicola's going to have a fit."

"They're quite the number, huh?" He doubles his pillow and shoves it under his neck.

"Definitely."

"So it's looking quite dotty around here. You almost finished categorizing?"

"Yep."

"And then what?"

"I'm going to put all the yellow stuff in one room and reevaluate the blue and green."

"What about the house?" he asks.

"What do you mean?"

"Blue dot or green?"

"I think you know the answer to that."

"You want to start looking for something else?"

"Not yet. I was thinking that a tennis court would be a good investment for resale."

"What?"

"Just kiddin', sweets. Just kiddin'."

I'm always shocked and overcome with thankfulness when Will walks in the door after school in one piece. The lady I carpool with, well, let's just say that if my bad driving is a cup of Folgers, hers is a triple espresso. She ran over Will's foot last week! Of course, he thought it was hilarious.

"It didn't hurt at all, Mom. No harm, no foul, right?"

Normally we meet in the kitchen, break open a bag of chips, and munch for a while. He tells me about his day, and I listen. Then homework time.

Can I say I haven't been this happy in years? I'm watching my family with new eyes, new hope, my own sense of purpose, present and future, mingling with theirs like the hands of long-lost friends clasped in reunion at the train station. And I'm so thankful these days! Put yourself on the thin edges of society, and you'll see how paunchy you really are!

The garage door slides up. Will's home.

He sets his backpack in the middle of the floor and starts taking off his shoes.

"Bud, how long has it been since you've changed your socks?"

"I don't know. Can I have a soda?"

"Sure. How's Nicola?"

"Unbelievable. Man, Mom, she's perfect."

Ah, remember the days?

"Why don't you invite her over tomorrow? We'll cook out. I don't have anything going on."

"Cool." He swigs his Sprite. "You know, it's been kinda nice not being caught up in church so much like we used to be."

"I know. But I kinda miss it, don't you?"

"Some. You know, I think Miss Laney's getting tired of the rat race too. Maybe we can do something with them or something? I mean, the woman has her PhD in the Bible! We could learn a lot from her, you know?"

"You're a genius."

Jace helps me with the dishes, our butts sort of swaying in tandem in front of the kitchen counters, and we catch up on our week. He usually swings home a little early on Fridays and we eat a family meal together. Will made homemade ravioli along with a home-made mess.

I turn on the tap and start scrubbing the pans. We work together in silence, listening to Will practice his trumpet. He has a very mel-low tone and could play jazz, I'll bet, if he wasn't such a rock 'n' roller stuck in the '70s like his father.

"I've been thinking," I say a few minutes later.

"About what?" Jace scrubs the spattered cooktop.

"I need to go away for a little while."

"Again?"

I look at him sharply. Turn back to my task. "I need to find Mary Andrews. Xavier was last in Minnesota. But he's in a remote area. The Boundary Waters. Ever heard of that area?"

"Great fishing spot. I went there in college. Hon, what good is this going to do?"

"It's Will. This year has been a turnaround. He's doing well, the stupid jerks are leaving him alone, he has the fair Nicola. I've got to make it up to Mary if she's not all right."

"Maybe you'll just open up old wounds."

"I've got to do this. Isn't there anything big in your life you regret, Jace? Things you wish you'd never done?"

"Not really, hon. But I can think of a lot of things I regret that I should have done, but didn't."

"Please understand this."

"Go ahead, then, hon."

"Just think, in a year from now, Jace, we might be sailing on a big old boat."

"I can hardly believe it," he whispers in my hair.

I wonder how many Jaces are out there. Men and women held behind in their calling because their spouses hold on to their ankles in one way or another, refusing to let them step out.

She pushes a light brown dreadlock crisscrossed with some kind of yarn over her shoulder. "And so I just parked my butt right there in the middle of the road. Almost got hit by a coal truck as it rounded the bend. And man, did he give me what for! Cussed me up one side and down the other, and I gave it right back to him."

I'm chopping onions and listening to Ashley talk about her latest protest. Her partner, Scott, stands there listening. He's the quiet one.

And talk about liberal! Oh my gosh! I swear, they're practically communists. Carmen would have a field day. But here they stand next to me chopping carrots at the Hotel.

I always thought people like this were evil. That's what the radio guys say. Well, sort of.

Then she starts in on her religious convictions. Or non-religious convictions. "God's doing a poor job if there is a god. Look at this earth! It's a stink-hole!"

She just keeps on chopping.

"Don't you think man's made it that way?" I ask, thinking that's a pretty good question.

"Of course I do! Which is why there can't be a god, if this god won't lift a finger to do anything about it."

I shake my head. "Why are you here, then? If it's all so pointless?"

"I didn't say it was pointless. We got ourselves into this mess. We're going to have to get ourselves out of it."

I've met more than one Ashley down here. I ask Sister J about it before I leave.

"What do you make of that?"

She sits down in her chair and settles a worn copy of the Douay-Rheims on her lap. "That's the crazy thing. Here God's using her to make things better, and she doesn't realize it."

"But God's using her nevertheless."

"He's not as choosy as some people tend to think He is. I've seen it over and over again down here. Frish, but I never turn away a pair of helping hands. It would be like turning away Jesus. And Ashley's a good person, doll. She needs to keep her mouth shut more than she does, but she's young. She'll learn someday the world isn't hanging by a thread waiting to hear what she thinks."

"That's a good attitude to have."

"We can't be picky here. And God's got Ashley here to be served as well as to serve. We can't forget Jesus shows up in all sorts of forms, even in people that don't give a rat about Him." She opens her Bible. "So we haven't had cake in a while."

"I'll take that as an order."

"You bet. If that's what it takes. Now let me share this verse with you. Have a seat. 'I thank my God upon every remembrance of you.'" She looks up. "You're doing a good job, Heather."

It was all I needed, just for her to take a little notice.

Yeah, I'm not that holy yet.

THIRTY-FIVE

Carmen corners me in the bathroom at Will's first band concert of the year. "Hey, freshman moms are doing a lunch bunch on third Tuesdays this year. Do you want to come?"

Don't these people have anything better to do with their time? "I can't. I volunteer downtown on Tuesdays." Drat, why Tuesday?

Brenda, who lives about a mile from me, applies a fresh coat of lip gloss. "Oh, come on! You can skip for one day, can't you?"

"Well, there's this girl down there. Krista. She and I always sit together for a while and talk. And I hate to let her down."

Laney, gorgeous Laney with five kids tucked in a town house, rubs my arm. "You knock 'em dead down there."

"Can we do it another day? My schedule is clear every day but Tuesdays and Thursdays."

Brenda purses her lips. "Let me work on that. Maybe next month we can switch it."

I head out of the bathroom, and Krista steps forward, looking scared and out of place. I invited her to go out to dinner with us and head to the concert. "Ready to go in?" I ask.

She nods. "Can I take this coffee in?" She holds up the cup.

"Sure. Let me get one before we sit down." The Booster Club is selling refreshments, and God bless those parents! They're hard-core.

A few minutes later we sit near the front at Krista's request. "I want to tell my grandmom everything about tonight. She be so happy I'm actually out with good Christian people."

A white turtleneck covers the "Playgirl" tattoo.

249

I grieve for her if her definition of good Christian people includes me!

The phone rings Sunday night. "Heather, it's Laney. Let's go out for coffee. I've got to get out of this house. These kids are about to drive me nuts."

I can see her standing there, her strawberry blond hair pulled back in a clippie, a sponge in her hand as she swirls it on the counter.

"Sure. I want to run something by you anyway. Wanna meet somewhere?"

"I'll come pick you up."

An hour later we're sitting at Starbucks. Yuck. But hey, this chai latte is pretty good! I may have to start coming here if they serve drinks like this.

"Thanks for doing this, Heather. I swear, I was about to become abusive."

Okay, so Laney doesn't wear a mask, and I *love* that about her.

"I've been there. Will went through the most horrible stage at seven. If you can't tell, he can be a little self-righteous."

"A little?"

"I know. But it would be worse if he didn't care about things. At least that's what I keep telling myself."

We both sip our drinks.

"Look, Heather. There's been some talk among the women at school about you."

"I figured. Carmen especially, right?"

"Nothing bad. They're just worried."

"Really? None of them have come to me with these concerns. Except Carmen. Which isn't surprising."

"That's for sure. Carmen says it like she sees it."

"I mean if they were worried about *me*, wouldn't you think one of them would come talk to me?"

"Oh yeah! Definitely."

"I mean, it wasn't like we were all the best of friends or anything."

"Oh, please. It's a gossipfest. I'm not worried about you, but I want to hear what's going on with you down there."

"I just didn't want to wear my good deeds on my sleeve. I mean, you're the Bible expert; you know more than anyone it's not what I'm supposed to do."

"Well, I'm asking you, then. As your friend. I've been praying for you ever since you started volunteering."

"Really?"

"Yeah. I can't believe it either. I'm not much of a pray-er, if you want to know the truth. I mean, I can go for several days and it's like 'Shoot! I haven't prayed in forever!' But God just keeps you on my mind."

So I tell her everything. The good, the bad, the boring. The funny and the sad. "You know what, it's the times that make me laugh and the times that make me cry that keep me going down there."

"Shoot. It's like that raising children."

"Definitely."

"Only nobody's going to end up in a shrink's chair someday if you don't show up. Well, I'm happy for you. I think it's great. I figured you must be doing okay at it since your crazy calls stopped."

Laney's right. Interesting. "Sorry about those."

"Are you kidding? I loved them! Actually, if I didn't have all these kids, I'd be right there with you."

"You've got your own 'least of these' right now, Laney."

She shakes her head and picks up a napkin.

"There's another reason I'm staying away. I've become so judgmental inside. I see all these women who have everything in life, and not only do they not reach out past the gates of the country club, but they act so miserable and wounded all the time. Like they're victims or something when God is blessing their socks off. Believe me, I'm one of them and I'm trying to change, but it's so easy to fall back into the habit."

"I know."

"It's hard for me to hide my feelings, so I just stay away."

"Yeah, but when you do that, it's easier to objectify these women. And they're people too. With their own pain."

"You're right, Laney. I know that."

"And you know, maybe some of them would actually like to help out too. Have you thought about asking them?"

"I did wonder if anybody would want to help paint the main room, but I didn't want to impose on them. Everybody's always so busy."

She begins rolling up the napkin. "I think it's worth a shot. You can't blame people for being farther back in the journey than you are, Heather. I mean, it took a kangaroo to get you on the road, for heaven's sake!"

Mercy, she's right.

"Maybe, Heather, you're supposed to be our kangaroo."

"Well, if that's the case, you're going to have to step up your prayers, Laney. I mean 'pray without ceasing.'"

"I can't do much outside the home, but I can pray. If I remember to. Man, don't you wish all this was easy? Some people make it look so easy."

"I honestly don't think it's easy for anybody. Some people are better actors than others."

She drops me off at home fifteen minutes later, and I hug her as we sit in the car. "Thanks for reaching out, Laney."

"Hey, you gave me a good excuse to get out for a good cup of coffee."

"No really. You have no idea how much I needed that. I've been isolating myself, I know that. I just have to learn to navigate these new waters."

"Well, you're not alone. Hey, and you pray for me too, okay?"

"I will."

See, it's like this. When God shows up, you never know what form He's going to take. But when it's Him, if you're at all awake, you know it.

"Laney, I've been meaning to call and ask you this. What would you think about our families starting a house church? Will came up with the idea, and it's all the rage, you know."

She barks out a laugh.

"Think about it. We shouldn't let your education go to waste a second longer than we have to."

She grips the steering wheel. "Really? Are you serious?"

"Definitely. Jace thinks it's a good idea too."

"Wow. I mean"—she presses her hand to her forehead—"I mean, I just figured God didn't want me to . . . well, didn't want me anymore . . . to serve Him like that . . . Oh, I don't know what I'm even saying, Heather."

She cries a cupful of very complicated tears.

I wave Laney off and turn toward the side of the house and the entrance in the breezeway between the kitchen and the garage. Someone sits on the porch bench.

"Jolly?"

"Hello there, Heather." His voice sounds sanded thin.

"Are you all right?"

"I just brought over some apples." He holds up a bucket. "And I just can't go home. I can't go back there, I miss her so badly."

He's been crying again. For a long time if I'm not mistaken.

"Come on inside. I'll make us a cup of tea and set up the guest room for you. You stay with us tonight."

"I'd appreciate that."

Jace, Will, and I gather around Jolly, and soon we're all drinking tea and playing a game of Trivial Pursuit. Jolly wipes us clean on the sports category. "I had no idea you were a sports nut," I say.

"Yes sirree. Helen and I never missed a game of anything if it was on the TV."

They must have enjoyed a lovely life. Really, really enjoyed it.

Will lays down *zaibatsu* using a *z* already on the board. On a triple word space. "Oh yeah. Oh yeah."

Jace bares his teeth. "No way. It's Japanese, and I have no idea what it means."

"It's a large Japanese business conglomerate." He leans back and crosses his arms over his chest. "And it's English."

"No way. It's a foreign word, bud."

I love watching this. It's only a matter of time before Will tallies those points onto his score. Hasn't Jace figured out what a pushover he is?

Jolly sips his tea, clears his throat, and looks down at his tiles through his pink half-glasses, Helen's old ones, of course. "Seems to me if a boy knows such a word rightly exists, he should get some points. I say give him half for even knowin' it."

"Done!" says Jace.

Our eyes meet. He knows I realize what a bargain he just got.

Will collects seven tiles from the brown plastic bag. "Hey, you were a topic of conversation in the cafeteria today, Mom."

"Figures. What did I do now?"

"You had to bring that girl to the concert, didn't you?" He smiles. "That's what the moms were saying. It was hilarious. You know the girls can imitate their moms dead-on!"

"You mean Krista?"

"Yeah." He dons a feminine affect. "'And she paraded her right up to the front. If she wants to slum it, fine, but does she have to rub everybody's nose in it?'"

Jace rearranges his tiles. "That's my girl. Making waves."

Will. "Yeah, boy. You should have heard Missy. She said her mom was talking about it with the other women."

Missy. Brenda's daughter.

No wonder Laney called.

"You must think you're so holier-than-thou, they say. And it's not only that—they heard the mission is Catholic. You're halfway to being a heretic too."

Mercy!

"I'm sorry, Will. I didn't think you'd be bearing the brunt."

"Me? Oh yeah, right. I think it's great. I mean, come on, it's not okay for you to bring Krista, but perfectly fine for them to talk behind your back, right?"

Well, honestly, I can't fault them there. Not really. I've done my share of gossiping. But somehow, when you're the one doing it, it just doesn't seem all that bad.

After settling Jolly in the guest room, I riffle through the day's mail and come up with a letter to Will. From Ronnie Legermin. Oh no. Bullying goes postal. I take it up to his room and hand it to him. "What's this?"

"Oh, cool."

"You want to explain why Ronnie Legermin is writing you?"

"I got a card from him two weeks ago. He apologized, which was totally crazy, you know? I mean, I never saw *that* coming!"

"Was it genuine?"

"Heck, I don't know. So I wrote him back and said, "Yeah, I forgive you," and all that sort of thing. No big deal, really. So I guess he's written me back."

"Well, open it, then."

"Okay, Mom. Sheesh. Can't I have a little privacy? I don't go asking to read your mail, do I?"

Okay, okay.

Liza outdid herself. A baked rockfish garnished with parsley and lemon rests on a simple marigold platter.

Anna sparkles in a new lime green sweater. "And don't you just love the gold trim around the wrists?" She twists her wrist back and forth.

"I do. You look wonderful."

"I know it's silly, a woman my age, but I couldn't resist it."

Liza sets down a bowl of buttered broccoli. "It was from Kohl's,

Anna. Nobody should feel guilty about buying something at Kohl's."

They've prepared for my coming, set out their best, and I feel as though I'm Christ Himself come for dinner. And knowing the way they think, I guess I am. "I could have brought my own fork."

Anna hugs me. "Do you use it?"

"Every day."

Liza updates me on her ministries, Anna as well, and she hasn't been arrested lately, which is a relief. I worry about her.

Liza sets down her fork. "I'm so glad you haven't forgotten us biddies."

Anna arches a brow but says nothing.

"Well, I do have an ulterior motive. Do you still have the plans for Alva's houses in Glen Burnie?"

Liza gasps. "Of course! Why?"

"I think we want to build one for ourselves, Liza. Sell the big house, live sensibly, cleanly."

"Like a true modernist would!" She smugly throws back her shoulders. "Right, then. They're in the study. This is quite exciting for me, you know. You'll have to keep us informed every step of the way."

"Oh, I will, Liza."

Anna lays a sweet hand over her sister's and smiles into her eyes. "I told you they'd be useful someday, dear. Dreams like Alva's don't deserve to die off completely."

"Anna, you were right, and this time I don't mind saying so."

THIRTY-SIX

Sly, the man who first helped me take my cakes to the kitchen, hasn't been around the Hotel very much. I ask Mo about this. Mo shakes his head above a bright red sports jersey. "Aww, Sly's using again. He's ashamed. I don't think he'll be back for a while."

"Where does he hang out?"

"Patterson Park. And do *not* go there by yourself, Heather. Don't be crazy. I see that look in your eye."

"Okay."

I should have reached out to Sly more instead of hiding back in the kitchen. The regret slams into my stomach.

Knox Dulaney breezes through the door. "Mo!"

"Knoxie." Mo doesn't smile.

"Now, man, don't do that to me. Is Aunt Jerusha around?"

Mo jerks a thumb around to the back.

A few of the guys sitting at the tables playing checkers or watching TV shift uncomfortably in their seats.

Knox disappears through the swinging door.

"Mo, I don't understand it. Krista told me how bad that man is. There isn't a month goes by that someone isn't dead because of him."

"He's bad news."

"Why does Sister J put up with him?"

"She loves him. Lord knows, she tried to bring him up right. But you know, sin is a dictator. Knoxie wanted fortune and respect."

"But it's fear, not respect."

"Not on these streets."

"But isn't respect earn—"

"Don't even try to understand it, girl."

"Okay. Well, I've got some cake in the car." I turn toward the tables. "Anybody want to help me bring in the cake?"

"I will." A man I've never seen, or perhaps never noticed, stands up. His words are quiet, hunched a little like their creator.

"Thanks."

We walk down the street to the car. "I'm Heather, by the way."

"Teddy Jamison."

"Have you been at the Hotel before?"

"I come and go. I try and find work when and where I can."

"What do you do?"

"I paint murals. That's my work down there on Lexington Street. Near the market on the parking garage."

"I've never seen it."

"Take a look sometime."

I open the back and load his arms with boxes.

"Sometimes I do sidewalk drawings for some spare change."

"Are you trained?"

"No. Just always knew how to do it."

"Do you take on commissions?"

"If I think I can do it."

I shut the hatchback. "I've always wanted a portrait of my son. It doesn't matter what medium."

I relieve him of some of the boxes.

"Sure. Just bring in some pictures. I'll do charcoal or pastel."

"I love charcoal."

"I'd appreciate it if you'd get the supplies too."

"Okay."

We're almost to the doors. Mo opens them and we deposit the cakes in the kitchen. Teddy disappears. When I deliver a fresh urn of coffee an hour later, he sits with the others, watching *The Price Is Right*, eyes glazed over, hands lying empty on the table, the memory of a syringe printed into their palms.

Oh yes, Knox Dulaney was here. One way or another he has that effect on people.

I'm scrubbing the oven again. Footsteps approach and a pair of expensive brown shoes comes into view. Nothing preppy or staid. Lots of European style.

I lean back on my haunches.

Knox smiles. "Hello, Mrs. Curridge."

"Hi. And it's just Heather."

"I just wanted to say thank you for coming down here. Aunt Jerusha has a hard time keeping volunteers, as you might imagine."

I drop my rag into the bucket and stand to my feet. "She's her own gal, that's for sure."

I know he's Jesus to me right now, but every time I talk to him, I feel like it's the first time.

"I'm regretful about my reputation to you."

"Yeah, I'm pretty much scared to say anything right now, Mr. Dulaney."

He nods. "No doubt. It's all right. You probably think I come in here to intimidate the clients."

I can feel my eyes widen.

"Ah, I read your mind," he says.

I nod.

"I don't do it for myself. I do it to let anybody know if they mess with my aunt, they'll have me to deal with."

"It's obvious you have a great deal of affection for her."

"She's saved my life more than once. Continues to. I try to help out here, keeping her safe, donating."

"She takes your money?" Mercy! Why did I say that?

"Yes, she does. You know what she says? She says, 'I'm not going to take the one good thing you actually do away from you.'" He chuckles. "I heard you brought cake today."

"Yes, I did."

"May I take a piece with me?"

"I'll wrap it up for you." Everything inside me screams, *Don't do it!* But a deeper voice asks, *Can you love as radically as Christ does?*

Yet as I tear a piece of foil off an almost-empty tube, I feel as if I'm doing something wrong and I wonder which voice is right.

But Christ never held Himself at arm's length, did He? He'd share His cake with Knox.

I might as well get it over with. On the drive home I plug my dead cell phone into the car charger and dial Carmen. She answers, thank goodness. I don't want to prolong this agony with the inevitable "Tag, you're it!"

That line has got to go.

"It's Heather, Carmen. Do you have time to talk?"

"I'm a little busy right now. Bart has a science project due tomorrow and I'm up to my elbows." Bart's ten.

It's two thirty. Will's going to Nicola's to study.

"Why don't I come over and help?"

"Would you? That would be great."

Half an hour later I sit with her at her kitchen island working on the project. I'm taping together construction paper cylinders to wrap around glass jars filled with water. We're going to drop in a thermometer and set them all before a heat lamp to see how quickly the jars heat up, comparing the temperature rise to the colors of the paper.

Or something.

Just hand me the tape and I'll be fine.

"Where's Bart?"

"He's got a game."

And here we sit doing his science fair project.

She looks at me, waiting for the inevitable "This is lying" speech, but I hold up my hands. "I can't say I haven't done the same thing myself."

"It's pathetic, I know. Okay, I'm setting in the thermometers. The water should all be at room temperature, so we'll let them get to the same level and then put the paper sleeves over and shine the lights. Want a cup of coffee while we wait?"

"Sure."

"I just got this wonderful machine that grinds the beans and makes a fresh cup in about thirty seconds."

Wow. It's great. Frothy and silky going down. I think maybe I should get one, but . . . get thee behind me, Satan!

"Carmen, I came over to set things right between us. I know there are a lot of hard feelings between me and the other women right now. And I know, believe me, I know it's my fault. I've been really caught up in things."

"It's true."

"I also want you to know I didn't parade Krista up front. She really wanted to sit there."

"Oh, that was just Brenda saying all that. You know her."

Of course, the obvious next question is why Brenda's gossiping criticism gets excused as "just Brenda." But now's not the time.

"Anyway, I just want to get things right. I can't jump back into all my positions, but I don't want to isolate you all either."

Carmen pushes the button and makes her own cup.

She sits down. "I guess I haven't been all that supportive. You've just always been in such a leadership role, Heather. And then to remove yourself."

"Can I tell you my story?"

"Maybe that would be a good idea."

So as we turn on the lights, write down data, try different light-bulbs, I tell her everything, just as I did Laney.

She pencils in the final temperature of the lightest cylinder. "I can understand a bit more. I think."

When I leave she hugs me at the car. "Be careful with that drug dealer down there. You might get shot or something."

"Maybe you'd like to come down with me sometime?"

She folds her arms across her chest. "Let me check my calendar." Then pulls me into another hug. "Of course I would!"

After having picked up the building plans from Liza, I pass my drive-way and turn down Jolly's lane. Almost six o'clock. The light is fad-ing, but it's easy to see he still loves his land. Fall mums bloom, brightening their square foot of dusk, lining the driveway with the promise of a nice person waiting at the other end.

All lights in the old home are off, save the kitchen, and the yel-low bulb over the porch shines in silent hope that maybe someone will ease his loneliness.

I hop out of the wagon, bound toward the door, and knock, antic-ipation hovering in the air around me.

Why didn't I think of this before?

He yanks open the door, and a smile peps up his face. Jolly pushes the screen door forward. "Heather! Why, come on in!"

"Guess what? I've got a great idea!"

"Oh, now?"

"Yes. I'm heading off to Minnesota to find a man named Xavier Andrews. I'll tell you why later. But he lives in some remote area called the Boundary Waters and you can only get there by canoe."

"Heard of it."

"At least I think he lives there. Anyway, would you like to go with me? I'm leaving in about a week, before it gets too cold. Would you like to go?"

"Yes."

I look both ways, lean forward, and put my hand against his fore-head. "You're not sick, are you?"

"No. You could have invited me to the moon without an oxygen tank and I'd have said yes to that too. I need a change of scenery, Heather. The sooner the better. Now Helen would say that's okay."

"She definitely would."

"Next week, you say?"

"Wednesday. I'll book your ticket along with mine."

When I tell Will, he descends into a full-blown sulk. "Man. You have all the fun, Mom. Going to the Hotel and being with Mo all the time, and now you get to go away with Jolly. It sucks being in high school."

THIRTY-SEVEN

Sister J stands with Mo, her handbag hanging from the crook of her arm. They both look a little stricken, a little angry, a little fearful.

"What is it?" I ask.

"Krista's disappeared again." Sister J. "She hasn't been back for three nights. Her stuff is still in her room. Nobody's seen hide nor hair."

"Where are you going?" I set my purse on Mo's desk.

"I'm going out to look for her. I'll see if Knox has heard anything too."

Mo tsks.

"Now don't you start with me! You know as well as I do that Knox knows more about what's going on in the street than you and I put together, Moses Weaver." She turns to me and jerks a thumb at Mo. "He's a rascal."

"Can I go? I just need to use the bathroom."

"You bet. It might not be pretty."

"I want to go."

The feeling of dread that pooled in my gut as soon as Sister J uttered the words "Krista's disappeared" begins to coagulate. Dear God in heaven, I hope she isn't dead! Sister J leads me out onto the street.

"Let's try that flophouse right there. LaQueesha lives on the first floor. She's tried to look out for Krista, but what can you do? We'll cut through the alley. Be careful not to step on the syringes; they can go right through your soles if you're not careful."

Mercy!

"And don't touch the walls if you can help it. Stay away from that cat carcass over there. Hold your nose."

Now I know why I've never gone down these alleys. And I could forgo the tour spiel if Sister J wouldn't mind. She looks right at home, though, I have to admit. I'll bet in her eyes, this is just the patio of the Hotel.

A brown door, paint scratched through, seems to be the only entrance around here

Sister J knocks. "This is LaQueesha's entrance. Nicest apartment in the building. The rest are like closets. But where else you going to live for fifty bucks a week?"

The door opens and a woman wearing a robin's egg blue sequined cowboy hat stands in the doorway. "Sistah J? How you doin'?" She swings the door wide. "Come on in! It's been too long, uh-huh."

"Heck yeah, it has. This is my friend Heather. She's a volunteer."

"Come in, come in, uh-huh."

We climb the three concrete steps and enter a dim hallway lined with frames surrounding copious cutouts: ovals, squares, and each one contains a school photo, a snapshot, or a ticket stub. She leads us toward the front of the building, past a couple of bedrooms—one set up as a prayer room with a kneeling bench and a crucifix—a bath, then a kitchen, all lined up along the corridor. And pow! Into the front room we emerge like spelunkers from a cave. Heavy venetian blinds accordion near the tops of the tall, narrow windows, and almost everything is light blue, matching LaQueesha's outfit, a sky blue mohair poncho over a shimmery tank top, jeans the denim god must have exhaled onto her, and turquoise cowboy boots with silver heels and mirrored decorations.

LaQueesha must love hoops! Ten heavy gold hoops lower each ear farther down beside her thin neck bound up with necklaces of gold and silver. Bangles, rings accent her graceful hands. She jangles and smells like peaches. I wasn't this feminine on my wedding day.

"Have a seat, have a seat. I'm just about to head downtown to the beauty parlor, uh-huh." Hands land on hips in a slouchy, runway fashion. So slender too. "Can I get you a ice tea?"

"Thanks, doll, that sounds good." Sister J sits on one of those wicker fan chairs Pier 1 sold back in the '70s when it was more the garage sale of the Orient than a trendy boutique anchoring upscale strip malls. This one is decorated with crystal beads that catch the sun coming through the window and throw tiny rainbows on Sister J's cheek.

"You look like a saint in that thing." I choose a seat near her on the couch, a cream-colored leather sofa running the length of the room. "Nice!"

"I love my couch. Now some tea for you too, uh-huh?"

"Please."

She walks into the first doorway off the hall.

Sister Jerusha taps her nose. "If anybody knows where Krista is, it's LaQueesha."

"What's her story?"

"Her grandmother owned this building. LaQueesha is one of the smartest businesswomen I know. Keeps the building up better than most landlords around here, although I wouldn't want to spend a night here if I didn't have to. Other than here at her place. Now this is styling, isn't it?"

"It's amazing. So nuns like a little sparkle when left to their own devices?"

"This nun does."

"Do you ever bemoan the fact that you've led a life of poverty?"

"You mean that I missed out on all the good things of life?"

I shrug. "I guess."

"Not one bit. Don't know any different. I went into the convent when I was nineteen. I was the youngest in my family—fourteen children. We didn't have much, but nobody abused us or neglected us—of course, we only expected a few minutes a day from each parent, so we had lowered expectations. So I don't know what I'm missing. And you know there are all sorts of good things in life. Maybe not things, but people, and places, and deeds, and families, and children. You know, life itself."

She folds her hands across her stomach and sighs.

"And then some days, you get to sit in LaQueesha's apartment and have some of her iced tea." She raises her brows. "Uh-huh."

"I heard that!" LaQueesha steps out of the kitchen with a tray of tea glasses rimmed in gold. She laughs. "I've tried to rid myself of that 'uh-huh' for years, and I just can't."

"It's who you are, doll." Sister J reaches for a glass and sips. "Ahh, best iced tea in Baltimore."

I take mine, sip, and by golly, she's right! "What's your secret?"

"One mint bag in with three regulars. Does it every time. Lots of sugar, uh-huh, and got to put in a good amount of lemon."

I raise my glass. "I'll remember that." Even Leslie Summerville would approve of this brew.

LaQueesha sits next to me. "So what brings you round today?"

"Krista's disappeared." Sister J sets her drink on the glass coffee table.

"Again?"

"Yeah. I thought she was gonna make it this time. I really did."

Our host's brows knit. "Oh, Sistah J, I wish I was as hopeful as you, uh-huh. But I seen that little girl for a year now, just struggling every day, and if you can't help her, I don't know who can, and the dear Lord knows that's the truth."

"Have you seen her, then?" Sister J leans forward. Her upper lip quivers so slightly I can hardly believe I noticed. And it hits me. She loves this girl. She loves Krista more than someone like me is able to give her credit for.

"No. I'm so sorry. I haven't seen her for a week."

"Any talk?"

"No, but I been busy, you know, uh-huh. I'll ask around."

Sister Jerusha leans back. "Something about that girl pulls at my heart, LaQueesha. God's marked her. I can see it like I could on you, like I can on Knoxie."

LaQueesha just nods and turns to me. "Sistah J was the first person to realize I could sing, Heather. I sing all over the place now, uh-huh, for Jesus too."

"Sister J, can you really see God's mark on people?"

"You bet I can. Don't know how or why, but there're some that get a special mark from God to do great things."

LaQueesha points a finger at her. "Now I seen you get it right nine times outta ten—yes, I have. But I think you missed it with Knoxie, Sistah. You have most definitely missed it with that man, uh-huh." She wipes a hand in disgust. "And you and I are the ones left picking up his pieces, we are." She points to me. "You stay away from him, Heather, if you know what's good for you. Don't ever talk to him outside the Hotel. Ever. You hear what I'm saying?"

I nod.

Sister J sighs. "It's good advice. I love my godson, but he's a dangerous man. What can you do?"

Is there a mark on me? No way am I going to ask. Both answers contain major drawbacks.

An hour later after various interviews on the street, including Zeke with his droopy pants, we return to the kitchen.

"I loved that lady! She's wonderful." I raise a bag of bread off the yellow plastic bakery tray and set it on the worktable. Garlic bread to go with Jimmy's "minestrone," which means cans and cans of vegetables dumped into water with some bouillon cubes, macaroni, and kidney beans. Donations have been on a diet lately.

"You gotta love LaQueesha. I'll be in my office if you need me, doll."

She turns and trudges through the doorway, flips on the lamp, and shuts the door.

Sister J is the Atlas of the North Avenue area. It's easy to say, "The poor aren't my responsibility. They got themselves there, they can get themselves out." And most people do say that, if not by their words, then by their actions. But then people like this woman give their lives, like Jesus did, to whoever will reach out and take them. Not because they deserve it, but because she has so much life to give away.

Serving God makes little sense down here at the Hotel, the last stop on the line for many people. But there has to be that last stop, doesn't there? And Jesus is here too. He can't help but be.

I had so many theories there on the hill, and none of them felt like bone or bled like skin. None of them were once an innocent little baby who cried out in pain or laughed in amusement. None of those ideas looked out of eyes glistening with the wet of life, looked out over used syringes and condoms and men like Knox Dulaney, eyes filled with anger because any other emotion costs too much.

My bed feels better and better these days. I'm preparing to leave for Minnesota in just a few days. Already it's almost too late in the year for the trip we're making, but it has been a warmer fall than usual up north, so Jolly and I may be just fine.

Jace climbs into bed looking like a once-wet dog now dried by a trek in the hot sun and ready for a long lie-down on the porch. I don't know how he does it. "How you doing, hon?"

"Tired. What you got going tomorrow?"

"Actually, a lighter day. And I'll go to the Hotel for a couple of hours in the afternoon."

I curl my fists around the top of the sheet. "Krista disappeared and we can't find her anywhere."

"I thought something was bothering you when I called earlier. No idea where she is?"

"LaQueesha's going to ask around."

He leans up and looks over at me. "LaQueesha?"

"Yep. She loves blue."

"Hopefully they'll find her soon."

I lean up on my elbow. "Why is it so hard for some people, Jace? I mean, here you've got kids born into the right family, all the right circumstances, and the only reason they amount to anything is because their parents buy their way out of their troubles until they're old enough to get with the program. And then you've got the people who come into the Hotel. I swear, they're not that different. They just never had the cushion."

"No. You're right there."

"I wish I knew what the answer is."

"If you figure it out, tell the world." He smiles. "You're the answer, Heather. Surely you see that, don't you?"

And yeah, I'm just one woman and all that. But maybe he's got a point.

Okay, he does have a point.

We can only change the world by changing ourselves. I guess that's always the very first step. Sister J tacked a Gandhi quote above her desk. *"Be the change you wish to see in the world."* Michael Jackson sang about starting with the man in the mirror. Good thought, even if the messenger creeps me out. And Jesus, my Jesus, said, "Inasmuch as you've done it to the least of these, you've done it unto Me."

Why must it be so simple yet so difficult?

I lie in the darkness listening to Jace's deafening snore and staring at the ceiling.

My grandmother, God rest her, used to say this to me.

Only one life t'will soon be past.

Only what's done for Christ will last.

Granted, she enjoyed a platitude spirituality, but she raised my father, so she did something right.

So here's the bottom line. Do I want to stand before God's throne and say I kept a clean house, I made sure my child was athletic, musical, artistic, and got good grades, I was present at all the important church activities, and I changed the oil in my car every three thousand miles because I was such a good steward of my blessings?

Is that all I will have to show for the gift of life?

Dear God, I hope not.

I won't be able to sleep with the hound dog next to me, so I throw back the covers, tiptoe downstairs, and pull out a fresh spiral notebook. It's inventory time. One column for blue dots, one for green, and one for yellow. And I begin to take a closer look at my possessions.

I set out the cereal boxes, bowls, spoons, and milk on our island. Gone are the days of bacon or sausage, eggs and biscuits. No creamed chipped beef or French toast.

And they're surviving just fine.

Who knew?

Will enters the kitchen and pours himself a cup of coffee. He takes it black. I wish I was half as cool as he is. Now if I could just get him to remember to put deodorant on every morning, we'd be doing even better.

"Did you put deodorant on?"

"Sheesh, Mom! Of course!"

I cock my head, and he sets down his cup and runs up the steps.

Okay, so he's not above the occasional lie. But neither am I, especially when Carmen corners me.

He rumbles back down the steps a minute later. "Okay, there. I was just prophesying before." He grabs the box of Cocoa Krispies and pours some into a bowl. "So what's going on today with you?"

"Last-minute trip preparations and then I'm going to take a quick run down to the Hotel to drop off a few things." Okay, more than a few, but they're going to sell some of this stuff on eBay.

He pours the milk, then, grabbing the bowl and spoon, heads into the family room.

I take a mental inventory of the purged items. Christmas China, sixteen place settings by Lenox. That'll fetch a pretty price, and honestly, does having holly and bows around your food make it taste any better? It would be one thing if this stuff had been passed down, but all my dad ate off of until the day he died was Corelle.

"And you know!" Will hollers from the couch. "I was wondering if you could maybe change one of your volunteer days to Saturday. That way I could come with you."

"You've got a lot going on Saturdays, bud."

"I know. But I've been thinking about it for a while now."

And he clicks on the TV to watch *Good Morning America*. He loves that show.

THIRTY-EIGHT

This morning the Petersons and the Curridges met at Patterson Park. In broad daylight. Near the pagoda.

Laney opened up the Scriptures, we shared Communion, Jace played his guitar, we prayed. Afterwards we ate cake and drank iced tea made with LaQueesha's special mix.

Church happens, I learned today. It doesn't always have to be programmed and planned, pulled out of the Body like a splinter from raw flesh, leaving bits behind to fester in its wake. The Holy Spirit put in a visit too. I know that because I'm a Christian, and sometimes, we just know these things.

Jolly brews me a cup of Red Rose tea. We sit at his kitchen table, opera music filtering in from the hi-fi stereo in the den.

"I never knew you liked opera, Jolly."

"Helen hated it. So I figured I might as well dig out my old seventy-eights. That's Caruso right there. Isn't he something?" Jolly's face lights up. "My father loved opera."

"Mine hated it!"

"Maybe he should have married my Helen."

"Okay, Jolly." I reach into my purse and pull out his ticket. "Here's your flight itinerary. I'll pick you up on Wednesday morning at 4:30 a.m."

He raises his brows. "That's cow milking time!"

"I know. But we have to be at the airport two hours before our flight these days with all the security."

He flips open the flap. "That so? Never been on an airplane before."

"Nothing to it. It'll be fun to do together. Now is there anything you'll need? We'll have to take a canoe ride to Xavier's place. The girl at the library found out the general proximity of his parcel. So you'll want to pack warm. Do you have a suitcase?"

"I do. In fact"—he points toward the door—"I'm already packed." An army green duffle bag rests on the floor.

"Oh, Jolly. I'm so glad you're looking forward to it as much as I am." I can't help myself—I throw my arms around his neck and give him a giant hug.

"Now, now!" he says. "Now, now!"

"You're just a treasure." I pull back.

"I was wondering if I might come with you down to that hotel of yours sometime. See if they might need an extra pair of hands."

"How about tomorrow?"

He scratches his cheek, the scritch-scritch of his stubble sounding like small maracas. "Well, now. I think that can be arranged. Of course, I'll need to check my overflowing social calendar first."

I do believe I see a sparkle in those eyes. Tiny, yes, but right there.

"Hey, Jolly. What happened to most of the dolls?" At least three-quarters of them didn't show up for duty today.

"I sent the ones I've always disliked to a doll museum. Helen's gone, Heather. And I never found her compassion for those ugly things."

"I don't think she'd mind."

"You kidding? She'd have had a fit."

I dial Carmen. "Hey, girl!"

"Heather! How are you?"

"Good. Listen, I've got a proposition for you."

"I haven't had one of those in years."

"Me either. So here's the deal."

I tell her about the paint from the Summerville Foundation just sitting there. "What do you think? Would the women of St. Matthews want to take a day and paint? It would be good PR for the school."

"Oh my gosh, yes! Are you kidding?"

My eyes blink of their own accord and my head is thrown back with the force of her enthusiasm. "Really?"

"Absolutely. You know, it's not that we don't care, Heather. We're clueless, not callous."

Well, that sure sounds like a different song than what they were singing awhile ago. I like it.

"Okay, then! Well, good. I'm going away for a week to find an old friend, so let's plan for something after that?"

"Great. I'll get the buzz going."

See, Carmen's not so bad. I don't know why I have such a hard time giving people a chance.

Okay, she deserved every bit of it, but still.

Jolly called at least four times today and came over twice, body taut with anticipation. His one duffel found a mate who came to the marriage with brand-new clothes from Target. Will is trying not to let his natural excitement show through the unnatural sulk. I watch him inspect and approve Jolly's purchases, see the longing in the movements of his sensitive hands, and I'd love to take him out of school to come with us. But I can't let him witness what might happen. It's my penance, my sin, and my time to face the consequences.

"Mom?" Will corners me in the bathroom, where I'm packing my travel bag. "I need to know why you're going."

"I don't know if you can handle it, bud."

"These people have a strong hold on you. Something's wrong. I think I need to know."

I take his face in my hands. "Will, a long time ago I was a terrible person. I'd rather you not know the ins and outs of it."

"Were you in school?"

"Yes."

"Can I ask Dad when you're gone?"

"I think that would be better."

"You know I'll forgive you whatever it is."

I kiss his cheeks. How does he know he has something to forgive?

THIRTY-NINE

Jolly and I climb out of the rental car, a soda can with bike wheels and barely upholstered seats. I've never seen car floors without carpeting before.

"Sorry I went so cheap, Jolly."

"I feel like I been on roller skates."

Me too.

"Sure was glad to get out of Duluth, though. I hate cities." He opens the trunk and starts pulling out our bags. "This'll be a nice little escapade, surely."

The drive took about six hours, Jolly talking about Helen, pointing out vegetation and naming it by botanical name and common name, never failing to express his delight at a well-planted field, a beautifully kept farm.

"Now that's a barn!" he said over and over again. "I always did favor the white barns for some reason."

"I like purple."

"I don't strictly find that hard to believe."

At the end of a flagstone path illumined by footlights with rusty iron moose ears sprouting from either side, a log cabin lodge sits against a star-filled sky. On a deep, wide porch, yellow light falls on settings of bent willow furniture.

"Who gets to run places like this? Who gets to live like this?" I ask.

"The lucky ones. That's for sure."

A young man with russet hair, a puffy beard, and an orange

276

sweatshirt proclaiming that the Mssrs. Abercrombie and Fitch have indeed taken over the world opens the door. "Ms. Curridge?"

"That's me."

"Have a good trip?" He walks behind the counter.

Jolly sets down his bag. "Yes, we did. Good drive. Pretty country."

"And you're Mr. Lester?"

"Yes, I am."

He turns toward a key cubby, just like in the movies. Pulling out two keys, he says, "Breakfast can be anytime you like. Eggs, bacon, that sort of thing."

"We'll want an early start. We're looking for a man named Xavier Andrews. I'm going to need a guide."

The young man shakes his head. "I've never heard of a man named Xavier Andrews. You know where he might be?"

"Runs a camp or something." I pull out the map the librarian printed off for me. "Somewhere around here. You all have the best guide in the area, right?"

"Let me call Ralph. He's the guide you're talking about. If anybody's heard of this man, Ralph will have."

The gist of his call is that Ralph hasn't seen Xavier Andrews in a couple of years, but yes, he runs a remote camp about twenty miles from here and as far as he knows, Xavier's still there.

Twenty miles? Mercy! I thought I was at least in the ballpark.

"It's a place for the hardiest of sportsmen. Ralph can't guide you tomorrow, but his nephew Grandy can. He grew up on these waters."

"Sounds good."

"He said he'll come by at 7:00 a.m. It'll take two days to get there."

Jolly and I stare at each other. He's thinking, *Is that right?* And I'm thinking, *Two days!*

The young man continues. "He said you'll paddle mostly. You'll have to camp for a couple of nights. We've got clean sleeping bags and all the gear you'll need. Grandy'll bring a couple of tents. I'll be honest, other than Ralph, there's no better guide than Grandy."

"Well, I guess that tells us what time breakfast is, then," Jolly says.

"You'll want to eat hearty. We'll pack up a cooler, too, if you'd like. Water. Two days there, two days back. You'll need the supplies. Grandy'll bring some things too."

I nod. "Thanks."

Jolly and I stand in the hall near our doorways.

"I had no idea, Jolly. I'm sorry. I just thought I'd come up here and find him easy. I don't know what I was thinking."

"Where was that last vacation you all took?"

"An all-inclusive resort in Belize."

"So there you go. It'll be fun. I needed an adventure, Heather."

"Well, we'll get one. I feel kinda stupid, very unprepared."

"Is that so? Well, he didn't seem to bat an eyelid, now, did he?"

"No, that's true."

"So stop thinkin' you're so dang special, girly."

I laugh. "You want to drive down the road and get a little supper?"

"To be honest, I'm exhausted. I'd just soon tuck in."

"Me too."

I love Jolly.

Tonight as I settled between plaid flannel sheets, I was thinking about the truly happy people I've known in my lifetime and how few there really have been, which seems so very sad. Miss Virginia was the crossing guard in our neighborhood when I was in first grade. I didn't start in at Christian school until second.

A joy shone from inside of her that made us kids want to be around her. And never once was I scared coming out of school, because Miss Virginia would be there, and she'd call me 'baby' and smile, her gold tooth gleaming. Nothing ruffled her, and even the mean kids smiled at her when they walked by.

Miss Virginia was happy, so therefore, Miss Virginia was safe to be around. I wish I thought of her more after I grew up. I want to be a Miss Virginia. I want to be safe—that place where people can fail and still be loved. Heaven knows, there are enough exhorters, enough admonishers, enough people with a lockdown on life, enough people who can tell all of us what to do and why and sometimes even how. They don't need me.

I rub some moisturizer into my hands. Raspberry.

But I want to be the person around whom people don't have to do a thing to be loved. Perhaps all of humanity can't fill that role, and maybe there's only room for a few of us on earth or all would be chaos. I don't know. But as I see it, there's definitely room for more Miss Virginias. And I aim to fill her shoes.

Tomorrow we'll be canoeing into the wilderness. I've never been in such a remote area in my entire life. Isn't that strange?

We set out in slim light, bellies full of a farmer's breakfast, as Jolly, rested and ready to go, called it. He sipped that coffee and gave out a long "Ahhh. Now that's good, strong coffee."

"You like it strong? I never had a strong cup at your house."

"It was hard on Helen's stomach."

The home fries were loaded with caramelized onions and cheese, and I ate almost a full plate, with Canadian bacon and a bunch of grapes.

I'm excited about the journey, but I really don't want to have to go to the bathroom out in the middle of nature. That's pretty much my single reservation here. Pathetic, I know.

Jolly sits at the front, I'm in the middle, and Grandy sits in the back, paddling, steering, saying nothing. We all paddle, and I think, *Two days of this?* Actually four days with the trip back, but I'm not ready to go there.

It surely makes whatever forgiveness I receive from the Andrews family, if I am even awarded it, hard-won. Even with this, I realize it's not enough penance. Not even close. For I remember the times we cornered Mary in the girls' restroom and smeared lipstick all over her face; I remember the time Julia B. and I told her the next day was red day and she showed up in red and the rest of us wore blue; and I remember Bryan stealing her lunch bag, opening it up, and displaying the contents to everybody in the cafeteria with a running commentary. "Ah, yes, the stinky egg salad." Or "Oooh, bread and margarine. The lunch of champions." After a while, Mary stopped bringing lunch, stopped eating lunch. Gary just sort of kept to himself—a silent pariah.

I can't tell Will this. I make Ronnie Legermin look like a saint.

I'm sure tomorrow my muscles will be screaming. I paddled several hours, although Jolly and Grandy were benevolent and took on most of the load. I even fell asleep for a little while as the waters slid by and we passed colonies of trees, their roots twisted through the banks, clinging to the earth, their upper surfaces carpeted in moss. But I didn't sleep for long. I didn't want to miss the great carved walls of rock, so ancient, looking as if the finger of God himself reached down and dug through the stone.

Pine trees lined the shores of the lakes we paddled through, open in the bliss of spaciousness, and they seemed to be guarding secrets inside their lineup. We haven't seen anybody since we left.

Grandy's a nice enough guy, but he carries some sort of heavy burden. Twenty-three and has lived back here all his life. I don't know what happened to outline him with a thorny crown, but I do know something did. With some people, I guess that's all you can know.

The men set up camp, and heaven knows where we are. They share one tent, and I'm lying here in the other. We had Spam and beans for dinner. Grandy brought out a travel guitar—I'd never seen one—and plucked some pretty strains. Jolly took over—never knew he could play—and we sang crazy songs like "You're in the Army, Mister Jones" and "I've Been Workin' on the Railroad." For a moment, Grandy's face cleared, and it was good.

Maybe that's part of redemption. Simply giving people the opportunity, even briefly, to allow their faces to clear and to be living for just one nice thing. I believe that's why I bake cakes.

And then Grandy had to ask why I was so bent on finding Xavier Andrews. Here's an example of when the truth can be a mistake. He told me he was a Gary Andrews, and nice try and all that, but the deed is done. Gary won't want to be reminded of all that anyway.

He's probably right.

He said if I was smart, I'd turn around.

But smart is Jace's department, not mine.

Hopefully tomorrow I'll see Xavier Andrews. I feel like the journey's really just beginning.

We actually had to carry the canoe about a hundred yards over land from one entry point to another. This is the most fascinating area I've ever been to. I can understand why people come out to places like this to find God. I never could before today. Out here you're so incredibly small inside the glove of His immensity and His beauty.

I saw some beaver dams and a few of the critters themselves. They're the cutest little things.

FORTY

My muscles don't scream, oddly enough, but surely tomorrow they'll voice their displeasure loud and clear. It is a chilly day, although Grandy assures me this is incredibly mild weather. Ice is beginning to form around the edges of the lake we camped by. By mid-October it can feel like a Maryland winter in these parts. I'll take the Maryland winter, I'm assuming, based on his description of what happens around here during the cold months.

I hate cold. I think that's what makes me happy about the Hotel. It's a place where people can go to get warm. Those nights will soon be coming. The city regulations say shelters can only open when the nights are below freezing. I can't imagine spending a night on a thirty-three degree street.

Now this morning, I almost could. A loon's call awakened me, that mournful warble that cut right down into the filling of my soul. When I climbed out of my sleeping bag . . . well, I dove right back in and dressed completely inside. I must have looked like a cartoon of two cats fighting in a sack.

The lodge loaned me a warmer parka and gloves and a hat. Thank goodness I remembered to bring some long underwear and thick socks.

So I dressed and met the men for some of Grandy's oatmeal, and glory be, a bull moose walked by not forty feet away. What next? Wolves?

I ask Grandy that very question.

"Sure, we got 'em. Timberwolves, coyote. And bobcat and lynx."

"Is it safe?" I ask.

Jolly coughs.

Grandy hands me a bowl of oatmeal. "Just sit still. They'll catch a whiff of your scent and most likely realize you're not a threat and pass on."

Those two words, "most likely," weigh about a thousand pounds. Just eat, Heather, why don't you?

The trees and their gnarled roots slide by, our boat lubricated by the water and the silence of Jolly, who's thinking about Helen, and Grandy, who's thinking about his childhood, I suppose. I'm thinking how the years go by so quickly and we sail right by so much, failing to recognize the intricate glory of it all.

Sometimes we fail to notice a shadow darting through trees and jumping over the river just out of our gaze, until one day, we realize how precious these years are, how more precious the next ones will be, and how we'd better confront the shadow if we want to live in peace.

That's what Anna does. Liza too. They live confronting the shadows. They know it does no good to ignore them.

Lunch consists of peanut butter and jelly sandwiches and some chips. Bottled water.

"Just another hour," Grandy says. He pushes his hand through his dark curly hair, and it stands up like a flame. "We'll probably want to make camp at Xavier's tonight and head out first thing in the morning." And then he shakes his head.

I sadden him even more.

That's the thing about sin. It's the gift that keeps on giving, as they say.

Perhaps Gary or Mary will be there. Of course, I've considered that thought, but Gary is forty-two by now and Mary forty-one. Surely they're not still with Xavier, are they?

No. That just can't be right.

True to Grandy's word, we pull up to the camp an hour after we resume our journey. A small dock juts into the rock-rimmed lake, thick legs reaching into the mud, and the men tie up the canoe.

Grandy jumps up onto the pier like the nimble youth he is, darn him. Nobody ever prepared me for how silly and ungraceful you feel when you reach middle age. Jolly climbs out next. Well done! But it takes both Jolly and Grandy to help me onto the boards.

A pebbled trail leads into the forest.

Grandy says, "I'll wait here with the boat."

I turn around. "Thanks. Jolly? How about you?"

"I'll go with you, but leave you to have your conversation alone."

I've never known a more thoughtful person. As I continue down the path, a little shrew runs across. Jolly stays beside me, and when I take his hand, he tucks it in the crook of his arm and places his other hand over mine.

"Thank you," I whisper.

He nods, a little teary. "It's just good to hold a warm arm in my own again."

After just a minute the trees thin out into a clearing, and in the middle sits a cabin that makes the lodge look like a five-star hotel: logs blackened by time and weather, porch sagging, whorls smoking out of a river rock chimney, scattering the aroma of a wood fire.

"Okay."

"You'll do fine."

We step up onto the porch, the floorboards, soft and forgiving, moaning faintly.

I slide off a glove and knock on the door, the chill wind nipping my skin with chiseled teeth.

Footfalls echo and my stomach drops.

I squeeze Jolly's arm as the door opens.

A man bent with scoliosis, waiting for rain under a thunderhead of gray and white hair, raises his brows. "Oh? Can I help you?"

"Xavier Andrews?"

"That's me. You all come to stay? We close at the beginning of October, but you can camp in the clearing if you'd like."

"Thanks. I actually just need to ask you a couple of questions."

Hard to believe this hermit was once the ladies' man Peggy described.

"Come on in. It's sure getting cold."

He swings the screen door wide, and we find ourselves in a living room filled with old furniture, lots of Naugahyde and plaid. Dust swims in the rays of sunlight streaming through a side window. Sadness in these walls too.

"Nice fire," Jolly says. He followed me inside, and I am grateful.

"A guy needs one on a day like today."

Jolly holds his hands toward the blaze. "So you going to winter out here all by yourself? My, that's something!"

"I been doing it for the last five years. Plenty of wood and water. Supplies laid up. It's not so bad. I do a lot of reading. I'm real busy in the other months with the canoers and fishermen and the like. It's a fine little break."

Xavier seems like a nice man. His voice still resounds with the warm suppleness of middle age. According to my calculations, he's in his midfifties now.

"How about something warm to drink? A cup of tea? Or some coffee? I put a pot on not long ago."

No electric lights, just gas lamps with some ferocious-looking fabric wicks illumining the room. "How do you cook here?"

"Got a propane stove."

"I'd love something warm," I say. "If the coffee's made, that will be fine."

"Fine by me too." Jolly.

He heads back through a doorway to the kitchen, and I sit down in a chair near the fire. Feels good. "So what do you think, Jolly?"

"Seems fine to me."

"I'm nervous."

"You'll do all right, Heather."

I hope I'm not adding yet another nail to this coffin of a situation. I'm under no delusion that this trip, this need to find these people, is by my own goodness. I lived for years without thinking about Gary and Mary. Now it's time to clean up my act, and God's helping me with the details. He needs to continue to help me, that's all I can say, because I have no idea where all this will lead. And Anna's question of whether or not this is for myself and my own feel-good needs screams like a cat between my ears.

He returns with a couple of mugs in his hands. "Here you go."

Black. Just assumed, I guess.

I'll take anything warm at this point.

"So what can I do for you all?"

Jolly points to me.

I clear my throat. I haven't practiced the question. I should have. I should have worded it carefully, written down a variety of options. But I didn't. Perhaps I didn't want it to really work out. What I really wanted was to find this camp deserted, Xavier gone, the trail ended, and that's that.

"I went to school with your kids, Gary and Mary."

He closes his eyes. "Oh, which school?"

"Bel Air Christian."

His face darkens. "Oh."

"I need to find them."

"Why's that?"

"To apologize."

He sits down on a straight chair and flattens the fluff on top of his head. "Truth is, I haven't seen Gary or Mary in years." He looks up, eyes moist but not overflowing. "I never knew how to handle those kids. I don't think I even knew how to try."

Jolly clears his throat. "Do you know where they are?"

"Last time I heard, they was somewhere near Amarillo. Gary hit the road as soon as he graduated high school and took Mary with him. I only heard from him once, and that was to sign over my rights to Mary's guardianship."

"Did you sign?"

"Uh-huh, and I was thankful to do it. Gary's a strong one. Now Mary. Oh, dear God." He tears up again. "If you'll excuse me. I've got some things to attend to. On second thought, you're welcome to bunk here for the night."

Jolly helps me to my feet. "No thanks. We'll just head on back."

Xavier leaves the room with only a nod. We depart from Xavier and his sad cabin on faraway waters. I guess we all escape one way or another; only some of us have more to escape from, sending us farther out and deeper in.

We turned around and set up camp a bit later than yesterday so we can make it back to the lodge by nightfall tomorrow. I paddled more often today despite the fact that my arms and shoulders finally feel like someone's trying to pull them apart with each stroke.

Something about being out here in the wilderness settles my soul. I can see why people yearn to retire somewhere remote, just live their lives in peace without their own expectations or anyone else's weighing them down.

I quickly slide myself into the sleeping bag and turn on the lantern.

If I could rationalize it as a way Jesus would have lived, I'd do it. He may have gone off to refresh Himself, but He always came back around. At least in His man-skin He did. I sure wish He'd come back around right now.

FORTY-ONE

I drop Jolly off and have to wipe away the tears as he lets himself into that lonely old house. The heat blasts out of the car vents, but even so, I wonder if I will ever feel warm again. Naturally, the cold hit like a slap-boxer on that last day. Jolly and Grandy took it like men.

I am not a man.

If anybody had wanted to see a woman complain and act like a delicate hothouse flower, they would not have been disappointed. Grandy almost pushed me out of his canoe. And surly? Mercy!

The Jacuzzi tub awaits. Now if I could blue-dot that thing, I would! I open the car door, yank my bag from off the backseat, and head inside.

Jace and Will practically trample over each other after I open the door.

"Mom!"

"Hezzie!"

We hug and kiss, and Jace, already having heard all about my chilly bones via cell phone, flips on the electric teakettle. "Hot chocolate all around!"

Will flips it off. "Dad, you gotta use milk if it's going to be worth drinking. I'll do it."

Jace grabs the sugar canister and hands it to Will. "I want to hear all about the trip."

"Me too!" Will. "I can't believe you camped out for three days. That's amazing. You!"

Okay, got it, Will.

"I liked it, actually. If it wasn't for the cold. We should all do that sometime."

Jace. "Big-time. I will remind you that I've been trying to talk you into it for years. Are you saying I was right?"

"Sometimes we just need to have things foisted upon us before we can really appreciate them."

"Ah-hah."

Will measures out the cocoa into the pan. "Dad gave me the basic story about the Andrews kids."

"Yeah."

"Gosh, Mom. On one hand I can't believe you were one of them, but on the other, it kinda gives me hope, you know?"

"I'm sorry."

"Yeah, well, you're a nice lady now, and you take up for the weird kids at school."

"You all are not weird!"

"See what I mean?"

"I thought you'd be angry at me."

"Why? You've only been great to me. I mean, if you were still one of those *ladies*, like some of them at school who've never gotten out of the mean girl phase, it would be different."

The phone rings. It's Laney.

"Hey, Laney. How are you?"

"Up to my eyeballs, but what's new there? Hey, I heard about the service project the women's committee is doing. Very cool."

"Did Carmen start promoting it?"

"Oh yeah. In fact, she's been calling everybody personally. She's totally on board."

"That's great!"

"Just thought you'd want to know. And I'm signing up too. Cade said he'd take off work that day."

"Thanks, Laney."

"Hey, you got it. So see you tomorrow, then?" she asks. "We're meeting at my house."

"Oh, you have no idea how much I'm looking forward to it."

Lark calls as I drive downtown Tuesday morning. "Hey, come by and pick me up. Mother's driving me crazy."

"Is she all right?"

"She is woman, hear her roar, Heather. She's been reading a book that's driving her crazy, and yet she won't put it down. Said she's always wanted to read *Gone with the Wind*, and so before she dies, that's what she's doing. Only she's already taken up with Melanie Wilkes, and poor Scarlett can't do one thing right."

"Wasn't that kind of the point?" I've never read the book myself.

"Beats me. But you should hear her yelling at that woman and Margaret Mitchell besides. I can't hear myself think."

"Sure, I'll swing by. See you in a few."

So this is a nice little sparkle to the day.

While Sister J leads Lark up to the transitional floor to show her what needs doing, I sit on a stool by the worktable in the kitchen and cut the black spots off of ten heads of broccoli. Cream of broccoli soup tonight with cheese that came in from one of the grocery stores, along with some outdated tubes of poppin' fresh biscuits. I'm almost tempted to take some home with me.

Honestly, I think Sly, who turned up last week, went Dumpstering and found this loot, but I don't want to ask for sure.

I hear Mo holler from his desk, "Now don't you be disturbing that nice lady back there, Knoxie."

Oh great. Why me? Why does he always want to talk to me? All I can think when I'm talking to him anymore is that I'm jeopardizing my family by even being around this guy, like if I'm caught in some kind of drug war and I die, then Will is left without a mother, Jace without a wife, and then who would be around to get rid of the green-dotted merchandise?

But then I remember that only the grace of God, in a general sense, keeps us all from being murderers and thieves.

"Heather Curridge."

"Hello, Knox. Pull up a stool."

He does, darn it. I was hoping this would be one of his breeze-throughs.

"What are you up to today?" I ask, then clap my hand over my mouth. "Forget I said that."

"Well, actually, I've been doing a little soul-searching. A very little, but any improvement is good."

"So what has your search dug up?"

"I was thinking about why I am the way I am. It's not like a five-year-old ever dreams of doing what I do."

"What did you used to want to be?"

"A fireman, of course. Then a policeman."

I hoot out a laugh.

"And then I suppose I was around ten years old when I found myself out on the corner and realized it was either us or them, and them was a lot richer and more powerful. It wasn't a hard decision for me, unfortunately."

"I'm sorry for you, Knox."

He picks up a broccoli floret and examines it. "How do you make up for it once you've done so many things to so many people?"

I tell him about Gary and Mary. The trip to Minnesota. His soulful eyes close. "It would take me the rest of my life to try and make up for my sins like that, unfortunately."

"Can you think of anything better to do with it?"

"Pray for me," he said.

And I assure him I will. "I already have been, in fact."

On the way home, I tell Lark about him. "Now what got into him? What's happening inside that man?"

"Who knows?"

"I saw the side of him that Jesus loves, though."

"That's good, Heather. I hate to say it, but I don't think you're through with him. Not by a long shot."

The three of us pore over five different floor plans from Alva's port-folio. I spread them out on the empty dining room floor. Yep, empty. The table and chairs, sideboard, and china cabinet brought twenty thousand at auction. I had no idea they were such good pieces when I bought them from an antiques dealer awhile back. Obviously he didn't either!

"Wow, Mom. These are great. Are we really going to do this?"

Jace. "Yeah. We're going to sell this place just before the hospital ship goes out, and this will be built when we're gone."

"Have you found the land yet?"

"No," I say. "But that will come. We have awhile to decide."

We all agree on the same plan, the Guggenheim. Lots of win-dows, three small bedrooms, and a wide-open space that envelops the kitchen, a family room, and a dining area, all on different levels under the same stretch of ceiling.

"And it will be done in white," I say.

"No arguments from me." Jace.

Will says, "As long as I can do my room in whatever color I want, I don't care what you do with the rest."

Teenagers.

Will points to a figure in the lower right-hand corner of the plan. "Look, this went for seven thousand dollars back in the '50s!"

Jace and I both gasp, then burst into laughter.

Will settles a hand on an indentation in the carpet left over from the buffet. "How much did you get for the dining room furniture again?"

Mercy!

FORTY-TWO

November is one of my favorite months because it brings my favorite holiday, Thanksgiving. The spirit of gratitude revolutionizes, so human in the good sense of what is human. I believe we are at the highest pinnacle of being completely human as God designed us when we are most grateful.

Will is grateful today because I'm letting him take off school to come help.

I have to remember to pick up the Thanksgiving turkey on the way home from the Hotel. Carmen really played this day up big. We'll be finished with that room in no time.

We pull into the school parking lot at quarter to eight, and judging by the look on her face, Carmen is anything but grateful right now. She storms toward me across the tarmac. "I'm so mad I could spit!"

"Why?" I'm doing all I can not to laugh. Carmen has been snippy, bossy, angry, but the expression on her face can only be categorized as outrage.

"Five of us, Heather. There's only going to be five of us . . . counting you!"

"That's okay. Will's here too."

"Okay, six. But still no. It's not okay. I'm beginning to think you were right about this stuff. Maybe we should keep this sort of thing to ourselves. Nobody wants to help anyway." She stomps her foot like a five-year-old, and I want to hug her.

"Don't listen to me about anything, Carmen. I'm finding out I don't know much about pretty much everything. And it'll be okay.

293

You did what you could. Some listened. Most didn't. Isn't that usually the way?"

She looks over at the school, shrugs. "Well, when you put it that way, you're exactly right. I don't like it, though. I mean, it's one thing to not show up when you promised to decorate the gym, but to paint a homeless shelter? After you said, 'I swear, I'll be there bright and early tomorrow morning, Carmen'?"

"Who else is coming?"

"Laney, who's more excited than you can imagine."

Knew that.

"Olive and Betty Hayes."

"Betty Hayes? She's eighty if she's a day!" Her daughter Olive has a son in Will's class.

"I know. She sidled up to me at the basketball game and said she still had a great painting arm."

I clap. "That's wonderful! Are they meeting us here? We can all drive down together if you'd like."

"They'll be here any minute. We can take my van."

"Sure. Can we stop for coffee on the way?" I wrinkle my nose. "The stuff at the Hotel is pretty bad. Jimmy doesn't make good coffee, and I don't want to tell him so."

"Sounds good to me."

Betty and her daughter Olive arrive together, both swimming in large khaki pants and loose men's shirts. These two define the word *delightful*. Betty lives with Olive and her family these days and does all the grocery shopping and makes dinner too.

"Hellooooo!" Betty waves her hands and scoots toward us. Betty smiles all the time.

Olive shuffles right on behind her. "Hey, guys!" She holds up a tray of drinks. "Thought I'd presume you'd all like some coffee."

Of course. Yes, the Hayes women are just the type. Why don't I ever think of Olive when I think about the other moms at the school?

Olive hands me a cup. "I remember you telling me you like those chai teas a couple of months ago."

"Bless you."

"Skim mocha, no whip." She hands another cup to Carmen.

Laney screeches in, executing one of those mind-boggling, high-speed parking jobs you see every once in a while, the driving antithesis of Liza. "Is that coffee?" she hollers as she extracts herself out of her old Windstar. "Because if it is, I'll take it!"

Nicola jumps from the passenger door. Will shoves his hands in his pockets and walks toward his real live girlfriend. Okay, I have to admit I'm relieved. When your son's a misfit, you do tend to think, down in the whispery portions of your mother-mind, that there isn't a girl alive who will actually appreciate him.

Laney looks as if she spent the night running through the forest. Her hair porcupines out from her scalp, and her clothing twists askew around her reedy body. "I swear, I'm going to leave at 6:00 a.m. next time I get a day off. It took us fifteen minutes to say good-bye. 'I'm only going for the day,' I kept saying to Hannah over and over again."

Olive holds out the gold. "I wasn't sure what you like, Laney, but I assumed with your slender figure you could afford anything. So I got you a whole-milk white chocolate mocha."

Laney sips. "And you figured perfectly."

"I didn't realize Nicola and Will would be here. Sorry I didn't pick them up a drink."

Laney shakes her head as she sips. "No prob. Thanks, Olive. How much do I owe you?"

Betty. "That look as you sipped was worth every penny."

Carmen claps her hands. "Let's go, then! Giddyup or something like that."

We all climb into her van, every one of us happy to be there, feeling a bit like we're heading off to summer camp. And that's why it was only us. Some jobs God reserves for those who are delighted to have them because He knows that's pretty much going to be the only reward coming anyway.

I pat Carmen on the shoulder. "See? It's all going to be fine."

Her eyes crinkle in the rearview mirror, and she turns on her CD player. The strains of Glenn Miller's "Tuxedo Junction" fill the space.

Betty smiles. So do the rest of us.

Mo hollers. "Ho! Here they are! Lookin' ready to do some business!"

Betty holds up her paint roller and gives it a victorious shake. The others do an equally endearing motion, and I swear, my face will split like a tree under lightning, my smile's so wide. Will and Nicola hold hands.

My old people meeting my new people.

I take a mental snapshot of their lovely female faces.

Mo picks up the phone. "Sister J? Paintin' crew's here!" He hangs up after her response. "She'll be right down. There's some coffee if y'all want some."

We all hold up our cups.

I chuckle.

Mo raises his brows. "Yeah, Jimmy's not the best at coffee, is he? Next time, though, you be bringing one for me, all right?"

I make introductions, and Mo shakes all the women's hands. Will introduces Nicola, and Mo acts like he's just met a princess. My son looks ready to zing even as Laney looks like she's going to pop like a balloon rising toward the trees. She gazes around in a state of almost wonder, and I have no idea what's going on inside her head. Carmen just looks ready to get to work.

"Big room," she says.

"Definitely."

She turns to the other women. "So I thought we'd have a bigger crew. Do you want to make two days of this, or stay until we finish the job?"

Olive sets her box of supplies on one of the tables. "We came to paint the room. Let's paint it."

Carmen points at Laney. "You're the one with the little kids. What do you think?"

"If someone lets me borrow a cell phone, I'll call Cade."

Olive says, "I'd better call home too. Sam has indoor soccer, but you know, he can miss it for once in his life."

I point to the pile of supplies. "Well, then, let's get ready. The stuff is over here."

Jace and the boys did a great job patching the walls last week. Looks good.

It has already been well established that we all know how to paint. The drive down was filled with our years of exploits in covering walls. Betty once painted a room puce; she took the prize for boldness. Laney doesn't need tape—good for her—she can cut in around the ceilings and the baseboards; she took the prize for finesse. Carmen used to paint for money in college; she took the prize for smarts.

Fabulous, right?

Olive never could see paying good money to a painter—after all, how hard could it be?

Yep, we are the chosen ones.

Nicola and Will still hold hands.

I dunk a wooden stir stick into the paint and begin to swirl. "Now that you're teaching our churchy-thing, how do you like it?"

Laney picks up a bristle brush. "I love it. I'm finally doing something with the gift God gave me. It's a responsibility, though. I really don't want to lead anybody down a wrong path." She grabs the can and heads over to the ladder.

No wonder cakes are my gift to the world. I don't want anybody listening to me at all. Way too much responsibility. And what I've figured out for today may not even stand the test of a twenty-four-hour time span. All I can do now is cling to Jesus. I wouldn't want to be in Laney's shoes any more than I'd like to be at the bottom of Loch Raven.

Laney's talking and joking with people from her perch where she cuts in the paint around the new ceiling, way more at ease than I am with the clients. I just watch her as I roll on the green paint, following the trail of Olive and Carmen the tapers of the baseboards. Betty's ahead of them cleaning the baseboards we'll coat with a thick white lacquer. Trim's my favorite part.

Will and Nicola are holding hands.

Laney understands how people are sinners. Everybody, everybody,

everybody. And she is no respecter of persons, herself included. At least that's my guess.

Sister J walks in. "Frish, look at you all!"

I set down my roller. "You like it?"

"You bet. Well, thanks be to God and all that good stuff! So introduce me to the gang, doll."

And I do.

Sister J touches her nose. "Jimmy's cooking up a special treat for lunch just for you all. Soup!"

We laugh.

"No, really. Obrycki's dropped off some crab cakes last night from a canceled catering job."

Carmen says, "I love crab cakes!" then claps a hand over her mouth. "Wow, that was loud!"

"Who doesn't love them?" Laney.

Sister J. "You bet. Every once in a while, the Lord throws us a bone. And if it comes in the form of a crab cake, so much the better."

Something happens to our little group. We solidify into a community, a single purpose ahead of us, a goal in sight, a small journey we agreed to take together. And that precious euphoria of doing good together reaches out and ties us close.

I love that feeling.

You know what I think it is?

God smiling.

Yep, nothing profound, just a few humans in relation to God and each other doing holy work that will bring themselves no benefit other than the joy of serving others. Now this is church.

A few minutes later, Sister J pokes her head into the room. "Heather? Got a minute?"

"Okay." I follow her back to her office.

"Not much news on Krista, doll. I thought you'd like to know. LaQueesha heard she got into some black Jaguar the night she disappeared. But that's all we know."

"Poor Krista."

"She's a baby doll. I'm still praying, though. Are you?"

"Oh yeah. I can't get her off of my mind."

"That's right. See, God knows where Krista is. And we know where He is, so it makes this silver triangle. At least, I always picture it that way. Anyway, thought I'd tell you."

"Thanks."

"Thanks for bringing down that crew. Nice gals."

I nod my head. "They're the best."

Carmen stands in line with her plate. "I feel guilty about taking one of these crab cakes. Maybe we should go out and get our own lunch."

I lay a hand on her sleeve. "Your presence here matters. It's not about you taking the food, Carmen. It's about you giving your presence."

"Are you sure?"

I laugh and so does Laney. "Sheesh, Carmen, you don't want the folks to think you think you're too good for them, do you?"

Carmen's face trims down into a look of horror. "Oh! I didn't think about it like that! Okay." She shakes her head. "This is all so new. I feel really uncomfortable."

Me. "I know! You should have seen me my first few weeks here. It was horrible."

Her brows rise. "Really?"

"Ah, yeah. *Really*, really."

Of course everybody ends up sitting together. "No, no, no, ladies, we go out two-by-two. Let's spread out."

Olive looks unsure, then says, "There are five of us."

Not counting Will and Nicola, who are still holding hands. They did manage, however, to pry themselves apart in order to mop the kitchen floor and clean the glass on the front doors.

"You're right! Okay, how about Laney and you and your mom. Carmen, wanna sit by me?"

"I'd love that, Heather."

Laney says, "Hey, I'm fine on my own." And she walks over to the table of the filthiest person there, Akbar Reynolds. His real name isn't Akbar. I don't think anybody knows what his real name is. He's a schizophrenic. And he smells like a litter pan on a humid day, and honestly, I just gag and gag if he's within ten feet of me. But with all the diapers Laney changes every day, I'm sure she doesn't notice.

She starts talking his ear off, and a few more people join her, a middle-aged couple—she bleached blonde, he with a long curly pony-tail—and a street guy named Brill who left a good job and family for heroin. They're laughing like crazy within five minutes.

Good heavens, some people are just naturals at this stuff! God should have called Laney, not me.

Then again, God called Moses, and Aaron was the one who could do the talking. Because there are a million miles between what God *should* do and what He does.

"You gals are great." Hands on hips, Sister Jerusha looks around. "I can't get over how you've been at it all darn day, with hardly a break!"

Betty waves a hand. "Us old girls still have it in us."

Sister J points at her. "You said it, doll."

Carmen says, "We appreciate the opportunity."

"Anytime. Believe me. An-ee-time. So how much longer do you think you have to go?"

"Another two hours," Olive.

I look at my watch. Seven o'clock. "Tomorrow, nobody'll know what hit them, it'll be so pretty in here."

"Already is. Okay, don't let me slow you down. I'm heading upstairs to the Bible study for the addicted men. Jimmy's leading tonight, and he's always good."

Carmen's eyebrows raise, and she looks at me. After Sister J exits, she puts a hand on my arm. "Addicted men?" she asks.

"Yes."

"Do they ever have those types of studies for women?"

"Yes, in the mornings."

"Okay." And she walks away, picks up a paintbrush, and sets to work on the trim. Second coat. And I'm standing there with my mouth open, wondering who in Carmen's circle needs such a study.

We all set to work on the second coat of the trim. Betty and Laney on the windows, the rest on the baseboards, and oy! My back will be singing the blues and the greens tomorrow.

Will and Nicola are not holding hands; they are threading curtains onto rods I'll hang in place next time I come down.

Knox Dulaney steps through the front door. "Hello, Mo!"

"Not a good time, Knoxie. We got these ladies here doing good charity works."

He holds up a hand of peace. "Not to worry. Not to worry. Just came to see Aunt Jerusha. She here?"

"Upstairs at the Bible study."

"Hmm. I think I'll take a pass." He laughs. Mo waves him on.

I shake my head and can't help but smile. Man, I wish I didn't like him. Why do I like him? He's a horrible person! "Hey, Knox."

"Ah, the good Heather. And bringing more good ladies with you." He shoves his hands in his trouser pockets and gazes around. "It looks good in here. Nice colors. Bringing a little county to the hood."

I wince.

"Well, I'll be going. Just thought I'd stop in."

I wonder how many people he's killed.

Glass shatters, metal crunches. I jump at the sound. What's going—

"Watch out!" Mo's shouts provide a baseline for our screams as glass shards spew forth before the ramming hood of a car crashing through the now-twisted front doors. The room envelops the entire car as it screeches to a halt, the smell of oil and burnt rubber imbuing the air.

All I can think is, *Thank God we were on the trim, thank God we were all at the edges of the room!*

"Will!" I scream, and the two kids run over.

"Don't move!" Two olive-skinned men jump from the car like crickets, hopping in agitation, and are they high on something dangerous? I'm terrible at judging nationalities, but they're not black, and one points a gun at Knox and yells something I cannot understand. He shoots at the new ceiling over Betty's head. She screams and cowers as plaster falls at her feet.

Obviously Knox has stepped on toes, expanded his territory where it wasn't meant to go.

Dear God in heaven . . .

I'm in the middle of an all-out drug war!

Oh Lord, oh Lord, oh Lord.

I put one arm around Will and tuck Nicola behind me.

The slow motion begins, two more men emerging from the backseat, and we're a breath away from dying, aren't we? Isn't this the type of situation where people . . . more guns are drawn, a kind of rifle . . . where people open fire, spraying bullets like water? And the words rise in pitch and volume, complexions are heightened to a flaring crimson.

Laney is as pale as a china plate. She's thinking about "all those kids." Staring at Nicola, telling her *Stay put* with her eyes and the grim set of her mouth.

One piece of me is bolstering up Will; the other is being boned by fear, its razor teeth pulling back layers I never knew existed. *Don't let my baby boy be hurt. Don't let this be it.*

Knox yells back in that same language.

I'm wondering about my life, knowing it's in these guys' hands and I can't even understand a word they're saying. And why do I have to be standing right next to Knox? If they shoot—

The other women press themselves to the walls, fear paralyzing their faces into blanched masks.

The first man out of the car steps forward, babbling his language and waving his pistol; he points it at Will, then at Knox, at Will, then at Knox. God, no. *Please don't let him shoot my baby boy!* Not the child who drew me a million robots. Not the boy who hugged me countless times without my asking, who keeps me in check.

Flicker, flicker, back and forth, and he's laughing now, a fast, sassy, *don't screw with me and yet I find this all extremely invigorating because I'm a coldhearted killing machine* laugh. More words.

I pull Will closer into my side.

"Don't move, lady!"

But don't you see? This is my child. I stayed up a bundle of croupy nights, sitting on the closed john in the bathroom while steam from the tub faucet billowed around us, mingling with our sweat, soaking us in a fine, warm descent. I couldn't breathe, but he could and that was the point.

Back and forth, the gun moves.

Don't you see? *He is the point!*

He laughs again. I look at Knox, at the fear in his eyes. And I know the other man will shoot. I know it like I already saw the movie.

Knox yells, "No!" Steps forward. Flings himself sideways, in front of Will, as the man pulls the trigger.

Knox pushes us onto the ground and falls on top of me as another shot blasts from the gun.

I am jarred with pain as my bones, compressed beneath his falling weight, grind into the floor. And Will. Will crumples against the old tiles, salmon and pink, found in a Dumpster. "Will!"

"He's shot!" Knox. "My, God, the boy is shot."

I scream and push Knox off of me. "Will! Will!"

The color has drained from his face. "Mom, I'm okay. I'm not dead." I lean over him.

And the gunmen scream at me, but I do not move. I look at them with all the hate I've ever known and I turn back to my son. The sound of sirens falls upon us. And the men, they're turning back around. No more shots fired, right? No more.

Another blast sounds as they shoot at the light fixture in the ceiling near Mo's desk; sparks fly.

"No more. Oh, Will," I whisper. "Call an ambulance!" I scream.

Shot? Blood? I close my eyes. No, I don't want to see blood right now. Not my baby boy's blood. My baby boy. I open them again and hold his hand as his eyes close.

"It's okay, Mom."

The men jump back into the car, back out through the glass, and squeal away, the crunch of tires over glass sounding in our ears.

My brain flounders in a knee-deep puddle.

No more shots. No more shots.

They're still gone. *Please stay gone.*

"Heather, are you all right?" Knox's voice enters my ear like the prow of a ship through the fog. And then.

Will. "I hope that guy gets a flat tire from all that glass."

Knox smiles, wincing in pain.

The women gather around us, pale, ghostly. Carmen shakes.

Laney shouts, "Call 911. Will's bleeding!"

"Already done it," Mo hollers back, thumping over.

Nicola and Will hold hands. Blood seeps through the shoulder of his shirt. I kiss his cheek. "It'll be okay, bud."

Folks are running down the steps from upstairs. I hear Sister Jerusha's shouts from behind them.

Laney holds Knox's hand. The dealer looks over at Will.

"Shouldn't it hurt more?" Will asks him.

But before he can answer, he loses consciousness, and I sit next to my only son, my fifteen-year-old son, waiting for the ambulance to come.

Sister J's face appears. "Oh my God, Heather. Will, doll, you're going to be okay."

"He's unconscious."

"Hit in the shoulder, thank God. It could have been a lot worse. Here." She reaches into her skirt pocket for that hankie she fumbles with. "Apply direct pressure."

Around me an amphitheater of faces above bodies spattered with paint and concern protect us from the rest of the world.

FORTY-THREE

Having a notorious drug lord at least try to save your son's life makes you wonder about a lot of things. Like what clicked inside of him to leap in front of Will? Was it God who did that, and does that mean He's got good plans for Knox? Or just for Will? Am I supposed to pour more of myself into this man's life now when the whole episode was his fault in the first place? I'd be a fool to think a hardened individual like Knox Dulaney is just going to turn around like that. Right. Like he really felt concern for Will.

Now that the adrenaline is gone, an anger remains that I can't begin to process until we leave this bedside and the hospital behind. I can tell you one thing, I'm not going down the hall to visit Knox Dulaney. He can suffer all by himself as far as I'm concerned.

Will sleeps in the hospital bed. The bullet has been extracted and he hasn't yet awakened. But I have deeper questions than the ones about Knox Dulaney. Jace sleeps in a chair beside me. It's 2:00 a.m. and there's nobody awake to call. So I ask them to myself.

Am I not doing the right thing by coming downtown? Isn't this partly my fault? Wouldn't God at least protect my son considering I'm trying so desperately to live a Jesus life? Can I expect some sort of divine intervention when it comes to stuff like this, and if I can't, what does that mean? Do I really have what it takes?

"Hezzie, go to sleep."

"I was asking that out loud?"

"You sure were, hon."

Will's eyes open. "So I'm figuring I don't have to go to school today."

"You're a nut." I reach for his hand, relief flooding me, filling the gaps behind the dam of doubt that he would come around at all after surgery.

"Hey, I'm living to tell the tale."

Breakfast arrives, and he sifts through the liquid diet all the while asking Jace about the particulars of his surgery. "It was a pretty straight-forward job. You've got some physical therapy to do, though, bud."

"What about Knox Dulaney?" he asks.

"Had his spleen removed. He's in far worse shape."

"Good," I say.

Will pushes the tray away. "Knox is here, right?" We nod. "Do you think I can walk down to his room?"

So, I didn't quite expect that. "No way!"

Jace sits forward in his chair. "I'm not sure that's a good idea, bud. Who knows who may come into that room?"

"Just for a few minutes."

"You shouldn't get up," I say. "Right, Jace?"

"Well, actually, hon, a little exercise is a good idea."

"Jace!"

"I'm sorry. It's true."

"Please, guys? And alone. Mom and Dad, you're great and all, but I've got to do this by myself."

"What do you want to see him so badly?" I ask.

"Mom. Can I go or not?"

Jace and I exchange an hour-long conversation in a glance. "Yes," he says. He touches my thigh. "In the medical sense, it's pretty minor, Hezzie. He's fine to walk down there."

Jace helps him step into a pair of sweats, then stand to his feet. He curls his hand around the IV pole, hands that seem to have become those of a man overnight.

"You okay?" I ask.

"Yep."

He walks out of the room, arm in a sling, face forward.

I look at Jace. "I'm dying to be a fly on the wall."

"Heatherrrrr . . ." He picks up the morning paper. "Actually, so am I."

"What do you think he's saying?"

"Well, with Will it's hard to say. But I can tell you this, we'll never know unless he decides to tell us."

"I'm going down to get a cup of coffee."

"Oh, that's convenient—you'll have to walk by Knox's room."

"What number is it?"

He sighs. "403."

I stand up and grab my purse. "Want something?"

"Yes. I could use the caffeine to clear my brain. Man, I just don't know what to think about all this."

"Me either."

I walk by Knox's room and quickly glance inside as I pass. Will sits in the chair, leaning forward, and Knox looks stricken. Not in a mountain-falling-on-you way.

The man is in for the battle of his life; it will make last night look like an afternoon at Chuck E. Cheese. And Will is leading the charge in a still, small voice. Mercy, but I wish I was more like my son.

Sister Jerusha arrives after the lunch shift at the Hotel. "I'm going to knock Knox's block off."

"Say that three times fast."

She hoots.

Will says, "He's right down the hall."

"Yeah, I know. But I just wanted to stop in first. Seems to me you're more of the victim than that rascal is."

"Oh, I don't know." Will shakes his head. "His injury is far worse."

I drag another chair next to mine. "Knox had his spleen removed in the middle of the night. I can't say I feel too sorry for him."

She nods. "Knox made his choices. I'd have moved heaven and earth to get him into a good college, on a good path. He knows that."

Leave it to Sister J to take away a drug lord's excuses and still love him.

She holds up a handled brown paper grocery bag. "And guess what I brought?"

I shake my head.

"Cake! And guess who helped me make it?"

"I have no idea."

"Come on in, doll!" she yells.

And in the door walks Krista.

"Krista!"

"Miss Heather!"

"Oh, girl, I am so glad you came back."

"Me too."

She hugs me lightly, and she smells so good.

"So where were you?"

"In Chicago."

"Really? How did you get there?"

"It's a long story. But I'm all right. I'll save it for the Hotel."

"I'll remember that."

She opens her eyes wide. "Oh, you will."

Sister J excuses herself to go visit with her godson.

Jace walks in with hot drinks round two from the coffee bar in the hospital lobby. Kristas is playing cards with Will, and really, she's still a kid, just two years older than he is.

"Krista! Would you like some coffee?"

"No thank you, Dr. Curridge. Are you comin' down to the Hotel soon?"

"In a week and a half, but I can come sooner if you need me to."

"I do."

"I'll be there the day after tomorrow."

She looks at me. "I got to make it work this time, you know?"

"Yeah, I do. We'll help you."

We sip our coffee, and Sister J walks in. Jace hands her a cup. "I saw you from the hallway."

"Good man." She sips, screws up her face. "What the heck is this?"

"A white chocolate raspberry latte. Will suggested it because Mo told him you love raspberries."

She sips again. "Hmm. Not bad once you know what it is. Thanks." She pulls out a little Bible. "I swore off Kings and Chronicles a long time ago. How about a little of that rascal David?" So she reads to us from the Psalms and reminds us, "Following Jesus isn't something we do because it's easy or even prudent. Sometimes it makes no sense at all."

"But then, God Himself being stripped of His clothes, beaten, tortured, and crucified makes no sense either," I say.

Sister J points at me. "You got it, doll. You've really got it. Will?" She takes his hand. "You were doing the work of the Lord yesterday. Sometimes we get scars from that, but someday they'll be badges of honor, stars in our crown."

I don't think I've ever been more proud of my son.

"What do you think, bud?" I ask. "Do we keep up at the Hotel?"

"Most definitely, Mom."

Jace smiles. I hear his thoughts, and to me they sound a lot like Jesus, who never promised loving Him would be easy or even secure . . . but free? Ah, yes. We shall be free indeed.

FORTY-FOUR

I stand on the deck, just under the eaves, my fleece robe pulled tight against the thin mist. The loch lies in peace, its waters barely visible through the low fog. Car headlights emit a cotton glow as they cross the bridge heading north. The waters seem to recognize that now is not their time.

Jace slides out through the doors and presses a mug of tea in my hands. "Nice nap?"

"Yeah. Really good. I'm glad to be back home. I hate hospitals. No offense."

"None taken."

"He's going to be all right, isn't he, Jace?"

"Yes, Hezz. I think you'll find he'll be better than he ever was."

"Why's that?"

"Life has become more precious. That's always a good lesson to learn."

"Still. Won't he be scared now?"

"Only if we let him be. I think the best thing we can do is continue on the course. It's like falling off a bike. Best to just get back on."

"I guess. I still have a lot of questions to ask God, but I'm so tired. Maybe they'll come tomorrow."

"You aren't too cold out here?"

"Just a couple minutes more. I'm remembering this place. It's safe here. When we leave, we may never feel safe again."

He puts his arm around my shoulders and draws me close. And he waits until I'm done, capturing the view I loved for so long. "We were never safe here, hon. Our souls were in greater danger than any bullet could extend."

"My head knows that. But so much of me cries out to stay."

"I know."

A wind blows through the empty, late-autumn trees, branches clacking softly, the almost dead revived through the breath of other.

I turn. "So you seem like you've got news to tell me. Is everything okay?"

"Maybe you should be sitting down."

"Oh no. What is it?"

"Hon, I found Gary Andrews."

FORTY-FIVE

"Let's go in, Jace. I'm cold."

He ushers me through the French doors. I sit on the couch, and he hands me a throw. "Where is he?"

"Just over in Howard County. He works for the Department of Health and Human Services."

"Are you sure it's him?"

"Pretty sure. I phoned him yesterday from the hospital and acted like I was from the alumni association of your old school."

"You didn't! Jace!"

"I know, but he bought it. He said he went there but wasn't an alumni."

He sits down next to me and pulls some of the blanket onto his own lap. We rest our feet side by side on the coffee table. "So I apologized for taking up his time, and that was that."

"What did he sound like?"

"Nice. Regular. You know, just a regular guy."

"Did he sound bitter or anything?"

"No, Heather. He didn't."

The call lasted two minutes tops, but my hand glistened with the sweat of two games of tennis in ninety-five-degree weather. I walk into the kitchen where the guys sit, ready to eat the meal Jace made. He really sets up a good chicken pot pie.

Two pairs of eyes question.

"He said he'd meet me."

"Yeah!" Will.

Jace sits back in his seat with a dramatic sigh of relief. "That's great, hon. What did he say?"

"He was very nice, actually." I pick up my napkin and sit down. "He remembered me, but I had to explain my way back into his memory. It was really weird. And really mortifying to have to say, 'I was that mean girl who used to sit halfway back on the right side of the bus.'"

"Is that right?" Jace. "Wow."

"I know. I'm relieved, though."

"So when are you meeting him?"

"Next Tuesday after he gets off work. He works flex time, so we're meeting early at the Hamburger Hamlet."

"Would you like some support? I could probably get Rick to cover my appointments."

I pick up my fork and look at each one of them. "No, but thanks. There are just some things a person has to do on her own."

Will picks up the serving spoon. "Let's eat."

Saturday afternoon Jace pulls up in front of a four-story townhouse, a looming house wider than most. "We're here!"

A For Sale sign hangs in the front window.

I look at him. "Is this what I think it is?"

"What do you think it is?"

"A possible home for the Kristas of this world?"

"Do you think it could work?"

I feel my heart race. "It's in the right location."

"The Realtor should be here in a few minutes."

I turn to Will in the backseat. "Are you okay to do this?"

He nods. "Yeah, Mom, I am."

It's like a narrow castle. Of course it's been cut up into apartments, eight of them, and maybe that's just the ticket. I'd dreamed of lofts, but why not one-bedrooms? Then if there are one or two kids with the ladies, there will be more room.

Woodwork hides beneath a thick crust of paint. The windows were replaced sometime in the '60s, I think. And the linoleum floor peels at the corners. Still.

"I think this could work." The first floor could have a gathering room and a training place for, well, all sorts of things, I guess: parenting, computer skills, ESL classes . . . hairdressing?

Well, why not? I still have a lot of contacts in the business.

Jace turns to the Realtor. "Are there any offers pending?"

The real estate agent, her sensible brown coat open to reveal a houndstooth suit, taps her day planner. "Not at this point. But you can't be too sure with these places. I wouldn't wait long."

"We'll get back to you tomorrow with an offer. Pending inspection, of course."

"Of course."

When we pull away, I can't believe it. "There's so much to do! We'll have to get some sort of funding, find a director for the home. Oh, man!"

My cell phone rings. It's Lark.

"He showed you, right?"

"Right."

"He made me promise not to say a word."

Jace.

"Just so you know, Summerville's on it. That place is going to need extensive renovating."

I breathe a sigh of relief as I end the call. "Ah, fabulous."

I turn to Jace. "This is amazing. Do you really think we can do this?"

"Would you like to?"

"I really would. Krista needs us to."

"Then yes. Absolutely, I do."

"What about the ship?"

"I'm figuring we get this up and running and stick to the game plan."

"I like it."

For the first time in many years, I'm glad I'm not some glamorous, skinny, glossy lady. I can't imagine showing up to ask forgiveness of somebody looking like life never dared touch me in a way that left a mark.

So here I stand in the entryway of Hamburger Hamlet. I hate Bethesda and pretty much anything right around DC. But I've never eaten a bad meal here, and they do a decent fudge layer cake.

I chose a simple khaki-colored wool skirt, a cranberry pullover turtleneck sweater, and mid-heel loafer pumps. My hair hasn't been colored since the beginning of the summer; it's too long, and I have to admit I look a little frumpy. He'll probably be glad to see I didn't turn out so well.

My purse hangs from double fists in front of me.

All of the bodily trippings one might imagine assail me. Dry mouth, heart beating like a Japanese drummer, brow a little sweaty. But he's meeting me, right? He could have said, "Let's just forget it. This is really creepy coming out of the blue." He must have turned out to be a pretty nice guy to agree to this.

A man in a barn coat, wire-rimmed glasses, and a ball cap walks in. He takes the cap off immediately to reveal wavy, dirty-blond hair. Computer programmer.

Nope.

Two women in ski jackets, high heels, and work skirts. Data entry or customer service.

Definitely nope.

Another man with white hair so thick there's no need for a hat, though the weather did turn quite cold yesterday. Charcoal gray overcoat. Financier.

Nope.

The door opens yet again. It's about five 'til four.

A grandmother, her daughter, and the grandbaby.

Cute, but nope again.

Maybe I should sit down and wait, or go to the bar and order something to drink. Or maybe not. If I'm not here when he comes, he may leave. But if I appear too eager, he might think I'm a stalker or something.

The door opens and he walks in.

Yep, it's Gary, loud and clear. He looks exactly the same. The wide cheekbones, slight nose, winged eyebrows that, seeing them as a functioning adult, are just beautiful. Without the overlay of dirt, Gary is handsome.

He smiles. "Heather Curridge?"

I step forward. "Yes."

"Now I know who you are! Heather Reeves, yes! I was remembering someone else."

"Probably Julia B."

"That's it."

"I'm surprised you came."

"It's pretty intriguing. Wanna go sit down? We can catch up and be more comfortable. I'm starving."

"Sure."

Now one would think I am relieved at this point. He's nice, accommodating, welcoming. But in truth my shame is utterly complete, having looked in the face of the person I sinned against and finding nothing but kindness.

I've never been lower.

The hostess seats us in a booth, the low, mellow lighting welcoming and yet offering me some sort of cover.

He really looks great. A wee bit overweight but in that nice-guy-who-wears-it-well way. His dark, straight hair, parted on the side like before, sparkles with a sprinkling of gray, and his brown eyes dance.

Now that's new.

"How did you find me?" he asks.

I told him about Jace.

He laughs. "That was your husband? Well, I was convinced. I mean, live in DC for long, and all people do is call for donations. Guess I don't have to send anything, then, huh?"

"Apparently not."

"So let's cut to the chase. Why in the world would you contact me after all these years?"

This should be easy, right? I've been working up to this for months. I've weathered canoes and forests, surly river guides and rental cars. "I wanted to apologize."

He shakes his head. "What? For the stuff on the bus?"

I nod. "And in school."

"You mean you've carried this stuff around for thirty years?"

"I guess so. I think so. I mean, it didn't start to really haunt me until about ten months ago. I was horrible, Gary. Especially to Mary."

"You've been watching too much *Jerry Springer*, Heather."

"I hate that show."

He smiles. "Me too. Look, I'm not saying what you did was right, but we were treated a lot worse right in our own home."

"But you all left so suddenly. What happened?"

"My grandmother just couldn't afford to send us anymore. She got laid off, and that was that. We all went up to Michigan—her brother lived there—so she could get work. I graduated high school, went to junior college in Amarillo, then got my degree from the University of Texas. But I always wanted to come back to Maryland. So I did."

"Are you married?"

"Was. Divorced now, but it's one of those situations where it's for the best."

Everybody says that.

"Any children?"

"A little boy. He's twelve."

"I have a fifteen-year-old boy." I tell him a little about Jace too. "But what about Mary? Whatever happened to Mary?"

I knew it was going to be bad. I could tell by the way he got quiet and folded his hands around his water glass.

"Heather, Mary's dead. She died years and years ago."

"What happened?"

"Some stories have crazy twists and turns. Mary was pretty beaten up by you guys, I'll admit it. But when we moved north, there was this lady next door who took a shine to her. She got her braces, permed her hair into some sort of style that looked good. You know, that"— he wiggles his fingers around his head—"sorta Farrah thing that was going on back then. Remember?"

"Uh-huh."

"She turned into a beauty."

"I'm honestly not surprised."

"Oh yeah. So she vowed she'd never be ridiculed again. And she got in with the fast sort of crowd. Dated a guy with a motorcycle, and to be honest, I couldn't blame her. Xavier, he did a lot of things he shouldn't have to her. If you get my drift."

I nod.

"Of course, I did what I could to protect her, but I had to work and go to school and couldn't be there all the time."

"I saw Xavier not long ago."

"Really? Where? On that river?"

"Yeah."

"You went all the way out there to find us?"

I nod and the tears gush and I cannot contain them and in the middle of the Hamburger Hamlet, darn it, in front of Gary Andrews, darn it, I weep and I weep and I weep.

"I'm sorry. I'm so sorry."

Gary scoots next to me on my side of the booth and puts his arms around me.

And isn't this rich? God, You are crazy. You know that?

I've finally calmed down. Gary has returned to his seat. We've ordered.

"Are you sure you don't want something stronger than coffee?" he asks for the second time.

"No thanks. I've got to drive back."

The waitress arrives with his soup.

"So do you mind finishing Mary's story?"

"No, not at all. Anyway, she ended up dropping out of school, getting into drugs, just a mess, Heather. I mean, it's the age-old story, you know. Some kids escape it unscathed and go on to live regular lives, and others never make it out."

"How did she die?"

"She OD'd. I took her to Texas with me after I graduated, but she couldn't kick the drugs. I honestly don't think she meant to OD. She was wild, and maybe sometimes a little crazy, but never suicidal. Not Mary. She was determined to make up for lost time."

"What about that neighbor? Wasn't she there to guide her? Before you moved?"

"No. She died of cancer not long after Delores passed away. Mary was seventeen. I think that was something else that tore my sister apart. Some people never seem to get any breaks, right? Mary was one of those people."

I drive too fast. Tears blur my vision, and I wipe them away with the back of my hand over and over. I call Laney.

"If salvation was all there is to it, perhaps God would just catch us up to heaven once we came to faith. It sure would seem easier that way."

"But He doesn't, Heather. That's pretty well established."

"So maybe we need to be there to give people those breaks. Not everybody seems to deserve it, and certainly, I don't. But I got that break through my dad, through Jace, and now through so many others, right?"

"Right, Heather. Are you okay? Where are you?"

I tell her.

"Oh, my friend."

Mary, Mary, where you going to?

Mary, Mary.

"But sometimes it's just too late, isn't it, Laney?"

Sometimes there's no way amends can be made, mangled piles of frayed rope retwined. Sometimes life must remain fragile, and sometimes forgiveness, while always sought, cannot be achieved. Amends cannot be made.

Mary, I'm sorry.

I'm so, so sorry.

It's all I can say. And nobody hears.

Do they?

Peace cannot be obtained. At least not about some things. Not here. Not now.

I pull off at the rest area on I-95 between Baltimore and DC, grab Will's car sketchbook and a graphite pencil, and scribble a note. Half an hour later Mo lets me into the Hotel.

"Yo, Heather! Kinda late for you ladies to be out and about."

I reach into Noah's ark and pull out the letter. "Could you give this to Knox next time he comes in?"

He eyes the paper with suspicion, then takes it from my hand. "If you say so."

"Sister J in?"

"She took herself an early night."

"She deserves it. I'll bet she sleeps like a rock, doesn't she?"

"Oh yeah."

The room is full. "Thirty-two degrees?"

"Just fell."

"Good."

I hurry back to the wagon, slide inside, and press down the lock button.

None of us really deserve forgiveness. Least of all Knox. Least of all me. But maybe in offering it to Knox, I'm giving Gary the greatest expression of gratitude for his own forgiveness I could possibly give.

Will would agree. Most definitely.

FORTY-SIX

At 5:00 a.m. Christmas morning the phone rings.

I lean across Jace and answer.

"It's Krista, Miss Heather. I'm about to run away again. I'm about to use and I know it. I know all the signs. It seems I get to this point of getting my feet underneath me, and then I throw it all down the garbage chute."

"I'm coming down to get you."

"I'll be ready."

"Stay inside the Hotel until you see me pull up. And pack a nice amount of clothing."

Jace touches my arm. "Would you like me to drive down with you? We'll be back by seven. And we can open presents then."

"Okay. I'll leave a note for Will in case he wakes up and wonders where we are."

Anna and Liza arrived around two for a big Christmas dinner. I left the sweet potato casserole and green beans up to Krista, and oh my goodness, she really can "throw down in the kitchen," as Jimmy says.

I called Sister Jerusha and told her Krista was with us. She said, "Merry Christmas, doll. You're a keeper. I still say I'm right about my God marks."

Mercy.

A pile of presents stood at the ready for Krista when we got home. Will had opened up ours carefully, picked out the ones we thought Krista might like, and wrapped everything back up again. When I saw the watch Jace obviously bought for me glimmering against her dark skin, I was happier than I ever dared to hope. It only deserved to be blue-dotted because it sat on her arm.

And when I saw the look on Krista's face, I thrilled. But when I saw the look on Jace's and Will's faces, I realized that God has big plans of grace and giving, shining light in the darkest of places, and my little family was being given the chance to be right there in the middle of it all. Could a Christmas get any merrier?

Bye-bye, house. Bye-bye, swim lessons and baseball. Bye-bye, tennis court and dinner out. Hello to so much more.

Perhaps some people can do both. Live high on the hill and down on the streets at the same time. But as Jace has always told me, "When you do something, Hezz, you dive in completely."

Flannery drove Lark and Leslie up, and Will, the creep, got the Christmas stocking. Carmen called to wish us a Merry Christmas. Then Laney and even Olive and Betty. We were tried by fire, I guess, bound together and purified in some way. I love these women. I really do.

Will and I stand in the snow at the cliff over the loch, looking behind us every so often to watch our tracks fill up with the falling snow.

We both suddenly look at each other.

"Did you hear that?" I ask.

"What? Yes. Did you?"

"Uh-huh."

"Mom, this is freaky. I heard a bell. I really did hear a bell."

"Me too."

We hold our gloves up to our faces and laugh.

"Did you really hear a bell?" I ask.

"No. But that doesn't mean we can't keep listening, does it?"

"Not at all, bud." I tousle his hair, put my arm around him, and pull him close.

If we listen for the church bell, really listen, we hear it chiming all around us, all the time, in every place the breath of God blows through like a silent breeze.

My ears are ringing with its music.

ACKNOWLEDGMENTS

Many thanks to Ami McConnell, Erin Healy, Rachelle Gardner, Claudia Cross, and Don Pape. Special thanks to Claudia Burney, who read the book in its original form and gave me the help I needed. And much gratitude to Ginny, Judy, Aaron, James, and Robbie at the Catholic Action Center, a ministry to the poor in downtown Lexington, Kentucky. Family and friends, of course: Lori, Jennifer, Chris, Marty, and Leigh; the good people of Communality who teach me the ways of Jesus and the ways of justice every day. As always, I appreciate my own family: Will, Ty, Jake, and Gwynnie. Here's to surviving an incredibly difficult year together! I especially want to thank my friend Heather, who cheers us on in our crazy ways.

WOMEN OF FAITH

Amazing Freedom
2007

"So if the Son makes you free, you will be truly free." – John 8:36

We often catch *GLIMPSES OF FREEDOM* but what about
the *promise* of being truly free? That's *AMAZING!*
Women of Faith...as always, *FRESH, FABULOUS,*
and *FUN-LOVING!*

2007 Conference Schedule*

March 15 - 17 San Antonio, TX	July 13 - 14 Washington, DC	September 28 - 29 Houston, TX
April 13 - 14 Little Rock, AR	July 20 - 21 Chicago, IL	October 5 - 6 San Jose, CA
April 20 - 21 Des Moines, IA	July 27 - 28 Boston, MA	October 12 - 13 Portland, OR
April 27 - 28 Columbus, OH	August 3 - 4 Ft. Wayne, IN	October 19 - 20 St. Paul, MN
May 18 - 19 Billings, MT	August 10 - 11 Atlanta, GA	October 26 - 27 Charlotte, NC
June 1 - 2 Rochester, NY	August 17 - 18 Calgary, AB Canada	November 2 - 3 Oklahoma City, OK
June 8 - 9 Ft. Lauderdale, FL	August 24 - 25 Dallas, TX	November 9 - 10 Tampa, FL
June 15 - 16 St. Louis, MO	September 7 - 8 Anaheim, CA	November 16 - 17 Phoenix, AZ**
June 22 - 23 Cleveland, OH	September 14 - 15 Philadelphia, PA	**There will be no Pre-Conference in Phoenix.
June 29 - 30 Seattle, WA	September 21 - 22 Denver, CO	

FOR MORE INFORMATION CALL **888-49-FAITH**
OR VISIT **WOMENOFFAITH.COM**
*Dates, Time, Location and special guests are subject to change.
Women of Faith is a ministry division of Thomas Nelson Publishers.

Dear Friend,

Thanks for taking the time to read *Quaker Summer*. My books are usually inhabited by strong-minded women who ultimately come to believe that God has called each of them to serve Him in unique ways. They also realize thay can't do it alone.

They have a lot in common with Women of Faith.

At a Women of Faith Conference, you'll find friends for the journey, encouragement for your soul, and affirmation that God has plans for you, that He's expanding the reach of His kingdom through women just like you, and that He'll provide the strength you need. Perhaps you'll hear His voice more clearly.

You'll laugh . . . a lot . . . for real. And you'll be blessed . . . for good. You'll be glad you went. Find a friend or go it alone. There will be plenty of others glad you came.

Peace,

READING GROUP GUIDE

1. Heather is struggling through two major dramas in this book: coming to grips with her past and the evil she perpetrated against Gary and Mary Andrews; and grappling with her future as she seeks to understand what is important and what her role should be in this world. How are these two themes related, and why are they happening at the same time?

2. What is the significance of Heather's flair for making cakes? Do you think Jace was right when he said she had "the gift of cake"?

3. Why did Heather get in the car and drive aimlessly around? Was she really aimless? What was she looking for?

4. How do Heather's spending habits reflect any behaviors of your own? What do these habits tell us about ourselves? What do we really want?

5. Which characters in the book impacted you the most? Which did you like the most?

6. Which character reminds you the most of yourself, and why?

7. What scenes or lines did you find particularly powerful, and why? How do they relate to your own life?

8. Why does Heather feel so insecure about herself with Jace, even though he clearly loves her?

9. Heather struggles between loving her "stuff" and knowing somehow there must be more to life. How is this similar to any of your own struggles?

10. What do you think is the main theme of the book?

11. What did this book say to you about church? About the church as a whole? About following Jesus and doing as He modeled?

12. Anna and Liza are the kind of characters who make you wish you could meet them. What purpose did they serve in Heather's life? Have you ever had anyone like them in your life?

13. Why is the character of Knox Dulaney so troublesome to Heather? What does he show us about ourselves?

14. This book is populated with a variety of interesting characters, including Sister Jerusha, Jolly, Lark, Laney, Carmen, Jace, and Will. How does each of these people contribute to Heather's transformation?

15. Heather is so concerned about appearances that she doesn't want to open up a salon for fear it wouldn't "look right." How does our concern about "what others think" keep us from pursuing our dreams and even following God's will?

16. Working at a place like the Hotel can be dangerous and even life-threatening. Would you do what Heather did and keep working there, bringing along your children as well? Why or why not? Do you think God requires us to put ourselves in harm's way in order to help where we're needed?

17. Heather's transformation began with her having thoughts and feelings that made her think she was going crazy. Have you ever had this happen to you or seen it happen in someone else? Why is it often true that when we really start listening to God, others may think we've gone nuts?

18. What do you think would have happened to Heather if she had not "coincidentally" found the Hotel? What might have happened in her marriage?

19. What was the significance of the church bell underwater? Why was it so sad for Heather to lose the idea of the bell ringing?

20. After reading this book, did you feel convicted or motivated to change your actions or habits in any way? What behaviors do you want to change? What do you think you really *will* change?

ML   2/07